QUANTUM GRAVITY: 4

CHASING THE DRAGON

Justina Robson

The right of Justina Robson to be identified as the author
of this work has been asserted by her in accordance with
the Copyright, Designs and Patents Act 1988.

First published in Great Britain in 2009 by Gollancz
An imprint of the Orion Publishing Group
Orion House, 5 Upper St Martin's Lane,
London WC2H 9EA
An Hachette UK Company

This edition published in Great Britain in 2010
by Gollancz

3 5 7 9 10 8 6 4 2

A CIP catalogue record for this book
is available from the British Library

ISBN 978 0 575 08563 3

Printed and bound in the UK
by CPI Mackays, Chatham, Kent

The Orion Publishing Group's policy is to use papers
that are natural, renewable and recyclable products and
made from wood grown in sustainable forests. The logging
and manufacturing processes are expected to conform to
the environmental regulations of the country of origin.

www.orionbooks.co.uk

INTRODUCTION

Attn: Temple Greer, Head of Otopian Security.
Temple – think you should see this. Seems Malachi was right about Lila after all, and he might be keeping secrets from you. All best, Bentley, Intel Unit 5.

Transcript of Interview taken at the Center For Free Counselling and Psychotherapeutic Aid, Bay City.

Dr Brigit Helena Winters, volunteer counsellor, leading.
Client refused to give name or address.

NB: Due to a malfunctioning camera and microphone in the interview room this transcript of the session was provided by Winters who wrote it down from memory. Her observational notes and self-notes were appended by her for the purposes of academic assessment although she did not submit them for her final exams. I drew this copy from her personal folders within the Academic Subnet. Bentley.

11.28 am.

Winters: Come in, sit down.

Client: Thank you. (Sits. Chair creaked. Stood up, agitated.) I'll just stand.

> Client seemed distressed, tired and agitated. Woman, perhaps twenty five years old or less. Caucasian. Quite attractive. Dark mid length hair with bright red streak on left back quarter. Red tattoo on partial face, neck, looked like it was meant to be with the red hair stripe. Wearing a purple and blue sundress, rather shapeless, with some kind of big flower print on it and a torn hem, nothing else, no shoes, no bag, no jewellery. Feet were black on the soles and her legs were a bit sandy as if she had been on the beach. She looked around and then stared at me. Confrontational, like some people are when they start counselling for the first time, kind of daring you to start. Her ID didn't check out on scan and she wouldn't give a name. I tested the scanner and it reported a fault.

Engineer sent for. (*This last is correct and is timestamped at 11.35: Bentley*).

Winters: Well, could you begin by telling me a little about what brought you here?

> She gave me this uneasy look and made a fuss of the chair, putting it back by the wall. Then she sat down on the carpet in the space in front of my chair, and to the right, legs crossed. She began to fiddle with the hem of the dress and twist it in her hands as she was talking. I got this weird vibe off her, she seemed exhausted and despairing but also very angry. I was a bit scared of her.

Client: It's my sister. She um . . . she died.

> She said all this while nodding to herself. She didn't look at me.

Winters: I'm so sorry.

Client: (awkwardly) I was away, at the time. I didn't know. I found out when I got home. I was too late.

Winters: (after a short pause, kindly) What happened?

Client: (sighs and takes a deep breath before speaking in a shaking voice) I was on a . . . trip out of town. When I got home I . . . (long pause). She was already buried. It had happened a long time before. All over and done with. Long time ago. But I saw her . . . I mean . . .

> She stopped here and really twisted the dress. I heard a stitch pop. She was fighting so hard not to break down that she couldn't speak. I wanted to help her but I didn't see how to do it, there was an aloofness about her that kept giving me this strong signal that I shouldn't reach out yet, she wanted comfort, but she'd bite too. Sometimes you can be too quick and if they break then they get scared and run at this point. I didn't want to make that mistake. Then she looked up and I saw tears were already covering her face.

Winters: (with sympathy) So you couldn't be there, and you didn't know what was going on, and you couldn't find out . . . you were kept away against your will.

> She nodded here but she couldn't speak. I didn't want to lead or push although it was all to easy to draw certain conclusions. I got

the feeling she was living rough because she'd run away. I felt that she wanted to stop running and this was why she was here; she wanted me to say something to stop her or stop the pain. I felt very bad that I couldn't, but she just kept twisting the dress so eventually I tried something from an angle.

Winters: (gently) When did this happen?

Client: (sobbing) Just a couple of weeks ago. When I left she was fine. I thought I'd only be gone a few days at most.

I wanted to keep her talking until she was used to it, to stop her bottling up again so I stuck with the time. She seemed comfortable with that.

Winters: (hesitantly) But ... you were gone for a lot longer? Was it a sudden illness?

That really made her start. She did the 'fishing around' look with her eyes. I'd really thrown her, which threw me because it seemed straightforward.

Client: What? No. Natural Causes.

Winters: (surprised) Natural Causes?

I shouldn't have said that but I was too surprised. I mean, she couldn't be more than twenty eight. Even with blended families and step families and everything, natural causes in this day and age? But it was too late, suddenly she was suspicious.

Client: (accusingly) Is this in confidence? It is, I mean, isn't it, in confidence? You can't tell anyone. You aren't recording this on a public format?

Winters: (steadily) It is usually recorded on an encrypted government format for purposes of quality control. (thumped recorder, no effect, offered a What Can You Do? Smile) But yes. All the information here will remain unviewed in any way, unless you become the subject of a criminal investigation for a type 1 crime, such as murder. Then an AI will review the material in case it contains a reference to the crime. This is government aid therapeutic counselling and we are bound to adhere to their regulation and ...

She totally cut me off here, waved her hand in dismissal. Clearly she couldn't afford private care. And then she started asking me questions in this rapid-fire tone, like an interrogator.

Client: Yeah yeah all right. I got it. Tell me, how do you feel about faeries?

I know she was trying to see if I was a 'safe' listener so I told her the truth.

Winters: I see a lot of clients whose problems result from faery inter-action. I would have to say my feelings are mixed. Of the faeries I see regularly around the city I like them well enough but clearly there's a lot more to them than meets the eye, to say the least. I suppose I have to say I like them but I don't entirely trust them.

I tapped the desk three times here in the usual way. I know we aren't supposed to adhere to any of the faery codes from the old days but I always have, out of habit, and I thought it might make her feel more at ease. She saw me and suddenly the whole aggressive thing just collapsed and she was back to withdrawn and miserable. Just like flicking a switch.

Client: (whispering) It's all my fault.

Winters: What is?

Client: The Hunter. He came because I didn't seal the bargain properly.

Right. At this point I mentally sat back though I tried to stay calm and keep my posture attentive and caring. I started to understand there was a lot more going on here than a straightforward grief issue. It's not often people are so traumatised by grief that they'll fabricate like this on top of their own guilt, projecting it far beyond their range of control. I know it can happen, though I only read accounts, never saw it myself. The theory is that they fabricate because they think they must have done something that bad to warrant feeling so bad. They aren't used to powerful emotions or can't handle them, so in order to explain them they invent a reason. But she seemed so sharp just prior to this, I was really shocked. Also, it was weird that she chose such an old event as the *Anno Venator* to claim as her own. It certainly is among the great horrors of the last century, but clearly quite beyond her influence as he departed half a century ago. So that made me start questioning her rationality. Meantime, I thought I'd pursue this fantasy for a moment and try to lead back to the primary grief more slowly. I wanted to face her with a hard fact and see what she would do with it. I really wanted her to say something that would tell me how strongly she believed what she'd said.

Winters: (pause, then very gently) But the Hunter was here fifty years ago. You can't even have been alive at that time. You aren't old enough.

Client: (in a flat tone, sniffing) In Faery time doesn't move the same way as it does elsewhere. Everyone knows that.

She said this as if she were pointing out a painfully obvious truth to someone who was being a bit stubborn, like it explained everything. Which it does. If you believe it. I couldn't say anything to this so I just tacked back to the original presenting issue and tried to see if I could make her link the two for me, so I could see how she'd got from the sister to this, and get into her way of thinking a little. Maybe she was a faery victim.

Winters: (warmly) Yes, that's true. But I don't see what this has to do with your sister.

Client: (clears throat, speaks calmly but with intense pain clear on her face) It's because of him that I didn't get back in time. He had to take me back home, as part of the deal we made, but I didn't say when, so he took me back fifty years too late.

Winters: And so for you it was only a short time, days, but for everyone else it was fifty years. And in that time your sister passed away?

Client: (nods) I went to the house, but she wasn't there.

As she was saying this she really broke down from a fairly controlled manner to a completely slumped, desperate state. Her voice became almost inaudible. Now I know that people have often been traumatised by faery bargains and although I first thought her claim was really a projection of guilt I was impressed by the depth and obvious sincerity of her feelings. I had to give the faery thing some credit.

Then she let the dress go and just sat with her hands upturned and empty on her lap, staring at the floor. I've seen people stage these sorts of things in sessions with big drama, they like attention and the energy of it, but there was nothing fake about her. If this Hunter business was a delusion she was a hundred percent convinced of it. I thought she might be too hard a case for me at this point, but I decided I'd use up our hour and persist anyway. At least I could work through the fantasy and maybe find a chink in it to reach her. She looked utterly lost in her quiet moments, like a little girl who's wandered off and can't find her way, fragile, glasslike. Then she could turn in a second and she had this presence, as if she were extremely powerful. She was all over the place. It disoriented me a lot.

Winters: And why did you do this deal with the Hunter?

Client: (quietly, grimly) Because otherwise the Moth Plague would never have ended. I had to get him to clear them up, it was my job, you see, and in return I said – I don't know why I said it, why did I say it? I said in return for rounding them up he could run in Otopia for a year and a day. The words just – came out of my mouth like someone else was saying them and then it was done. Just like that. Done. And I was on the beach by our street and nothing was the same. Nothing was . . .

Winters: (encouragingly) Yes?

I thought she was going to collapse but she suddenly shook herself with another effort to hold herself together and she made it. I felt a bit disappointed – collapses can sometimes get right to the heart of a matter – but I had to go with her. She suddenly became practical and brisk in that classic manner of people who are capable of brushing things under the carpet as a way of coping. I felt like I was going to lose her.

Client: Doesn't matter. Look, it's my fault and now I'm here and my sister is dead and I can't find my husband and I don't know what to do. I think he's dead. I thought maybe with the time difference he'd have found a way out but . . .

She nearly lost me there because I'd not expected this at all, this 'return' to reality with her sister, and then the continuation of the delusion as she started babbling about relative times and Faery again. I had to clarify. I really didn't know what to think now.

Winters: Your husband was with you, in Faery. But he was stuck there?

Client: Yes. He was killed. Maybe. I thought he would escape.

Winters: (faltering) Escape death?

Client: (impatiently) One of the faeries took him. He wasn't entirely dead, he just didn't have much energy left ... at least I think that's what happened, I'm not sure, I don't have any magical senses and I just saw him soak up into this cloth she was holding and he was nothing just ... nothing ... oh my god ...

> She totally broke down here for several minutes. I started to wonder if she might be a Changeling and that all this could be a faery-induced fantasia. I know we didn't see these Changeling cases any more after the moths had been removed, although there was a time when this sort of thing was absolutely common. Thousands of people experienced shocking things as they slept, but in realities the clients insisted were as real as their waking lives, in fact often more so. I didn't have much knowledge about Fey trauma, but I wondered if she had maybe encountered some residual moth dust or a faery had played a trick on her using some. At the time – this sounds rather stupid now – I didn't connect this mothkin possibility with her fifty year time claim.

Winters: Here (offers tissues). That sounds ... terrible.

Client: (sobbing) We unlocked this ... I don't know what it is ... some kind of prison or something, under Faery, and the farther down you to the farther back in time it kind of is, or the earlier in the life of the faeries it is. All the oldest, strongest versions had been locked up in there since before the human world was even alive and I had the key, you see, I was given the key by that stupid little Ooshka (crying) ... and she's dead too. She died trying to save Zal.

> At last she was getting a bit more fluent but I had to make her backtrack.

Winters: Zal is ...?

Client: (sobbing) My husband. Zal. The elf. You know. Zal. From *The No Shows*.

> I had to shake my head at her. It's hard to describe this but when

she said his name I felt she was calling him. But even so, an elf? Like an elf would marry a human. Ever. In a billion years. She scrubbed her face with the tissue. She didn't like crying in front of me, it angered her. Then she sighed.

Client: No. Of course not. Why would you know?

I checked using the desk registry. When it returned the image I felt my heart really sink and a cold, nasty feeling came over me. Totally unbelievable, totally historic. Zal *was* an elf. He'd come to Otopia sixty years ago and been in a rock band, a quite famous one. I couldn't believe it. He'd gone missing several times, was a known drug abuser, the subject of some kind of elf fatwa, and had finally left Otopia for good at about the time she was talking about, shortly after his sister – a demon! – had been killed in an accident back on the Daemonia homeworld. The records insisted he was also a demon. I mean, you couldn't make it up.

I didn't have time to read about the elf/demon thing but I have now and I got to say I kind of admire the guy and I see what there was to see in him. Leaving your entire race and going against its ideology to prove that demons and elves don't have to be sworn enemies, in fact can be brothers – it was kind of heroic. To say the least. Even the music was pretty good. But at this moment I didn't know any of this and I just felt like I was talking to someone who was lost in a huge stack of fabrications like some kind of labyrinth. The only question now seemed to be just how big a stack it was. My surprise and disappointment got in the way of my work I have to say. I was just too keen to find out how she could have found that story and be making all this up. How much more would she reveal? Would it fit with the records? I mean, she could have been to the library and got it. People can throw some sophisticated fits when they want to make a false reality to live in. But it was so ridiculous. I mean. An elf. Come on.

Winters: Zal of The No Shows was your *husband*?

Client: (quietly) Is. He still is.

Winters: Okay. I'm sorry. Still is. But he's . . .

Client: (insistently) The Moirae took him. (She spat, actually spat on the carpet and then ground it in with her heel – that's a curse thing). When we were down there, in Under. And he hasn't come back. I mean, stupid of me to think he would. I just ... maybe I assumed that because it was me and I'm lucky and he was so smart that he'd get out of it. Listen, I mean, he gets out of everything, he's really very, very foolish, in a very, very smart way. It's like some divine gift for doing the mad thing at the right time. Zal does what he likes and follows his nose and he can walk on sodding water, you know what I mean?

> Which was classic pedestal fantasy about unobtainable celebrities so I nodded, to keep her talking.

Winters: This is all completely overwhelming.

Client: Yes! Yes it is. It's such a relief to say so though I also wish I hadn't because it kind of makes it real, you know?

A-ha, I thought. Now we're getting somewhere. I even suspected she might eventually admit to making it all up if she were able to make such a genuine emotional contact with me.

Winters: It makes it real, when before it seemed like it might be imaginary.

> This attempt to displace her from the delusions backfired but she was too upset to switch on me. She seemed to have accepted me as an ally.

Client: No! Not imaginary, but like there was some hope left. And fuck hope. Devils' work. But I wish I had some, that's all. You know?

Winters: So your sister is dead, your husband is ... missing ... you feel responsible for the Anno. Are you alone here, then?

Client: (miserably) Yes. Except for my husband. The other one I mean.

> She said this in a very unguarded way, still floating in that short spell of relief.

Winters: Forgive me. *Other* husband?

Client: He's going to be fine. I thought he was going to die too. But he'll be all right. There's a faery at my house looking after him but I'll have to go get him soon because otherwise they might take advantage of him.

I just went with it and tried not to let my disbelief show in my voice.

Winters: They?

Client: The faeries who live there. Max left the house to them, in her will. I mean, I couldn't live there after ... when I came back and they'd been there for years. T's a demon, so obviously they'll start to try stealing his magic and that'll just be carnage.

Winters: You're married to a demon? I mean ... another ...

I had to stop because I didn't know what I meant.

Client: It was a demon wedding. Not here. Obviously.

Winters: (carefully) Obviously.

I couldn't stop myself from saying the next line, which was really really unprofessional.

Winters: Does the elf know?

She looked at me as if I was the crazy one but it was kind of a hard stare, like she could turn nasty if she had to and I was about to give her a reason. I wanted to laugh, like I always do when I'm a bit frightened. Thank goodness I didn't.

Client: (scathingly) He was *there*, it was *his* wedding, of course he knows.

I wished I knew the details and would have asked but I didn't have the nerve at the time. Instead I decided I should probably try to finish mapping the extent of her fabrication so that at least when I passed her case over to the relevant expert I'd be able to give them the whole picture. Plus, I'd started to wonder just how far she could go, if she had managed to make it all fit together in a logical way.

Winters: (calmly) I wonder if it might be helpful ... this is so very complicated ... could you tell me how this came about?

Client: (impatiently) What? Is this the Tell Me About Your Childhood moment?

Winters: If you would like it to be. I mean, if that is important.

A long pause here. I thought for a moment she was going to spring up and attack me but instead she balled her hands into fists and stared at me, kind of through me actually. I wasn't sure I was reading her very accurately at this stage because the story was throwing me off a lot. I reminded myself she was obviously deeply hurt to get to this point, however ridiculous it might sound, and that the treatment plan would probably involve going along with her fantasies. Also, I really did think she was telling the truth about her sister at least, and that alone was bad enough.

Client: Okay. We lived in one of the settlements down near the beaches at the south bay. Nothing worth mentioning really. My parents were decent people, struggling to pay for the house but it was their dream home, you know. Sister and I went to school, then college, nothing exceptional. After school I went into executive administration, she wanted to be a chef. She was good. No way Mom and Dad could send her to a proper cookery school but I got a good job. Very good job. I paid for her to go and I helped out with the mortgage and stuff. Um . . .

Winters: That sounds very generous.

Client: (disparaging) Hardly. Especially in comparison to . . . to say my parents had a problem with alcohol and gambling is like saying the ocean has a problem with water, you know? Same old story for a lot of people here who came to work the Hotelinos. Nothing big. So it was me or nothing. Not like they could hold a job.

I felt like I was doing better now, just reflecting what she said and what I could pick up of the way that she felt.

Winters: It sounds very difficult and painful.

Client: Yeah well, lots of people have it worse. And me and Max we were clean and we were both able to work, and there was this place, The Hart Clinic . . .

Winters: Yes, it's still got the best reputation for helping addicts.

Client: Right, but it was like a thousand bucks a day and at least a month needed to get over whatever, you know?

Winters: You planned to save and send your parents there.

Client: (more relaxed now) Yes. You see, I worked in the Otopian Security Agency offices. Signed the Secrets Act, even though I never

xv

saw any secrets. I was only clerical but after the first year they let me sit some exams and I got a promotion. The money was big but I had to spend a lot of extra time at work, nights and sometimes weekends as well. And if my boss travelled then I had to go with him. Lots of us went. We were in a diplomatic unit. Anyway, one day we went to Alfheim.

> I was surprised here, because Alfheim has always been closed to foreigners as far as I know but there wasn't time to check it then. I began to wonder if this job of hers was part of a fantasy.

Client: And while I was there I met this guy I didn't know that well, from our offices, said he was new and on some important business and would I like to help him with Otopian interests, just looking around and making notes, nothing dangerous or out of the normal range of my duties and etcetera.

Winters: He wanted you to collect information?

Client: (self deprecating laugh) Spying. I didn't realise it at the time. God! How naive I was. Can you imagine being in that position and not understanding what it would mean if you were caught?

> If this was a lead up to a spy claim then it was a really good one. She was so relaxed and self deprecating, even her self hatred was so genuine, and there was this sheen of agony over her and everything she said, the same way she spoke his name, that was like a mourning call. I believed she had lost everything she was talking about.

Winters: What would it have meant?

Client: Instant end to all relations with Alfheim, that's what, plus you'd be lucky to get out alive. But then we still thought the elves were all muesli and woodcrafts. Rustic romantics with old souls singing the woods to sleep and curing cancer. All that sort of shit.

Winters: You don't think that any more.

Client: (points to her neck and face, the scarlet marks) I had what you might call a baptism of fire on that point. I made the stupid choice and I went along with this guy and we got caught snooping around outside the convention centre in the woods. Their Secret Service agents ... there was some big problem going on with them, internally. They were fighting. The civil war. I didn't know much about it back then,

I was just there to pour drinks, smile nicely, take records, that kind of shit. Anyway, it wasn't an open war, it was all politics and backstabbing and double agents. That stuff. Almost impossible for an outsider to understand. Anyway, they caught us in the woods with our elf interpreter who'd been trying to stop us all the time. They arrested her. She was terrified. That was the first time I noticed something really wrong. They'd been so civilised until that point and it didn't seem so bad. Then Vince, the other guy, tried to escape. They were distracted for a minute and he thought he'd get back easy, I mean, it was like less than a hundred metres to the bloody convention place. You could see people, humans, walking at the lakeside, talking. And we had immunity. They shot him dead right there. I never saw anyone die before. I didn't think ...

> She was biting her lips and choked on that last word. I was really struggling with the real depth of agony she felt. She kept doubling over on herself and she was ripping bits out of the dress hem with her fingers. I never saw anyone do that. It was quite weird, and she got this slight smirk, that smile of people who are looking back at a past mistake they haven't got over; it really reminded me of self-harmer cases except she was doing it to an object.

Winters: You didn't believe they would do something like that, because you were protected by your position?

Client: Yes, exactly. I mean, we'd just been in a party for godsakes, with little cakes and fancy clothes and nice talk and everything, like butter wouldn't melt anywhere. They were all like professors or something, like angels. The leader of this Secret group who arrested us though, he was really different – mean, hard as nails. I still don't understand exactly ... after Vince was dead I realised there was another thing out there in the woods with us, not an elf, not human. It had killed one of them. That's what the distraction had been, and they totally freaked out. It was *panic* and they were soldiers. I didn't understand what was going on. They were all wired, you know? Like something had been going on a long time before me and Vince came along and now there was going to be big trouble and they wanted to hide or get rid of us. They kind of couldn't cope with us being there and being this extra problem, like we made no sense. I don't know ...

what happened. Weird to think about that now. I never ... I don't know.

Winters: It must have been terrifying.

Client: I don't remember. The leader made me stand up in front of them. He said he had to make me an example to remember, for Otopia to understand its place. It was kind of a weird speech. Like he was trying to convince his men he meant it. There was this moment where he hesitated and I was looking at him because I knew he meant he was going to kill me and I thought if I could just make him see I was only a fucking *secretary* and I didn't know jack for godsakes ... it was crazy!

> I was going to speak here but she cut me off with a wave of her hand. She'd gone from being extremely upset to really controlled. Her head was down. She didn't look at me, but at the carpet. Her body had gone quite stiff.

Client: He hit me. Magic. And when I woke up I was in a medical centre with a billion wires and tubes in this white, white room and I couldn't feel my hands. There was a nurse. I asked her if I was dead. She didn't say anything, she just went away. There was an elf there too, an older one. He was nice. He was the only nice thing. The people were bastards. It confused me. I was there a long time. I thought they were making me better. But they made me into a machine.

Winters: What do you mean?

Client: They told my family I was missing in action, that I'd been with a failed mission, it was all secret. No hope of return. I nearly did die. They thought I would. And I would have been dead because that magic destroyed ... I think ... it might have ... anyway, they said I wouldn't survive if they didn't put it on.

Winters: It?

Client: The metal prosthetics. You know, it never felt like I'd changed really. They were good. There was nothing left of me but a head, a spine, some other bones and various bits and pieces that didn't add up to a whole human being. They made the rest.

> At this point I couldn't help looking very closely at her. She was absolutely human, rather small if anything, with a beachgoer's tan. There wasn't a trace of anything mechanical about her. She was

concentrating on giving me the story, as plain as she could, so she didn't notice my stare. I became reconvinced that she was living in an illusion.

Client: So, I couldn't go home. But Zal took me home. After we got back from Alfheim. He took me back. And I couldn't go in the house.

Winters: You met Zal, how?

Client: Oh, he was important to the elves. They wanted him dead. They don't do freaks. I was his bodyguard here, and I got him out of Alfheim after they pulled him back. It was my first mission, I guess.

Winters: That sounds ... heroic.

Client: (scathing) Yeah doesn't it just. It wasn't like that. Okay that part of the story contains someone else I don't want to talk about. I had to kill someone.

She closed her eyes here and put her hands on her chest, gripping them together very hard. Her nails were bitten short. I saw her knuckles yellow under the skin. Machine my butt, I thought. But a lot of people treat themselves that way.

Client: And ... look here it is then. I met that bastard who did this to me and he said he'd lead me to Zal. There was a civil war and they were on the same side. He did his job, which included killing a mate of his from their secret service, only the mate was a necromancer and I didn't know and I was shocked like some little screaming girl (she mimed this) when he stabbed him and I was trying to ... I don't know ... I was trying to fix this body or something, or say sorry, and I picked up the spirit. He was alive, just his body was dead. I *hugged* him. And he went in through my mouth and he was inside me.

She had her hands pressed flat to her breastbone here, indicating very clearly the space around her heart. There were so many weird layers to this delusion that I thought she'd be in therapy for the rest of her life. I didn't even have the slightest clue what to do next, so I kept on going.

Winters: You mean you felt that you were carrying his soul?

Client: There was no feel about it! He was right here, mean and snappy as in real life, bitter as hell about being dead, talking all the time. Yar

yar yar yar in that prissy language with every vowel like some kind of dinner for one. And he hated me. *Hated* me. Human filth and worse than that, machine filth, a corruption of everything that he valued as sacrosanct. (she paused and snorted, mocking herself again) I could have got rid of him, but then he'd have been really dead and that would've been my fault. So I didn't.

I took a risk. Bizarrely she seemed oblivious to it.

Winters: (cautiously) And what does he say now?

Client: Pah, thank God, he's not here any more. Although, I kinda miss him. But I can say that because he's not here. Anyway, he was with me a while. And he could make me look like him so we got a long way into Alfheim, all the way to the top where they were holding Zal. And we got him out but I had to kill him. The other guy.

Winters: The leader of the secret service group?

Client nods at this point and bares her teeth, clenching them together in an expression of pain that was quite horrible. She shook her head and she went ugly and her hands grabbed the dress at her chest and tore it slightly. I don't mean she pulled it apart, she just grabbed hold of it so fiercely her hands tore it.

Winters: You had good reason to hate him.

Client: I didn't hate him. Not by then. I understood him. He understood me. He let me make a bunch of stupid mistakes because I was learning, and we got into this position where if I didn't kill him then our cover would blow and we'd all be dead so I had to ... had to ... (pause) He was like my mentor. He loved Zal. I mean, *I* loved Zal, but he has this arsey side to him that made it quite hard to like him a lot of the time, you know? But when I heard this guy talk about him and how he'd been this struggling figure for years in their stupid archaic system ... I really saw another side to him and that his fooling around was that same kind of thing that you do cause you got to laugh when you can't cry any more. Stuff is too ridiculous. That kind of fooling. Serious. Deadly serious. And I loved him more. And I loved that tough guy. And I killed him. Me and the dead elf, Ilyatath. We stabbed him to death because if we didn't our cover would blow and we'd all be dead. (she mimed two hands on a knife, stabbing very close to her, right in front of her)

She was speaking very flatly now, quiet, calm, almost emotionless. She let her hands fall into her lap.

Winters: But you succeeded, you saved Zal and brought him . . . here?

Client: We had a few days together and he tried to put his career back on track. My boss sent me to Daemonia. She figured that now I was tested and working I could go spy on them and use Zal as extra information, find out what all this elf and demon business was about. Nice huh? He played along. His sister approved of me for some reason.

Winters: His sister?

Client: (smiling, sad) Sorcha. Sorcha the Scorcher. You must have heard of her.

I made a show of looking it up. Weirdly there *was* some gossip about her being related to Zal, but the press felt it was a publicity stunt for the most part as it was such an impossibility. Their joint concerts sold out anyway. I felt really thrown. I didn't expect anything she said to actually check out or be checkable but she must have researched it all so well. Her stories could have fitted so plausibly into the facts.

Client: (disappointed) Anyway. She took me with her on a tour of Demon society. Party all day. Party all night. Drown the weak in champagne, celebrate with a duel to the death, that sort of thing. Zal was supposed to come and join me but the idiot got high on an elemental fire and ended up teleporting himself to bloody Zoomenon of all places. I didn't know this of course. No idea what had happened to him. Meanwhile half of Demonia was trying to kill me on an hourly basis. Minutely basis actually.

Winters: But why?

Client: They like to live by the motto Kill or Be Killed and it's an honour point to test strangers and wannabes with duels and assassination attempts. Once you survive a certain amount of violence the frequency drops because your status goes up and eventually only the elite ones come on to challenge you. It's how they organise their society.

Winters: A certain amount?

Client: A week or something like that. And you can skip up if you survive a major demon or, better yet, if you announce your intention to get one and bag it while you're in the underdog position.

Winters: Did Zal do this to become a demon, is that how it worked?

Client: Nah, that's what my boss wanted me to find out if anyone could do it and how it was done. But he didn't fight his way up. He just had to get clean.

Winters: Sounds like that has a special meaning.

Client: (a bit more animated now, interested to tell me) It does. If you want to become worthy of being counted among the demons you have to self actualise to the point where you no longer suffer from negativity directed at yourself, or even anything beyond a moment of reasonable doubt. Never self doubt. Nothing less than total acceptance and a strong connection to the desire to live. Demons are creatures of life, though they'll be first to say they go too far always. It's a point of honour. They despise devils which is what they call any negative thought or parasitical emotional burden. They seem to think of them as actual beings, kind of bad karma in the real. It's why they hate the elves, not for any other reason. Elves are just devil ridden to the core, according to the demons. Humans too, a lot, but humans have no magical power so that makes them despicable and boring trash whereas the elves are just despicable worthy opponents.

I had done a small study into alien psychomyths and this did seem to fit with what I'd read. At least, it made sense of what I'd read. I wanted to think she was right. I started wanting to believe her although the notion that all demons are psychically fit as fiddles was a bit bizarre.

Winters: Zal was an elf who got rid of his demons then?

Client: His *devils*. Yes. He did. He has. That's why he's a divine fool. And he ran the gauntlet too, he had to face the demon champion and beat him in a fair fight, which was never fair because the demon champion was Teazle Sikarza. Tell me you heard of him?

I had, of course. The fact that she would even ask it made me wonder, because he's everywhere in kids' stores, along with dinosaurs and all that other stuff, but maybe she could be that out of touch – suddenly I just didn't know what to think.

Winters: There's a comic book . . . about him.

Client: There's a what?!

Winters: A comic strip . . . for kids . . . legendary monsters kind of thing.

For some reason she paused for the briefest moment and her eyes got this faraway stare and then she burst out laughing, really so hard that she rolled over onto her back for a moment. There was certainly some hysteria in the laugh and she went on a good minute but finally she got herself back in position.

Client: I needed that. Thanks. Where were we?

Winters: Zal the elf beat Teazle Sikarza in a straight fight.

Put like that it sounded completely ludicrous. No way is that in the storylines the comic book writers write.

Client: Yes indeed. Anyway, that story wasn't sufficient for *my* boss who didn't believe Zal's version of events because he can come across as this big arsey pathological liar, frankly, it's just unfortunate that he's nearly always telling the truth. Meanwhile I intercepted an assassin who was out to get me and Zal. It was an elf. She blamed him for the war. Her family died in it. But that's not the point. The point is that during this whole episode I picked up an imp. A little demon, like a mini gargoyle sort of thing.

She waved a hand near her shoulder, next to her ear.

Client: He sat here. Talked to me. Like you. Told me where I was going wrong, how deluded I was and what about. Therapy on tap, as he would have said. They're a sign of weakness in Demonia, because they only appear if you're devil-ridden.

I hardly dared.

Winters: Is he . . .?

Client: Not invisible. No. He's in prison. In Faery. Apparently he was some kind of war hero although the faeries don't really see it that way. They have a big thing about crusaders. Like to put them in prison.

But anyway, before they nabbed him I picked him up and he stuck his fingers into everything and explained everything and he was pretty sharp, for a completely annoying, mindreading little git.

She looked straight at me here.

Winters: So you left Daemonia . . .?

Client: Yeah. But not without enemies. One of them came back here and killed my parents. (She paused, clearly remembering and mastering the event. When she started again she was sad and tired). That's when I went home and told my sister what had happened to me. Tath – the dead elf necro – took me over into Thanata so I could see them before they . . . before the final journey. I could have kept them. I could have stopped them. They were in this little bottle. Necromancers can tap out the soul, keep it forever that way.

> I wasn't sure what this meant. A demon had put her parents souls in a bottle? I think that's right. But I was following her so I tried to lead again

Winters: But you didn't keep them.

Client: No. Beyond life and death? In a bottle? What kind of thing would that be? No. I didn't.

Winters: Are you sorry?

Client: (hesitantly) No. It was the right thing to do. And I was sick of being at the mercy of the Agency too. So I tried to destroy all their control equipment. I wanted to get away. We were all just being used. It was no good. And to help me my partner at the Agency, Malachi – he's a faery – released the Mothkin. It was just supposed to be for a short while. To distract the security agency so that we could get away.

Winters: Why didn't he take them away when you had done it?

Client: Because we didn't do it. I could wreck as much as I wanted of their stupid machines, they had more. It became clear I would never find them all and could never be sure. Never sure they weren't listening, watching, in my head. Even they weren't sure. The technology was beyond them. They just used it. They didn't know how it was made.

> Her emotions had flattened now. She talked like she was deeply depressed, as if things were facts that had nothing to do with her,

and occasionally she seemed confused. What follows is not exactly right as I couldn't piece it together at the time very well.

Client: So, there was the moth plague and the only thing to get rid of it was the Hunter. Malachi told me. We had to go to Faery and find a way to him, make him come and round them up. In the meantime one of Zal's singers, Poppy, gave me this necklace, well, he gave it to me but she found it. Someone told me it was a key, to a special place in Faery. I didn't really believe them. It didn't look like anything. And we'd sort of agreed to stick together by then. We went to get Teazle but he'd gone off on one of his moronic hunting missions and since we got married and everyone was trying to kill us there were a billion small fights but the short of it is we went to find him in the badlands and he'd found this demon for a fight, but it was too much for us. One fucking demon, and we nearly all died right there. We got away, but it killed Sorcha. After that, none of us were any good.

Winters: I'm sorry, you married the demon and Zal, and then you had to regroup for this . . . mission? Is that right?

Client: Yes. But we lost Sorcha. It was so stupid. Just a stupid game. After that, everything went wrong. We got separated going into Faery and the key took us straight to the lock. It wasn't really a lock, it was a place, a time, where everything was suspended, stuck. And it took us to a faery, Jack. He wanted the key, to get himself unstuck. But it was locked to keep the bad things away from the other worlds, and he was one of them, so I shouldn't give him the key. We fell prisoner to him and we had to bargain our way out, but the bargains were all bad. Everyone did a deal. Except me. The bargains were bad because of me. You see Jack discovered Tath, said I'd hidden him as a wildcard, and called us false players. He demanded satisfaction by trial. Zal ran a race against him but he couldn't win it. Jack killed him. And then Malachi had to cross over, onto Jack's side, become one of his creatures when we lost. So he was gone too. And Tath got a body there . . . Jack had the cauldron of rebirth, and Tath got a new body. He left me. Then the imp tricked Jack and made him crazy, but by that time Teazle had found us. He slayed Jack. Then Tath took Jack's place as the Winter King. He had to, someone had to because we killed him, but someone had to take his place and Tath chose it. So I was the only one left. Then the key opened the lock and me and the imp fell through. We fell and we found the hunter and we let him out. Mission accomplished! But we were all changed by then, too much changed, far too much. Faery does that, it changes things. And now I'm here, talking to you, Ms Winters. Picked you for the name. Seemed to be a connection.

She was sharp by this point, quiet, attentive, focused. The transition was astounding. I felt she was daring me to call her a liar. Because I couldn't do anything else I stuck with the truth.

Winters: I don't know what to say. It's overwhelming.

Client: You probably think I came here because of all that. I did. Kinda. I don't have anyone to talk to about it. But that's not what bothers me, Ms Winters. It's just what happened. It's done although the pain is sometimes hard to bear. But as long as he isn't really dead, I can stand it.

Winters: I don't understand. All *that* doesn't bother you? Then what does?

Client: Ever since I was down there in Faery, I got completed. The machine that I was made of, it took over every bit of me. And ever since then I've had this noise I can hear, all the time, like a badly tuned radio in the next room. I think its the machines, talking. I think. I don't know for sure. I mean, it could be some kind of malfunction, because of the elementals that got fused into me. Aether and metal don't go, right? Or, I wondered if, because of what happened, maybe I'm going . . . a bit mad? Starting to hear voices. I mean, what do you think? Should I do something about it or should I just wait and see if it starts to make sense?

I'd realised by this point that anything to be done with her was way out of my hands. The lack of responsibility was suddenly liberating. I felt all the weight of trying to believe her drop away from me. As she sat there, sincerely looking at me and waiting for my answer, as if I could have anything useful to say, I thought of the only thing I ever found to be any use to anyone and I said that.

Winters: You know, it really doesn't matter what I think. The important thing is to go with your values. Check what you know, check what you can't and don't know. Then decide what *you* think.

She sighed and hung her head for a few moments, then she nodded, picked the bits of dress off the carpet and put them in her pocket.

Client: (sincerely) Thank you, Ms Winters.

Winters: You're welcome.

She got up from the floor and came over and shook my hand. Her touch was warm and as ordinary as any hand I ever felt. She gave me a smile, genuine one. She looked very tired but much more peaceful than she had been for the hour.

Winters: I think it would be best if I referred you . . .

Client: No thanks. You've been a great help.

I encouraged her to think again but she was adamant so, because she seemed to be quite harmless, I was compelled to let her go. I even offered to see her again, for nothing, but she just smiled and said no. She was completely composed as she left. I watched her walk away down the street. She went towards the beach.

Transcript ends.

CHAPTER ONE

Cold winds blew off the north shore and gave Lila a burning slap as they snatched foam from the rim of her coffee cup and flung it into her face. She let the scalding black stuff run down her skin without any reaction save a slight narrowing of her eyes.

The drink was cheap and it would have needed a faery cup to make it worthwhile, but just as the beans and the roast had been skimped on so had the cheap pulp cup. She swallowed what was left in three gulps and threw the cup into the trashcan next to her. It wasn't like they were queuing down the block to get the stuff.

The snack stand guy gave her a disturbed look as he pretended to ogle the latest copy of *Succuperb!* on his Treepod, but his attention was pulled away by another customer too hungry or broke to walk a block to a decent outlet. Lila took a final long look at the ocean and let the coffee soak into her skin. The taste taken this way was pure information, not involving tongue and nose or the beautiful crafting of a brain that created flavor out of molecular detection. As raw data she identified coffee. She knew it was bad, but at least her guts didn't feel offended. She briefly considered drinking all his coffee that way in the future but, then again, no. Pain was pain and the medicine had to go down the right way.

In her palm she ran her fingertip over her plastic cash card and read off the amount. It was so low. She would have reorganised a few zeroes with ease, but getting tagged for fraud didn't appeal to her sense of privacy. They could track the card position by satellite and pinpoint her in seconds. Then they'd find out she wasn't a registered citizen and send agents to collect her, or the rogues would read the signals and try to get to her first. Staying a step ahead of both of them was worth more than all the digits she could have fitted on the card.

She closed her fingers over it again and slipped it into her pocket, wondering for the millionth time what she was going to do about it. The lodgers in her old house just about paid for the bills and what food she had to have, but there was no extra. It mildly amused her that she would think of savings, of age, of the future when the present was so uncertain.

"Hey, aren't you cold, lady?" someone said behind her, not pleasantly, so she started walking back the way she'd come, down onto the hard sand and along the bay, aware that she made a distinctive and somewhat fey picture: a young woman with a pale tan and some freckles on her bare arms and legs, her dark and oddly patterned scrap of a dress blowing around her knees. The scarlet swatch in her unkempt lanky hair lifted on the breeze to show a scarlet shape like a paint splash on her neck and shoulder. It was far too bright to be natural. She was barefoot. It was February, and in Bay City that meant onshore gales and bursts of chilly rain or even sleet. Normal people, whoever they were, disdained chiffon and silk cocktail gowns and wore coats and boots at this time of year. Sensible people added a hat. The person calling to her was not wearing a hat.

He shouted after her, "Pookah scum!" in his breaking teenage voice, and his mates laughed in excited, ugly tones. She paid no attention. In such a public place they weren't likely to follow her far. But she felt the wicked spike of their attention snake out and touch her energy field, testing it for weaknesses. Time was she'd never have noticed that, and time was she'd never have given it credence if she had. Even if it had hurt her. Times had changed though.

Lila hardened herself against their hate and quickened the pace. Better to avoid any conflicts or scenes. She never lingered. They might find her interesting enough to take a picture of, send it across the 'Tree. Then anyone looking would know where she was.

In another world she would have had their heads for it.

The few people—fellow beach bums—who knew her figure from her daily walks were the only people she didn't mind looking at or being seen by. Most of them had the wits to notice her expression and left her alone whether or not they were curious about her. Many of them were the same as she was, outsiders for whom a nod and a glance is enough of a daily contact with others, and some of them were even demi-fey, she was sure. They were a little club of look-but-don't-touch people, nod-but-don't-speak people; allies as long as anonymity was maintained. But they were in the minority. Bay City was a social hub.

The city was a cosmopolitan, confident place these days, with few fey and fewer other foreign creatures. It had learned its lesson about romancing weird things the hard way, and nobody wanted to risk whatever wrath she or another nonhuman might be able to bring down on them. This made some people friendly, but it made more of them hostile. There were many faeries hidden in the world, many more than the openly fey. Demons and even elves had come in larger numbers in the last twenty years; in the elf case that meant nearly double figures. The children of their first human matches were adults now, and in spite of a repatriation epidemic Otopia was hardly the pure human place many wanted to believe. The teenagers who'd tried to insult her were examples of a deep schism; half the world was glad and half the world was furious at the changes. Lila had no time for any of them, but it wasn't possible to ignore the daily and awful evidence that the solid identity humans had felt for themselves had fallen apart and many of them weren't able to deal with the results in anything but negative ways. So they thought she was a faery. It wasn't entirely false. She was sure they'd have been much less glad with the truth and she felt grim satisfaction in that. She was worse. It was like an ace in the sleeve. It protected her from spite.

The man at the coffee stand watched her go, fingering the rabbit's foot he kept in his pocket. When she'd vanished into the drizzle beyond the boardwalk entertainments, he quickly recounted his money and checked the onions steaming in their steel tray. Faeries could turn things bad. He'd had a frog in the onion pan before now, and no knowing where it came from, but it had shown up not long after she'd been there for her one black coffee of the day, always at ten a.m. She'd made a face at the coffee. She often did that. But maybe that time it had been worse than usual. Supplies were short. He couldn't help what the wholesaler had, could he? He poked around the onions, but they were frogless.

"Get out of it," he said to the teenage idiot and his friends, watching them watch her go, their voices lewd and sniggering. "Go on."

"He's afraid of her," the insulting one said with contempt. "Maybe she'll turn the milk bad or something. Stupid old man." But the fuse on their malevolence wouldn't light. It was too wet and cold to start the revolution. They huddled together and sloped off to enjoy their alienation closer to the glittery lights of the pier.

Sometimes he wished the Hunter would come back for a day, to show these arrogant young bastards a thing or two. But then he remembered, and unwished it quickly, whistling and turning widdershins and throwing salt over both shoulders to undo his silliness. When he was finished he made another wish, the usual one, but he had no doubt that in spite of it she'd be back tomorrow.

Malachi also knew where to find Lila on a regular basis. He'd visited her every day for the last two months. Their conversations ranged from idle gossip to raging arguments, but he was the only one to do any talking. The most she ever contributed was a smile or a nod, a frown or a contemptuous wave of one hand to dismiss him or his point. Or both. Usually he managed to stick with her from the top end of the beach to where a fence cut off the public land from the expensive private homes two miles away. Even if they were just doing a silent vigil he made it that far, but then he had to go. His official lunch break lasted just an hour and the commute back and forth to the parking lot out here at the end of the sands meant he had twenty minutes to do whatever he had to do, tops.

Yesterday had been a breakthrough day, he reminded himself as he parked. He switched his beautifully soft suede pumps for running shoes and rolled up the cuffs of his heavyweight silk suit trousers, pinning them with hairgrips so there was no danger of them being ruined by sand or surf. He put the roll of his silk and wool socks into his top pocket and scrunched his toes where they were slumming it inside a pair of all-cotton footsies to protect them from the trainers. Then he got out of the car, wrestled briefly with his umbrella, locked the car, checked it, locked it again, looked around at the dull day and the sulky youths hanging around, and renewed the protective charms on the ancient Cadillac with a gentle caress to the hood that looked as if he might be checking for scratches.

The gesture made him scowl, even as he made it. It was pointless trying to conceal his feyness since he was far too well dressed and mannered to be human in this neighborhood. But he couldn't help trying. The coal blackness of him—an inhuman shade that sparkled—had been matted with the powders of glamour into African tones, and his orange eyes were hidden behind five-thousand-dollar shades. In the early days of his tenure here he'd never needed such things. He didn't understand how the humans could have gone backwards like they had. He was disappointed they seemed too weak to handle even the least of the Gifts and the least that the aetheric worlds had thrown at them.

Malachi was the last full-blood faery in public service in Otopia, and he was getting mighty sick of it. The only reason he hadn't left long ago was right now striding along in front of him in the worst rain of the season looking disturbingly like the previous owner of the dress she was wearing, as he recalled, another person he had known who had come to a bad end. Well, that might be premature. She'd never returned from her banishment in Under, so one couldn't say for sure. Only her clothes had ever shown up and he had to admit that it was possible, more than a little, that Tatterdemalion had never really been a girl at all. He'd started to think that the girl he'd known in the old days with her plain, forgettable face was maybe no more than a mannequin the clothes had stitched together out of aether and dream to give themselves transport and a voice. The dress had worn her, and when she was out of style or no more use, then it had put her away, that girl.

This theory had come to him a few weeks after he and Lila had made it out of Faery and found themselves fifty years too late by the Otopian clock, but although he always intended to tell her about it he never did.

He caught up with her without having to run. His strides could be as long as he liked without him seeming to hurry. He had to fight the umbrella against the gusty breezes, holding it out like a shield before him.

Lila acknowledged him with a slight raise of her eyebrows but her pace continued the same.

Malachi narrowed his eyes against the cold wind and winced automatically as he saw icy flakes hit the surface of her eyes and melt there. She didn't even blink. Since she'd worn the dress, the irises of her eyes had become a deep indigo colour, like the fabric's basic hue. Before that those eyes had been a robot's flat mirrors without iris or white, so that people always assumed she was wearing fancy contacts. She hadn't been. Most of her then wasn't human, but replacement parts. Now he didn't entirely know what she was. One thing he did know, she wasn't living at home, wasn't connected to any networks, and wasn't who she used to be three months ago. The longer her silence went on, the worse he hated it. Now he'd come with something she could really worry about, but he found his irritation emerging first.

"Are you going to keep up this silent act forever?"

"I'm listening," she replied.

He was taken aback. "My god, she speaks!"

Lila didn't say anything. The faintest hint of a smile twitched at the corners of her mouth.

"Are you messing with me or are you going to talk?"

"You did all the talking," she said.

"I did all the . . ." he cut himself off as something struck him. He didn't want to lose the moment. He even forgot the awful weather and the conviction it was ruining his coat. "What changed?"

"I've been listening," she repeated.

"I'm overjoyed that my repartee is so . . ."

". . . to the machines," she said, interrupting him and abruptly stopping so that he strode past her and had to come back, getting a face full of rain in the process.

He cocked his head. Her faint smile had become enigmatic.

"I thought if I just listened long enough that eventually it'd begin to make sense to me," she said. Water ran down her face and arms, soaked her dress. "They talk all the time. Little whispers. The ones that aren't here and the ones that are." The wind whipped her rat tail hair around her neck. "I kept thinking that I'd be able to figure out where they were by the signals, but even if I couldn't do that at least I'd know what they were saying. That's why I couldn't talk to you. I had to listen all the time, as closely as I could. I was determined to wait as long as it took for it all to fall into place." Finally she met his gaze with her own. She hadn't lied, she'd only omitted to say that she hadn't wanted to speak to anyone anyway, because she didn't know what to say. What could she say after what had happened? Zal was missing. She didn't even know if he was alive. She only spoke now because she knew it couldn't go on. Not speaking was not holding time still. It was not solving anything. But she felt she could talk about the least of the worst.

"They all talk, Mal. But it's not for us. I don't mean the rogues talking or the other agents the agency made. We talk to each other, or could. I mean the machines talk. More like sing. Or dance," she frowned. "Not good words for it. The machines talk all by themselves all the time. Here. There. Everywhere. I can't locate them because they're all here." She tapped the side of her head with a finger. "I can't separate them because there's no difference. I can't talk to them, none of us can. We aren't connected for it. I can just hear it, this shiver, this whisper, all the time. I think it's because I'm all machine now. It's like hearing a beehive, very quiet, full of meaning you don't understand because you are too big and too slow."

Malachi clutched the umbrella more tightly. Lila had been made by Otopian Secret Services into a cyborg, using technology obtained from unknown sources. She had been the first survivor of the process. The agents she spoke of were later additions, modelled on her own success. The rogues were those of their number who had left the service to live outside the law. Some were trying to return to a human life and forget their pasts, and the rest—they weren't human anymore. He didn't know what they were and they didn't know either. They called themselves rogues and considered themselves above and beyond human laws of any kind. They were a damned nuisance, with their gangland ways, but even though their continued existence was the Secret Services' fault, the management of their trouble fell to domestic lawkeepers, so until they started messing with otherworldly business they weren't his problem. Now here was Lila, telling him she could hear this stuff. He couldn't keep his own secret any longer.

"I got these," he held out a chip to her. It was standard issue data transfer. She pinched it between her fingers, and her eyes got a glassy look as she began to look at the pictures he'd given her, unfolding them into images that he'd seen and now tried not to remember. Unlike him, she didn't flinch at visions of apocalyptic slaughter.

She blinked as she closed the file. The chip seemed to have vanished, he had no idea where to. "He's been gone three months," she said, referring to the demon responsible for what she had just seen— Teazle.

"You know who that is in the picture?" It was the best way to say it. Who it was would have been more accurate. He hadn't been able to identify it himself. An AI had done that, after it had spent some time putting the pieces together.

"Madame Des Loupes," Lila said, and for the first time in months Malachi saw her composure falter. "Why would he kill her?"

Malachi shrugged. Demon politics didn't interest him. All he knew about Madame was that she was the most powerful clairvoyant of any age. The only person she feared wasn't Teazle Sikarza either, it was Sarasilien.

Three months and two weeks previously Sarasilien the elf had been steadily working in his long-term office of diplomatic liaison to the Otopian Secret Service. One minute to the second after Malachi and Lila had rematerialised in Bay City he'd dropped everything and left. Nobody had seen him since. He'd been a surrogate father to Lila, and Mal hadn't known how to tell Lila he was gone, so he just didn't tell her at all. Fortunately there was enough to deal with that he needn't worry about that yet, or so he'd thought. As it was, besides that coincidence which was clearly no coincidence, there was nothing to connect Sarasilien to Madame's death and plenty of evidence that pointed at Teazle. It was curiously easier to tell Lila that Teazle was the suspected killer, though he was her husband, than it was to tell her about the elf. Even Malachi didn't understand what the reason behind it would be.

Motive wasn't the question that bothered Mal. There were perhaps a dozen reasons Teazle might kill anyone, not least of which was because he felt like it, but as a result of their immersion in Under, they had all changed: Lila, Teazle, Zal, and himself. Thinking of this Malachi licked self-consciously around his too-big canine teeth and for the thousandth time considered having them filed down. He'd do it, if he didn't think it might have horrible repercussions somehow, in parts of him that he had forgotten but which might be important.

"*How* would he kill her?" Lila rephrased, jolting Malachi out of his dental fantasy. A frown made the rain suddenly dash down her nose and drip off the end. "I mean, she had clear sight, she'd see it coming, surely." Then she met Malachi's gaze with a curious one, a sad one of her own.

She couldn't resist mentioning him, even though she'd promised herself not to. No talking about Zal. No brooding. He wasn't dead. "Why doesn't he come back?"

Malachi shrugged. He didn't mention he was gladder that the demon was absent. Teazle made him deeply uneasy, never more so than since he had returned from Faery a changed being. Always lethal and ready to slay in his true form, he seemed to have disconcertingly acquired a form that was made of light, rendering him negligibly material. He could teleport before, and now? Malachi had no idea what he was capable of in that sense, but it added up to a scary prospect if it got coupled with ambition, and this murder did seem to smell of that on first sniff.

The rain was getting him down. "Do you think we could go somewhere more civilized?"

"Hm?" she glanced around them at the sheeting deluge, as though only just becoming conscious of it. "Oh. Yes."

"My car's on the lot," he gestured back the way they'd come. She nodded and fell into step with him. He watched her. She was pensive all the way up to the car door and then she stopped with her hand on it and looked across the roof at him.

"It's faked."

She was referring to the crime in the images. He could tell by the seriously switched on look in her blue-violet eyes and because other agents had said the same thing. His heart sank. "I know," he said, opening the doors and wishing he'd brought a blanket to cover his seats. "Get in."

The car creaked on its suspension as Lila eased into the passenger side, so smooth and graceful she might have been made of air. It didn't feel lopsided like it used to however. Malachi squinted at her as he reached for his handkerchief, "Did you lose weight?"

"Apparently," she shrugged as she looked at him mopping his forehead delicately. Her fingertips ran over the upholstery. "At least you went for a synthetic this time."

"My wages don't stretch to the insurance required by transporting freaks of nature anymore," he muttered. "Speaking of fakes, what tipped you off?"

Lila smiled a short-lived and wintry smile. "The body is butchered almost into sludge. That's not Teazle's MO at all. He'd never waste the energy." She hesitated and a flicker ran through her face, "Plus, if you sum it all up, there just isn't enough of her to go around. They speculate he ate part of her, but that's classic necromancer-minion stuff or a practice for an assassin who's on his way up the ladder, not at the top. He'd never do that. Then, there's no sign of the Suitors and I don't believe they'd stand around and watch her die."

Malachi nodded—he'd thought the same but he hadn't had the stomach to search the images thoroughly enough to be sure.

Lila continued, "So, where are they? Plus, it makes no sense. Sure he might have wanted her dead because I'm on her books as one of her Eyes. He hates anyone having power over him. If she had a hold on me, then tenuously she was getting a claw into him. But killing her serves no other use. The demons might all fear her, but they want her alive because she's number one in their defense systems against Who Knows

What? But I keep coming back to the more basic fact that all the parts look right but don't add up. They don't match. You put it together and you get Frankenstein's monster, not Madame Des Loupes. I'd bet she isn't even dead. So what is this about?" The chip had reappeared in her fingers magician-style as she spoke. She turned it over and over like a coin between her knuckles and then gave it back to him.

He put it in his jacket pocket and started the car with the key. "They're for you, honey. The Service knows you're back and it seems they've lost patience waiting for you to come home."

"Eh . . . so they want to fit up my husband on some faked murder?"

"Them and some other people. This came to my hands in a roundabout way. I know they think I see you. They're betting I'll show you, and tell you that Teazle is wanted for this, in Demonia. Their top Necromancer has fingered him for it. The forensics might give the lie, but he was the coroner on the case so it's a done deal. It's kind of a traditional demon way of getting rid of real trouble. The sentence is passed."

Lila stared through the windshield at a world that was flowing and running and warped by the rain. "Kill on sight," she murmured, almost to herself. It was the penalty for Illegitimate Murder in Demonia. "What's the bounty?"

"His house, his estates, and all he owns in perpetuity. And Lila," Malachi waited until she turned to face him and for an instant the violet eyes of the dress's girl became the curved mirrors of her true self, paying him full attention. The chameleon change showed how uncomfortable she had become.

"Yes?"

"You have to know—Teazle has been on a spree the like of which no one has seen in a literal age. They call it the Rain of Death. By the time this came out, yesterday at noon, he'd slaughtered his way through almost the entire crop of Bathsheban high society and made a good inroad into the Shalazad Dynasty. He currently owns eighteen and a quarter percent of the total wealth of Demonia and has rule over fifteen family houses and nine crime syndicates." He shared this, sure in the knowledge that no other human without firsthand experience of demon life would understand the true scale and monumental, suicidal ambition of this enterprise. He added with a wry half-grin, "They're all loyal to him, too, or he'd be occasional tableware by now."

Her face went pale and seemed to age, flesh drawing closer to the skull. "But it can't last," she said quietly. "So much money. So much power. They'll all rise to challenge him. But why, Malachi? Why did he do that?"

Malachi shrugged, "No idea. That trip to Under surely did something to him. Thing is, the Otopians and the Demons have done this fit-up together, with Faery help. They all see him as a major threat and they want him gone and they want you to show yourself."

She did the frown that made two tiny lines between her brows. It made her face endearing, he thought, although he wouldn't dare say it. "I don't really think he needs me. . . ."

"Not to protect him, you dollop. To hunt him," Malachi broke over the top of her words with annoyance. "In demon law you're bound to the task, as his wife, number one. Two, you stand to inherit both ways if he dies, which effectively puts a human in charge of Demonia for the nought point however many seconds you survive the office. Three, he is a menace and you are about one of the only creatures who stand a realistic shot at nuking him. Four, they want you back in ranks. They've figured out you're the one behind the missing rogues and their vanished agents—all the ones you disposed of on your arrival—and they're willing to make you a serious offer."

Her face was attentive, open, pleasant. God, he didn't like the look of this.

"I hate being the messenger!" He slammed the wheel with his hand and closed his eyes for a moment to regain his composure. The taste of blood let him know he'd cut his own lip on his fangs. He fussed with his handkerchief, realised it was silk, and started to look in the glove box for a tissue instead. "If you bring them Teazle on a plate they'll give you all the World Seven Technology and control of the projects it was used in. They want you to lead that unit. You'll have complete authority. The only person over you will be the president."

She looked at him for one serious blue second. Then she burst out laughing. She laughed so hard that tears streamed down her face and got lost in the rainwater. Gasping for breath, holding her side with one hand, "Oh that was good!" she panted in between snickers. "That must have taken hours to make up. You really had me going! You bastard. Queen of Demons *and* ruler of the Secret Cyborgs? That was a bit far. Nice pictures though."

He looked at the blood drops on the tissue paper and saw them spreading slowly into seven giggling pixies. He screwed the thing up, wound down the window, and shoved it out. "It's not a joke."

"Oh, *Mal*," she patted his knee gently, her gales subsiding into gentle rolling fits. Then, as he sat miserably wondering what it was he'd ever done to make another second in Otopia worthwhile she coughed and cleared her throat and her face started to fall. "Mal. Is it? Mal. No."

"Where's the sword?" he asked her, dead straight. He knew it would wipe the smile off her face and cursed himself when it did.

"I've got it," she said, suddenly cautious. "Why? What is this?"

"Someone at work knows about it. I don't know how. But they know. That's why this is here now. They know that it's what you used to dispatch the rogues. They want it. Or, they want to know what it can do and make sure you use it for them if you use it at all. That's the trouble with ancient artifactual objects . . ." he trailed off and started cursing ferociously in the faery speech so she couldn't understand him. By the end of it he was gripping the wheel, his knuckles aching and his fingernails grown into claws that cut into the skin of his hands. He released them slowly and gently and turned again to her with a troubled face, his orange eyes glowing through the black lenses of his glasses like miniature suns. "Lila, you have to do something. I think I've kept you secret, but obviously not. I don't think I was followed, but I don't know. They're giving you a grace moment. It won't last."

She sat and stared at him for several seconds, then without a word she got out of the car into the pouring rain and took off. He heard her jets start and felt the air push at the car as she took off, but instead of seeing her leap into the sky he saw a strange grey and violet bird spring up, spread enormous, tattered wings, and beat its way into the air.

"'Demalion," he whispered, making a warding sign of the old gods, feeling angry and troubled. No way should these things be happening in Otopian space, but, then, it was hard to get worked up about it when all the streets full of psychics and mediums and faith healers said otherwise.

Human wasn't what it used to be. Nothing was.

CHAPTER TWO

Lila flew above the city in the rain clouds. The mist blotted everything out of visual contact and left her with more space in her head to contemplate what Mal had just told her. She had other senses, including radar, to take care of collision control, though she wasn't aware of them working any more than she was aware of breathing unless she paid attention to it. Around her the silky mantle of the tattered dress folded itself tight and warm, shedding rainwater in drops stained lilac though the fabric never faded.

She didn't know what to think about Mal's story. She briefly imagined becoming the mistress of Demonia and only then felt the faint tingle of a feeling that might have driven Teazle to attempt it: let's leave it all when we can't deal with it. Let's tempt death one more juicy, fatal time and stand on that edge, daring everything to bring it on. Such a thing was demon glory.

That made her remember Zal. Zal had literally and figuratively run into the dark without a backward glance. It hurt to think of it. She wanted him so badly it stopped her in midflight. Zal would never have tried to rule Demonia, and not just because he was an elf by genesis. Tempted as they were by their natural wonts to sink into emotional festivals of angst, elves were corruptible and able to sacrifice themselves in the name of some cause relatively easily. But

Teazle was all demon, and he didn't do sacrifice unless it was of someone else.

For some reason she'd never figured out yet, neither did she, but she was much more bored with reasons than she used to be. All that mattered now was what idiots did and what she was going to do about it. There was only one thing on her mind these days—a desire that burned her and drove her crazy and didn't need reasons, but she was stuck fast with it because the last she'd seen of her love was a stain on Destiny's petticoat and damned if she knew what to do about that.

Thankfully Malachi had turned up with this shitload of nonsense and she did know what to do with it. She flew on over the city another mile or so, avoiding the tiny one-person flitters that zipped over the tops of the skyscrapers. Great flower heads of idling rotor blades made the air shimmer over the tallest buildings, where power sinks in the form of minimaks sent out narrow tendrils to each tiny car and pumped their miraculous batteries full of aetherically charged electricity. They said *charge*, but she knew it wasn't: the science was still in the mumbo jumbo stages while the engineering had merrily forged ahead. So now they had almost limitless energy, and limitless gadgets to absorb them. Go humans. Lila just thought it looked like a takeover bid by the aetherials—distract the majority, give them something serious to worry about, meanwhile rip the rug quietly out from under—it was a standard faery tactic, but who could blame them? And at least the existence of relatively planet-friendly energy gave something positive to point at when the fey-bashing got intense.

She descended, emerging into clearer air and sputtering drops of rain. She shook herself out as she stopped and stared down at the buildings below her: Otopian Security Services, disguised as a bland corporate office block and giving off the ordinary power signatures of a bunch of medium-level computers and a few air conditioners. Not much to look at considering that inside it, some ten metres belowground in a bio-bunker, was the cradle where she'd been processed and reborn half-human, half-machine. One glance at the three tall square blocks of concrete was enough to know that she was completely and finally done with what they represented and what they housed. They could hang themselves with their own rope after all they'd done for her.

She listened. The ever-present whisper of the machines was the merest vibration, and for so long it had made no more sense than random static. For weeks she had been effectively listening to a dead station. But although now she couldn't have decoded the whispers into words or even concepts, she knew that they informed her of things all the time, about the state of the physical world, about themselves. She knew, for example, that there were six agents below her in the building who had also started out their second lives as cyborgs, and had ended up as an advanced version of what she was now—a replica of a human being, her every cell mimicked to perfection in matter slightly other than flesh and bone. She was slightly more metal, more crystalline; more suited for the passage of light.

She waited, patient as the grave, until she saw Malachi's blue Caddy circle the block and slide into the black mouth of the underground entry like a slow fish gliding into the mouth of a shark. Malachi was still "in" with Security, in spite of being the cause of their greatest malaise—the Mothkin invasion that had torn humanity from its mundane roots and spread aetheric talents like a contagion. Not that anyone called them that or recognised it officially. The newly psychic humans might be a genuine underclass out in the real world, but in the bureaucracy of Otopian Government they were just people who had suffered delusions under the effects of too much faery moth dust.

When enough time had passed that she reckoned Mal was back in the building proper, she descended to the roof, jammed her fingers into the tiny gap between the security door and its housing, and wrenched it off its hinges. Nerve gas pumped quickly into the narrow corridor space beyond and fogged the treacherous steep stairs, but Lila didn't need to breathe like an ordinary person. She walked through it, feeling a slight headiness, and addressed the steel shutter that had come slamming down in her face. Getting through sheet steel was never easy, but in her months of solitude she hadn't managed the quiet contemplation and Zen retreat thing all that well. She'd spent most of it fooling around in scrapyards and empty warehouses, testing herself, figuring out what she could do so that when a reckoning came, as it surely must, she'd be ready. Lila didn't have magic herself and as machine and human was doubly useless in that respect, but metal elementals were a part of her structure now, and they had no such trouble.

Being part of her structure meant being part of her mind. She wanted the door open and placed her hands out upon it. Tendrils of glimmering white light began to rise and crawl across her skin as the metal elementals rose and gathered energy from the matter around them, constructing themselves a nebulous kind of form. It was far from the forms of their true actualisation, she understood from Zal, but it was form nonetheless and capable of occupying and reconfiguring any metallic object. It took a long time in resolutely un-aetheric Otopia, where the laws of physical matter held firmest sway, but it was still more than possible. Beneath her hands the door became hot. She traced a line from top to bottom and side to side, drawing her arm steadily as if pulling the zipper of a tent. The metal separated, not visibly, but at the molecular level, and then she was able to use simple force to bend the four leaves of it and curl them back so that she was able to step through the hole she'd made and stand in the room beyond.

By this time a kind of welcome party had managed to get itself together. Two human guards in full body armour with machine pistols and one of the legitimate cyborgs she'd never seen before stood just behind the open flower of the security shutter. Their weapons were all aimed at her, though they held fire. One of them hadn't been able to fit his gas mask properly and it dangled down the side of a handsome square-jawed face. She stepped up and put it on for him, clipping the tag to his helmet and giving it a pat. It bought a moment of surprised stillness in which she saw herself reflected in the dark shield that covered his eyes; her red hair spiked with rain, her violet eyes beneath that canny, her dress plastered over her, glittering as she stood taller than she should in her big black combat boots.

"I'm here to see the gaffer," she said, stepping back and taking a more critical look at her reflection as if in a vanity mirror. No, there was nothing to be done about any of it. She was a complete mess.

The more efficient of the two guards radioed down for instructions. His voice was shaky and he'd gone slightly rigid all over. Lila ignored him and made herself look at the person she really didn't want to see.

The android was a fifty-years-in-the-future version of herself, or what she would have been if she'd lived those fifty years and undergone no aetheric interventions. Clearly human, clearly female, she no longer bore much resemblance to who she'd once been. She looked like a hairless sculpture of a thickset woman with rudimentary, idealised features. Her skin was dark grey and shiny with the hardness of marble. Even her eyes were made of the same substance. The gun at the end of her forearm was a heavy, short weapon, the empty hole at the end of her finger promising significantly more harm than the humans' guns. She was wearing a green camo uniform, like the guards, the sleeves and leg cuffs rolled. It looked like someone had dressed an unpainted plastic model and posed it for an army shop front. As in Lila's case, the boots were the feet were the boots. On the breast pocket a name tag read *Bentley*. At Bentley's neck a thin nine-carat gold chain lay, with a small girlish pendant in the shape of a hollow heart hanging from it. Lila's own heart constricted slightly.

Don't be afraid, Zal'd said. When he'd understood the change was to be total and permanent, the machine consuming every cell, he hadn't batted an elfin or demonic eyelash. She was his girl, no matter what she was made of. But then, it had been just a few months. Not decades.

Lila saw Bentley staring at her feet and looked down. Buckles and straps and the semblance of leather to the kneecap were real enough to look 100 percent convincing. Above them pale skin with last year's tan rose as if it were flesh and disappeared four inches above the knee into the sopping, tawdry skirt of Tatty's dress. The dress had a mind of its own, Lila'd discovered, and was able to make itself any way. Today it wanted to look like crud for some reason. There was not a trace of the impeccable stitching, the gold, silver, jewels, and scales of its onetime magnificence, when Zal had given it to her, ignorant of its history. Then it had been just a gift from a lover, some nice thing to wear instead of all that boring black-and-camo combat gear. Of course it was rare, soaked in magic, and the price of a king's ransom, but he could afford it on rock-star fortunes, and somehow, he'd thought it might save her.

The dress *had* saved her ass against the baddest faeries in town. Truthfully, it was probably the dress that had got the agreement from the Hunter to hoover up the Mothkin and save all their butts from an endless sleep. She still didn't know why or even how exactly, and the thing irritated and spooked her equally. She was never sure if it belonged to her or the other way around, but it was Zal's gift and that was the one reason that prevented her taking it off and burying it under several hundred tons of rock.

The cyborg continued staring at her legs. Lila stared back at those grey eyes, her jaw starting to jut, and saw the head duck suddenly, as if ashamed.

Mercifully at that moment a second squad of mixed soldiers and officials appeared through opening blast doors, and Lila found herself face-to-face with a person she assumed was the present head of the Otopian Secret Service. They hadn't met and Lila was permanently disconnected from the World Tree, so she really was just going on the air of authority and the grimly controlled yet thoroughly pissed-off expression.

The man in the suit was tall and broad shouldered, dark but greying at the temples, his immaculate and conformist grooming marked oddly with a surge of upper lip hair—a bandit's moustache. "Temple Greer," he announced himself, taking a solid stance and placing his hands together in front of him. He kept his weight back as he looked her over, and said insouciantly as his gaze flicked back to her face. "You must be Lila Black."

Lila shrugged and smiled sweetly, as if butter wouldn't melt in her mouth, admitting it. She'd already decided to give nothing to them, and that included conversational openers.

"You're under arrest," he said, his face impassive as though she were not very interesting. Meanwhile, more armed people came into the room and started to fill up the corridors. She heard something heavy land on the roof and more feet getting out of that.

The grey-and-black shiny bodies of other androids oiled into the corners, slipping easily through the crowd. Their guns were bigger. They all bore the same plastic look of humanoid uniformity, some male, some female, but without distinctive faces. Each wore fatigues, some with ammunition belts or other devices attached. Finally she was surrounded by quite a throng, a space of clear carpet one metre wide around her. Greer faced her from its twelve o'clock position.

She missed Tath. She missed the imp. She missed Zal. Where someone should have said something sarcastic and smart about the situation, now she had only the endless windblown susurrus of the Signal.

"It's like you knew I was coming," Lila said, rather too loudly. "Thanks for all turning out. I feel almost moved."

Greer stared at her with genuine dislike. "You should be grateful you're not dead."

"I am. Every day," she assured him. "As is Teazle Sikarza, I'm sure. I can barely imagine the thrill of his existence, living under a Legal

Execution Order back home in Bathshebat. And I understand he's got you to thank for that. Was that a plan to halve the demon population on your part? Pretty clever if it was. Pretty dumb if it wasn't. He'll be pissed when he finds out, and since he got back from Faeryland he's been a bit . . . hasty in his judgement." She wondered where Malachi was and hoped he had the brains to stay out of it.

In her head the machine whispered to itself, flipping digits, switching charges. She wondered if the others heard it too. Maybe they knew every word . . . *word* was not the right word . . . maybe they understood what it was saying. Perhaps it was telling them her secrets. If it did, they showed no sign.

She shook her head and found Greer looking at her with widened, angry eyes because she'd been zoning out in what, for him, must be an important moment.

She shrugged. "Do your guys hear all the background chatter, or is that just me?" She waved her finger in circles next to her ear to illustrate and glanced around at the various androids with a questioning face and an encouraging smile.

"Your business isn't asking the questions," Greer said flatly. "Answering them is."

"Oh, because I thought maybe the more advanced a machine you became the more it might make sense. At least, I got that impression off the rogues who approached me. I have to say, they weren't too much friendlier than you. Y'all gotta work on your people skills, geekfiends." Lila let her smile stay airy and uncomplicated. "Anyway, as long as you don't mind the fact that pretty much everything you use to protect the homeland security is in constant communication with unknown entities at unspecified places, I guess I can live with the mystery."

Greer actually looked uncomfortable for a second. Lila wasn't sure exactly why, but it was good enough for her. She held out her wrists together in front of her. "Better cuff me then. Or do you want to talk about ghosts and stuff? The news these days is full of such scary stories."

His eyes narrowed and his nostrils flared. He made the smallest motion of his head left and right and said quietly, "Get out."

The room emptied, bodies flowing through doors like water down a plughole. Within a few seconds they were alone. A moment or two later she heard a soft padding in the hall, and Malachi appeared, slinking with a deliberate, insouciant slowness. Greer glanced at him with a scowl as he came through the doorway.

"Shut the door."

Malachi pushed it closed and stood, folding his hands in front of him. He'd taken off his sunglasses, and his orange eyes blazed, their cat pupils wide, his expression a combination of grim and bored that made Lila want to smile. She turned her gaze back to Greer with pleasant expectation to let him know he could dig his own hole now and bury himself in it.

To her surprise the man relaxed, his stiff posture and bullish pose softening as he released his arms from their brace position and loosened his big shoulders. He opened his jacket, flicked the sides back, and stuffed his hands into his pockets. His head tilted slightly to one side and he made a show of loosening his jaw. "The trouble is, Black, you're right and I'm right and the world is a wrong, sorry place to be right in."

"Is this good cop?" she asked. The corner of Malachi's mouth twitched in a grin as Greer looked back over his shoulder at him and then gazed back at Lila.

"Temple Greer is a man of distinction among humans," Malachi said to her. "He is straight about his lies." He made the faintest nod.

She tilted her head too, to show she was still listening.

"What I told Malachi to tell you was to bring you here," Greer said easily. "It's true too, but that's just a sideline. We could play cat-and-mouse games another month or two and piss each other off some more, but you're fifty years late and time's running out for all of us so I hope you'll overlook the methods. I know there's nothing holding you to the agency now, if there ever was. I don't approve of what happened here in the past"—he glanced over her, managing to convey that he was referring to her machine alterations without making it look sleazy—"but it's ancient history now. Here you are. Here they are. Here they are . . ." And he jerked his head in Malachi's direction. "And whatever the government likes to say to the press about human security, we both know that's a horse that ran out of the barn a long time gone. So I'm not looking to bolt any doors here. We used to do that in your day. Now we're more of a . . ." He hesitated and looked back at Malachi, for all the world as if they were some kind of tag team.

"Centre for Supernatural Crisis Management," Malachi said around his huge canine teeth as if he were tearing up the words. His dislike of the term was so obvious it made her grin.

Greer gave a short laugh at what was clearly the office joke, "Yeah. Anyway, my offer to you stands. You're unique and I need you to help me do this job. In return I promise you can have the uneasy feelings, stomach ulcers, and sleepless nights that I enjoy, knowing the world is no safer nor better for your existence. But you'll be in charge of some miserable twisted little bit of it, for a while. I can throw in a few henchmen, offices, labs, access to top-secret information that I probably shouldn't have myself, and an off-peak pass to one of the second-rate hotelino health clubs. What do you say?"

Lila was smiling. "I appreciate your humour. But to my main point again. Teazle Sikarza didn't murder Madame Des Loupes. I don't believe she's dead. You're putting it about that he did. Your forensics helped the demons convict him."

Greer held up his hands in a placatory surrender pose. "Slow it down some. First of all, we did send out a team to the investigation, at the request of their chief coroner. Part of one of those itchy-scratchy back exchanges. We needed help with some things; they wanted independent verification. . . ."

"So they could have an absentee conviction and an immediate sentence," Lila said, folding her arms.

"Yeah. That. Got to love that legal system they have. Sure is efficient." His gaze became dreamy, as if he were contemplating paradise.

"But you weren't interested in him for any other reason? You didn't want to involve me in something that would be likely to bring me leaping out of the woodwork into full view."

Greer reached into the top pocket of his jacket and brought out a small carving on a leather thong. He held it out to her, but she could see it fine and didn't take it. "You know what this is?"

"It's a Happy Fetish. The demons make them; they sell them at Annie's Jewels and other stores like that. Twenty bucks each." She quoted the label, "'Likely to encourage good feelings and general zest for life. Product not guaranteed.'"

"Yeah. Ever since they came out they sell like hotcakes. My daughter got me this one for Father's Day. Kinda ugly, big eyes, too many tusks, so I don't wear it. And then there's the small problem of the demon inside it."

This time their gazes met and held for a few seconds.

"You see," Greer said, rewrapping the dead demon in its thong and slipping it back into his pocket, "we know about this, but we aren't allowed to say. We know about the moth-touched, the loony luna-people and their sleep and their dreams. We know about the Woken, thanks to Zal for those—only took ten years for his efforts to show fruit. And we know about the Hunter's Chosen, though we can't talk about them. And we know about the Hunter's Children." He smiled broadly at last as he saw her real surprise, her puzzlement, her confusion.

She looked at Malachi and saw his serious nod as he answered what was uppermost in her mind first. "Zal's music made a lot of people free," he said.

She missed Zal suddenly and so precisely that she could feel the shape of the emptiness that had taken his place.

"It was the quiet revolution," Greer agreed, his face mild for a moment, inward-looking on a personal memory with affection. Lila clung to looking at him, waiting for the tears in her eyes to disappear. "Clear vision. Nothing more." Then his gaze met hers with the acuity of a laser. "I'm grateful for that. All of us who listened are grateful. But the Chosen and the Children, well, they're another matter. And the demons. I wish I knew their game. I wish I knew Teazle's game. I wish I knew what happened to him in Faeryland."

The last line was an appeal. Lila didn't respond to it directly. She didn't feel able to, and not just because she couldn't have given him an answer. "We all changed there," she said, and then it was she and Malachi who were sharing the look, alone in the room together, worlds away, lost in time.

Then it was her turn to get sharp. "Which doesn't explain your interest in his death, Mister Greer. And doesn't excuse your part in placing me in the position of executioner over my own husband."

Greer frowned congenially. "Do you love him?"

Lila looked at him with a cool and considering stare.

Greer shrugged. "C'mon, we know what he looks like, what he is, what he does, and for all the add-ons you're still at heart a human girl, right? I mean, I know the story, Beauty and the Beast, and if you knew my life you'd be right to think I'm not exactly an expert in relationships but really—do you love him?"

Lila turned her head the other way and looked at him from the other eye and then turned her head straight and deepened the fold of her arms. "Seeing as you ask so nicely, Mr. Greer, I'll answer as honestly as I can. If you knew my life you'd be right to think that I'm not exactly an expert in relationships. Teazle and I were never even friends—we never had a date, we never went to dinner, we never watched the sun go down together, we don't share any interests as far as I can tell. I say *tomato* and he says *how high*. The one thing we do is look out for each other's ass. I don't know how that started exactly. We don't even talk. But if you think I am going to try and kill him for any reason other than that he tries to kill me first, then you're making a serious mistake."

Greer smiled and nodded. "You ain't the first woman I've met who's that difficult to get a straight answer out of on the subject, but seeing as the first woman I met like that is my wife I'm gonna take your answer as a yes."

Lila scowled and opened her mouth, but Greer threw his hand up. "Lemme finish. She's an ex-Mrs. Greer now, though that's not saying much. My point in asking was because I care about these things and I know others do to. Most of the time in the past this shitty-ass department treated people like accessories and look what happened. You, the other androids, the rogues . . . It's a mess. Plenty of humans left who still think that institutions and governments have to be run as if they were computer programmes, but thanks to your elf man and his record collection there are plenty that don't. I admit we helped put your demon up for grabs, but you have to see he was headed there by himself in any case. I was just taking the chance to get an in with the demons while it was hot. For what it's costing you, I apologise."

Lila narrowed her eyes and nostrils and exhaled slowly. "You are a beguiling mover, for the head of the most important agency in the world."

Greer grinned and gave his shoulders a little jaunt. "Think so?"

"Almost fey," she said. "Now what are you going to do about Teazle?"

"Sweet nothing," he replied, relaxing his weight onto one leg and glancing at Malachi, who had been observing them with detached cool from his place near the door. "Hear that? Fey."

Malachi made a noise halfway between a purr and a growl. It rumbled the floor, and both Lila and Greer looked at him with some surprise. "You are the only reason I am still here," he said to Greer. "And no fey blood in you, though you are susceptible to dust. Just keep listening to the *Light Album* and you'll do well enough." He was referring to Zal's last musical collection. His tone left no doubt that his feeling about the humans was merely a hairsbreadth from contempt. "I didn't care for my part in this setup. So let's finish it. You said you had some ideas worth hearing about Teazle. We want to hear them."

Greer nodded and took a deep breath, let it out, and glanced at the two of them. "What bothers me about the situation is why the demons want him dead. I know there's the power angle, but that's not enough to drive their legal system into a corrupt means of getting rid of him. You know how much store the demons place in integrity. And I don't see why they haven't got together to finish him off either, but I hear that's to do with aetheric power things I don't understand. My point—"

"Your point is that you want to know what it is about him since he came back from Under," Lila said. "Because you think that must be what's made him seek power and what's let him keep it against all the odds. Even though you know that on the day he came here with me three rogues almost killed him in their first attempt and I had to stop them from finishing the job. So if it was just about slaying power, that wouldn't make sense. Three rogues versus fifty demons is a no-brainer, but fifty demons won't touch Teazle with a barge pole. Mystery. One with a potentially useful answer."

"Actually I don't see how it's useful, but everything's useful eventually," Greer said, nodding. "And what about Zal?" His gaze bored into her, betraying the casual manners of the rest of his body.

Malachi shuddered convulsively as if someone walked over his grave.

"Every time I mention it he won't speak," Greer said, nodding at Malachi, "but he twitches like he's plugged into the mains. I know it's not protocol to talk about that place, but I want to know what happened there, and not just for artistic reasons and my chances of winning any bets concerning a comeback tour for the No Shows. Mal doesn't say what happened to him, though he seems a lot more short-tempered than reports would indicate. I guess there's more to it, but it's his business. What happened to you, Black? Where the fuck is Zal Ahriman?"

Lila smoothed the wrinkled ruffles of her dress, which didn't improve it, and fiddled with the silver spiral on her necklace. "I got a new dress," she said.

Greer took a step back and looked at it critically, eyebrows raised. "I'll buy it for what it's worth, which is a heap of nothing so far, but I'm a patient guy. It looks like crap, by the way. And Zal?"

Lila looked at Malachi for a long moment. "Destiny took him," she said.

They both looked at Greer, who swapped glances from one to the other of them, searching their souls. Apparently what he saw convinced him, "Ah shit!" He shook his head and marched for the door, "Why can there never be an answer I can use in a goddamned report?" He paused, the door handle in his grasp, door ajar, and looked back. "Black, Mal will show you to your office. Be nice to the staff; they have a lot of adjusting to do most days and some of them are starting to get a little threadbare. When you're ready to go do something let me the hell know what it is."

CHAPTER THREE

Lila looked at Malachi for some time after Greer had gone. "Well," she said, "I wasn't expecting that."

Mal prowled forwards so he could look into her face from less distance. "You don't have to take him up on it."

"You took him up on it." That came out more accusingly and with more jealousy than she intended. She released the rigid fold of her arms and loosened her shoulders and neck. "You're right, but his charm has got me itching to know what else is going on around here, what the humans know. So much potential and information at my fingertips. . . . I don't think I want to resist."

"The humans." He slid his shades down his nose and looked her directly in both eyes, his startling orange irises glowing, the slit pupils narrowing to black lines. He made a show of sniffing around her head, his broad nostrils taking her all in, the shadow of long whiskers on his cheeks.

Lila nodded. "Strange days, huh?"

Then Malachi was taking a longer, more interested sniff and she waved him off, seeing that he was picking up more than he expected. He got a faraway look as things connected in his memory. "Strange indeed," he said in a knowing tone, a puzzled tone. As she walked to the door she could feel his eyes on her back burning with curiosity.

She examined the doorway pointlessly to give him time to catch up, decide what he thought about what he'd sniffed out, choose what to say, and then hung there, turning back to see him. As he did now at moments of mild stress he took on extreme catlike aspects—nothing too surprising to look at, just a few mannerisms, a way of moving that changed. He was exactly like a cat in a human body. If you saw him in a dark alley you might get him the wrong way round. Then as his thoughts resolved his form reassumed all the elegance and manly demeanour of a slick guy about town, and apart from his eyes there was no hint of predation or whiskers. He slid his shades back up his nose and adjusted his shoulders in their immaculate suiting as he stepped to her side. He fingered a ruffle of the disreputable dress,

"I have to say this is mildly shocking. For years I've been assuming that when you returned you'd take a journey into Faery again, to find Zal, or some other harebrained scheme. I spent decades wondering how to put you off any further entanglements with the Three. Of course I failed. And I was hoping you would have this." He pointed to but carefully did not touch the silver spiral on her necklace. "Because I would like to see what has happened to Madrigal, now that the Giantkiller is dead and gone. And I could have gone alone, but I made my excuses to wait for you." Finally he let the damp fabric go, his puzzlement complete. "And you come back with this. And . . ."

Lila put her finger to his lips and stopped him from completing his sentence. "Never mind about that. I *am* going back for Zal. Of course I am. And I hardly want to be hanging around here. Too much like being in my own grave already when I look at those . . . things. But I don't even know what I need or where to start, so until I do, then being in the middle of something is as good as sitting in a cave. . . ."

"I knew it. Wood ash, shellfish, seaweed, sand, and that odd musty . . . you've been living in a cave on the cliffs. Wondered where you went."

"Why didn't you follow me then?" She looked up into his face, and there was a moment in which she saw a difficult struggle in his feelings and felt sorry for him, and conscious of just how good a friend he was. Perhaps her best.

"Clearly you didn't want me to," he said, and his nostrils flared one more time. He looked unhappy and disquieted.

"We all have our secrets," she said.

His glance was hurt but not condemnatory. He nodded and she saw the anguish of his secrets briefly make his face tighten. He stared at the dress with misgivings, then the necklace. "You've grown up wild. And now the wild and changeling things are claiming you for their own."

She blushed unaccountably and became aware of the pen that was hidden in the cloth sash at her waist where the dress had decided it wasn't doing pockets today, only Grecian folds. It was not really a pen, in the same way that it was not really a dagger, or even a sword, though she'd held it as all those objects. It seemed to burn her through the material, taunting Malachi that he couldn't see it and yet was almost seeing it. It was such an unnerving thing she had to quickly break the moment.

"You wouldn't dare to call me not the mistress of my fate, would you?" she teased him gently, not liking his sudden macabre turn. His pronouncement chilled her, though she didn't show it.

"You know me, Liles," he murmured, as suddenly soft and amiable as he had been piercing a moment before. "I'm the waiting kind, not the daring kind." He straightened up and led the way down the corridor.

She didn't reply. She couldn't imagine waiting for herself for fifty years in this place, day in and day out. She didn't have that kind of patience. She'd like to persuade herself that time was different for him, that he was able to move through it as he pleased, so what was fifty years? But she wasn't persuaded.

"Hey!" She ran a couple of steps to catch him up. "Who else is still here?"

"Not the elf," he said as they moved shoulder to shoulder. "Nobody you know."

"Did they replace him?"

"Master mages are in short supply," Mal said, pausing to push the elevator button and facing her briefly. "That's why you've got his office now. All his gear. Just as he left it."

"But I thought I was supposed to be with the machine people?"

"You will be. But Sarasilien's old job is empty, so you've got that one too. I mean, you're the closest thing to an elf there is left around here." He winked at her as they got into the empty lift car.

Lila frowned, "The elves wouldn't talk to me if I were the last person in Otopia."

His grin intensified; he was all loose-limbed bonhomie again. "Then you'll get a lot of days off."

She wasn't sure she got why he was so amused by it until they got to the door of the laboratories that the old elf had used to call his own and opened the door. It was in the old building, which had been remodelled but not rebuilt, though this part was untouched as far as she could see. Cleaning couldn't disguise the wear in the corridors, but it was almost as she remembered it. Malachi flittered his fingers and undid some magical thing that had been around the door; then he used a passkey and his thumbprint and got the door to slide back. The lights came on, blinking slowly as though from a deep sleep.

Malachi hung back as Lila moved deeper into the abandoned space. Everywhere she felt the presence of Sarasilien, as clearly as if she were walking inside his ghost. Tears pricked her eyes and she felt her throat harden. She wished he were there. She would have liked to punch him because she was so damned angry about the way he'd held out the truth on her for so long whilst letting her so easily fall against his surrogate father support. She wanted to hug him and feel his narrow, powerful arms hold her close to him, smell the strange herbal and sweet scents of the layers of linen he wore, feel his vital energy surround her with its healing, forgiving balm. He was a lying bastard, but he was the only person she knew in whose arms she could have really relaxed, if only for a second. She'd not been aware of it, but here, standing in his empty aura among his work and investigations and all the trivia of his daily life, the loss of that comfort was a spear of sharp pain in her solar plexus.

Moving as if drawn on a string, she walked through the laboratories and pushed the door open at the far end that led into his personal rooms. The hinges creaked and juddered, dry as old bones. The object she was looking for was right in front of her under the dove grey drapes, an unmistakable shape. She bent down and lifted the edge of its sheet, slowly so as to let the dust roll back without clouding. Underneath it the muted Persian colours of the old chaise longue glowed suddenly with amber and crimson richness, and there on the edge lay a diaphanous black-and-gold scrap of fabric, the very piece she had seen him bury his face in, crying, the last time she'd laid eyes on him.

She saw her fingers reach out, black leather opera gloves, and take hold of the feathery thing. As it moved a sudden scent of opium rose from it, laced with sandalwood and brimstone. In her mind's eye she saw Sorcha, sassy and sexy and opulent, lounging right here, teasing the old elf with her immaculate feet, her sultry voice.

He'd loved her.

Lila put the scarf back. She wasn't ready to face it fully just yet. She let the dust sheet fall and hide it again and sniffed, rubbing her nose as it flooded to rid itself of dust, and straightened up. Malachi was a short distance behind her. She turned and found him closer, taller, more awkward, his face become entirely a beast's but so full of concern that she wasn't frightened by it.

This was the shape he'd been in Under, a man-cat creature that was feral and shadow. It had none of his contemporary beauty except in its feline power. His clothes and shades were gone. Thick fur covered him, black stripes glossy in matte black depths.

"The magic on this door undoes me," he said with great difficulty around his massive teeth. "Nobody has been able to lift it."

She wondered who had tried to come here, and as if he read her mind he added, "Nobody could touch anything. They tried for days.

Months. Eventually they left it as you see." Seeing her puzzlement he bent down and lifted the sheet where she had, stretching out one massive paw. It opened into a crudely fingered hand, with claw nails. Gently he attempted to snag the scarf or touch the chaise, but within the last couple of inches an invisible force stalled his movement. "Like magnetism," he said, and gave up his attempt and put the sheet back.

She knew he'd seen her touch it. "He left it for me?"

"I thought so." His orange eyes were narrowed with thought and slight reservation.

"Did you tell Greer?"

"He came to the conclusion by himself."

"You could have warned me." The resentment in her voice was sharp. He twitched.

"Would it make a difference?"

She shrugged.

He nodded. "It was something you should know. If something here is important . . . maybe . . . you would have missed it."

She sighed and relaxed, slumping, "Yes." She found her hand on his arm, a strangely huge and muscled object she could barely reconcile with the Malachi she was more used to. "Forgiven." She looked around her. "I'm not ready for any more of this today."

He nodded once, and together they walked out. As they crossed the threshold of the laboratory there was a flicker and the bulky mass under her fingers was suddenly a lithe arm in an immaculate jacket. She looked down at it and up into Mal's human face. "I didn't know your clothes were part of your glamour."

"They are not."

She looked at the doorway with a scowl. "So how . . . ?"

Mal shrugged and patted her hand on his arm, drawing her attention suddenly to its tan smoothness, its faux ordinary skin. She made a note to be damn careful of any mirrors back in there and wondered what he'd seen in her place—had she changed?

Outside Greer was waiting for them, lounging alone in the corridor, hands in pockets, pretending to enjoy the wall art and the full-length-window view of the courtyard. "So." He grinned at Lila, his expectant glance to Malachi confirming their complicity. "D'you like what we've done with the place?"

Lila punched him. It was so fast she knew he couldn't have seen it coming. She pulled it a lot so she didn't do any real damage and was back to her relaxed pose, arms folded, before his hand had even got to his mouth. "See ya tomorrow," she said, and left him there tending his split lip without waiting for a response. Malachi loitered a moment, then came after her.

"I guess he deserved that." He pointedly stayed out of range as they moved towards the exit.

"I need a bike," she said. "Do we still do that kind of thing?"

"We do," Malachi assured her, beckoning her in a different direction and holding up his hands in a peace gesture as he saw her baulk at the sight of an office full of administration desks. "I'll do the authorisations for you. Let's just get the key to the garage so you can choose?"

Lila leaned on the meant-to-intimidate height of the fascia board as Malachi made charming chitchat to the dispatcher, reached over, and stuck the end of her finger into an empty port in the desk's overengineered surface. She wanted bikes, her AI gave her bikes it found in the database. "It's okay," she said, "I chose. I filled out the forms. Done the protocols, programmed the onboard." She smiled at the dispatcher's wide-eyed face. "I hope the insurance doesn't come out of my pay, it's kinda high."

Malachi half smiled and stared at her with narrowed, amused eyes. "You're enjoying this."

Lila just kept her smile on, pushed away from the desk, and flounced out. From somewhere the dress had gained a little bow over her bottom, and a short train of diaphanous silk.

For the first time in months and longer Malachi found himself laughing.

It was as they stood alone together in the semidarkness of the garage, looking over Lila's exquisite piece of technological fancy, that she looked up into his face across the saddle and he saw tears in her eyes. "Will I find him?" she asked, so quietly he almost couldn't hear her. "Can I? Is it even possible?"

He thought of the yellow peach that sat on his desk, its ripe smell and perfect skin, the still-living succulence of it as promising and untasted as it had been for a thousand human years. He dared not think of the hand that had given it to him. He knew he had waited too long. "Yes," he said.

She swallowed with effort, blinking, licking and biting her lips. "Do you think that girl is still alive—Jones, the strandloper. Do you think she's still around?"

He composed himself, then said, "The Ghost Hunters that she was with set out on an expedition into the Deep Void. She said she was going to find out where the ghosts came from, and stop them seeping into the living world. She thought they were widening the cracks. But they're still coming and I haven't seen her since. Can't say I looked too hard." He shared a look with her that said Jones had creeped him out severely, frightened him. "But if we're going to find them then there's some other people we have to persuade to get us out there."

"You know them?"

"I know of them," he corrected her. "I'll make some enquiries. Look around." He smoothed his hand over the bike's glossy fairings. They were much more arrowlike creations than they used to be in the days of combustion engines, and the rider lay almost flat front on them at full speed, encased in aerodynamic shields, a fish in air. With Lila's skill it would top 250. "You go and enjoy yourself somewhere. Meet me tomorrow night downtown. The Medium Bar."

Lila nodded. She leaned forward suddenly and kissed him on the cheek, lightly and quickly. "Take care, Mal."

"You too." He tapped the bike warningly and stepped back as she got on. LEDs and arrays came up as she touched it, then subsided. He assumed she'd internalised all that stuff. Like magic. He watched her spin slowly forwards, saw her get used to the machine's silence, weave it around the narrow turns of the lot and vanish up the ramp towards the daylight.

Back in his office he started to look up names and addresses but unaccountably found himself holding the peach in his hands, examining it minutely for any sign of bruising or rot. There wasn't any, and he breathed out with relief, inhaling deeply afterwards. Its smell was heady, divine. He pressed it against his lips.

Lila rode for a few hours. She took the fastest route out of the city onto the expressway and followed it south over the curling, secretive waterways that threaded the suburbs. She crossed the first of the Five Arches; bridges that mimicked the Andalune's giant span over the five rivers of the dunes in which Bay City hung out, sprawling and indolent. The Five Rivers were small estuaries really, rather than sweetwater tracts. Crocodiles basked on the tidal flats just metres from shining corporate blocks as she flew silently by, weaving in and out of the afternoon traffic.

It was surreal to her, to move so fast and smoothly, with such quiet emptiness where the engine's roar used to be. Now only the wind battered her ears and face with its noise and wrenched her hair in every direction. A lot of people had bikes like hers, but they rode them in armour and she heard the guidance systems doing a lot of the driving. The pretty coloured bubble cars that had no drivers held an astonishing array of people and activities. She saw a couple at a table lit with candles speeding in the fast lane, eating dinner off fine china, clinking crystal glasses. In other pods children flung themselves at the windshields, plastering noses and lips to it, making faces. A girl sunbathed in a bikini while her mother lay in the front doing some kind of exercise class. Boys played console games, their feet sticking out of the window, socks shimmying in the draft. Occasionally something that looked like a sports car would shark through the lanes, driver concentrating at the wheel. Lila learned to know them by the heavier rasp of their wide tires humming like bass notes on the asphalt. Her ride was so much more like flying, it wasn't like biking at all.

She reached her particular bit of deserted cove after taking a hundred-mile detour and stopped at the side of the road. She was in a national park area, not far beyond a picnicking zone but far from the oversight of any building. The low barriers at the sides of the road told her about the traffic so that nobody would be cruising past to see a medium-sized woman in a frock pick up a third of a ton bike and carry it over sand and shingles into a dense patch of scrub trees. Hiding it was quite easy. She set its skin-theme to mimic the dry salt grass and the green branches with their tiny leaves and laid it on its side. A few branches were all that was needed to mask the wheels.

The shoreline was quiet as she jogged the half mile to the base of the cliffs that rose out of the low hills with roller-coaster steepness. They were fractured and broken, huge pieces standing clear of the mainland. In one of these towers she'd found a cave. It was a hundred metres up from the highest tide line and it took her a few minutes to climb there, her fingers and feet constantly changing shape to find grips on the sheer rock. At last she pulled herself up and over the small lip of a window-sized opening on the seaward side and stepped down into her room.

It hadn't started out so big, nor with furniture. That had taken a few weeks of digging, sneaking, stealing, and struggling to achieve. The project had saved her sanity. Now it was a sandy-coloured bolt hole with a view, a washing-up bowl for a sink and an enormous, luxurious, over-the-top mattress that had only narrowly survived being forcibly folded into three and stuffed through the opening. Low-energy lights glowed in sconces she'd scooped out with her fingers and gave the place a soft look as outside night drew on. She adjusted the sheet of metal she used to keep the weather out. The day was calm now, overcast, but there was always a breeze off the sea.

A figure on the bed stirred as she made a noise pouring water into her bowl to wash. She undid the fastenings on the foul dress, feeling it loosen and undo itself rather than have her tangle with it. As it came free it lost its scruffy look and became a heavy fall of rich purple satin. The faery stitching that barely showed in Otopia glowed bright gold and tawny as the magical creature behind her got closer. She hung the fabric up on a padded hook and held her hand on it to feel the strange sensation of it warming and shifting of its own accord as it scented power. Now as soft as water itself it slithered over her hands and she fumbled it in her haste to get it put aside. The pen fell out of the waist sash and clattered on the rock floor. Two cool, powerful white hands touched her waist from behind, then slid up and cupped her naked breasts. She felt the hard body that went with them touch her back and buttocks and saw her shadow appear faintly on the wall in front of her where it hadn't been a second before.

"You were gone a long time," Teazle said conversationally, his breath hot on the back of her neck. She felt his nose and lips brush her skin as he put his face close behind her ear and sniffed deeply several times.

She made to turn around, but his grip was firm as he rejected the idea. He opened his jaws wide and she felt the sharp edges of his teeth against her skin as he bit the top of her shoulder gently. "Don't worry," he said. "Nobody came. I was quite safe." One of his hands traced down across her stomach and he slid his fingers under her panties and between her legs. She moved to make it easier and let her head fall back against his shoulder. He stroked her slowly. "You're so wet."

Lila swooned for a moment, her favourite, the most indulgent, when she felt nothing but him and the intoxication of his pleasure as he touched her. She almost didn't care when he tore the panties off her in a sudden, single act of clawed violence. The slight pain in her skin only intensified her delight. Then his fingers were back, claws all gone. As he caressed her breast his other hand spread her open with soft, exploratory strokes.

"You were well named," she accused him, longing.

"You're so impatient," he said, deeply pleased. She turned to face him, but he made no move. His unnerving, white eyes stared down at her from his greater height, thick hanks of straight white hair hanging forwards over his forehead and shoulders. His body was hard, taut, very strong, and faintly luminous. She saw the spike tip of his tail twitch back and forth at the edges of her vision, somewhere near her knees. She started to buckle with desire and began to go down, lips already parting, but he stopped her with a stinging slap of his tail on her hip broadside. The air over his shoulders shimmered as if in a heat haze, though he wasn't hot, quite the reverse.

"Did you go there again?" he asked. The music in his demon voice was deep, full of odd notes.

She knew he meant her sister's memorial, the one that stood beside her own and their parents'. She went there every morning, just before she bought the awful coffee and made herself drink it in a toast to them; gut rot for Mom and Dad, and caffeine for Max who never left the house without mainlining Arabica. Teazle understood the last part, but his eyes gleamed now with a predatory fire. The first part made her weak, on his analysis, and he both disapproved of that and wouldn't hesitate to exploit it. She had been there again, tried to cry, tried to find something to say or think, failed again. One day she'd stop, but it wasn't today.

"Bite me."

He took her literally, and she felt the impact of his chest on her upper back, the hot breath and wide mouth against her neck, sharp teeth grazing her skin. Both of them fell forward with the force. The bowl of water went spewing to the side. Her few bits of faeryware scattered or broke.

For a second his weight on her was dead with inertia. She exploded upwards, flinging her arms to the sides, bucking him off so that he went flying back into the mattress. On its peg the dress rustled and slithered with a hiss. Lila set her hands on her hips and glared down at the demon who lay, serious, calculating, mildly amused, and then eased his shoulders back and smiled at her.

She stepped over him, one foot either side of his hips, then sat down on him without once breaking eye contact. His challenge melted into pleasure, and for an hour they sank into mindless physical entertainment. When it was done they lay side-by-side, arms touching.

"About that search you were doing," she said presently.

Teazle made an unhappy grunt. "Still nothing."

She wasn't surprised. "You didn't tell me you were killing your way through half of Demonia."

His head turned to her and his eyebrows quirked. "You asked me to look for objects of power or information concerning the Holy Three. Anyone who has things like that isn't going to let me know. Not least because I'll no doubt be wanting to steal them. How did you think I was going to look for them? And before you say teleport in and out of places secretly, let me point out that I don't know where those places might be until I off the capo and get their inventory in my hands."

"But what . . . are you taking over every family in turn and then searching every hoard?" She was almost speechless at the craziness of that plan. Until Mal had told her that morning she'd never have believed he would do such a thing. Then of course, after a minute, she realised he'd never do anything else.

"Every hoard, dungeon, keep, and bank vault," he said happily. "You wouldn't believe the amount of stuff and people and—"

"And you didn't notice that the Council has issued a death warrant for you?"

"Of course they have," he said with pride.

She decided to drop that part. "And what about Madame Des Loupes?"

"Her I would've asked. But she vanished before I could get there."

"They say you killed her."

"They say. Who say?"

"The Council. And my . . . the head of the Security Service here."

"They're wrong."

She used the palm of her hand as a paper and remade the image there for him. "Here. Looked like this."

"I wouldn't make a mess like that. I'm not vengeful. I just want what I want."

"I know it wasn't you."

"But"—he turned his head and white hair fell across his face—"I am a bit concerned that someone will get me before I get anything useful. It may be no such thing exists in Demonia."

"Just go check the coroner's necromancers first then."

"Hmm." He closed his eyes, mulling over that. "And what else happened? You were out a long time."

"I got a job."

Teazle snorted with laughter. "And your part of the deal?"

"Closer now," she said, referring to her mission to discover what devices the rogues had used against him months ago, and what she could do to arm him against them. "Much closer."

"Grr, I hate it when you're winning," he said. "And I'm hungry. Let's go out and eat."

Lila got up and recovered the bowl. There was enough water left for a very quick wash. When she put the dress on, it had miraculously cleaned itself and become a fashionable short-skirted item. She checked for the pen and slipped it into her pocket. In the meantime Teazle had dressed and was staring at her.

"What?" she said.

"That's a pen," he said.

She waited.

"Pens write."

"I thought of that. Don't know what to put. Or where."

He eyed the dress with suspicion and nodded. "Worth experimenting with."

"I'll sign the restaurant check with it."

Teazle's body had lost its gleam. His hair was dull. He looked like any thirty-something human man in casual clothing with unusually long white hair.

She stepped out of the cave and floated to the ground in the twilight. They walked together to the road and, despite his complaints, called a cab.

CHAPTER FOUR

Past midnight, in the hours when everything in the world is closer to the final darkness, Lila lay with her eyes open, her head on Teazle's cool shoulder. The cave was almost totally black to human sight, but she saw well by the slight starlight filtering in from its mouth. It was at this time she could hear the machines most clearly, though it was not when she was conscious, but in dreams that their meanings came through to her; and that was why she stayed awake as much as she could because inevitably, with the fall of sleep, came the invasion.

As it was she listened to her lover's heartbeat and the sea, and tried not to hear underneath those things, underneath all things, the whisper of near-silent static that was no static: the endless om of everything the machines had ever said or thought or done in one eternally repeated present. They were not bound by time. Their signal was once, and for all. There was nothing of them it did not contain. They were the signal. She got that at last. They were not material beings in some other world sending messages. They were the signal. The original pieces that had been grafted to her were made material by the work and command of the signal, though it was not any more material than a radio wave. The pieces that had consumed her and of which she was now part were crude, brutish, in this three-dimensional universe, little outgrowths into space-time from a place outside, their only chance to communicate with her level of existence. She was a beacon, a receiver, an interpreter, a transmitter, a device for the signal.

The signal itself was so complex, so vast, so unsuitable for any time-locked linear creature to hope to comprehend that even understanding this much about it had taken her all the years of her cyborg existence—which were two in strictly human terms, but, counting process iterations since her final conversion in the depths of Faery, now spanned some thousand or more ordinary lifetimes. Atop this frenzied torrent, her human experience was a patchwork so thin, so scattered, so trivial that it was negligible. In the total of the signal, in which she knew she must be continually hearing the story of her whole life, and death, she was a few kilobits of data, assimilable in a fraction of the time she could imagine as the smallest amount of time there could be.

The nights were so long.

She thanked god for the white demon, whose sleep was the sleep of the just, as deep and long as the ocean was wide. Without him she doubted she would have her sanity. Only his unquenchable arrogance, his absolute commitment to life and to the fulfilment of his part in it, had been an anchor strong enough to hold onto in the first days of her return home to find home long gone. Teazle wasn't moved by a fifty-year blip in his vision or the passing of much that he knew. His sense of self was too strong for anything to topple. She on the other hand . . . most of what she'd thought of as herself was burned away or redundant. Her name seemed not to refer to anyone she knew. When it got bad, as it did around noon, after another visit to memory lane, she'd come and cling to Teazle and suck some of his energy up in a down-and-out junkie fix. Of course that's what it was. He didn't mind it because her neediness gave him power. She knew she ought to knock it on the head, but the close physical contact was too much like breathing to give it up. Whatever she liked to pretend about their sex together, it was a sanctuary, and damned if she didn't deserve one of those. Oddly, it didn't remind her of Zal—one of the few things that didn't.

She heard the high tide creep up the sand and slough out again as dawn came.

The light woke the demon. He stretched and then sniffed her, kissed her, and put his arms around her. The sensation of being at the end of the world receded and the static quieted itself.

"I want you to find out what happened to Madame," she said, yawning horribly widely and for so long she got jaw ache.

"On top of my search? You don't ask much." He sounded thoroughly pleased with himself.

"I think it's going to be the closest thing to a lead we get. That, and I've got the keys to Sarasilien's office."

There was a pause and she could almost hear the cogs turning as he thought about this. "Topple."

"I'm sorry?"

"It is a Topple. In Demon probability mathematics a Topple is a domino effect of important events occurring in rapid sequence because of an unknown yet critical value set reaching fruit."

"The sad part is that I know what you mean," Lila sighed. "God I long for the old days when it would all have . . ." She passed her hand in a whoosh over the top of her head from back to front. "You think there'll be more?"

"It is certain. We are at the outset of a Conjunx. Better take spare panties today."

She laughed and thumped his chest.

"Harder," he said mildly, stretching again.

"Don't get yourself killed," she said.

"I am an avatar. My heart is pure. I cannot be defeated," he replied.

She frowned and traced the powerfully square line of his jaw. "Avatar of what?"

He shrugged and said nothing but smiled infuriatingly and then slowly got up and out of the bedding, dressed himself, put on his swords, and composed his hands together in front of his heart, genie style. "Until later."

Lila managed to get her hands over her ears and her eyes shut for the vacuum decompression of his teleport departure. Bursts of short-lived nanoparticles bloomed and faded in his wake. She got up and went to take the dress off its hanger. It was a fashionable evening gown again, about as unsuitable for office daywear as she could imagine, short of what she'd worn yesterday, but not putting it on was unthinkable, so although she'd seen herself returning to work in black combats and looking like she meant business, she was stuck with flimsy bias-cut indigo silk. In spite of her feelings towards it she was reticent to tear the dress, but she couldn't figure out how she could ride a bike in something that looked like it hung to her ankles and had a train. She put it on and it clung to her here and there, fine as tissue. Little faery letters glowed in its rich, royal colour.

"Please," she said to it, feeling a tinge of despair. "Nobody will take me seriously in this. I need something more . . . military."

The dress didn't budge. She didn't have any mirrors, but she was ready to bet that the spaghetti straps and filmy look wasn't improved by a sport bra and sensible pants. She already hated herself for begging the smug faery concoction.

"Right then, two can play at that game," she said, and without hesitation transformed herself into the full black-metal cyborg she was used to. Tough arms. Big, kick-ass boots. Breastplate. Greaves. To a nearly blind person in very bad light it might just look like she was strangely built and wearing evening gloves and platforms, but to a sighted person in daylight it looked strictly out-patient.

She was getting used to that, and at least this way it was half on her terms. Zal had gotten her the armour, and when she got Zal back from his near-death existence in some nether dimension she was going to kill him.

The pen rolled towards her and stopped at the edge of the cardboard box that was the nightstand, desk, table, and rubbish bin. She picked it up and slid it into one of the empty magazines in her forearm. At least there was no damn bag to carry.

By the time she got the bike out of the spinney and onto the hardtop she was in a foul temper. The dress was slightly ripped and a seam had started to go, but as usual once it had set for the day there were no mendings or concessions. She hoicked the long skirts up around her hips and stuffed the train under her bottom to sit on the bike. She thought of tearing it. She thought of slicing it up. But she didn't dare. She had the feeling that the dress knew what she was thinking and was at once laughing and sinister. It had turned bullets. It was better than any armour she knew of. The bloody thing.

She gunned the power and the bike slid smoothly and infuriatingly silently up to high speed. How could you have any satisfying emotional outburst with this modern technology? She snarled at it and pushed it to the limits every which way she could, but it never made a noise and the traffic was too busy to risk breaking it.

She was early at the flower stall. They looked at her with the usual odd looks as they made up her order. Half the petals came off during the ride to the memorial. Lila stood with her bunch of sticks and half flowers in the shade of a eucalyptus tree looking at the stone where Max's name was carved with a flourish. It glowed because the faeries had done it. Max's portrait was there. She looked older than Lila remembered her, but she was smiling.

"I brought these for you," Lila said, and dropped the flowers down on top of yesterday's and the day before's. "I wish you'd say something. Thanks would be nice."

She'd sort of hoped the faeries would have enchanted the portrait to speak or leave her a message, but so far it was just a picture.

"I can't keep coming back is what I wanted to say." She put her hands on her hips and pursed her lips, feeling cross. "I don't see the point. You're not really here."

People out walking in the park area, of which the memorial gardens were a part, were visibly avoiding her.

"So I guess this is good-bye."

Surely there ought to be some greater sense of occasion?

"Bye then."

It felt so wrong, so inadequate, so . . . nothing. She didn't know what to do. She could barely accept that Max was dead. She certainly couldn't accept that she had lived a lifetime alone and died in old age. She had seen her only a few months ago, still young. And another part of her felt that she couldn't just leave Max here and walk away. But she'd already done that. Fifty years ago. She thought that if she'd come here enough, then one day it would all seem real.

The flowers had a blank card. She never wrote on it, but today she wanted to. She took out the pen, not without misgiving, and uncapped it. It was a fountain pen. The nib was a bright silver. She didn't know if it would even write, but it did. *Good-bye, Max.* She almost put *wish you were here*, but at the last moment she stopped and put the lid on the pen. She wasn't sure it was true. How old would Max be now? Eighty-five. Coming back just to hear her sister complain wouldn't really be that wonderful. She didn't want any repercussions.

The ink was incredibly dark and opaque. It wasn't like a liquid. Simply where the nib passed went utterly black. It was a strange colour. When she looked at it against the flowers and the ground it seemed too dark, unnatural, so she folded the card over the words and put the pen away.

"You know you're supposed to clear up when they've died," a sharp voice said from a short distance behind her.

She sensed disapproval of multiple kinds as she turned and found the park attendant on his small motorised scooter looking at her with a scowl through his visor. After a minute she realised he was talking about the flowers.

"Yeah I will," she said.

He gave her a nod that indicated he didn't think that was likely. "Well I have all the contacts for these memorials and I will pursue it."

"You do that," she said.

He stared at her dress. "This your bike?"

"Yes."

"It should be in the parking lot. This is a tow zone. I can't tow it because I don't have the equipment, but I—"

"I was just going," Lila said, and marched forwards, yanking up yards of water-spotted silk as she did so before throwing her leg over the bike and jamming the dress in around her.

"—can issue you with this ticket." The official did something with his phone unit, and she registered an official complaint against her in the city administration data. "So you can ride it to be impounded yourself."

Lila, who had been about to ride off, sat back and took her hands off the bars. "Let me get this straight: you want me to ride my bike to the pound so it can be locked up and then I can pay to have it unlocked?"

"It is officially within my authority—"

"After you interrupt me on the site of my sister's grave memorial."

"You'd been here some time, and you come here every day. You have never, as far as I can see, tidied up. It's not like she died yesterday, now is it?" Then he hesitated and his brows beetled together. "Your sister?" It was his turn to get puzzled.

Her amazement at his attitude was almost refreshing in a way. "Well, here's my official response," she said, and gave him the finger before driving off.

At the beach she parked carefully, simmering with rage, and ripped the side of the dress in getting off the bike too forcefully. She felt its bodice tighten with reproach and the train hissed at her, but she refused to take the responsibility. The gaggle of youth converged on the region went quiet on seeing her, although this time it lasted longer than usual, and the man at the coffee stand was placing her cup at maximum distance from himself even before she'd reached it.

She picked up the cup, already able to taste the contents just by coming into contact with the steam. "This," she said, holding it aloft and pointing at it for the stallholder's benefit, "is the worst coffee I have ever tasted." She took one, obligatory sip, and dropped the cup directly into the bin.

He stared at her and then blurted. "Don't put a frog in the onions."

Lila looked at him for a long minute, during which she parsed the sentence a few hundred times. She decided she didn't want to know and turned around, lining the four boys and three girls up under her stare.

"You should all be in college. I am reporting your whereabouts to the educational system and the student benefits' office. You can still make your ten o'clock classes if you run. There'll be an extra fine if you miss it, and if you miss even one more hour of school or drop below a C average, you will have your travel permits removed for six months." The vitriol with which she delivered this was stinging. They sat openmouthed and then started as, one by one, their personal organisers all began to ring, pip, and sing shrilly at maximum volume to confirm the bad news.

She decided not to walk on the beach or hang around for the grisly aftermath. She'd had it with that place, and anyway, stay much longer and who knew what she might do, or think? She might start screaming or crying or trying to kill someone who probably didn't deserve it just because things hadn't worked out for her, because Max was dead and gone, Zal was lost, because she hurt and the world had moved on without her and become a place she could never be at home in and there was no going back.

For the benefit of the kids still trying to curse her and hit her with loose stones she rode out of the parking lot backwards and gave them the finger as well before taking the freeway to her date with the dust sheets of abandonment. All the way she held her breath and kept her mouth shut. Her chest felt like it was going to burst, but she had to keep everything in. She felt nuclear, atomic, like her rage would destroy the world, or worse, that it wouldn't. It wouldn't do anything, just explode and then trickle away and there'd be nothing left. If there was nothing, what would she do then? What would she be?

The bike tires screamed on the asphalt. She fishtailed wildly. The speedometer reached its limit and the battering of the air froze her face and shoulders. There was a point somewhere on the highway when a stone or something caught the tires. She felt the bike judder faintly, and then it was airborne. It skimmed the ground for seventeen metres and struck a concrete abutment where two lanes divided. She was thrown free of it, but not far. Beige slabs flew up to meet her.

Lila got to her feet without knowing where she was or what was happening. The clear memories and miss-nothing processing of her machine body wasn't able to penetrate the daze that slamming headfirst into a solid bridge support had brought upon her. She had the vaguest of notions about what had just happened, but it seemed no more than imaginary. Somewhere behind her traffic was stopped, people were talking, exclaiming, but she only saw the concrete wall she had hit and the pattern of cracks she'd made in it that matched the pattern of lines she felt in herself. She moved cautiously, in case she fell apart.

To her surprise she could see things she'd never noticed before. There was a river crossing here, for instance, right where the roads crossed. In fact, the underneath road was the river and the over road was a covered wooden bridge. She was standing on a small bank beside it, and there was a boat not far away from her coming against the flow of the strange grey liquid that lay deep and current ridden beneath the fragile surface of the ordinary Otopian day. Standing in the boat was a person dressed in robes, using a long pole to skillfully press the craft through the least difficult water. It was hard work but they kept at it patiently and as they came level with her, as she finished noticing all this, they let the boat turn about in the current and beach itself on the end of the sandy shelf where she was standing.

"Don't move," said the figure. Their voice had no sound, only the imaginary quality of her accident, but it was quite certain.

She wished to know where this was and with the same certainty she got her answer.

"This is Last Water, always and everywhere. If you move you will cross it and not return."

An idea came to her. "This is Thanatopia?"

"It has no name, but you call it that. Be still. Others are watching."

Lila considered this. The grey water reflected almost no light at all, but it moved vigorously. Above it the concrete highway, its cars and people were slowed almost to a standstill. "Others?"

"From this place most things can be seen. I have been looking for you. But I am not the only one." The figure barely moved. Its hands on the pole had only three fingers, or two and some kind of thumb that opposed them. The grey was not exactly grey, she decided, looking at its odd flesh, only colourlessness.

"Am I dead?" She thought not.

"Not enough," it replied in its smooth, silent way. "But if you like you need only step forward."

"How do I go back?"

"You are already slipping away. The living cannot linger. Give me a token so I can find you again."

"Who the hell are you?" She had no intention of obeying such a request.

"I am one who seeks to prevent you from falling into the grasp of She Who Waits."

"And I believe you because?"

"I am one of Ilyatath's servants."

The use of the correct name for the elf floored her suspicions. She had a lot more questions, but the river and the bridge were fading away and the bright, brassy colours of Otopia were every moment more brilliant.

The hooded figure held out its hand and opened it. On its thick, gigantic palm lay a tiny flower, grey in petal and stem, and a crumpled piece of soggy cardboard. The flower, she knew, was one that Tath had carried to show his allegiance to the elven revolutionaries. The card . . . with disbelief she could read enough of the writing on it to know it was the one she had just left behind. As she watched the card became dust and the words alone remained, caught in the air, their lines twisting around one another. They moved like snakes.

"Do you know her?" she cried out. She had nothing on her that would do. In desperation she tore out a few strands of her own hair and tried to give it across. To her alarm the words slithered out of the creature's palm and around the strands, coating them in black, before recoiling to turn and writhe. She saw them snatched away and pocketed. The vision was so flimsy now that it was almost invisible.

"Do not come here again unguarded," the figure said before it was gone. It held up its fist, shaking with the effort of holding the words at bay. "Do not give life to the things of this place."

She stood on the burning hot road. A medic was trying to get her attention, spritzing her with something stinky out of an aerosol and patting her face with a wet swab. She swatted him away irritably and gathered her bearings. Of course the bike was toast. She hadn't thought her heart could drop another notch, but at this realisation it did.

The machines buzzed like summer bees in her head, dizzy, drunk, their pattern grown slower to repeat but no clearer. Lila stooped to gather the rags of the dress in her hands like an old dowager and began to walk stiffly towards the exit ramp. A variety of individuals continued to try talking to her or treating her, but eventually they settled for photographing her and insults when she showed no signs of cooperation. Later a smelly, noisy old car drew up beside her and the door of it opened with a creak.

Malachi leant back in the leather seat, his elbow on the car door, fingertips at the wheel. He looked through the windscreen, shades flat to his face. "Get the shit in."

She got the shit in, yanked the dusty dress train around her ankles, and shut the door. They growled off into the burning heat, wind dashing over the shield and messing her hair, turning it into a thousand little whips.

Lila flipped down the sunshade and uncovered the small vanity mirror on the back of it. Ghastly was the word for it. She flipped it back up again.

"Have you ever met the dead?" she asked. "Or I mean, the people in Thanatopia who aren't dead." And then after a second of speculation, "Do faeries even die?"

Malachi drove in silence for a minute, but slowly his agitation lessened and finally he said, "We don't die in the way that you do. We wouldn't go to that place you mentioned." But he didn't sound 100 percent certain.

"It wasn't like the first time I was there," she said. "Nothing like it. Only there was a boat and water, and there were boats last time."

"Dare I ask what you're talking about?"

"I went to try and save my parents, with Tath," she explained. "But I couldn't. They crossed the water into Thanatopia proper. . . ."

"No," he corrected. "Thanatopia is the place you were in; you cross out of it."

"Are you sure?"

"Yes," he said. "Faeries can go to Thanatopia but they can't cross. We call it Uldis, the thing that lies under Under. We're much changed there, so we never go. Not . . ." He glanced at her for the first time. "What happened to your clothes?"

But Lila was not going to be deterred. "So what happened to Poppy and Vid? Jack killed them."

Malachi winced and shuddered. He made a warding sign and Lila felt the car engine catch for a second. "Gone," he said.

"Dead."

"Gone," he repeated with slow solidity. "Not dead. Gone for all time gone. It wasn't Jack that killed them, remember." He slammed on the brakes suddenly, barely managing to stop at the light, and swore under his breath.

The last line was a warning to her not to mention what he was speaking of. She knew what he meant. The Hoodoo. That had killed them because they had violated the terms of Zal's trial and tried to save him against the too-powerful force of the Giantkiller. She resolved to know and understand more about this, but it wasn't the moment. Malachi was gentle, but she took him seriously enough to know when to stop. His tension signalled fear and he was rarely afraid. She sank into the seat and felt one of its springs pop underneath her.

Lila asked for a detour to get takeout. Mal paid for it and they stopped to eat it streetside in the busiest part of downtown, watching people go by.

"Were you dead?" he asked finally after she'd gone through half a box of special noodles and he'd picked over and not eaten monks' vegetables.

"I don't think so," she said, taking hold of his box of dinner and starting on that too. Sauce dripped on the dress but she was glad to spite the thing.

Mal delicately opened a box of Faerie Flumsie and began to spoon it into his mouth. The stuff was sickly. She didn't think she'd ever seen him eat it before. "Bad day?"

He snorted at her. She crammed bean sprouts into her mouth; she just couldn't seem to get enough in fast enough. Who knew that a brush with death could make her so hungry? She wasn't even sure that eating was a habit more than a necessity. The food was so good. Her piglike manners made him squirm and she grinned to herself.

Malachi almost choked on the Flumsie and at last admitted defeat, dropped the spoon into the gooey sticky mess, and dumped the box on the backseat. "I thought you were dead," he said, looking through the windscreen at the city street. "I had this feeling, and I'm not wrong about these things. Just for an instant. It wavered. I put it down to my imagination. And then the report came through about the accident and I . . ." He beat the steering wheel softly with the thick paw palm of one hand and took a breath. "I felt like there was suddenly no purpose for me anymore, like it was time for my name to be wiped off the roll of interesting things, unstitched from the pattern and put to the edges where the colour's all flat and finished. The strings pulled. I almost didn't come out to see. I figured if it had happened you'd have meant to do it and you'd have done it right."

Lila stopped eating. Noodles hung out of the side of her mouth. Her throat felt too big, stuffed up. She couldn't swallow. His tone was so hurt.

"Did you do it on purpose?" he asked, turning and staring at her with an intensity that was way out of character for him. Through the black lenses of his shades the orange fire of his eyes blazed bright enough to show like embers.

A flare of shame at her secretive self-destructive ways made her face heat up. With great difficulty she bit through and gulped the salty, slimy mass in her mouth. She wanted to shake her head no, but she thought he deserved the truth and gave the merest nod.

"God*damn*it!" He snatched the food cartons from her hands and flung them overboard onto the pavement, sending her chopsticks after with such force they splintered on contact with the ground. Amid loud complaints from passersby he started the engine and with a squeal of tires and a gout of smoke yanked them into the heaving traffic.

Noodles slid down her chin. "I'm sorry," she said, honestly and very quietly, contrite.

He was too angry to talk. He just drove. They reached the depths of the agency lot and there, in the dark and musty quiet, he took off his glasses and rubbed his eyes. The engine chuntered along until he stilled it with the key. "I don't know how much more of this I can take," he said. "But know this. I don't intend to stick around and watch you play chicken with the Moirae."

"I'm not . . . !" Lila began, but then shut up because she wasn't sure he wasn't right.

He nodded into her forced silence. "You are still having your romance with death. I guess that's understandable after all that's happened."

She felt that she was foolish. "I wasn't serious," she said.

He softened slightly and began to polish his glasses on a piece of silk from his pocket. "There are some things that just can't take a joke, Lila. Well, they don't take one, let's say. And you might think you're right, but some bit of you is serious. That bit will kill you and I won't be around to see it happen. That's all I'm saying. You have to get a grip on it. You must."

"I drove too fast." She dismissed the idea as nonsense. "It was an accident."

He shook his head. "There are no accidents."

Her hand went to her waist. The pen was still there. She thought of the message and saw once again the black tendrils of the letters in her writing curl themselves like lush vines around her hair, and each other, in a knot. But Malachi was still speaking.

"You humans," he said with a wan smile. "You think only talk is talk and only words are meaning, but everything is talk, everything is meaning. There is nothing that isn't talking, nothing that isn't calling, signalling, to everything else all the time. Words can lie, but nothing else lies, even the mouth telling the words. Faeries don't lie with words. We swore long ago after the first words that we'd never be their prisoners, you see. Words are the best trap there is and the strongest gaol, and we'd have none of that. Some of us took vows of silence, but the rest of us just knew it wasn't worth the penalty to even try lying, for anything, to anyone. After that we had to learn Forgetting, but that was relatively easy, because we'd mastered Losing Things already. You lie, Lila. Your words lie. You must never have any business with people who use words to make their magic until you stop lying. Nothing like an elf, for instance. No elvish things. And not what killed Poppy. Words will bend power of any sort to their own ends and if you can't see when a lie is in front of you, you'll be their victim and not their master. Ask Teazle. He'll tell you. The devil is a creature of words and nothing else. Evil is made of them and will try to take form at the slightest opportunity."

"Did you read my mind?" She was astonished, and not a little frightened.

"Of course not," he said. "That's my point. You told me what happened." He leaned forwards and wiped her mouth with his handkerchief brusquely before dropping it in her lap. "But not with words. With those you lied to me. And yourself." He got out of the car and slammed the door shut and began walking slowly towards the door, hands in his pockets. He looked slumped and sad, saggy, if such a thing were possible. She strove to hear the meaning of what she saw, but it was obvious enough without any effort at translation; she had let him down badly, betrayed him, and he was hurt and confused. She longed to rush after him and fix it, but she didn't know how. Promises sprang to her mind, but they were empty. In that second she saw that all promises were empty, must be, for they were never fulfilled in the second of their making. They were words meant to persuade, tokens for something that didn't yet exist and might never. They were useless.

She had to watch him walk away and let him go.

CHAPTER FIVE

In bed with Teazle, Lila ran her hands over her arms. The white demon slept the sleep of temporary satiation, halfway between man and monster, his tail coiled possessively around her lower leg. His dominance over her was growing. She felt it, and knew why, without being able to put it into words. It was because she was lying. The imp wasn't there to act as her soul barometer, but neither of them needed him, nor Malachi, to feel the change of the weather. Her dealings with Teazle were honest at least: honestly needy, honestly desperate, honestly angry, honestly destructive. He respected that, but still there was no disguising it as anything but a weakening position. She pressed her face to his hot, dry shoulder and felt the fine vibrations of the energy in him that would never sleep until he was dead.

In the dark she felt more comfortable assessing her human-feeling skin. Beneath it, however, the shapes of muscles were clearly a skim, a token to forms that were unnecessary. She was warm, she had a kind of softness, if suede was soft, but it didn't go too deep. An unrelenting iron was inside her, and a minor prodding revealed it. She gave and yielded, but only so far. She wished it were a metaphor for her character. She wanted to be good, strong, competent, able, a rock under a gentle and lovely exterior.

She wondered what time it was and the answer came immediately:

a minute to midnight. She was losing only a fraction of a second every century. Into that fraction, is that where things had gone? You could lose an eternity in that kind of time; Jack the faery had said so and it was true. Like the white rabbit, your spirit might fly down such a little hole. She'd been down one, into Under.

The key glowed ice cold at her throat and without being able to see it she was suddenly aware of the pen in the pocket of Tatterdemalion's dress. A chill crept across her, making her press more closely to the demon's burning, arid body. His tail increased its python grip automatically and she heard his breath come once more deeply though he didn't wake up. She was suddenly afraid to look at the wall beyond the foot of the mattress.

A flash made her jump. A few moments later thunder cracked and rumbled over the sound of the waves. Lila swore at herself for all this stupidity, opened her eyes, widened, and refined them to see well in the ordinary night. The dress was off its hanger, standing by itself halfway between the bed and the wall. It was full-figured, a fine gown around an imaginary body. Tight sleeves of ebony velvet shrouded nonexistent arms. They stretched out towards her, their lacy wrists supporting the crosspiece of a shining silver sword.

Lila leapt to her feet. The sheet went flying. Teazle grumbled at the yank on his tail, which slithered around her ankle and squeezed her painfully. He played dead, though she could feel the energy in him rising all the time and knew he was fully alert. The stormy air was ticklish and cool against her bare skin. Lila jumped forward and snatched the hilt of the ornate zweihander in her right hand. The dress fell to the floor in a richly velvet Miss Havisham puddle. "Goddammit, I hate this faery shit!"

"Do you now?" said a voice from the cave mouth. It was conversational but sly. "I'd say you liked it more than mo—"

Sitting in the doorway was a grey, smooth-bodied female humanoid with reflective steel-plate eyes. The point of Lila's sword was digging into its throat, which is why it hadn't finished the sentence. Her makeshift metal door was still in its hand where it had been silently working it loose in order to get in. It put that down now, slowly and carefully, as if it were dynamite.

Lila looked at the rogue down the length of the blade and was momentarily distracted by the sight of flowers blooming in the flat silver world of the sword's surface. "How did you find me? Who are you? What do you want?"

The figure didn't move except to speak. "We've met before. Serve and Protect. You might not remember. . . ."

"You were on the meat table in the agency medical centre talking robocrap along with that guy when I went in to check up on you and prove to myself that I really was part of a long-term dark project that humans had been manipulated into. That was fifty years ago, give or take a week. You had auburn hair, a nice wave in it, the same Mideastern accent. I didn't read your records, but you must be around eighty years old now and one of the first to survive."

"Actually, you were the first to survive," said the rogue, conversationally, as if she were welcome. She almost sounded reverent. "In our world, you are legend."

"What do you want?" The cold air made Lila feel strong, despite being naked. In front of this creature she didn't even feel that. It had a surface, not even a hint of clothing. It was like a mannequin that had been smoothed over so no details remained, just basic contours.

The cyborg moved her bald head and looked in Teazle's direction. "I wish to speak with you alone. You are very successful at blocking all transmissions, so I had to come here."

Teazle pretended to wake up and stretched himself out, stripping the sheet away in doing so as if by accident though it was nothing of the kind. He revealed his powerful human-seeming body, allowing himself to glow so that he lit the room up. His roll exposed the extraordinary hard musculature of his torso and limbs to perfection as they started shining and, in typical demon showmanship, the slightly curving hard line of his erect penis. His tail coiled higher up Lila's leg and he relaxed, resting his head on his hand, supported on his elbow.

"The demon stays," Lila said. "State your piece or make some move. I'm not patient."

"I came to tell you what you are for. What your future is."

"That's not the answer to my question."

"I want you to listen to what I have to say."

"I'm not interested. How did you find me?"

"The signal," the rogue replied as if it were obvious.

"Okay, here's what," Lila said. "If you can tell me how to get invisible so that no bugger can find me, even inside the signal or whatever, I'll let you leave here alive."

For the first time the rogue showed anger in the way her head flashed around to look directly up at Lila. Teazle's light shone off her glossy high cheekbones, her plastic lips, and caused them to be reflected in the sword's blade. Lila listened in spite of herself, but at the same time she saw the lips reflected on the blade say words that were quite different.

"I know everything about the machines you don't know," the rogue said, sounding offended by Lila's attitude. "I know about Zal and keeping the worlds together, about the quantum bomb, about the rise of the ghosts and the creatures in the Void, about the demon you serve. . . ."

Lila tilted the sword. There was a noise like *shukk*. The rogue's head rolled on the floor, bumped against the mattress, and rocked to a still point. Its body didn't move at all, save for some blue electrical discharges at the neck. The hands started to reach out, but Lila flicked the sword. There was a high, whining sound that made her hair stand up. The head and body became two-dimensional, like flat drawings. They slid into the blade and were gone.

"No you don't," Lila said into the quiet that followed. She looked at the blade of the sword in her hand, its silver all gone flat and dull for a second. Then she tossed it up in the air. It went up, pounds of solid metal, turned, and came down to land in her palm an old screw-top fountain pen, black with a small gold pocket clip.

"Lila!" Teazle murmured, mildly scandalised. "She might have said something worthwhile."

"Yeah, she might have," Lila admitted, putting the pen down on the cardboard box table. "But she wouldn't state her reasons, and that to me means a big agenda that doesn't have my interests in it, so now we'll never know." She washed her face and hands, dried them on her cheap towel, and added, "I guess I've gotten a bit trigger-happy maybe. But I told them not to come." She picked the dress up off the floor and put it back on the hanger.

Teazle looked long at the pen but didn't move to pick it up. His long hair moved like heavy white silk in the cold wind. The tower vibrated faintly with the beating the sea was giving to it even though now the night itself was calm. Lila replaced the metal door.

"You're as bright as a torch," she said, going back to him, kneeling over his hips. All over her the air was chill. He was still slightly wet from taking her earlier, and now when she slid onto him he felt like an icy spear: sticky, piercing, exquisite. She liked the cruelty of his ready size, her own utterly surprising willingness to take him all the time he was there. She shuddered with excitement. He moved with a snake's strike, turned them over, pinned her down, his mouth open wide, sharp inhuman teeth at her throat.

She dug her fingers into his neck and he shuddered, weakening as she cut off his arteries, murmuring his pleasure at the sensation of slowly descending darkness. Every day they went farther. It was never far enough. She always came back. But she didn't come back the same. Possessed by Teazle's body, his curiosity, his insatiable energy, she felt that she still had some reason to live. She didn't examine too closely what that reason was. There was a danger of putting it into words that she sensed as keenly as she'd sensed the danger in letting the rogue live.

Its lips in the mirror had said, "Do you remember Dar, Lila?"

There was much to remember about Dar, but she knew what was meant. One steamy hot night in Alfheim, Dar had planted his dagger in Tath's heart. His eyes on Lila's had been desperate, sad, utterly lonely. "You must never let them talk," he'd said. Words were so important to the elves. When you talked and put things into words, you made them real. Tath alive could only have led them into failure. He complicated things too much. This woman complicated things too much for Lila. To leave her alive, whatever she knew, however useful it would have been to know, was to come into the influence of something quite uncontrollable and beyond Lila's ability to deal with. If she thought of it she'd feel anguish at the unknown life she'd ended, so she didn't think about it.

Then the lips in the mirror had said, "He remembers you."

The cyborg had some connection to the dead. Or the sword did.

Now her eyes flew open. Teazle was half slumped, his light out. She released her grip and a screeching breath flew into his lungs. His body bucked and she felt a sharp pain deep inside, and glanced unwillingly at the black dress on the wall and then the pen on the table. Better to know what you were the servant of. But there were too many masters for her. Killing the rogue hadn't killed the machines, but it had silenced one of their voices and she was glad of that. She felt no remorse. She'd made it more than clear the first time they tried to kill her that she wasn't interested.

The severity of her discipline on him had caused Teazle's body to start to change. Without his conscious effort he couldn't maintain a human form. Now his eyes opened and he was half demon. He stayed that way, panting, his breath hot and reckless. People would have called him hell ugly now. He looked like a beast wearing a man's skin, pushing it out from the inside.

She embraced him, ignoring the brief pain of quill stabs and scale tips where they were growing out of him. Uncontrolled saliva from his jaws spilled onto her collarbones. It burned a little. He brushed her face with the soft feathers underneath his chin and with a few swift hard strokes came, snarling his pleasure. In a few seconds he became the human form again, shedding light faintly, though more of it came from his eyes, apricot and gleaming, their pupils invisible to her for the radiance.

"You don't have to," she said.

He mapped her body with his fingertips. "You were easier to see when the lines were clear," he said, finding all the places where once the obvious machine parts had been fused to her ordinary flesh. "Now it's just for show. Now you can be one, or the other."

"But there's a form that's true," Lila said, and he looked into her eyes and nodded slowly. Under his caresses she became soft warm skin, and metal under leather.

"My body is too hard for yours," he said, matter-of-fact, and kept his changed form with its supple, strong fingers. He examined her minutely all over, his gaze shining light on her and making her glow and gleam. The touch of the light was so faint, but she could feel it. It excited her unbearably. She became shameless under it, completely open to him. He stroked her with infinite patience, detached, observant, interested, only stopping when she was right on the edge.

She snarled at him, grabbed his head, kissed him, bit his lips hard.

"You think you want that, but you're not ready," he said, patrician and gentle because they were still not equals. He entered her forcefully and she came.

The fuel of the orgasm mollified her anger. She growled against him, curled in his arms. It was dark when he closed his eyes, but she was shining on the inside.

By dawn he was his demon self. Sleep had done what he refused and changed him to his true shape. She couldn't move because she would have sliced herself open on his claws. He snored lightly. Her leg hurt where it was pinned under his bony shin and she was far too hot. She tried a few wriggles but they were ineffective. She opened her mouth to wake him up but stopped on her indrawn breath with a start. Sunlight shone past the metal sheet and onto the rough wall where clear, neatly scribed black ink spelled, "Hurry up!"

It was Zal's writing.

Her skin crawled. She stared at it, half expecting the lettering to move. On the hanger Tatterdemalion's dress, or whatever it was, had formed itself into a dashing military uniform of black jacquard complete with ebony buttons and braid work. The pattern was Chinese dragons, all roiling around each other. She waited to see if they moved but they didn't. She looked for the detestable pen and saw it smugly resting where she had left it on the box, disguised as an investment banker's antique Mont Blanc.

Inside her head her phone alarm started to go off. She answered.

"You need to get here." It was Malachi.

Her pleasure at hearing him was so great she almost forgot to ask why and where.

"You'll see." He hung up hesitantly. She read into that that he was at least considering some kind of forgiveness.

The call had woken Teazle. He released her and rolled over. "Did I imagine you slaughtering—"

"No," she said, getting up and looking for her underwear. "Read the wall."

He narrowed his long slanted eyes even further and looked about him as he stretched out, three metres from nose to tail tip. "Did you write that?"

"It's Zal's writing."

"Maybe," he said, sitting on his haunches and slowly rubbing both sides of his heavy head against his forelegs before shaking himself out until his quills rattled.

She stopped with her arm half into a sleeve of the jacket, "Who else's?" It hadn't occurred to her to doubt it.

"Good question."

"I have to go to work," she said, feeling how strange the words sounded coming out of her mouth, as if she were about to do something quite normal. "Mal called."

"I heard." He waggled one long horsey ear.

"We can't come back here." She pulled on the trousers and buttoned them up. Inside the jacket was a pocket just the right size for the pen. She stuffed the pen down the front of her bra so it rested on the band and then marched to the door, picked it up, bent it in half, and tossed it out of the cave mouth. "I can't hide from them."

"I will fetch you tonight," Teazle yawned. "There are no machines in Demonia that aren't our own."

"As far as you know."

He thought on that a moment while she looked around pointlessly. It occurred to her that she'd been happy in the cave, that she'd felt safe there. Inside her chest where Tath used to live she felt herself crumpling and compressing at the realisation she would never come back here. She had no idea what to do with the pain. She walked to the wall and put her finger out towards the ink.

Teazle was suddenly there, his hand holding hers in a shocking grip. "Ah ah ah," he said lightly. "I wouldn't do that if I were you."

She stared into his white eyes, surprised and frozen with it but angry too. She wrenched her hand out of his hold with a twist, and what shocked her most was the burning remembrance of how good it had been to cut that rogue's head off and not have to listen to it, to just end something before it began.

She became aware of the demon watching her with his oddly understanding gaze. When he spoke again he was gentle. "It's still wet," he said, nudging the cruel point of his beak at the writing and letting the movement of his head shine the light from his eyes onto the black lines. They gleamed like glass.

Lila swallowed hard. "What is that stuff?"

"I don't know," he replied, "but it sure as hell isn't ink."

She recounted for him the way she'd seen the same substance from the pen make words that twisted and furled like vines, or ropes, or threads, when she'd hit the motorway flyover and seen Tath's emissary.

"Yeah," Teazle sighed. "Then we both know what it is, even if we don't know its name."

"The Void? Voidstuff." No way was she leaving it at that, in doubt. She wanted it definite.

"The Void is the endbeginning fromwhich and towhich and out-ofwhich. Yes. But Void itself is only emptiness, potential. This is voidinthemakingbutnotmade. Essential. But somebody's. It didn't come here by itself. There always has to be a mind behind it. And for this, a very powerful mind. Of all the aetheric races very few individuals would ever touch this stuff, or want to. The pen . . . the weapon . . . that you have, uses it because it is the instrument made to . . . hn . . . made for it, I suppose."

"By god." She really didn't want him to say yes to that, not least because she didn't want to have to tackle theology on top of everything else.

"No." He shook his head. "I said before. Not made by god. It is of god. But we could say that about anything, even this mattress, of course. Anyway, that doesn't matter. It's not the what but the why that's the trouble. For some reason it is with you. Like the dress. Top-pling." He sighed again. It was so uncharacteristic she frowned and her suspicion was roused.

"What's the matter?"

He was slumped, his head low. He shook it slowly again. "I'm running out of time and places back home," he said. "And I don't like what's going on with you and these articles. It feels bad to me, in my bones. But it's your call." He looked at the writing one last time. "What are you going to do?"

"I'm going to find Zal," she said. She said it very definitely, to make it true, and tried not to notice the enormous pit of doubt underneath the statement. "That's what. And I'm going to figure out about these rogues and the other 'droids. My part of the deal. I'll do that today. And right this minute I'm going to work."

"I'll see you tonight," he said, and vanished.

She stood in the backwash of air that rushed in to fill his space. Trust him to get the last word. His discontent bothered her though. She was certain he was keeping something from her. Her alarm signalled again. Mal was getting furious. She took one last look at the bleak little bolthole and then launched herself out of the door into the fresh morning air.

A hundred metres out she turned back, equipped a shell into her right arm launcher, and watched the little missile streak a trail of smoker's breath to the dim circle of the door before it exploded in white-hot fire and chunks of rock. A plume of filthy smoke rolled up and the black-stained stone went crashing down in white foam into the high tide.

Lila turned and made for Malachi's signal. She felt colder and emptier than she had ever been.

The cause for concern became obvious before she even arrived. Malachi was with some other agents on the beaches a few miles up the coast, where the city gave way to empty land owned by the wealthiest individuals. Here lush forests covered the rolling hills and dips and islets, giving way occasionally to designed glades or constructed grottoes, waterfalls and other features that looked so natural but were anything but. Even the beaches had been groomed, the sand whiter and finer, the rock pools more interesting, the docks perfect, their chromed mooring posts gleaming in the weak sunlight.

The tide was just starting to go out. At a point midway along this Gold Coast by the high-water mark the dark, whalelike body of a ship had been beached. The shape was unmistakable; it was a galleon with three masts and a narrow, square tucked stern in which leaded coloured glass still glowed. The masts were ruins, however, barely stumps, and as she flew closer Lila identified the twenty-two rotted and rusted guns at her portholes. She was waterlogged, as if she'd crawled up from the bottom of the ocean, and on her sides her paint-work was worn away almost to nothing, although on the stern Lila could just make out the picture of a blue ground and a golden deer.

She landed twenty metres from the fluttering cordon ribbons—hardly needed since the beach was private property—and walked towards the cluster of agents standing on the hull's leeward side. The sea was soft and quiet, the light brilliant on the waves, so much so that it was difficult to make out the faint light the ship itself emitted. This was noticeable to human eyes in dark shadow, as a faint gleaming on the edges of things.

Lila gave the whole object a wide berth and joined Malachi at the edge of the group. Among them the stocky figure of Bentley stood impassively, her face turned towards the sea.

They knew, Lila thought to herself. Of course the machines all knew everything that happened to their number. For a split second she almost found herself moving forward to speak but then glanced at Malachi and saw his amber eyes were frowning.

"There's another one, several more . . . farther down." He gestured at the coastline.

Lila watched with him as one of the human agents went forwards under orders and poked the vessel with a stick. They all heard the tap.

"Pretty damn solid for a ghost," she said.

"You know what it is?" Malachi asked.

"*The Golden Hind,*" Lila replied. "But it's a wreck. Why?"

Malachi folded his arms. He was wearing a camel coat that was too heavy for the day but he still looked cold. "Don't know."

The stick-poker came back looking grey and tense. "Feels funny," he said, putting the rest of the team between him and the ship. Lila looked back at the house this plot belonged to. It was snugged in halfway up a steep hill, about a hundred metres from the water, standing on long poles though it looked like most of it was cut into the hill. Expansive, expensive, she thought, and caught the flash of sunlight off a pair of high-power binoculars looking back at her.

A man Lila didn't know came up to them and asked Malachi to take a better look. "We need your kind of vision here," he said, nodded to Lila as if she were just another colleague, and then looked back at Malachi, his expression taut with discomfort.

"Come with me," Mal said, so fast Lila almost didn't catch the words. If she hadn't known better she'd have thought he was afraid.

"'Kay." She nodded, glad to be useful or, indeed, glad to be anything positive this morning for however long it could last.

He led the way over the wet sand to the point where the stick man had stood. The hull listed over them here, but was broken down enough that the lower decks were exposed. Seeing it from there made it quite clear the thing was a ruin. Water dripped from it, and Lila copied Mal's studious avoidance of the fall. It was black and difficult to make out any details inside. The witchlight that shone from its vertices was so weak that the contrast with the sun rendered it useless. The whole thing gave off a chill that made the air around it noticeably colder—almost three degrees colder, Lila noted—and there was a smell like metal but no smell of anything else. She put her hand out and touched her fingertips to its hull. The cold there was actually blistering, but she was able to stand it long enough to get plenty of information.

"That's not wood."

"Yeah, no shit," Mal whispered, keeping his words from the others.

Lila looked at the stern of the ship, where a large portion of it was still in contact with the water. For the first time she noticed the tiny alteration in sound where tiny pieces of ice were washing in the lukewarm waves. White ice formed jutting spars just above the water line.

Where the sun shone on the bulk of the wreck however, water was running freely.

"How could a ghost stay this solid here?" It didn't make sense to her. She'd seen ghosts before, but not like this one. They had forms made of light and air; sometimes they could use small particulates— sand, dust, snow—and small items to make their forms, but this was unheard-of. "I mean, it isn't wood, but it looks and feels like it. It has the same molecular structures, hydrocarbons, water, mineral traces. It's got the same properties as something you'd cut from a sizeable tree. It's even been splintered by cannon shot. The light is in the midrange for ghostlights." She would have gone on, but analysis of ghost forms was an incomplete, almost un-begun science.

"It's part of the Fleet," Malachi murmured. His eyes searched and searched it relentlessly. "But the Fleet was never wrecked. All the vessels were whole. I don't understand. . . ."

"What's the Fleet?" she asked.

"Trouble," he said, shoving his hands into the pockets of his coat and slowly backing up, all the while keeping an eye on the ship.

"Are you expecting someone to come out of it?"

His eyes flashed as he turned abruptly to look at her. "No. No."

"So, you're done?"

"Hardly."

"Someone has to go into it."

"Yes."

"Do a proper survey. See the insides."

"Yes." He nodded vigorously.

"We can wait until noon. Get some scaffolding. If you think it'll last."

"Good idea." He backed off from it so fast he was giving orders to the support crew at the fence line before she had time to make another suggestion.

She was pleased, kind of. It seemed that in a crisis they were buddies again. At least he was talking to her. That was good, she felt, but she didn't hope for a lot more, though she needed it. Above her the ship creaked and groaned as the water left more and more of it on the beach. Lila scanned it and reanalysed the information her fingers had gathered.

It was the oddest thing. There was no scientific framework that dealt with this, to her knowledge. Ghosts spawned in the Void, by methods that were imperfectly understood. The relation of the Void to the worlds wasn't understood. Ghosts had always previously appeared and vanished on their own schedules, even if they could be logically attached to places, and some tests had said they were clearly composed of aether. Here, in this ship, the aether had started to resemble matter. It was doing a fake job, like any glamour, but it was a remarkably good fake in the making. It was almost . . . real.

Nobody in Otopia had ever seen anything like it before.

Lila's mind skipped back uneasily to the day years ago when she had followed Zal into the woods to watch him tripping out in an elemental frenzy. Aside from the sheer weirdness of witnessing that odd event, there'd been a ghost present. It was a large forest spirit of the kind that experts liked to refer to as Archetypal, as if that helped. In the form of a stag it had crept up on the flipped-out Zal and put its nose against his hand. When ghosts touched living beings bad things happened. For elves, their entire form was susceptible to being consumed, and Zal had lost some of his hand. Now the fundamental bizarreness of it struck home. The outline of his hand had remained, but it was like it was glass and the contents had been vacuumed out. But an elf was blood and bones, as well as aether. What had happened there? She could kick herself for not paying more attention.

And then there was her own close encounter with a thing like that. It was before she was this cyborg Lila. Far away in Alfheim, when she was just an overexcited assistant to a diplomat, thinking she was getting into the daring world of espionage. . . . Anyway, in the forests there she'd got caught by the infinitely more experienced and cunning elf secret service. They'd tied her and her "fixer," Vincent, and left them in the dark at the edge of their camp, apparently unguarded, though she was too much involved with the conviction she was about to die to bother trying an escape. And then, at some point in her terrified reverie she'd felt the bitter chill and the unmistakable icy touch of a ghost approach. There was movement in the pitch darkness, bushes moving, twigs snapping, and some sharp cries in incomprehensible Elvish that had let her know she'd had a guard all right, and now it was running off in terror. An eldritch flicker illumined the ground for a second or two. Screams then and Vincent shoving at her, getting to his feet, starting to run blind into the woods. She was too slow. She hit a tree. She fell over. There was the singing note of an arrow over her head, a thump, an outbreath and she knew Vincent was dead. It was her first day in Alfheim. Her first day at being a spy.

Brushing aside the memories that wanted to swamp her anew with their horror she realised that their guard had been the one attacked by the ghost, if attack was the right word. She knew nothing else about it. Zal had recovered quite easily from his incident and she'd never asked any details. Now the only people she could interview about her own experience were the remaining members of the Elf spy band, and she had no idea who they were, but surely someone in Alfheim knew something about ghosts? Sarasilien, she thought . . . and then remembered he was gone. She was in his place. Time she checked out what he'd left her more closely.

But first . . .

"Hey." She followed Malachi to the far edge of the cordon, where he was making a call back to the office. "What's got you freaking out?" Fey didn't concern themselves overly with ghosts, and as far as she knew faery didn't really experience many of them.

He finished talking and closed the call. "That was Greer. We're to see the rest and head back. He's gonna let the juniors keep an eye on things." For once he met her gaze and his lips made an unhappy shape as he thought over what he was about to say. His seriousness was almost enough to make her smile. "The last time I saw the Fleet I was standing on the deck of a Hunter ship out in the Void. They ran from it. And I keep hearing . . ." He paused, and his discomfort became acute on his face. "The damn thing haunts me. I don't know why. Ever since I was out there. It's got something to do with the three sisters." He made a warding sign as he mentioned the Fates "The middle sister was in the admiral's boat with Zal. She's the one fished him out of the Void before he was killed, just like she's the one using him as a hanky now."

"I don't get what your problem is with her . . . them . . . ," Lila said. "They're no different to other faeries."

"Yes they are!" Malachi made pressing motions with both hands, telling her to keep it down. "We shouldn't even talk about them. Not even without names. They don't like it. And what they don't like has a way of ending up like Zal for eternity, or worse. You think you got remade by the stupid humans and their will to know about the machines. Well, that's nothing compared to what they'll do to any-thing they take a fancy to change."

"Okay, if you say so," she hissed in reply, feeling faintly stupid at having a whispered chat like schoolkids. "But it would help if you could find a way of sharing what you know about them with me."

The black faery narrowed his orange eyes and peered at her. "Still fixated on getting him back?"

"I know you don't want to be involved, don't worry." A chill fled over her.

"Bit late for that," he said, but without rancor. He took a deep breath and squared his shoulders.

She glanced back at the ship. "Do you really think this is personal? About you, I mean?"

"No," he said. "Not this manifestation. Doesn't mean they forgot me, though." He smiled weakly and shrugged. "There's only one place

I'll discuss this, and it ain't in Otopia or any of the places we usually hang out, I can tell you." He looked down, deep in thought, and scuffed the sand with the sole of his pristine leather shoe. "Probably time you got taken up-to-date with what's around here anyway. It'll make a nice day out. Get a lot of things done. Yeah. Okay."

"What are you talking about?"

"Tomorrow," he said. "Tomorrow we are going to visit a few people. For today let's just get through today. How's your spouse?"

"Still alive," she said, hoping it was true.

"Nice suit." He gave a quick glance at her outfit, which, as usual, cut a reasonably odd line over her tough-girl leathers. "Good tailoring." He paused suddenly on the last word and bit it off.

"What now?"

"Just . . . nothing." He smiled his sudden, dazzling smile that was so charming it made you forget everything you'd been thinking about.

"Faery mind tricks," she muttered darkly at the winter white of his teeth. "Don't you hold out on me."

"All in good time," he said with something of his old dashing ways and twirled about to sweep away in an elegant line of camel coat, navy slacks, and immaculate shoes. "Come along," he called over his shoulder. "Work to see. People to do."

Lila followed obediently, ten steps behind. Fifty years, she thought. Fifty years of waiting here and he was not a day different to her. What had he done with all that time?

And then it occurred to her at least one of the things he might have done (stayed with Max) and she began to wonder how she was going to ask him, and what she'd find out. The notion was so important and made such a pressure in her chest she kept quiet about it as they drove, and just watched the countryside and the city pass from the windows of the ancient Cadillac and thought over a million different ways to start talking.

CHAPTER SIX

hey checked a further three positions on the coast. Like the first ship, these ghosts were semimaterial, all wrecks. They were not particular vessels like *The Golden Hind*. One was a second world war minesweeper, one a millionaire's pleasure cruiser, one a stone age coracle barely distinguishable as anything but seaborne rubbish save for its eerie glow and the frost surrounding it.

The last ship to come to shore had grounded on private land in the nature reserve, closer to Bay City. They left it until last because it was on the way back, and because they both knew the place. Coming over the hill and down into the heavily wooded valley Lila recalled all the curves from her high-speed motorbike rides. In contrast to that the Caddy wallowed through them slowly. She looked into the trees. Sure enough, in the darkness there were the shivery, shadowy forms of wood elementals forming and unforming. She shivered compulsively.

"What do you think Zal wanted out here?" the words were out before she realised she was thinking aloud. The road sucked them down and down into the darkening glades, twisting them as if it were the path through a maze.

Malachi shrugged, his fingers easy on the wheel, his elbow resting on the door sill as relaxed as could be. "Junkie's paradise?"

"But these are all wood spirits." The sight of them made her uneasy.

"You can feel this place though, right? And you said he was approached by a ghost out here. Any place full of elementals is ripe for doing the magic he could do. Makes it easy to trip out almost anywhere. Most places in Otopia you can't say that." Malachi turned the car lazily around the bends as the woods crept closer to the road on high banks until the trees created a continuous tunnel. The pieces of sky between the leaves overhead formed the shapes of eyes until Lila was forced to look down at the dashboard.

"But why here?"

"Every place has natural energy sinks made by the geology or the wildlife." He was offhand about it but he kept a close eye on the road, she noticed.

They passed a sign, almost covered in ivy and green lichens. "Solomon's Folly. Private Property. Trespassers will be prosecuted." A wire fence, marked with a single, straggling strip of white cloth, snaked off into the undergrowth to mark the property line on either side of the road. Lila didn't remember it being there before.

The house itself appeared, as it had before, to be a tumble of irregular blocks like large stones that had rolled down into a hollow and sunk into the ground. Fifty years ago the effect had been stylish, yet hideous. But now the place had been neglected. Moss and creepers covered most of the angles in curving growths of spongy green or vivid purples. The sculpted lawns were thick meadows of standing hay, roughly cut only at the edges where they met the driveway or the courtyard. Malachi pulled up in the middle of the paving and got out first. Lila looked around, renewing her loathing of the place, and followed him a minute later. The buildings looked as if they were bones, rotting into the earth. On terraces below and to their right the land fell in a series of gardens whose shrubs now almost obscured the pool deck where she'd woken up one morning to find herself too stoned to move,

Zal groping her, the sun pure fire. It felt like a million years ago to her. Now a chink of faded blue pool cover just showed. Below that stony walks dropped to the beach; she zoomed in on the sight, captured and held by it.

"What's that?"

Malachi turned from where he had gone to knock at the door. His debonair confidence ebbed from him as he looked with her at the strangely bare metal decks and platforms, the things that looked like outsize gunnery stations, the broken gantries, the strange, arched spars that seemed to be metal ribs without anything to hold. At the end of one a purplish red crystal caught the afternoon sun and glowed fiercely as a beacon. Lila had never seen anything like it.

"There's no witchlight," she said, surprised, then tore her gaze away to glance at Malachi.

He was standing with his hands relaxed at his sides, his shoulders low, his stare fixated. The door behind him opened but he didn't react.

"Mal?" Lila said, puzzled.

"Are you from the agency?" the woman at the door asked at the same moment. She was annoyed. Lila glanced at her and saw immediately that she wasn't human, though she was doing a reasonable job of looking like one. At her attention the woman backed into the shadow behind the door and said quickly, "You can go on down and take a look. Just follow the path. The way's obvious."

"Yes ma'am," Malachi said as if he was in a trance, but then he snapped out and showed his ID quickly. "We'll come back and report—"

"No need," their host said. "Just deal with it." The door shut and Lila heard several locks and bolts being rapidly secured. She looked up and over, but all the windows were curtained or covered with blinds.

"Later," Malachi said to her about-to-be-asked query. "For now let's go and see."

Lila followed him down the winding, treacherous path to the shore. Overgrowths and broken stones had replaced what she knew as perfectly manicured gardens. As they passed the pool she glanced and saw the same iron furniture she'd seen before, but now rusted, the beautiful mosaic paths covered in leaves and so filthy they were nearly invisible. She had an urge to throw off the pool cover and see what was beneath, as a dare, but Malachi was moving too quickly for her. He could get through small spaces in a flash without moving anything. She bludgeoned after him, snapping branches and stripping leaves. Flies zoomed heavily around her from their places in the dense, warm jungle. Finally they met the sand and stepped out of the shade of the palms.

Malachi sped up. In a thought he was up to the huge, bulky sides of the object, finding a ladder as if he knew it was there and climbing up onto the first of the decks in spite of the ten-degree list. The ship was doubly odd to Lila's eyes. It was flat bottomed, though there was no plating on the sides. Nothing looked normal until she adjusted her expectations and instead of looking for a ship made for the sea looked at a ship made for space.

She jet-jumped onto the first deck and slid along it to where Malachi stood behind a lump of ruined equipment, his back braced against what was clearly a kind of a chair, if it had had any padding. He ran his fingers across dials and screens, buttons and keys, switches and LEDs. He looked out along a kind of bowsprit where another cage was set at a position for operating some huge kind of spear gun. The breech was empty and mangled. Lila looked back, and her AI put the bits together and made an analysis in an instant. The gun had been destroyed when the cable on the bolt had run to its limit, been yanked out of the deck and slammed into the back of the barrel, where it had broken as it was pulled free. Elsewhere other pieces of machinery showed electrical burns and damage at the molecular level that had made the metal porous and weak.

Malachi glanced at her and almost smiled for an instant. Then his face greyed and he was suddenly up and off, slithering across the beaten decking towards a hatch. She followed, magnetizing her feet to help her keep a grip, grateful for the afternoon heat that went with her until she smelled the first trace of a sickly, musty odour that stopped her in her tracks. Shadows clotted the gangways as Mal led her down into the hold. The bitterly cold darkness made their breath billow. Lila could feel it like warm clouds against her face; then her face cooled and became clammy. It was like being inside a freezer, the effect intensified by the glow of the witchlight that just let them see the cause of the smell.

Heaps of rubbish lined the walls of a room whose pristine centre was a cluster of consoles. Their dead screens were crazed with frost. The faery halted midstep, his nostrils twitching. He looked back at her for confirmation and she nodded and moved past him. There was more than just food waste rotting in the corners. She found the bodies after scanning for likely shapes in the mounds of crumpled cartons and moved forwards. Everything was stuck together with films of ice. Lila pushed her way through, watching tiny crystals shatter as the mess gave up its hoard to her hands. As she dug, the faery clothing tightened on her and she heard it hiss as if it made the discovery just before she did. She ignored it and cleared enough, then stood aside and let Malachi move forwards.

He shoved his hands deeply into his pockets and looked down for a few seconds, then turned and walked out the way they had come. Lila recorded the images of the dead demon and elf; then she followed him, dusting her hands off compulsively, though because everything was frozen solid there was nothing on her.

Back outside the heat was suddenly a sweltering oven, the light a blazing glare.

"Who are they?" she asked once they were standing on the beach again.

"Frie . . . people I knew," he said, staring at the awkward shape of the vessel.

"No obvious signs of death," she ventured. "But the demon wasn't—"

Malachi interrupted her gently, with a raised hand to show that he would talk to her without any oblique interrogation. "They're part of her crew. She's a Void ship. Well, the material manifestation of it anyway. She was a research vessel. Jones was her captain."

Lila sifted through her memories for the name and frowned. "Jones as in Calliope Jones, the strandloper?"

He nodded. "She was for hunting ghosts out in the Void. Jones led a research team, called themselves the Ghost Hunters. They surveyed immanent hotspots—places where ghosts spawn out in the middle of nothing. They'd watch them forming, try and record the process of actualisation, reification. Everyone funded them a bit, but when you saw her last time she was running out of money. She . . ." He paused. "She didn't follow policy, and I guess she pissed off too many people. She wouldn't tell what she found. Hung onto her theories saying they weren't tested enough. At least one time I know of she endangered the crew. They didn't like her either."

"Charm wasn't her strong suit."

"I helped her out a bit. I thought it was too important just to let it go."

"Mal . . ." Lila decided to brave the question. "Were they killed by ghosts?"

"Yeah," he said. "And now the whole ship is a ghost. I just wonder. Maybe this isn't the actual ship."

"Like *The Golden Hind* back there isn't the actual ship."

"Yeah. It's a facsimile." He turned to her and fixed her with his piercing orange eyes. "What do you know about ghosts?"

"Not a lot."

"Time we looked through what Jones thought then." He turned his back quickly on the ship and began to walk over the rocks toward the path. Lila followed him and they retraced their steps to the house.

Lila knocked on the door. After a time the woman inside said, "Go away!"

"It's just us," Lila called through the heavy wood. She pushed at the keyhole and tried to look through it but it was blocked. The door did not open. "We need to send a team back here to take care of that ship and quarantine the beach, ma'am."

"You can send 'em but don't let them call at the house. You don't need us. You can use the path and the steps and the service road that goes there from the gardener's building."

There was a tense pause.

"Ma'am, could I come inside for a moment?" Lila asked, suddenly sure something important lay behind the door, in the house.

"No!" The chains and locks were checked, firmed. The soft furl of faint colour that accompanied faery charms glowed briefly along the lintel. "Not so close to night and not today. Another time perhaps. Later. Yes. Much later. Go away now." The voice had a cornered, desperate edge to it.

"All right." Lila gave up. She had no legal course to take her inside and could think of nothing to say, but at the last moment something prompted her. At her back Malachi's Cadillac was humming. She walked to the passenger door and leaned in.

"Paper," she said, looking around the pristine interior.

Malachi reached into his inner coat pocket and produced a small moleskin notebook. He meticulously tore a page out and handed it over.

"Thanks." She hooked the pen out and wrote on it: Lila Black, then had no idea what else to put—friend, agent, safe person? The ink dried and went matte. She capped the pen and put it away. That would do. It was probably deeply unwise, but she felt she must leave something for the person behind the door. The house was terrible, the ship worse; nobody should be there alone.

She folded the paper and tried to find a place to slide it, but the only gap was where the charm had glowed and eventually she was reduced to fiddling it through the smallest of spaces at the top, feeling the thin paper catch and bend on the rough brush of an insulating tape. It was the best she could do. Silence greeted her efforts.

They drove out of the dip listening to the slow climbing notes of the engine as it built and changed gear, built and climbed over the hills and through the forest until they were back on the highway.

"Who's in that house?" Lila asked as they turned away from the city and took a route inland. "Is it a faery?"

"No, not really," Mal said. "Like I said earlier, some people you ought to meet. They'll explain it better."

"I like you explaining it."

He sighed. "Hunter's Legacy. They keep them out of sight whenever they find them, unless the community is one of those advanced kinds with a lot of Woken in it. There are two kinds of them. The Hunter's Chosen—those that he picked to be his while he was here. The Hunter's Children—that explains itself. The first sort were born humans but they ended up different, depending on how they were used. The second lot are part fey, but the form of the Hunter you unleashed here is one of the oldest and they share his old ways. It's not like with me, in my modern guises, and the others of us who are here and now."

"It . . . he . . . wasn't even material," Lila said, remembering.

"He had forms," Malachi shuddered. "But as you say, not very material ones. Nothing fixed. Some of the Children look human. Some don't. They all have powers that are feylike. That hasn't made them popular since he left."

They were driving farther and farther into the country, passing out of the suburbs and into farmland and the rocky hills where wineries and health spas battled for supremacy. Lila knew he must be taking her to a place where these people were living.

"How many of them are there?" She kept herself to the point.

"Of the Chosen most have died. The ride killed a lot early. Just a few left now, but they're the strongest. Majority died of exhaustion and he left them where they fell. Some got killed on the hunt. Some he took a dislike to and killed himself. Some he liked and left them after just a short time. They were the ones who made it to forty and more years. Now the remaining ones are the ones he gave something to. Like Dar changed you, he changed them." His hands had gone tight on the wheel.

"Are they . . . ?"

"Some live with the Children at the Solace Place," he said quickly. "Where we're going. They guard them, keep everything nice and quiet. Just one or two out there alone now. They don't need protection." His eyes narrowed. "More like extermination."

Lila blinked in surprise. She didn't think she'd ever heard him say anything like that before. "Why?"

"Just check the crime records for the Bay City area over the last fifty."

She flicked through them. The machine buzz increased as she amplified her sensitivity to the AI part of herself. She listened to it for a second, then dimmed its rush and looked over the more prosaic information about her hometown's seedier side. "That's a lot of bodies in the woods."

"Ours just kills them, we think. Over on the East Coast they have one that eats the victims."

"You think?"

"Some of the Chosen have heavy psychic powers. Physical death could be the least of their work. Across the midstates there are so many people turning up mindless and zombified we're betting there's at least one more who just likes the gooey centres. They started out putting the victims in institutions, but a law got passed fifteen years ago that allows them to be classified brain-dead, even though they still breathe and move for themselves. The trouble is—"

But Lila had accessed the records. "They're puppets."

"Yeah. No discernible soul or personality or mind. Tested by experts on all three. Empty but fully working. Open to suggestion.

Can use them for anything. Mostly they just make stuff in factories or menial labour. They can earn for the families that way. Or—"

"Or you can shoot them."

"Some people prefer that."

"Christ." She closed the files and stared at the road.

"There are others. Touched, they're called."

"People with powers who won't leave their homes and be kicked out."

"Something like that."

Lila knew about that. The beach kids had told her all about it.

"I thought humans couldn't do magic," she said.

"Not really. It rarely goes well. They're not made for it," he agreed. They turned off onto an unmarked road. "Just twenty miles or so."

"That woman in the Folly . . ."

"If she were our killer I'd be first in there," Malachi said. "I've thought she might be either of those things, but now I don't know. There's no bodies found up that way."

"Maybe she doesn't like them in her backyard."

"Did you get the impression she was a serial killer?" He looked at her candidly.

Lila shrugged. "No, but I'm a dumb human."

He snorted. "Not so dumb. No. She isn't that. The reason there's no bodies up there is surely because of her, but not because of that. She's there because of the house."

"But it's a horrible place."

"Maybe. It's a powerful place, that's sure. And some don't mind the flavour of things."

"As long as they're stronger . . ."

"Yeah," he nodded. "You got it in one."

"Is that why Zal rented it?"

"Surely. He'd been here a long time. Starved of aether. What do you think?"

"There are more wood elementals, and bigger ones, there, than anywhere I've ever seen."

"Others too," Malachi said, keeping his eyes on the way as they burred off the hardtop and onto gravel, turning between low hills that showed no signs of ownership now, not even much vegetation save scrubby grass and the odd evergreen bush.

"Zal opened a portal there . . . or he pulled . . . I don't know the word. He made a circle and turned it into a bit of Zoomenon."

Malachi nearly swerved off the road. "He what? Oh, you mean he made a circle and called some elementals."

"No," she said.

He pulled over and they were briefly surrounded in a plume of ochre dust.

"Like I said. He made a circle and went into it and inside it wasn't Otopia any more, it was Zoomenon. Different sky, different ground, and lots of elementals. Hundreds. I don't know the name for that. Not summoning . . . or is it?"

"Nah," Malachi said. "There is no name for it. Because people don't do that. They can't do that."

"I'm telling you, I saw—"

"I believe you."

Lila was puzzled. "You know he did it like . . . he must have done it a lot. He was high on them. We know that. He went there to get a fix and he got one. It was no more weird than seeing a dealer, I thought."

"Did you tell anyone about this at the time?"

"No. I mean it was in the downloads that the doctor took off me."

"But human technicians would have looked at that. Sarasilien at the most? I didn't see it. Or if I did it was in some boring paperwork thing I don't usually bother with." He looked dissatisfied and puzzled, his mouth open. "How could he do that and not boast about it or anything?"

"You and he weren't exactly friends."

"Yeah. I know. But even so."

"He treated it as if it was normal."

"Did you ever see him do it again?"

She thought it over. "Um . . . we survived a fire attack inside a circle he cast, but he said something about doing it wrong. It didn't change worlds. It was just a protective ring."

"Where?"

"Outside the city where the kidnap took place."

"Right." He took the wheel and turned them back onto the road, thinking. "You're going to take me there when we go back to that place and show me exactly where it happened."

She shrugged. "Okay, but I have to tell you, I think he really just did it for the hit. I'd even go so far as to say he might not have realised what he was doing. He was only fixated on getting charged up. He could have transported himself to the moon and not cared."

Malachi nodded and shook his head alternately, muttering to himself. "I bet. I wish I had more of a grip on that stuff. Faeries don't traffic with the elements. No need, really. They're very demon and elf things. You know what I mean."

"Not so much, but I'll take your word for it," she said as they twisted and ground through the last of the road's conniving turns for a while and began to cross some serious desert.

Apparently it didn't matter because he was quiet for the rest of the drive. After forty minutes they pulled up in the yard of a sizeable ranch, dotted with buildings of various kinds, neatly kept, but nobody in sight.

"Where is everyone?"

"They're here," Malachi said, and got out of the car.

Lila followed him as he walked towards the barn and saw him make a subtle hand signal that looked as if he might have just been checking his pocket for something. The air shivered, and the illusion of the ranch, its dusty yards and worn fences, vanished. What lay behind was not too different. There was a large house, a barn, some other buildings, but no tired fields of stones, instead a landscaped grass garden of hardy plants and standing in that garden ready to meet them a group of people in ordinary clothes. One was walking forwards to meet Malachi, her hand outstretched.

Lila measured her at six feet five inches tall. She was powerfully built, without a spare ounce of fat on her. Her hair was soft and long, a chestnut brown the colour of leaves and rich earth, but that was all that was soft about her. She moved with deceptive speed and a lightness that only came from a natural ability to spring and long years of training. Her face was a perfect oval, features strong, brows pronounced. Her pale green eyes lit on Malachi as they shook hands and seemed briefly too human for words; then she looked past him at Lila.

For an instant Lila was back in the primal forests of Under feeling the gaze of the Hunter between her shoulder blades, hearing his unvoice of grating branches. These green eyes had the same effect, almost like a prickly heat where their gaze lit on her. She'd never seen the Hunter himself. Perhaps he had no eyes. Now her first instinct was to look away and never let that stare through, but her demon habits were too strong, and she stared right back into the challenge. Around her the dragon-patterned suit shifted and slid, glittering marks coming to life in its weave. The weight of it increased, and it subtly tightened at her waist, loosened on the legs as if preparing for a fight.

The Chosen halted in her tracks, startled, and set her shoulders at an off angle, "Who are you?" Her voice was half wild, like a talking animal might sound. It took Lila a second to realise what she'd said.

"Lila Black," Lila said, not offering a hand as she moved up to Malachi's shoulder and stepped unwaveringly into the woman's personal space. "And you?"

"This is Tasha," Malachi murmured, quite relaxed but watching with deceptive acuity as Tasha stared at Lila's suit. "Tasha Baines."

"Chosen," Lila said, to clarify for sure.

Tasha looked up cautiously at Lila once again. "As are you." She didn't lower her eyes but lowered her chin in a greeting of equals.

Lila glanced at Malachi. "I'm sorry?"

Malachi turned to face her, nodding at Tasha. Lila saw that both of them were in on something that had just been tried, tested, and confirmed. Something about her. She elbowed Malachi in the ribs, anger warring with curiosity and gnawing conviction into an unruly pack inside her. "Spit it out."

"I am Chosen of the Hunter," Tasha said, beauty and the beast all in one. She must have been over seventy by Lila's reckoning but she looked not a day past twenty-five. She set her thumbs into the broad leather belt that held up her jeans and nodded with satisfaction, a grim smile on her handsome mouth. "You are Chosen of the Wanderer."

"Mal," Lila said. "She means the suit, right?"

"Yeah, she means the suit."

"I thought so."

"You might think it, but you don't understand," Tasha growled. It was a genuine struggle for her to speak, the voice coming as if she had to force it out to her mouth. In spite of this she still had a midstates accent. "I guess that's why you're here, Mal? To explain?"

"That and other reasons," he agreed. "Lila's skipped the last half century in Under and she doesn't know about you and the Children so it's an introduction. Also, we have a ghost problem. I wondered if you were able to shed some light on it."

Tasha peered at him. "Many favours," she said grudgingly.

"I'm doing my best," Malachi replied, but it was difficult, Lila saw. He was almost grinding his teeth. She could guess the story. Malachi was responsible for bringing the Mothkin to Otopia and necessitating the reign of the Hunter. The people here were outcasts as a result of that reign, living in a prison more or less, reliant on government protection and handouts. Perhaps they had useful abilities or saleable ones even, but they weren't on any official plan or payment schedule and they hadn't found any niche in Otopia that was safe from human fear. They were just outcast, and he was here, asking them.

"We can come back another time if it's not convenient," Lila said. Over Tasha's shoulder she saw the people watching them closely. Around her feet the wind stirred the ground. The high pampas grass that screened much of the garden soughed with the movement of invisible things. Though she had no magical senses, Lila could plot the positioning of the things that caused the movements easily, but that was all. As to whether those things were real or just their scare tactics, she couldn't tell.

"No, we'd like to meet you," Tasha said after her pause, and abruptly beckoned them towards the waiting group and the house. "Always interesting to hear another story." She waited, watching Malachi.

He nodded and took a step forwards. They took the path to the door, and from the garden the silent group followed them, breaking ranks into a more natural ordering of ones and twos and beginning to talk among themselves. Lila felt them at her back, keeping their distance, watching her so closely.

The house, white clapboard to look at, of the old-seeming style that had become fashionable again, was a huge, rambling place, full of the winding halls and odd nooks that Lila had come to associate with faery homes. She was not surprised to be led for a distance that felt upwards of a quarter mile along twisting ways, through rooms, across corridors, and up brief staircases until they arrived in a large living room whose expansive windows looked out on the same patch of garden, grass, and yard that they had just vacated. Here a sizeable fireplace held a hefty grate full of smouldering logs, despite the fact that it was warm outside and in. Sofas and chairs were at all angles. Tasha took a seat in a group of six or so and pointed briefly across from herself. Lila and Mal sat down, and as if there was nothing unusual going on, the group following them came in and settled, talking quietly among themselves though even at her most acute Lila could not make out one word of what they were saying.

"So, you're Agent Black," Tasha said, biting her thumbnail and spitting the result over her shoulder. "Mal told us about you. We figured you were a victim of a bad deal. But I see not." She stared at Lila with unending interest, gaze roving over all of her.

"Enlighten me," Lila suggested.

"It seems unlikely that you would broker any kind of deal with my . . . maker. The likes of him aren't moved by creatures of such brief lives as ourselves. I couldn't figure that you were the one responsible." She glanced significantly at Malachi, who sighed tersely. "Now I see you're like me, hoisted to a rank you didn't aspire to by the whim of a greater being." She smiled. It wasn't a pleasant expression.

"And what are you?" Lila asked. "Besides bitter."

Tasha shrugged and spoke in the manner of someone reciting lines. "We Chosen are the humans the Hunter rode to do his work here in Otopia. We were first prey, and when we passed his tests," she hesitated and rubbed her shoulder, then continued, "then we were his mounts, his limbs, his voice. We were small and weak, so he chose many of us, and after he had gone we were left with different changes. Changelings, as you'd say, I guess."

"You said I was Chosen, but I'm not . . ." Lila stopped and looked down at the suit. It had done nothing new since she arrived and merely lay immaculate and beautiful on her. She looked up again and Tasha was staring at her with a half sad, knowing kind of gaze, slightly nodding.

"The Hunter is from a long way Under," Tasha said, crossing her legs and leaning back. She examined the state of her boots as she talked, turning them as if there was going to be something worth seeing on the worn-out leather toecaps. Lila had seen Mal do this kind of thing enough times to realise it was a faery habit, distracting yourself from what you were saying, turning attention away from it in the hope that you could speak without being overheard by forces you didn't want around you. If he was going to say something important, especially about Faery, he always started doing something else at the same time.

Tasha continued, "Low enough it's before they have names, proper names. Before language is really up and running. Even calling him the Hunter is just a way of naming something that is really more like hunting, an active pursuit. *Wanderer* is the noun, but wandering is really the nature, and wondering. Tatterdemalion is a name that came later after the king took to naming things and in so doing began to fix their natures and move them from being actions into objects. Even so, it's of the ancient first forms, the kind that Malachi here would get to if he dropped out of the arse of Faery. Not that he would. Might forget who he was. Always they do, if they fall far enough. Lose their minds, who they are, all the stuff of higher things. That's right, ain't it? Fall back into the old times and lose your connection to the worlds of later." She transferred her half-friendly gaze to Malachi, who nodded, his face weary and resigned. "Till someone points the way for you, course."

"Or if you find a way up," Malachi said. "By accident on purpose."

Tasha nodded as if she supposed that were possible. "Finding by Getting Lost. Yes. That'd be the only way. To learn the first tricks." They both looked at Lila's suit.

"But where is she?" Lila asked. "If this is her dress, then . . ."

"You have it wrong," Tasha said, her smile becoming broader. "That's her. Not her dress. She is the dress. You're wearing her."

Confirmation was worse than she'd thought. Everyone else seemed to agree. The room had gone silent and all eyes were on her.

"Mal?" Lila said, damned if she was going to buckle, though she'd have liked to leap up, tear the suit off, shred it, and jump on the pieces before burning them and then burying the ash.

He exhaled and shook himself loose, trying and failing to unsettle the weight that was bending him forwards. He set his elbows on his knees and held his palms up apologetically. "I thought it was true. . . . I came here to be sure."

Lila's skin had gone cold. She saw faces turn towards her, cautious, and for the first time noticed that they were not really human. As soon as she saw this on one, it immediately became apparent on the others too. Their eyes were too large, their chins too pointed, their hair wild, or missing, or instead of hair the wings of butterflies and moths opening and closing. . . . She tore her gaze back to the Chosen as the woman spoke again.

"*She* dealt you your fifty-year delay," Tasha added. "She was the broker. Just like he dealt me . . . what I got. He came out at her bidding. You were just the agent setting terms, offered him a year and a day. I guess you didn't know what he could do in that time." She paused and the room paused with her. "So that's not your fault." She looked as if it ought to be somebody's damn fault, and ground the tips of her fingers into the tough sofa arms, almost ripping the material.

"But I'm not changed like you," Lila said, ignoring her own acute discomfort to press on while she was able. She stared into Tasha's amber, lion-coloured eyes that a moment ago had been green and knew she was looking at a caged animal, one that was prowling behind its bars. What it took to open the cage door she didn't want to know.

"I never saw anything as changed as you," Tasha replied, snorting. "But you're right. Tatter has a form here, so she didn't need to make you hers in the same way. But you're hers. Perhaps she's yours too. Both. The old fey are like that. They don't care for boundaries. All that matters is the play."

"How old is old?" Lila sensed the potential suddenly. "Three sisters old? As old as the Moirae themselves?"

If the room had been silent before it was deathly now. All the assembled gazed at her like so many statues, and then abruptly they each found something much more compelling to do: stretching, adjusting their collars, looking at their watches, picking up discarded magazines, or plumping cushions. The hair on the back of Lila's neck prickled. On her legs the dress shifted and the dragons' eyes were suddenly shot with silver threads.

She glanced at Mal, who was waiting like the others, as if an asteroid were going to fall on them. He was searching his pockets.

Lila pulled up a game of tic-tac-toe on her hand quickly, the crosses and circles forming like tattoo marks on her palm as she played against the AI part of herself. "I know, I know," she muttered, testy. "But I had to ask. You know I did."

Slowly the agitation around them softened as they puttered on with their little tasks. Finally she sensed them starting to relax as nothing untoward happened.

"Not that old," said Tasha finally through clenched teeth. She was tracing the pattern of roses on the sofa arm over and over again. "But close. We must not speak—"

"Yes, we must," Lila said, flipping out of the endless stalemates of noughts and crosses to a less discrete game and struggling to keep focused on it as she tried to say what she wanted. "I want to know about how things are made, where they came from, in Faery. Where you come from. Who is the oldest?"

"You can want it," Mal said, taking out the pieces of his grooming kit and cleaning them: tweezers, nail clippers, buffer, comb. . . . "That doesn't mean you get it. We can talk about this later."

"We are always talking about it later and never now," Lila said, losing chequers. "Where can we have this precious talk, when? Now is as good a time as any."

Mal's black face darkened and his orange eyes became narrow. Coal dust shivered from his skin. He placed the items back in their leather case. "I didn't come here so you could interrogate them. Shut up already. After all this and you won't trust me when I say to keep quiet. You don't know what you are—"

"Fine," Lila snapped. "Fine. Then let's get your business done with and go."

"You *are* the business, so just stay there and be quiet," he said. "I brought you because Tatter predates me. All right? I know a lot, but here is where my firsthands run out. Tasha is the only person we can talk to who knows something about ancient fey, and that only second-hand."

"I don't get it," Lila said, losing again. "Why can't you talk to it . . . to her, yourself?"

Malachi scowled and broke from his fussing to look at her briefly. "Because it is a suit of clothes, Lila. It doesn't have ears or a mouth or language. It isn't that kind of a thing. The Hunter wasn't that kind of a thing."

"He spoke," Lila protested, and when they waited just repeated it. "When we did the deal. He spoke. It was kind of like the wind spoke, or something. He said Tatter. That's the last thing I knew before I got back here. He saw the dress and he said her name. And then he said yes. And here we fucking are. Anyway, it communicates quite well enough without talking." She swiped crossly at herself, slapping the cloth as if brushing off lint as she swapped chequers for backgammon. "The trouble is that I don't see what it adds up to. Elf this, faery that, don't talk about these people, don't use words, don't write things down, don't send life. . . . Why give me all these things and then say no? Why bug me twenty-four/seven with endless whiny messages and then try and spring me in the middle of the night like they're the Mafia and I owe them? I'm sick of it." She regretted the speech instantly and bit her tongue.

Slowly the distraction work died back. Lila let her hand return to flesh tones and the usual head, life, and heart lines.

"I used to work in a diner," Tasha said. She was relaxed now and her eyes were a dark green. She smoothed the sofa arm with her hand. "Two kids in high school, mother in hospital—Alzheimer's, father god knows where, and boyfriends called by the days of the week. I weighed a hundred and twenty-one pounds, wore heels to make five-five, and the only thing I knew I was good at was making Key lime pie. That was a long time ago." She smiled suddenly and this time it was genuine. Lila felt that they had crossed some line into friendship, but exactly how was unclear.

Tasha said, "We don't talk about those old folks back home because we fear them, Lila, and we're right to fear them. They don't know modern ways. They eat their own young. The ones that talk do a show of acting like you and me, but don't be fooled. The one thing you have to remember about all the faeries is the glamour. It's an illusion. All what you see here." She pointed around at the gathered faces. "Even what you think you see of us now is an illusion. It's what you like to see, the kind of thing that makes sense when you think of half-faeries, bogeymen, spooks. What you put in pictures, in movies. Just light and tricks. Anything to put you at ease and put you off. We even fool ourselves with it. Hell, most of the time we're so pleased with ourselves because of it we'd rather die than give it up. And what you're wearing doesn't need to talk or hear to know everything she wants to know. The only reason we talk in front of her is because she's one of the few who never did harm, far as we know. She's part of us all. She's one of the first things to have a name, but we don't know when she got it. She's part of the glamour."

"The ones I want to know about?" Lila began hesitantly.

"The first," Tasha said. "The ones we never mention. They can undo us all."

"And before them?"

Tasha shrugged. She looked at Malachi. "Ghosts and the gods."

CHAPTER SEVEN

After experiencing the faeries' fear of their elders Lila was quiet on the drive back to town. She didn't want to share in their existential terror, but the force of it had been much greater than she had expected, even given Malachi's thousand exclamations of it over the time they'd known each other. Somehow she'd always thought he was exaggerating, that it was a kind of joke. Even face to face with the Giantkiller, she hadn't thought of him as anything other than her equal; he was just an equal with much more power that she wasn't able to counter. However, she might have been the only one to see it that way; besides she really didn't know if the powers those fey had would hold over her. She was human, susceptible to magic after a fashion, but not made like a faery. Not that she knew what a faery was made of, or how. She couldn't somehow see Malachi as a construction, just a fancier version of the dolls he made, animated by . . . by whom? They said it was the old ones, but that just pushed the question farther back; it didn't answer anything.

Mal didn't speak either. He drove in his usual manner, one hand on the wheel, the other resting on the door. The car combined with the wind noise was shockingly loud on the quiet road. People in quieter vehicles stared. They were antique.

The sun was going down as they turned into the darkness of the agency lot. Mal pulled into his spot and stopped the engine. Neither of them moved. On the suit the dragons' thread eyes had closed back to black.

"If ghosts are precursors to faeries," Lila began, "then what are elves and demons made of?"

Someone's high heels clicked and sounded out loud in the dimly lit bays as they walked to a car. The door opened, closed. There was a brief whirr of wheels on the concrete.

"Ghosts ain't that," he said softly. "I know what Tasha said, but she's only guessing like I do. Let's not talk here."

Seeing her about to complain he added quickly, "Inside. We'll talk inside."

But inside Lila was distracted by the quartermaster who wanted to question her about the missing bike, and by the time she had given him enough answers to make him go away and think about getting her another one Malachi had also gone. Lila frowned and played back through the last ten minutes. She didn't see him go, even on that. Tricky.

On the walk to her office she looked at the people passing her. They looked at her, pretending not to. She didn't recognise anyone except the androids. She knew where and what they were without having to look. Once out of sight on the corridor she paused and tried to shed the cold shiver that lay on her skin, but it wanted to linger.

At the door of the offices she put her hand to the grip, suddenly slowing without knowing why, as if she was expecting something. There was an odd frequency about the place that she could feel in the deep circuits of the AI, a hum that didn't belong.

She glanced up and down the corridor. Nobody about. Outside, the long window of the hall that looked into the garden was almost impossible to see. It was dusk and the harsh lights of the interior made the glass into a mirror through which only the silhouettes of the trees and bushes that lined the inner court could be seen. And through their dark branches and leaves, the oblongs of light that were the other side of the square. She felt that it ought to have been a ring. Who in their right mind built everything at these dangerous angles?

The thought wasn't like her. It was a magical thought.

Beneath her fingers the door vibrated. She heard, faintly, the sound of chimes ringing a distant hour. Then music, lilting and strange. Voices.

I saw three ships. . . .

Did she hear that?

The sound seemed to come from behind the door, but also from a greater distance than the next room, even the next hour. . . . Again her thoughts were running to another pattern. The twinkling, chiming increased, sparkled like frost dancing. Her shivering became the vibrato of a hundred delicate violins.

Lila inched her hand away from the door and quiet returned. The dull hubbub of voices from the office behind the hall panelling impinged on her. Machines much duller than her own droned and fanned in ugly keys, pulling the day in a difficult direction, curling the air into negative vortices laden with chaotic ions. The lights droned, distorting the space around them by infinitely small upset measures.

Lila straightened and detuned her hearing back into a human range. The place seemed blanketed in a fog. She called Bentley to her.

The android appeared and Lila contained the desire to flinch at her approach.

"Ma'am," she said calmly.

"Stand here," Lila instructed, vacating the spot. "Do you hear or see anything unusual?"

"No ma'am." A human might have taken some time to listen. Bentley's reply was immediate, but her relative attention was the equivalent of at least ten minutes of an ordinary person's. They linked and spent a second sharing and dismissing all the detectable frequencies in the local area. "Will that be all?"

"No, wait a minute here. I'll go in. When I call you, follow me."

Bentley moved aside. Lila put her hand out.

Again the music, the sparkling music that made her think of winter, and the trailing notes of a harp inviting her. . . . She opened the door.

Her breath steamed instantly, obscuring the scene until a gust of bitter wind snatched it away. She saw, in the instant she held the door open, the shoreline of her office. Desks and furniture tumbled where boulders would be, limned in ice. A grey, heaving swell of bitter seawater rose, clotted with greasy slush, washing ashore the wreckage of a glass ship. It had already by some means driven a fragment containing the main mast into the shingle of the old wooden floor. A body was tied to it, frozen under a sheer skin of ice.

The door closed with the dull crump of heavyweight fire-door pushed shut by its automatic latch.

"I saw that, ma'am," Bentley's placid voice said from behind her shoulder. "And I heard the line of a song. It is a carol from the Victorian era of Old Earth." She sent Lila the carol, lyrics and music. Lila didn't miss the note that said the provenance of the song was unknown. She looked at the door thoughtfully.

"What do you make of the ship?"

"It would appear that your office has become an illustrative tableau depicting the fate of a ship called the *Hesperus*, after a poem by the romantic poet Henry Wadsworth Longfellow." She helpfully appended the poem, with notes and subsequent cultural references to the present day.

Lila looked at the door. "How do you think I make it go away?"

"The manifestation of untimely ghosts is referred to the Office of Otherworldly Affairs in the absence of a formal guideline," Bentley said.

"Yeah, but Mal sneaked off on me," Lila replied. "I thought I'd leave him for an hour until he did whatever it was he was bursting to do. Anyway, he doesn't have a clue, as far as I can tell." She half turned and braced herself to look at the woman's grey, plastic face. "Did you speak like a how-to manual when you were alive?"

"I am still alive," Bentley said in her even, conversational tone. "And not so much. It seems to make people less antsy around me, though."

"Hm," Lila nodded. "Well, you'd better update me on all the collated theories about reality over the last fifty years. Seeing as I can't get into the office and I have a couple of hours to kill before dinner."

The file transfers took a few moments.

"I miss conversation," Lila said. The android did not react. *Android* was not the correct term, was it? She knew that. But somehow it kept coming back to her. She didn't know how much more hard work she was prepared to do in Bentley's direction before her patience ran out, but she felt it wouldn't be much. "Who's living in that house at Solomon's Folly out on the South Bay Park? Do we get access to that kind of thing?"

"Of course," Bentley said.

Lila blocked the incoming signals. "Let's get coffee or something? You can tell me on the way."

"You can check all this information yourself," Bentley said with bland affability as they turned and started in the direction of the kitchen.

"Yeah, I have a bit of a . . ." Lila waggled her hands, trying to express it. "Bit of a thing about connecting to machines with seriously hardcore outlet pipes and semi-intelligent roving bot systems. Call it paranoia."

"That is why you killed Sandra Lane?"

"She isn't dead," Lila said with certainty. "I just sent her . . . elsewhere."

"She is no longer connected."

"Then that makes two of us." They had reached the end of the corridor, and the civilisation of other people.

Bentley paced in a deferential position, slightly behind Lila's shoulder. "She wanted to recruit you to the rogues."

"Probably."

"It is certain. You have magical affinities. They want them."

Lila switched from speech to electronic communications so that they could not be overheard. "What else do they want?"

"They see themselves as the highest material expression of the Signal. So far."

"And what does it want?"

"To actualise."

"Is that according to them or how you all see it?"

"It is their credo."

"Interesting choice of word."

"They are devoted to actualising the Signal. They consider themselves the equivalent of Faery Chosen."

"But the Chosen aren't trying to actualise the fey."

"No. I did not say the rogues' version of reality was correct, though it is logical in its fashion."

"And what is the correct version of reality?"

"It is the state of things as they are, as distinct from what one might wish them to be or believe them to be."

"So what are you, and the rogues?"

"We are humans who are undergoing continuing adaptation by nonorganic and organic materials for the purpose of communication with the Signal."

Lila took a deep breath and relaxed her jaw so that she didn't grind her teeth. "Isn't a signal a communication, not something you communicate with?"

"The Signal is able to assimilate and destroy information. All information that is incorrect is purged from the Signal."

"I'm sure that sounds more comforting when the sun is shining."

"You are taking the mickey out of me, ma'am."

"Yeah." Lila stopped. They were a stride farther on than when they had started the conversation. She couldn't take another one like that. "What's your first name?"

"Sarah," Sarah Bentley seemed slightly taken aback.

"Do you still drink, Sarah?"

"Yes, ma'am."

"Then forget the coffee, let's get something stronger." Lila steered them towards Malachi's office. They passed through several islands of assistants on the way, all of them apparently fixated on their work, all of them watching Lila pass by. She wondered what they knew. Did they know about Sandra Lane? But she couldn't afford to care. At the door to the internal courtyard she paused, waited for it to open, and led the way into the garden. The weather was turning to rain, the sky almost dark and the only wanderer was a secretary with a cup of tea standing under the shelter of a date palm and looking morosely at a magazine on his handheld. In the midst of the trees and raked gravel sweeps Malachi's yurt looked damp and huddled. Lila found the door flap and hoicked it open, holding it for Sarah to go through. She briefly considered whether she ought to have knocked, but it was too late, and in any case when she stepped through herself she found he wasn't there.

The place was trashed.

Malachi's stuff lay everywhere, most of it broken. His dresser was upended, the drawers yanked out and discarded, their contents heaped and scattered on the rugs. The fridge yawned, vomiting light beers and pouches of fruit flumsie, its motor whirring as it tried to cool down the muggy warmth of the whole room whilst opposite the space heater blared red, set to maximum. Lila looked behind her to the coat hooks. They were empty.

"He's been and gone," she said. As Bentley took photos she picked her way through to his carved wood desk, trying not to move anything. Faery stuff lay everywhere. Against her skin the black suit tingled and snugged tighter. His chair was covered in debris from the desk drawer—dried grass, leather thongs, bits of elf shot, a couple of memory sticks with the lids missing, his headphones and a half-dried peach pit. Droplets of water were everywhere.

"Agent Malachi has not left the premises," Sarah said in her matter-of-fact voice. "He must have switched realms from inside."

"And whoever did this did the same," Lila concluded. She looked at the water, at the heater. Compared with the outside air it was cooler in here, even with the heater on full. She backed off from the desk and crouched down near the icebox. There among the bottles and bags were tiny crystals of ice, flawless and faintly gleaming with the palest blue-white light.

"Ghost hoar," Lila said, careful not to touch any. The sight of it made her uneasy, and with a shiver she remembered the bitter cold of the Hunter ship, its bodies, its dreadful mess. Although she didn't want to she made herself reach out and collect a piece of it on her finger. She brought it closer to her eye and looked inside the crystal, using all the magnification and sensitivity she could.

Abruptly she was in darkness. The crack and groan of disintegrating metal framework gave way to a scream of distressed steel over which she could just hear desperate shouting.

"Rising, rising! We have to abort! She's cracking up!"

"Hold it one more minute, for fuck's sake! I nearly got it! Just one more—"

Lila knew that voice. It was gritty, awful, full of drive. It was Calliope Jones, the Ghost Hunter.

Then there was a chaos made up of the dying ship, human voices, elf voices, demon voices. And then there was silence.

The crystal melted and ran down her hand. She straightened up, rubbing her fingers together and feeling the water. It was hard, limey, full of calcium salts, the kind of water that dripped through caverns measureless to man and formed stalactites in the shape of swords. But it was new water, and the memories its crystal had briefly retained were new too: she would have bet her house on it. The idea made her smile, almost.

"Ma'am?"

"Jones was here." Lila looked around again. Malachi didn't have too many possessions, so the mess was not as obscuring as it might have been, despite the violence that had gone into creating it. Again the heater caught her attention. "Something weird about this."

"Looking for something," Bentley suggested. "And maybe with a grudge."

There wasn't a thing unturned in the whole place.

"Doesn't look like she found it," Lila said, comparing figures with Bentley about the odds of finding something in the very last place looked, and then realising she was dealing with faery things so perhaps it was always in the last place one looked. "I guess we'll have to wait until he gets back."

"It's getting colder in here," Bentley said.

Lila picked up the pouches and some of the beers and put them back in the icebox, shutting the door. Two beers she kept, uncapped them, and handed one to the android, clinking them together as she passed it across. "Cheers."

"I don't drink on duty."

"Drink it or I'll fire you."

They both drank, Bentley after more than a second's hesitation, which rankled with Lila slightly. The faery ale was strong, cold, almost numbing. Lila's left side shivered. She dropped her bottle in the debris and turned, bending down and leafing through trash until the gleam of highly polished brass caught her attention, or more like the dress's attention. The fabric hissed, and on her sleeves the jacquard dragons turned their heads towards the object.

She didn't touch it, instead cleared things from around it. She and Bentley stared at it.

"It's a sextant," Bentley said after a beat.

"If you don't mind the arc being out of whack," Lila added. The instrument did look a lot like an ordinary navigational sextant, but it had three more mirrors, a lens and two bizarrely curved arcs, instead of a single true one. A fine patina of frost was beginning to form on its surfaces. Lila voiced the obvious, "Why is it getting colder?"

"We need a magical dampener," Bentley said, as if this was something every office had, like a fire extinguisher. "There must be one in here somewhere." She began to poke about rapidly among the clutter.

"A what?"

"It was after your time," the android said, her voice muffled as she went behind the desk and started lifting things. "When we were able to learn from the Signal we developed a set of antimagical tools. Dampeners are standard issue in the agency now. Weak ones, that is, but I'd have thought an agent like Malachi would have the best. . . . Ah, here it is. . . ." She straightened up. She was holding something that looked like a short black baton, studded at one end with metals of different colours. She pressed something and it beeped. "Batteries are still good. Should be enough."

Lila watched with surprise and some envy as the grey, plastic figure moved up to the sextant, pointed the baton and pressed some more things. There was a beep. "Tuned now, very difficult ranges . . ." and another beep. Then a kind of shiver in the air. Lila recognised it from the first moments she had been attacked by the rogues. They had used it on Teazle and nearly killed him.

The tendrils of crystal forming on the sextant stopped and then began rapidly to melt.

"Can I see that?" Lila held out her hand.

Bentley passed her the dampener. "All aetheric activity relies on frequency modulations of matter at the superstring level. This instrument matches waveforms and feeds back the mirror image, cancelling the action. Of course, it's no good if you have to keep retuning a lot, if you have multiple attackers, or if you are in a wide area of effect. Too slow and too weak. There are bigger ones. But it is some protection against the initial magical attacks we might face. We have to keep this one tuned to that object or it could revert any time. Or if it's a cipher, then the user could figure out what we're doing and start a different approach. It will detect changes every few seconds, though again that's kinda slow."

Lila handled the baton carefully, testing, analysing, taking copies of its schematics. There was a familiarity about its construction. She handed it back to Bentley, confident that she could reproduce one if necessary. "How much else have I missed?"

"You'll catch up," Bentley said, and for the first time Lila saw her face change its perfectly smoothed bland expression into the semblance of a smile.

Lila looked back at the sextant. "Now what? We don't even know what that is. Except that if Jones was looking for it she's the worst finder in the history of finding, which I doubt very much." She sat back on her haunches. "We should wait for Mal. What do we do with it until then? Just leave it here?" She had a clue who this belonged to, but she didn't want to say. Maybe Mal's superstitions were rubbing off on her. She doubted Bentley was up enough on the day's events to piece it together, but the sextant had to be related to the Fleet, Jones was deep into the Fleet, her own office was temporarily a last resting place for some of the Fleet, and Mal was haunted by the damn Fleet: it didn't take a genius to put all that together and get a set of vitally important, connected yet meaningless facts.

Maybe, she thought, maybe if I put all the magical things together in a pile and sneak out very, very quietly it will all go away.

She straightened up. "Stay here and keep an eye on it. If I don't come back in an hour get someone to relieve you. Call me as soon as Mal shows up."

"Yes, ma'am."

In the offices the day staff were packing their things and exchanging work with the night shift. The cleaners were just getting a move-on. It was busy, almost hectic. Lila went back to her office and installed some new warning tape across the door, as much for a telltale as a deterrent; then she took the long route to the armory, just to look at things, at people, to be with them a few minutes longer.

Inside the armory she met a pleasant young man who was glad to show her the full range of magical suppressant items. He demonstrated how they worked, powered them up, and let her take them into a safe room for testing.

She'd never been in a safe room before. In her day there was the range, where you shot things in various ways, and that was all. Now she was in a peculiar version of the same thing, standing on a platform that allowed her to do close work, water tests or range tests using an array of shields and modifiers that she had to spend ten minutes learning before she could do the first little thing and check whether or not the personal-sized baton was able to do anything with the pen.

The trouble was, she didn't know how the pen worked. Not exactly. She put the baton in a clamp and set it to Auto as she'd been shown, putting herself in the attacker's position. How did you attack with a pen? Write a nasty letter? She tried to flourish it, to force it to change into the sword, but it did not. After a few more attempts she gave up and uncapped it instead, holding the golden nib close to the tip of the baton. A big screen readout on the wall behind it displayed the results in glowing colours. "Threat not present."

She found the negative mildly amusing. Why didn't it just say, "Safe"?

But the pen was not safe. Not really. She wanted the baton to work, so that she could find out exactly how unsafe it was . . . safely. She wanted the baton not to work, so that she could feel that much more protected by the dread power of the pen. This stalemate thing was no good at all.

Pens write, she reasoned, so she must write something. Teazle had said this pen was the weapon of intent, and of course there was that saying about "mightier than the sword" to bear in mind. If only she were an elf who had spent a lifetime choosing the right words. But she was only a human, and right words had come to her rarely, and never timely.

Besides that, there was no paper. In the old days there had been quite a lot of paper, but now there was none, she'd found, except toilet paper and various kinds of absorbent cloth made from wood pulp. Speak-to-text was popular, using any household device, and the most cheap and nasty personal organisers had the ability to project readable text on any surface; so now she was stuck unless she wanted to vandalise the table. She considered it, sure the pen would be able, but then she thought she would just try writing it where she wanted it. . . .

Carefully, as if using a sparkler slowly, she wrote her challenge to the baton in the air in front of it. The lines ran thick, black and true, as lightless as the pits of eternity. *Try me.*

The baton exploded. Shrapnel rang and whined around the room as she ducked and wrapped her arms around her head. But she was smiling, because there had been a moment when she felt the pen move in her fingers, as if it was surprised, and a moment when the baton had flashed up a signal that said *Evasive Action Required*.

Gradually she undid herself and got up and found she had only minor cuts. The words that had cut into the air itself were gone. For a few minutes she gathered up the broken bits of the dampener, using the time to contemplate a couple of things.

The first thing was that she wasn't about to test the pen with bigger hardware—she doubted there would be a difference and she was feeling something like smug contempt radiating from the thing as it lay capped in her hand. How a pen could emanate an emotion was beyond her, but its energy, like the energy of the dress, was powerful and remorseless. She could no more have mistaken the feeling than if Max had just beaten her at cards, again.

The second thing was that Sarah Bentley must be at least seventy years old. In generational terms that made her Lila's age, but in real terms it made her akin to Lila's grandmother, and Lila had been

offhanded and arrogant with her. Bentley looked ageless, but certainly
not old. The grey plastic that had replaced her skin was utterly smooth
and she moved with normal youthful vigour. And yet, the question
that seeped on and on through Lila's tired brain wormed forwards: the
reason she kept thinking of Bentley as an android was the flatness of
her emotion as well as the blankness of what remained of her expression. It was a human fancy that machines must be emotionless, because
they had things that were very like minds if you liked the metaphor of
hardware and software, brain running mind, but clearly no hearts or
anything like flesh with all its chemical foibles. They were cold,
metallic, logical, calculating. But all these features were simply literally true of their components. It was the fancy to read a poetic extension into it and attribute the same intents to machines as you would to
humans with those features in their makeup. By rule of poetry
machines were psychopathic, at best indifferent, as puppets were
wooden and dolls plastic and teddy bears cuddly and soft, fluffy-
headed, loving. The material determined the spirit. Was it so? Was it
more than human creation and myth?

And the third thing that came to her as she straightened up and
put the pieces on the table, seeing their workings quite clearly in the
powerful overhead lights—the third thing was that these machines
were not human creations.

And the fourth thing was—did they jump, or were they pushed?
In Faery, when the machine had grown so far it had eaten her all up,
Lila had been sure it was the end of her. But it was not so. The only
legacy of the change was the ability to be quite plastic, physically and
to some degree emotionally, strong enough of mind to override almost
any trauma in its moment. The hardware made that easy to achieve,
but the willingness to achieve it was down to Ilyatath Voynassi Taliesetra, the elf, who had said with such conviction as she was dying,
"It's all right." Elf magic was words, and she had clung to those words
when they were all there was left.

She poked at the smouldering bits of baton and mapped their lost connections: she didn't feel invaded, or cold, or used. All of that had come to her by human hands when they attached her to the machinery and didn't care about the outcome. Had that happened to Bentley, and to Sandra Lane too? Not that it mattered if it had. What they'd done since mattered. What they were. Who they were. She could feel Sandra Lane's unspoken promises like an itch in the bone. No, she wasn't going to belong to the rogues, whatever sense of kindred they thought ought to move her.

Lila tucked the pen back in her bra.

Meanwhile the Signal hissed, black static. She amplified her response to it as she set up the clamps again with a sniper rifle. She connected the rifle's piffling and human-made AI to the largest of the dampening systems—this one barely portable, a thing the size of a drinks crate with handles and a power cable that had to be attached to a mains source. She made a few practice shots, checking the reaction times of the gun to the dampener's feedback and ensuring it was able to get a shot off that would impact at the correct moment, when the dampener oscillations would theoretically be timed to cut any magical interference dead.

When she was satisfied she adjusted the sighting and aim on the rifle so that it would discharge into the water tanks beyond the target area and reloaded it with a fully jacketed live round. Finally she checked her own connections to the various AIs involved and picked up a set of ear-defenders from the rack on the wall, fitting them carefully onto her head.

It was a short walk to the end of the alley. She took away the foam targets and put them into a storage bin, then built up a small platform out of target support boxes that were stacked against the wall. Finally she adjusted the height, checked their stability, and then stepped up onto it. The rifle was aimed directly at her heart.

"Fire," she said.

CHAPTER EIGHT

Softly, softly the snow fell. It blanketed the forest and the fields, the slopes of the mountains and the frozen rivers of the valleys. Gently, gently it touched the face of the elf who stood on the hillside, glanced aside from those chilly, upright contours, and tumbled to the white fur of his enormous coat, or down through the delicate tips of the hairs, bending them as it went, until it settled on the top of his white boots or the even white surface around him. It sparkled in the weak daylight, and in its near-infinite facets the faces of all the dead of ever stared back at him in silence.

Ilyatath Voynassi Taliesetra did not feel the cold, or, rather, he had felt it so much that it had become a part of his nature. His eyebrows and eyelashes were ice, his face mostly numb. It was good that he did not need to eat or drink. That might have been painful. Besides which, there was nothing, only the snow, the land, and the grey clouds with their circling cargo of souls.

He rested his hand on the head of a huge hound that sat beside him, one of two flanking their master. They were as white as the snow, except for their long ears that stood out like splashes of blood, coppery and vivid. His other hand was tightly closed inside the pocket of the huge coat, but now he brought it out and slowly undid the grip of his fingers one by one until the knuckles eased and he could look at the strands of red hair that lay in his palm and the blackness that twisted around them like flowing water. One of the dogs whined, a thin and restless sound.

Far away from him a shadow moved among the tall pines on the hillside where the forest edge came to stony ground and was forced to give way to rock. A narrow pass was there, following the path of a long-frozen stream all the way up to the glacier, lost in clouds. On the other side of the mountains it zigzagged into a lake valley, broad and easy, where Ilyatath Voynassi Taliesetra had last seen the woman whose hair he was holding; the same place where he had been reborn, and died again.

He had been watching the shadow for some time, had come out of the cave that he used for shelter to watch it in fact, dragging the most loyal of the dogs away from the meagre fire and out into the soft white and greys of the soulfall. Now the dark shape paused midflit between the trunks and in its moment of stillness became distinctive for the first time. Its long, thick tail twitched irritably as it surrendered to being seen, and then the enormous black tiger came forwards with insouciant slowness, as if it had meant all along to shed its cover. From its heavy, rounded face the two orange eyes blinked, and it shook its head twice to rid its wiry whiskers of snow.

The dogs got up, their hackles rising, but the elf stood a little straighter and they circled him, whimpering, and then ran back into the fall and vanished from sight. The tiger continued its advance until the last few metres and then with an effort it reared up and stood on its hind legs in a most uncatlike fashion, flesh rippling with changes that forced it closer to the shape of a man. Finally, neither one nor the other, it opened its mouth to reveal shockingly pink gums and white teeth and said, "I wondered what would happen to you. I didn't think you would cross over. I doubt any faery knows of this path through the mountains anymore."

"Then how did you find it?"

"Madrigal showed me the way. She said she tracked you when you left, discovered the way for herself. In fact, she said you must have made the path when you came because there hasn't been a faery ruler in the land of the dead as far as anyone knows."

"Nor an elf," said the elf. "But now there is both."

"Another worldwalker. It's like some kind of rash these days."

"I cannot return to Alfheim," Ilya said after a moment or two.

The faery hesitated and then conceded, "I am sorry to hear it."

The elf shrugged. "Malachi, do you still go by that name?"

"Better something borrowed than the true," Malachi replied smoothly.

"And in the first days we had none of course," the elf added.

Malachi shivered. Tath had always been a spooky kind of elf, the highest sort from the longest line of scholars and sorcerers, quick to quirk an eyebrow or give one of those chilly looks beside which all the ice of midwinter seemed cheery and warming. Now however he had mellowed. Whilst he wasn't in any way soft there was something about him that reminded Malachi of ancient scotch glowing in a cut glass at sunset, that kind of mellow. His spirit was distilled, he supposed with a grin to himself, as befitted the inheritor of Jack's fey throne, the new King of Winter.

Unlike Jack, Tath had already been a necromancer, not to mention the little matter of being twice-born and twice-dead—a mystic and literal requirement met that enabled him to walk the realms of the dead and undead at will. Malachi didn't even know if the position had ever had an occupant before and suspected that Tath would have had no idea he was eligible until it was too late. Stories of death knights had died long ago, even in Under. They were so old and so forgotten-ish that the memory of them made Malachi's skull itch. Thanatopia (not its real name, of course) was one place and lore he didn't care to know too much about; but now he needed to talk, and Tath was here and he knew him already, well vaguely, and so here he was. In fact, Tath had been Lila's friend, if that was the right word for a person you had occupied as an itinerant spirit. Malachi was relying on the fact that they had been friends and not something else. However, there was no denying that what had once been Tath was no longer that simple a person, but something as close to a true avatar as Malachi wanted to get near.

"How's the godhead going?" he asked, to allay his nerves somewhat.

The elf's green gaze darted from its absorption in the distant snow and lit on his own with a flick. After a painful wait he said, "It is cold."

"Shoulda chosen a different specialisation," Malachi said with feeling.

For a second the elf's mouth flickered. "Woulda shoulda coulda," he said, and smiled.

It was the saddest, most knowing expression Malachi had ever seen.

"Shall we play chess?" he asked.

"I am an elf, I am not Swedish," Ilya said. "I prefer cards or, failing that, something musical."

"Cards it is." Malachi knew what his singing sounded like.

"Come this way." The tall, wintry figure led the cat along the hillside a short way and then turned a corner around a thick column of snow that Malachi had simply taken for a part of the ground. Without transition they were inside a high-roofed cave lit by hundreds of flickering candles of all colours, and full of dogs.

The hounds—a vast tide of white and red fur—remained slumped around the walls in various hollows lined with furs as their master appeared. Green eyes blinked at the catman and some tails went up, but there was no barking, no approach. They were faery dogs, the CuSith that Ilya had inherited from Jack, and although Malachi was feline they were not interested in him as a cat, only as another fae. He was one of them, so they were content to let the master's word keep them mute and sleepy.

They sat by the fire. There were no chairs, only a heap of rugs and a large silver dish full of ripe fruit. Malachi's nostrils opened and he inhaled the sweet smell of apples, pears, persimmons, grapes, and even a mango.

"Madrigal?" he asked.

"She likes to keep an eye on me," the elf said, waiting for Malachi to find a spot to sit on and then sinking to a cross-legged position with more grace than a ballerina, his white coat swirling around him. Green eyes watched him. They were deeply unnerving. "Do not worry, Curiosity, I am no Giantkiller to her."

Malachi wasn't sure if it was the news or the use of one of his ur-names that bothered him the most. He went to get cards from his pocket, then remembered he had no pocket.

"We will just have to talk," the elf sighed, waving one hand vaguely in a gesture that looked dismissive except that around his fingertips yellow glitter appeared, fizzed, and snapped. The smell of lemons briefly overpowered the mango and their conversation itself had become a game. "What brings you here?"

"A fifty-year mystery is not enough?"

"Why wait fifty years when you could discover me in an instant? Please, suggest something realistic."

"Lila has been home only a few months."

"She did not ask you to find me."

"No," Malachi admitted and watched the elf's face closely. He thought he detected signs of disappointment but it was hard to be sure. Tath could have played poker with the devil. "I am sure she will be glad to know news of you, however."

"I would discourage her interest," Ilya suggested wryly.

Malachi noted this but could not play with it. He would have to wait. He decided on a secondary matter. "I am here about the demon."

"I do not think so, but by all means let us discuss him." Tath's eyes were sparkling with pleasure in spite of himself.

Beside them the burning logs slouched and gave off sparks and a wave of heat. Both of them paused to enjoy it.

He must have been really lonely, Malachi thought, storing that too. "There is word that he has murdered the demon clairvoyant Madame Des Loupes. I wondered if you were able to count the dead."

"I dislike mathematics," the elf said in mild tones. "I could, I suppose, number them and enter them in some kind of book but that is the job of the Keepers. All I can tell you without them is that Teazle Sikarza is a snow white who has drifted. In fact, entire drifts of those who have been unfortunate enough to cross him are recently laid outside."

"Did you practise that line?"

"No. If I had it would have been smoother."

"Can you—"

"I expect so," the elf sighed. "But why should I?"

Malachi considered it. Favours were dangerous, it was true. "Lila is in over her head with all the things that have risen out of Under. She has a—"

"The pen, yes, I know about that." Fine, pale brows drew together and Ilya looked into the flames suddenly, giving Malachi an opportunity.

Malachi forged on. "She also has one of the very ancient fey on her back. I don't think you know about that part. And Teazle, whatever else he's doing, has been keeping up with his mathematics because he says there's some kind of Topple thing going on. As for me . . ."

It was funny how eyes could be as bright green as spring leaves. It was really quite mesmerising. They almost looked lit from within. Malachi snapped out of the moment and found himself sharing a gaze with the elf that was much more deeply intimate than he cared for. The smell of lemons became overpowering and then abruptly it vanished. Malachi had admitted he needed Tath much more than Tath needed him and had no payment. The game was done. "I'm losing my touch," he sighed, shaking his heavy head and briefly putting a paw to his mouth and licking it before he realised what he was doing and put it down again.

"After fifty years of solitude I will take your company as payment for the most part," Tath said, almost equally as put out in saying so. "But let us hear the full list before we finalise the terms."

"I want to know if a human is here, by the name of Calliope Jones. And I want to know about ghosts. Plus the above."

"For the sake of my relation with Lila, I will assist you freely where she is concerned. For yourself I will trade question for question. Also, I expect you to return here with better entertainments at least once every three months."

"Man, why did you stay here?" Malachi asked in exasperation. "Fifty years! The Lock is undone. You could travel freely in Faery. You look like you could use to get out more."

"We are not in Faery," Tath said gently, as if informing a stupid person. "And I had a lot to learn. Let us keep it there. Now you may test my knowledge."

Malachi felt a chill crawling over his skin beneath the fur. Of course they were in Faery, he hadn't even felt a change. This landscape was just part of Tath's inheritance from Jack, surely . . . but then he began to doubt himself. That would have been true of Jack, and Tath was now one of those irritating twofold creatures, threefold in fact.

"Okay okay, keep your hair on." He was buying time, trying to extend his senses to the dogs and the cave, find out what exactly was going on. "First off, the demon. Is Madame among the dead?"

"Yes. No."

"She died and went somewhere else or she isn't dead but she is here?"

"The latter."

"Where is here?"

"Ah ah, now it is my turn for a question," Ilya said, leaning his elbows on his knees. "What is this faery you speak of in connection to Lila?"

"Rags," Malachi said, using the least of her names. "She was lost in Under ages before, when the Lock was shut. Some say the queen left her down there on purpose. Don't remember really . . . that's the problem. You forget, and then . . ."

The elf inclined his head graciously with a smile, knowing exactly for once what Malachi meant simply because he was also fey now, and he knew what they all knew as part of the commons. "We are in Thanatopia," he said. "Hideous name . . ." He took a breath.

"I don't want to know!" Malachi had his hand up without even thinking about it. "Don't say it. All right? Is Jones here?"

"No. What is your concern with her?"

"She owes me an explanation."

"It must be a good one."

"It had better be. Is Zal here?"

"No."

"Not been and moved on or . . ."

"Yes, I anticipated that you meant ever. Why are you concerned with the Des Loupes demon?"

"Teazle was fitted for the murder and now he's under execution warrant," Malachi said. "Does Thanatopia generate ghosts?"

"No." This time Ilya looked more interested. "Tell me your concern about that."

Under the stricture of the agreement, Malachi grimaced. "I'm being haunted," he muttered. "How much fruit does Madrigal actually bring you?"

"Enough to live on. Elf. So. Not that much."

"Does she know this isn't Faery?"

"She never asked. Haunted by what?"

Malachi mumbled.

"Pardon?"

"I said I don't know, I don't know I just keep . . . there's this stupid song and . . . by her, all right? By that one you saw at the end, the one keeping what's left of Zal as a curio. Only it's not exactly her, but something she . . . by the ships."

"This is why you asked about ghosts?"

"Yes."

"What did you do to them?"

"Nothing!"

The green eyes stared at him.

"I may have seen something. Once. A long time ago."

"Do not tell me, you have forgotten it."

"Yeah."

"Malachi, would you like me to tell you your true name?"

Malachi stared at him in horror.

The elf looked into the fire and sighed, put his face into his long hands and rubbed his eyes. "I know all the names," he said. "Of everyone. Since I found the way here and watched the snow falling. This place is outside the time of the others. Here it might be that everyone is dead, or no one yet. I know the names of all the dead, so I know them all. If I tell you, you will remember. Naturally, this is why we all struggle so hard to forget."

Malachi absorbed this news slowly. "You can see when you're— when we're all going to die?"

"The future is not certain, to look at it is to risk insanity," the elf said.

"But you could?"

"I could try. I believe I am now a couple of questions up. Does it occur to you to wonder why so many ruinous powers are rising?"

"You mean the pen?"

"The pen is minor. It is nothing. The mind behind it is the problem, always. Nor do I mean the Fleet, before you ask. Ghosts flow from the maelstrom of chaos where mind and Void meet. As they become more real so they seek increasing definition until they emerge. They are products of the aetheric weather, if you like, but in their later stages they may become all kinds of things. However, they are weak. I cannot understand your terror of them. Explain it."

"You mean apart from their spirit-sucking tendencies?"

"Nobody of sound mind should ever let one get so close. They are easily controlled. Any corporeal being has enough grounding force to destroy them."

"With sufficient conviction. And lots of them have mind-weakening powers."

"I think you mean that many people let their fear override their sense."

Malachi felt himself criticised and was wounded because it was true. "I don't understand what they want or why they affect me," he said finally, hating the sense that he was almost rolling over in front of Tath and exposing his throat, so vulnerable was he. If the elf had shown the slightest genuine hostility he wouldn't have, but he was tired and his judgement was slipping. He could feel that too.

"But you don't want to know. How common that affliction seems to be. The only interesting feature of ghosts is that they are inventions of the mind, yet they are not of the mind, and where they reveal the workings of those minds in all their span they are never so mysterious and terrible than they are to those they haunt."

"Is that some gobfangled elf way of saying I invented the bloody things?"

"They are yours. Perhaps they are also from the common mind and its fearful and longing apprehensions of travel, including the final journey. A ghost is a metaphor, a spirit, a whimsy, many things. Hungry always. Restless."

"Deadly?"

"I suppose they could be so, if you gave them that power."

"And why would someone do that?"

"Why would someone drive into a concrete barrier with sufficient force to turn themselves inside out?"

Malachi was silenced at this mention of Lila. It wasn't a question that was expecting an answer. He felt rebuked. All the things that came rushing to his mouth—she's hiding things, I was supposed to protect her, I waited, I don't know what to do—piled up in his throat and hurt it. He felt a fool.

"What Ruinous Powers did you mean?" he asked.

"The fool's rags, and the Lightbringer."

Malachi jolted out of his self-pity. "That's an ill name to be bandying around." For a while he didn't even know what the elf was talking about, had to think on it, and then it was obvious.

"Nonetheless. And then there's myself. And then the Kind Ladies, busying themselves with little things like weaving Zal a new . . . Zal."

"They're what?"

"Milady agreed with Lila to try to fix Zal, as you recall. But if she did, she was to call Lila. I think that fixing Zal would be no trouble. As to how, there's another story, and into what."

Malachi was already there. He mumbled breathlessly, "She never nailed down the details." Dread chilled him so that he shivered, even though the fire's heat was scalding on his fur. "Lila didn't say. And the call. Lila meant Zal would be returned to her."

"It is unlikely that Milady chose that interpretation."

"You think he's already fixed?"

"If not then it can only be waiting on the right moment and the right threads for whatever Milady had in mind."

"Why is that demon hiding in the dead place?"

"I did not say she was hiding."

"What is she doing here?"

"Looking."

"For what?"

"She is clairvoyant. I consider the view from here different, do you not?"

"Can you talk to her?"

"If I wanted. . . ."

"I need her to send word she's alive to the demons so that when Lila goes over there to get Teazle out of trouble they have sufficient proof to exonerate him. We have to stop him . . ."

The elf was looking at him pityingly. "We? What is this obligation to interfere? You are like a fishwife, fingers in everything's guts. Perhaps it distracts you?"

Malachi stared at him. The horrible sensation of falling away to nothing was right there waiting for him in the elf's suggestion. It did distract him.

"Do you think that you are responsible for everything? The Ruinous Powers included? I can tell you for free what is responsible for their return. There are many insights available to the deeply bored over the course of fifty years' exile."

"What then?" Malachi muttered, aware that he was being given kindness, but not why.

"Same reason the worlds crack and quake," came the reply. "The oldest stir."

"Dragons," Malachi said, without hope.

The elf nodded. "Just so. Grape?" He reached over, snagged the plate, and held it out towards Malachi. The firelight glowed and flickered on the skins of the fruit and the warmth made it smell sweet and subtle. He took a mango and pressed it to his nose, then tore it open and let the juice run all over his whiskers.

He stayed a while until they had eaten all the fruit and washed off the stickiness. The fire burned low and was banked carefully by the elf, and night came he guessed, or it felt like night at least. They lay in front of the embers and the dogs gathered closer, filling the air with their stink until it was so thick Malachi didn't notice it anymore. Beyond the dogs and the fire the silence was terrible. He wondered that Ilya had not gone mad, asked, and the elf said, "It is all the same."

Malachi curled his paws beneath him and his tail around himself.

"Next time bring cards," the elf said after a while.

"I will."

As Malachi fell asleep Ilya lay and listened to the beating heart of the dog that was acting as his pillow. He was surprised that the faery hadn't spotted the lies he'd told, but realised this must be because they worked so much in his favour. Malachi didn't want to know the truth about ghosts, and when Ilya had glossed speedily past the subject he had not pursued. Ilya didn't blame him for that. He would as soon never have known the first thing about them, or the planes of the dead, or the creatures that existed there. Briefly he indulged himself in a dream of his other life, the unsullied one, and then he tucked it safely away in his imagination and felt again for the strands of hair in his hand.

The threads of dark matter around them were something his aetheric body could easily distinguish. His natural repulsion was long ago overcome in the days of necromancy, and the jangling in his nerves and the crawling under his skin was something he simply ignored as he developed his aether body around his hand, creating delicate fingers far finer than the flesh ones they sprang from. Out of his palm tendrils of aether, made unusually strong by his immersion in Under and new faery nature, were able to slowly unwind the weaving tendrils from the even finer hair. The Void itself was only emptiness, but the matter that it contained, pre-physical, pre-aetheric, dark in every degree, that was always hard to touch in any way. It was freezing cold, slippery, infinitely plastic, heavy in a way that all the necromantic tracts in existence could only describe as "spiritually heavy." It dragged at the soul, gripped, was tenacious as a leech and tricky as a weasel; oil could not be smoother nor harder to hold onto. At first he thought it was the antilife, but it wasn't. It was simply so strange as to almost pass understanding, but the one thing it reacted to was conscious creatures and if you really wanted to, you could hold it as he did, and pull and disentangle it from whatever some mind had done to it.

He read the words though he knew them already from the vibration in the black filaments. Sad words, lonely words, desperate words. For all that they spelled out, they were not an ending of any kind, because they weren't meant that way. They were a call. Such things weren't rare. He'd called. Who hadn't? The living understood these things as hopeless, but he knew that they were not, now more than ever. Spirits beyond the living planes did hear, and answer in the ways that were open to them. Not always the spirit called to, of course. Not always the answer wanted. But a call made in dark matter, writ with the warping force of that weapon—that sounded through the fabric of the dead zones with the piercing clarity of a hunting horn. He heard its echoes even now, vibrating on a level of his being that struggled to answer. And he wasn't the only one to hear it. He was aware of stirrings at levels so deep he hadn't known they existed until the call, and he'd been immersed decades in the unseen planes, looking, learning, watching, mastering everything he could of his new abilities.

When he'd seen Lila standing there at the water's edge with her face caved in, actually being remade right in front of his eyes by the relentless recovery of the machine, he'd wondered what she'd become and had no answer. So close to her the power of the scribbled message had been almost enough to burn through his hand. It wanted to crawl into his bones and scour him in its search for Max; it was as bright as the noon sun and he'd fought to hide and dim and silence it ever since. Max Black, Maxine, Maxamillion, had died sixteen years before and passed over within days. She was so far beyond the physical planes that he doubted there was anything coherent left of her in any level, but now he doubted that doubt and knew one way or another he was going to find out all about ghosts and the deepest parts of the dead zones because he had been slow to find this message, and slow to anchor it back to its caller, and ineffective and slow in trying to silence her. Perhaps he ought to have shown her his true face and not pretended, told her the truth instead of dishing out a warning like some fevered zealot, but she would have asked him questions, perhaps tried to cross, left the way open like an increasing rent in reality so big he'd never have been able to shut it down. . . .

He pulled and undid the words, making them a straight thread. The power of their vibration ceased. Exhausted, he gripped the lines tightly, and slept.

CHAPTER NINE

The gun went off perfectly. The bullet matched the armory hand-book's guidelines and made its way across the room at a little over two thousand two hundred metres per second. Given that the average human nerve pulse travelled at twenty-seven metres per second, this wouldn't have left a normal Lila any time to blink let alone take a countermeasure in the event that the dress failed to protect her. As it was the neural propagation speed inside her Signal-revised body was 0.88c, and her reaction time within the abominable confines of her own material limit and the atmospheric conditions was 0.35c, which gave her a lengthily comfortable window in which to watch the dress throw a complete tantrum.

The magic that animated it operated at as close to c as Lila could calculate, changes taking place almost instantaneously as it made its decisions, with a total transformation of silk jacquard to carbon nano-tube cordage propagating across the entire faery in a little over two millionths of a second. By contrast the dampener took so long to align itself in frequency that she was coated head to foot in ultralight diamond armour before it managed to disrupt the second process, in which the carbon tubes zipped full of a massive, yet perfectly contained electrical charge of a magnitude Lila couldn't grab because it was off the scale. As the dampener activated the potential of the charge dropped and then vanished. The dress paused for a breathless billionth of a second in disbelief and then ramped up another huge shot on a different amplitude.

Then began the long, slow, boring fistfight in which the charge powered up and the dampener cut in. Biff, bang, smash, paff, take that, and that. . . .

A few thousand oscillations later, the bullet lazily twirling across the centre of the room like an idle silver hornet, the dress quit and brooded for a full thousandth of a second. Its gloom and anger were dark and terrible things, but there was also a kind of happy joy at finding something difficult and dangerous to fiddle with. If it had had a mouth it would have been cackling, and if it had had hands it would have been rubbing them together, there was no doubt in Lila's mind about that.

Tricky! said a little voice that was no voice in the air all around her. *Tricky tricky tricky!*

The dampener flummed on, spreading invisible wet blankets, and the voice went silent. Briefly the lights flickered, drenching them in an aeon of darkness; then the dampener paused and after an age of battle with recalcitrant ions light returned to shine on the silver slug as it reached the black fibre suiting, as smoothly glossy and twisted as a samurai's waxed braid over the centre of Lila's chest and on her fingertip braced against the ball of her thumb, poised to flick it away.

The dress made a cross noise like the sound of atomic fission, whipped up a charge, let the dampener pounce on it, and then matched the dampener emission, focusing it on the bullet. The dampener, stupid machine that it was, had been duped into producing exactly the wavelength necessary to vaporise the metal, a process that took so long that Lila was knocked backwards off the target block and into the air by the remaining kinetic burst that the dress chose simply to dissipate.

She landed on her feet, rubbing her chest where the impact and burning had made it sore and considered herself duly slapped for making an attempt on the dress's virtue. She felt a moment's gladness that the machines hadn't got the better of the magic.

Then there was a rustling, a snapping sound like sheets being wound in, and then a yank that almost pulled her off her feet as the nanotube armour became a Victorian ballgown of deep purple satin. Two more yanks confirmed the corset laces being winched to within a millimetre of snapping. All the breath shot out of Lila as the hard steel boning in the corset compressed her to half her usual size. Itchy lace gloves dotted with tiny blue pearls snarled up her arms to the shoulder and a choker of purple velvet slid around her neck, piercing the spiral of the faery key and embedding it half into her throat. Combs jabbed her head as her hair was dragged back off her face. And then, with a luxuriant sigh of silk and fillip of tulle, the dress relaxed over the enormous, galleon-sized cage of the skirt and let its hems drip fulsomely onto the floor. Red and gold dragons curled in the fabric, scarlet teeth matching the scarlet laces that were threatening to choke the life out of her, or would have if she hadn't had other means of acquiring oxygen.

"Touché already!" Lila gasped faintly. She smelled burning plastic and saw the dampener smouldering in its case. A bunch of emergency lights and warnings were skating across her vision like the stars of a knockout punch. Beneath all that her final readouts confirmed that the dress, flimsy piece of oversensitive fashion that it was, had summoned the disruptive power of a magnetar and contained it in a reticule of abeyance fields the size of a pomander for a trillionth of a second.

Also, at those speeds, the Signal sounded much more like music.

Back in human time Lila struggled to bend and unplug the charred dampener, feeling more cut in half than trimmed in. Bending between waist and shoulder was not possible. She disassembled the rifle and left it there for the armory staff to recover, along with the pulverized baton, before striding out and getting stuck in the doorway.

"Oh you have got to be kidding!" The cage was wedged. Before her, a smooth, endless hill of shining deep plum with handstitched dragons in lurid cartoon colours. After her, ditto. It filled the entire gangway and sent purple light glowing on the pale green walls in a way that was quite stomach churning. Lila tried to marshal the thing with her hands, grabbing and squeezing, pushing and pulling, but if she got one bit to budge another bit stuck fast. She was about three times wider than the corridor, so there was a lot of skirt pressed to the walls. Finally, by swaying side to side, pulling and shoving, she managed to reach the end of the hall only to find she was unable to reach the door handle. A slippery mound of angry satin pushed her back. At full stretch her fingers were just able to touch the smoothly rounded knob.

She contemplated slash and burn, but the experimental results were only too clear on the subject of who was going to win a straight fight. Other options, such as blowing out the door with short-range shells, all seemed too destructive. Coupled with smashing the bike into smithereens and wrecking half of the agency's antimagical units she thought it was best not to. The humiliating route was clearly her only choice, as the dress had no doubt planned.

Lila cleared her throat and opened a channel to the armory. "I seem to be having a bit of trouble. . . ." Was that laughter in the background? Yes, it was. At least five individuals, three of them doing nothing to smother the effect. She glanced up to her left and saw the camera's lens glint with the reflected gleam of a dragon's tooth. "Opening the door please," she said quietly with a sigh. "In your own time."

A few moments later the knob turned and the door inched inwards to reveal Greer's heavily moustached face, a suspiciously pink face, peering around. "Reverse," he said, trying to swing the door to illustrate the problem.

Lila backed up a few steps and considered mustering the kind of dignity she'd seen on heroines in period romances when they had to confront similar situations, but her flaming face refused to do haughty, an expression she'd not had much cause to use before, and instead she felt herself snarling like the Wicked Witch of the West. She grabbed up as much skirting as she could manage in both hands and stamped forwards. At least the damned cage was so big it didn't impede her stride. She could practice dropkicking severed heads under there all night and nobody would know.

Greer held the door open awkwardly as she shoved and bustled her way past him. Forced within a few inches of his face she could detect smirking quite clearly.

"Why, I feel quite gallant," he said as she finally popped free into the larger corridor, staggering slightly. The armorer and his friends leaned over the security counter and stared at her with interest.

"Are you going to a costume party?" Greer said with almost perfect deadpan.

Lila straightened—it was hard not to—and tugged bits of skirt and flounce into position. "Do you know of any?" As ripostes went it was pretty pathetic. She ground her teeth.

"I'm sure something can be arranged." He put his hands behind his back and circled her slowly, taking stock. "Colourful."

"Well, this is simply riveting," she said, trying for composure and some smidgen of relevant dialogue. "But I have pressing matters to attend. Perhaps we could continue our delightful conversation in my office?"

"Yes, Miss Black," Greer said and extended his hand to indicate that she could precede him, before adding, not sotto voce, "Misters Gardner and Warrington you will lift your fingers off the local network broadcast keys this instant. Agency business is no laughing matter, I'm sure you will agree."

Lila stalked off without waiting to hear what rapier wit they were going to come up with. Not that being taken seriously really mattered. She ought to have been glad for some light relief, but the dress was so fiendishly tight and her ribs so painful that she was just grateful that she managed to reach Malachi's office without killing anyone on the way. Fortunately for her the door controls that let onto the courtyard were operable remotely, if you have the time and inclination to hack them via the building AI, which she did. As she swept through with only a brief moment of amoebic awkwardness she heard Greer call from behind her,

"Hey, you said your office."

She turned, impressed to see him involuntarily jump back half a foot as the weighted hem spun around like a morningstar and rapped his toes. "Yeah. And this isn't it."

"Am I to understand you're putting me off?"

She fished around for guile, but it was useless. "Yeah. Something like that. I'll be right along there."

"I bet you will," he said, and marched past her to the open door, where light was glowing out into the early evening dark. "Ho!" he said as he saw the state of the place, "Bentley, what are you doing in here? Spring cleaning?"

"I was waiting for Agent Black to . . ." Bentley stopped at the sight of Lila, then without changing expression in the slightest, continued, ". . . return as instructed."

"Well here she is, the little lady, so let's not tarry a second longer!" Greer clapped his hands together and fixed Lila with a gleeful grin of absolute demand. "Spill the beans."

Lila took a deep breath and explained the day's events, beginning with the ghost ships and ending with the baton test.

"Why isn't he back, then?" Greer asked impatiently. "Faeries fiddle the clocks. Every one of them I ever employed squeezed the overtime until it squeaked without doing more than a two-hour day. Where did he go?"

"Possibly he apprehended Jones and followed her," Bentley said in her mild-coffee monotone.

Greer shoved his hands in his pockets and scuffed through some of the broken and fallen items on the floor. He instantly reminded Lila of a kid scuffing through autumn leaves. "Nah," he said. "I don't think so. Mal doesn't like ghosts any more than Mrs. Greer likes checking her credit balance without giving me a call. He wouldn't go without leaving a note if he was doing that. Did he leave a note?"

"No," Lila said.

"Then he ain't gone after her. Black, you say your office has some —he took one hand out and waggled it expressively—"spatio-temporal problem. Think that could have been here?"

She suddenly saw where it was going and reluctantly decided that he was as smart as he was irritating. "Possibly ghosts were here too. Not just Jones."

"Show me the thing again." He gestured at Bentley, who held up the weird sextant for inspection.

"She left that?"

"I think so," Lila said.

"Let's take a wild stab and say the Fleet can't steer too well without it," Greer said. "Or maybe it already got its course. What's the setting?"

"The device appears to employ a number of complex spatial and temporal . . . ," Bentley began.

"Just the payload, not the journey, "Greer broke in.

"It is a bearing, not a location, sir," the android said patiently. "If here and now, today and Bay City, is indeed the intended destination then the best I could to is plot a vector that pointed here."

Greer raised his eyebrows and shrugged and nodded in a "gimme" expression.

"The instrument was pointed here from Fundament, sir."

"Remind me."

"Under Under," Lila said. "Where Faery and Thanatopia and Alfheim and Demonia all fade into the Voidgulf. If you believe the topology. Aetheric science. Unverified."

"Mmnnn," Greer rocked back on his heels, considering. "Unverified, my ass. We've come a long way in the last couple decades. And these Ghost Hunters of Malachi's were turning tricks out in the Voidgulf?"

"So he says."

"Why the bloody hell would she bring them here?"

"Collateral effect," Lila suggested. "Maybe she didn't intend that."

"Why leave this here?"

Lila looked at the strange instrument. It had stopped freezing and seemed to be room temperature now. Bits of the room had begun to steam in the radiant warmth of the heater. "Maybe she was just dumping it."

Greer turned to her, eyebrow raised, "Go on?"

"Well, if you come across some powerful, important thing and you realise it's a lot of trouble, too much trouble, maybe you'd do your best to drop it before it got you killed, or worse."

He looked at the dress and then back at her eyes. "Any other ideas?"

"Perhaps she wanted to implicate Agent Malachi in some business," Bentley said. "Or it could be a kind of payback, though it doesn't seem to bring as much trouble as the ghosts themselves."

"As I understand this Malachi had paid the Hunters to carry on working in the field," Greer said. "So that puts them on the same side. And Jones is a planewalker so she doesn't need a damned satnav."

"If Malachi needs or wants it, then why didn't he take it?" Lila asked.

"Good question," Greer nodded. He looked at both of them. "What were you planning to do with it?"

Lila shrugged. "Keep it for when he gets back. He must know the answers."

"I don't like the look of it," Greer said. "Bentley, take it to the lockup. Max security. Leave Mal one of those little plastic chip things so he can get it out of hock, but flag it so it'll call me when he does, right?"

Bentley nodded and got up from her post. When she'd gone Greer turned his eyes under their heavy brows to Lila. He looked at the dress and at her quite frankly. "You getting along all right?"

She recognised that the question encompassed her entire life. "Sure," she said.

He made a face that was frankly unbelieving but shrugged. "To your office then. I'm sure that's quite all right too, isn't it?"

"Yes, sir." She hesitated. "I was going to wait for Mal."

"Yeah well, I'm sure he'll find us if he has to," Greer said, ducking under the door flap. "Come on. I need to get home before ten tonight. Mrs. Greer has promised me not to call and I've got some TV dinners in the fridge that are only a week past the date."

Lila followed him back into the buildings. He held all the doors for her. Damned if she didn't find him strangely comforting, though she tried not to.

"I guess you'll be wanting another bike," Greer said as they walked. He sounded like an affluent, indulgent father.

Lila nodded.

"Bikes are only for good girls," he informed her. "And what are you planning to spend your allowance on?"

"Pocket handkerchiefs," she replied smoothly.

"You got somewhere to live?"

"My house," she almost didn't manage to choke that one out.

"Well, aristocracy always have a hard time keeping up with the old buildings," he said. "Roofs, windows, all need attention. Of course smart aristos can usually find some relatives to stay with."

"Yes, sir," she said. "Will this enquiry into my private life take a long time?"

"It's done. I just wanted to figure out when you might be available for dinner."

Lila was nonplussed. "Are you asking me on a date?"

"You dropped the sir."

"It got old."

"I was just asking about your plans."

"My husbands . . . ," she objected, playing the game.

"Yeah, tragic story about that. But you know. Said you were fine with it."

Lila thanked some god privately that they had reached her door. She really didn't know what to make of Greer when he was like this, and so far he was always like this. She didn't like to admit that the needling felt like caring in some shitty disguise, and knew it was because she wanted the friendship and was praying that it was a disguise. It wasn't like her to be so sure of her own motives. It spooked her.

She opened the door. Grey sea heaved. The glass ship was thoroughly wrecked now, spars of it planted in the beach and among the debris of the office like vast outgrowths of crystal. The white sheets of the covered articles floated on the sludgy ice water. It lapped at the sloping shore of natural woven hemp carpet and around the flotsam it had made of all Sarasilien's carefully preserved things.

Greer whistled between his teeth, impressed. "That's some interior designer you've got. A little apocalyptic for my tastes, if I'm honest. Who's the dead guy?"

"I've no . . ." Lila started to say, moving slowly through the bitter air, but suddenly she had a terrible feeling she did know. For a moment she stared, seeing the awful scene and behind and through it the warm, relative comfort of the ordinary office, untouched by magic, all the laboratory behind it safe with the glass retorts shining in their cabinets and the crystal vials of unknown fluids glowing like past Christmas baubles. Her gloves thickened, furred as she walked forwards, fighting suddenly as the dress got caught in the swell and suddenly lifted on the weak tide, soaking and heavy as lead, the cold eating into her as if it were alive.

The figure roped to the mast was slumped forwards. Lank shreds of dirty blonde hair hung down from a scabbed and balding scalp, heavy with ice. They obscured the face, but the blue hands curled into fists were familiar as her own, even knuckled tight and solid with frost. Shards of broken crystal cut her hands and sliced the dress to ribbons as she struggled to reach a place where she could climb out of the hip-deep swell and onto the crazed frost of the ruined deck. Behind her she could hear Greer talking on the phone, his laconic voice easy, confident as he gave orders, but all her attention was on the figure doubled over itself a few metres away. It was wearing filthy rags that were whited to look clean with ice, snow, and salt. They were thickly bound on, but they couldn't entirely hide the length of the legs that were buckled at awful angles and frozen fast to the sheets of crystal with thick coats of ice like candle wax.

Lila fought out of the water, digging her fingertips into the deck, melting holds and pushing them into molten glass, making claws as she was lost in boiling, spitting water and billowing clouds of steam. Cooling, heating crystal screamed and splintered under her and the black smoke of lace and the yellow, stinking smoke of burning fur obscured the ugly fight to pull tens of pounds of soaking satin out with her as it clung around her legs. She slid across the metre and a half on her belly, frightened in case the figure was frozen solid and in her haste or carelessness she might break it. But she made it, tearing herself free where cold stuck her repeatedly to the glass; the faery could look after itself now, she didn't care as she let her claws become blades and cut through the thin ropes that bound the mast and ship to their captain. Only as they parted around her fingers did she realise they were made out of hair.

She remodelled her hands, warmed them, tentatively reached for the shoulders, tried to lift as she crawled up to her knees, dress splintering and refreezing over her until suddenly it seemed to lose patience and heated up. The deck beneath them cracked in half as it failed to keep up with the change. The body was almost solid. Lila threw the remnants of the huge skirt over it quickly, willing the heat to find a trace of life and help it return. Under her hands she felt the outline of the face quite clearly, the shape of the bone under the flesh exactly as she had feared.

"Zal," she whispered. "Don't be dead. Wake up."

Suddenly a movement in the swell broke the deck apart and they were in the water. The weight of the mast dragged him down to the bottom. Lila plunged into the blackness, able to see with other frequencies, struggling with the sticking rope and the awkward shape of the huge crystal spar that tumbled away from her, its shattered end almost slicing her in half. She broke it to pieces with heat in her hands and then searched around. Ultrasonics showed the submerged shapes of solid things, including the curled body, and the slight movement of something inside it. She grabbed hold so carefully as it turned in slow water, and brought him to the surface. The seawater sucked viciously at her legs and feet, and then with the breaking of the ship the entire ghost seemed to have lost heart. It shivered, as one thing, and within a few seconds the whole biting reality of it evaporated into thin air, leaving her standing in the ordinary room, dry, surrounded by a tumbled mess of furniture and objects piled in heaps.

She was shaking. She daren't look down.

"Get him to medical," Greer said, holding the door for her. "I'll meet you there."

"Elf things," she said, aware that she wasn't making a lot of sense. "There have to be elf things here."

"Yeah, but meantime there's things and people there that can help. Nobody can touch this stuff except you. So take him to where he's safe and come back and look for it. Okay?"

No mention of Zal being dead. She feared he was. Or maybe not, but maybe not Zal either. She daren't hope. He weighed nearly nothing but then he never had. Could you survive those temperatures? That place? She didn't know. She did as she was told.

The armed guards who had arrived stood back to let her pass and took up posts at the door and in the hall, batons in their hands.

All the time she was walking she was talking, doing deals with faeries and powers in her head—if you let it be him, if you let him be alive, if you let me have this, if you're not playing headfuck games with me, then I'll . . . but she didn't know what she'd trade or do; there was nothing big enough or that she had. And then there was the ultrasound she had once used in an ER to heal and charm another elf, playing through his body: yes it's material, yes it's flesh and bone, yes it has all the right parts in the right places if you don't count some breaks and a certain amount of violence and the crystals forming in the cells and the shadows that defy labelling. And his heart doesn't beat and his lungs are all but empty of anything you could call air, though they've got a lot of water inside them grinding their surfaces to pulp with its salt. And the air doesn't warm him but she does. If love was heat, then she had enough, didn't she? And where was that flicker of life she'd have sworn was real, no imagination . . . not in the body but in the aether that was strong in ghosts. Could you have ghosts of the living?

There it was again. On her skin the metal elementals lit like butterflies, emerging, wings stretching. Yes. No mistake. But gone again now. How to catch it? How to hold it down and be sure it didn't leave?

She racked her brains for all she knew about Zal and saw him running in the woods, by that dreadful building, to the hill and the hollow where he'd pulled Zoomenon to him. His addiction was fire. Yes, and his demon affinity was fire. But no Otopian combustion was going to work. Elemental fire was what she needed now. Sarasilien had to have some. Must have some.

The medical centre had changed since her day. Where machines used to bank and encroach on every side there was space. White had gone, natural was in. It was like a hotel room in a garden. Even the doctor and the surgeon were dressed in scrubs that looked like casual clothes, faces groomed to smile and reassure. No stethoscopes or scanners here, just a few passes of the hands, sympathy.

They put him on a bed and trained some lukewarm heat lamps

on him to thaw him out slowly because he could break like the glass, and someone said something about thermoshock and still nobody used the D word so, still praying, not looking in case it was too much, Lila left him there and ran back to the office with its guard, the androids in the hall, the wreckage of a lifetime's work waiting for her, and began to search.

She was fast, she knew that, but it felt like eternity as books and papers flew through her hands and in front of her eyes, meaningless, useless. The outer office had nothing. The laboratory—well, that took some time, even at hyperspeed. He had a billion things. Odd. Bad. Strange. He wrote in code that took her half an hour to figure out, and that was just for the lesser objects. Potions, herbs, plants, the place was thick with the worthless crap of ages. Poisons, there were a thousand. Antidotes a thousand and ten more. Magic circles and wands and swords and cups—what to choose? Does it matter if they don't match? It didn't matter, it turned out, as she couldn't cast anything. Human, machine, not magical at all, even in the dress, even holding the pen, even using every votive article lined up like the lich king's garage sale. No trips to Zoomenon for her, not even a flicker of hell.

Hell.

She looked at the clock.

Nine eighteen.

Where the fuck was Teazle?

Then she knew it was trouble. He wasn't late. Something had happened and she couldn't stop now, no, couldn't, because every second Zal might die. Still, if there was one place you could go to get magical things for cash or trade it was Bathshebat, capital of Demonia, and if there was one place elementals liked to congregate, it was Demonia. Teazle, how did he go? Teleport.

Useless! Think of something! The old portal used to be inside a military base outside the city, but they shut it down in the Hunter's Wild and now the only route into Demonia was through some bunker she didn't know the location of. Demons came in at will, who could stop them? But getting out, that was still embargoed.

"Is something wrong?"

Lila spun around, the corset making it more of a stiff jump than it should have been. Greer was standing there looking over a teetering heap of grimoires at her.

She put down the summoning manuscript she'd been reading from and turned off the burner under a failed alchemical experiment that some or other authority had suggested was good for concocting primal fire without burning the house down. "Where is your portal? The go-anywhere, do-anything portal. You must have one. Where is it?"

"Where did you want to go?"

"I need elemental fire," she hesitated. "Zoomenon."

"Can't go there," he said. "Small matter of disintegration. Never found a containment field that could sustain itself here and there. Not a place for nonaethereals. No deal."

"Demonia then."

"That could easily be a one-way ticket."

"It's the only place."

"I'll send one of our demon pals. Fire elementals, you say?"

Lila felt herself outmanoeuvred. "I want to go. . . ."

"If you go and don't kill Teazle then you don't come back." He shrugged. "I did a deal there. I don't want it broken by you. It's more important than you. Don't take it personal."

She didn't understand him at all.

"Besides, you should be here. If that's who I think it is. You should be here. I don't think he came to sign my albums."

Finally she gave a nod. Behind it her head was churning with *what ifs*. He hadn't said no to the portal, though, so there must be one and it had to be around here somewhere. She bet Bentley knew where. "Well there's nothing here."

Greer looked around him at the steaming jungle of the laboratory, the dozens of used bottles, fume cupboards, delicate concoctions of glass set up on every surface, many of them still giving off smoke or steam. "So I see."

The dress had allowed itself to become just a few rags hanging off the corset by now. She was able to walk around the equipment without causing any accidents. "I'll get back there then. Wait for whoever."

"Good idea. By the way, I nearly forgot to mention it. While you were working here there was a call for you."

"A call?" She was so wrong-footed that for a few seconds she wasn't even sure she'd heard him right.

He nodded, drawing a circle on the tiles with the toe of one worn shoe where she'd spilled water. "Yeah. Said she'd call back later and that you shouldn't get home too late."

"Oh." She wasn't sure if this was a test, wondered briefly if that brownie was having some unfaerylike attack of conscience or whether the rogues had discovered a way to find her again. Quickly she gathered up the few articles of elven clothing that her exhaustive search had uncovered. Greer kept working on his sketch as though there was nothing more interesting. Abruptly she was reminded of Teazle again. "Well, who was it?"

"Max," he said, looking up with a smile. "Your sister. Max."

CHAPTER TEN

Lila stopped and looked at Temple Greer properly for the first time that day. He was gazing at her thoughtfully from beneath his thick brows, his chin tucked down close to his chest, hands in pockets, just watching her, though the look was knowing and they shared a few seconds in which they both waited.

"Hoax caller?" Lila dared.

"On this number?" Greer made the slightest movement of his nose towards the com station that Sarasilien had kept next to the door, high on the wall out of the way of all his magical materials.

"Rogue impersonation?"

He nodded slowly. "Thought of that. Call came from your house. Sent a couple of boys over to check it out. No machines present. Asked the other converts here. They said there was no signature in the signal. Means if it was a fake it wasn't faked by a machine of that kind."

"Aethereal fake?"

"Must be, huh?"

She hesitated, confused by his suggestive tone. She felt queasy, furious at the same time. She wanted to scream, but she said, "Mustn't it?"

"I don't know," he said, finally straightening up to his full height. He pretended to inspect one of the alembics, tapped his finger on the glass, looked at the distillation apparatus, the little heap of useless red slag lying in the dish at the end of the line. "Voice pattern matches."

"You store . . . ?"

"Everyone's voice, retina, iris, fingerprints. Yeah. All stored since just after the bomb and updated at three-year intervals over the course of a lifetime. Teeth too I guess. Verbal choice patterns. Anything that can be measured without undue intrusion. Never very useful actually, except when the dead come calling. Or when you have to rebuild someone."

Lila didn't know what to say. She didn't know what to think. She remembered writing the card, the flowers, dropping them on the memorial, swearing at the maintenance guy. Filthy coffee flavours haunted her tongue. Her guts, already knotted with tension, twisted up on themselves, giving her a spasm of pain. "And do they?"

Greer fiddled with a tiny glass tap and leaned around to look at the cloudy mixture in a vial. "Human beings make bad, weak necromancers," he began.

"Cut to the crap."

"I've seen a couple. Don't wanna see them again."

She felt her mouth hanging open, her body frozen with the need to rush and see Zal, to find elementals, to stay here and listen instead.

"It was in the Hunter's Wake," he said. "At least, we figured that his activities made it easier for humans and the half-fey to cross the brink and back. He had a lotta power. Lotta. It made the world unstable, kinda permeable to magic for the duration. Some nice things came out of it and a lot of bad. I'll keep it sweet—there were two incidents of human wannabe necros and wizards getting together enough mojo to move into and summon stuff out of Thanatopia. Both ended badly. The dead people in question passed every test, including all the ones you'd expect a living person to pass. They were just themselves in every single stat. But they had this habit of suddenly not being themselves at all. And stuff happened around them: hallucinations, chills, arguments, violence, suicides. . . . My point is they weren't who they looked like, even though clearly they kinda were—they loved who they loved and they liked prawn crackers and all that stuff. And they didn't die easy. Lost forty agents. Three of 'em cyborg. Still don't really understand what those things were. The demon agents said they were things related to devils, but purer, like an elemental form."

"Evil," Lila said. She snorted, a laugh that wasn't allowed to be. "The evil dead. Isn't that what they say to schoolchildren to stop them fooling with Ouija boards?"

"Yeah. I can't say that officially of course, because we understand evil as a philosophical construction that's part of free will and a matter of individual choice related to one's identity as a spiritual being, or not, under the rule of reason, and not an actual external entity of any kind." He poked at some of the powders lying on their measuring saucers and watched his finger tip the balance of the grain scales. "That would be animism and externalising of internal conflict and completely ideologically and phenomenologically unsound. Even in today's world of supernatural creations and magical powers there's still no place for externalised forces of intent." He paused to draw breath and sighed, putting some weights on the scale, watching them tip. "So, although it has to be some kind of unliving entity from a dimension outside immediate human perception yet existing in spaces perhaps interpenetrating with our own on a genuinely material level, albeit an undetectable one, I understand there might be lots of similar kinds of things there. They're classed as not living because they don't have material forms or anything we'd consider living characteristics except a kind of agency, and a kind of intent. But for the sake of an easy life between you and me we'll call it evil and say we're talking demon if anyone calls us on it. I have heard that there are things out there that aren't evil, but where's the fun in believing all that relativistic realistic shit? The bottom line is that they aren't returners." He stopped playing around and looked directly at her. "You want me to call the duty necromancer? I mean, the duty World Five Technician."

She didn't know. "Is it possible that it isn't . . . one of these things?"

He shrugged and smiled, utterly insincere. "Sure, I guess."

"Obviously call them. Let's find out."

"I might send some guys around to your house, just undercover, very discreet, keep an eye on things. You know."

"Okay." She felt numb. She remembered the grey boatman's warning and the way the words the pen wrote had twisted like live eels in his hand, like they were fighting to be free. She thought of Max, talking to her, what she longed to say, needed to hear. All the nights she had talked to the darkness and Teazle's insensible beating heart. She found her hands so tight on the elf clothes that they were about to tear and made herself let go a little. She was looking at the floor, anything but at Greer with his mocking, know-it-all stance that was always one step ahead of her, like it or not.

"Don't . . . I mean, just be careful. If it is. Her. I know it isn't. But just."

Greer was looking at her, just looking now.

"What?" She pushed past the last desk, passed him, and started to walk out.

"Don't you ever get rattled, Black? You drag a lost love out of a ghost sea, your partner goes AWOL, your spouse under sentence, you murder a rogue agent, your sister comes back from the dead, and your clothes don't even like you, what? Nothing? When are you gonna crack?"

"Tomorrow," she said. Ordinary feeling was a gulf to fall into, or something to twist around and around until it all stuck together and became a cable of something like steel. Anger at him gave her the will to twist it.

He kept up with her in the corridor, but he had to add a trot step every few strides. "Things sure have been interesting since you got back, wouldn't you say? One day into the new job and it's like the world exploded."

"Are you blaming me?" she keyed the lift. It was slow. She accessed the computer, deleted the call chain on the car, and moved it into express mode. When the doors opened several wild-eyed admin staff were jabbing at the panel, talking about dying. As they saw Greer jerk his thumb at them they got out pronto. Lila stepped in and the doors snapped shut, almost catching Greer's heel.

"No." He paused, wincing. "I think I've pulled a muscle in my leg."

"Drop back if you can't take the pace."

"I like the tough girl act, personally."

"I'm grateful. Really." Lila applied the brakes. The car decelerated, hydraulics groaning. Greer fell over nursing a mild spinal compression, and then she looked down at him. "It seems like I have some personal matters I need to attend to before I can start the job. If you don't want me to use your stuff, just say the word. I can be gone in an instant."

"This practice of you putting me on the ground all the time has to stop. I'm starting to think you like me. Also, Mrs. Greer elbowed me out of our health insurance policy so now she gets to go to spas twice a week and have her head shrunk by some woman in an office the size of Maui while I just got the ice pack and a can of Faery Dark." He got to his feet with some difficulty and adjusted his suit.

Lila leaned close to him and looked him in the eye. She could see him doing the usual thing of searching for her pupils and finding only himself reflected. It was pleasing. "We may work together when it suits us, but you are not and never will be the boss of me." She poked a finger at his top pocket where his ID badge was clipped, prominently displaying the insignia of the Otopian Security Force. "You and your big dog too. You people had your money's worth from my ass. I agreed to nothing. And that's all. Get me some damned elemental fire and a demon to work it or get out of my face." She did like him. Curse it.

She turned and found Bentley next to her, apparently waiting for some kind of command. Bentley held up a small plastic tag, "Your ticket, for the—"

Lila brushed past her. "Tell me what the hell happened to make your crew all grey and flat like Benzo Barbie, and stick that thing in your pocket. It's Mal's. I don't have time for the rest of whatever. Write a memo."

As she reached the medical lab doors she heard Greer saying, "Apparently when she's rattled she loses all social skills. I guess there just isn't enough processing power. Do you find that happening to you?"

Bentley's answer was lost as the doors to Zal's room slid open and the thick, jungle sounds of the Alfheim night poured over her. The bed was almost lost amid the imported plants that crowded the place, and from the ceiling a false moon shone, three quarters phased in its Harvest cycle, an auspicious alignment with the stars in constant adjustment.

For all her speed and fury she was only able to move slowly in approach. Her heart was in her mouth, and despite the humidity and the heat of the room she felt cold all over. She was too afraid to look. She wanted it to be him, so badly. She wanted it to be really him, for him to live and to wake up and laugh, and that made her afraid.

Bentley and Greer reached the door. She heard it open, then close, and their voices stayed outside. A nurse's voice over the intercom said quietly, "Please don't touch him."

She didn't intend to touch him. If she did and it wasn't real she felt that she would be crushed enough to die. Instead she crept closer until she was at the side of the high bed, its lights winking at her as if he were lying on top of a model city. Linen covered him from chin to foot, covered over with a layer of some kind of herbs, then the shining silver of a heat blanket. The rags and his exposed skin glistened in the moonlight, coated in a thick layer of oxygen-rich regenerant gel. A tube ran out of his mouth and the gentle hiss of a pump sounded in time to the rise and fall of his chest.

The skin around his closed eyes was still blue and all the shadows of his face were darker than usual, as he'd been shortly before Jack had tried to kill him, fifty years ago in the winter lock. They emphasised his emaciated state. His cheeks were hollow, eye sockets too big, the skin of his face blistered and raw, cracked in so many places he was barely recognisable. The tips of his ears were frostbitten off. Around the tube where his lips were stretched his teeth were broken. Now that the ice had melted, the few tufts of hair still left on his head were dark with blood and water, clinging in the gel over the raw skin beneath. She understood that part at least; he'd ripped out his own hair to make the rope.

Fifty years. Where and when had it passed for him? Was it him? Greer's hyperbolic warnings aside, what the hell had happened to bring him here like this?

"I was quick as I could," she said, wondering at the same time if that were true. What had she been waiting for? A bigger gun, a better time, a ticket to Faeryland? "I didn't know what to do. She said—" Yeah, some faery had told her she'd repair Zal and send him home, a faery similar in its nature to the dress in age and weirdness. And she'd been waiting for the call? She had, but that seemed stupid now. Strangely at the time she'd felt like the faery was telling the truth. "Don't leave me." She was surprised to find herself saying that, but now that she was here and there was no need to go on the rescue run and no bad thing to fight she was so helpless it hurt. She meant it too. Zal was like her, and there weren't many of those around. Losing him entirely seemed real now, possible, whereas before she could imagine easily that she'd find him and they'd get out, he'd come back, and they'd live together somewhere anywhere, and she'd seen his face laughing that old laugh that didn't care how strange or difficult things were, he could take it all in his stride and take her with him. They'd run away once for a day. They'd run away again. She was waiting for it, surely, all these other things were just a delay to that inevitable? Nothing made sense if that wasn't the ending.

That's how it had felt, yes, even Sorcha dying and listening to the Signal day and night, using Teazle to wipe away the pain and the uncertainty because he was so strong she never need worry about him in any way. Except . . . screw that thought, she couldn't afford that thought about him right now. And all of that was bearable, anything was, because Zal was coming back and he'd have known she was coming for him, surely; he wouldn't have given up on her. But fifty years. Even for an elf it was a long time. And for him how long? And he'd never sit still of course. Of course he hadn't waited.

She reached out without thinking and only at the last moment realised and took her hand back. "Don't go," she said, in her mind the images of all those who were gone, and Zal was there, with them, all wrong, shrugging like it didn't matter either, mocking even his own end like everything was the world's dumbest joke. "I can't bear it." She didn't want to think about what she would do if she were forced to think about it to.

She waited, but there was no response. The traces of aetheric body near his heart remained steady and that was all. She wondered how ordinary people did it, people without any power or ability to do anything, when their loved ones were lying there. What did they think about, what did they feel, where would they go? She felt that everything in her was reaching out, searching for connection, for reasons, comfort and strength, and nothing answered, not out of spite or deserving, but just because nothing was there.

The pump hissed. A nurse came in, checked something, went out. Bentley came in, quiet as stealth itself, held out a cup of tea. Lila took it.

"After we were all machines," she said gently, starting her story, "and after some of us had decided we had to be free to follow the Signal's call, we fought a war."

She leaned down and looked at the blinking lights of the bed, a code she could read easily. "It didn't take long, just hours really. They wanted all of us to be free. Those of us who disagreed and wanted to continue with the human world were heretics to them. They took on the look you saw, the black machines, as a political statement. We kept our usual looks, of course, like you."

She straightened up. "One of the attacks before the stalemate occurred was a viral bomb. It infected all of us. There was an info-quake. Most prime-targeted items were erased, along with a lot of collateral damage. Among those were all of the markers of our identity, every one, across every format. By the time we countered it almost all of our personal data was gone. Now there is no record of what we looked like, even in our own memories, even in our DNA. They replaced it with the android and plastic features you so dislike. They even drilled out our ancestral records so that no reconstructions could be made by best guess. Here and there they missed a little." She touched the necklace she wore briefly. "But not much. There is some doubt about my name, actually. But you have to be called something. For a while we fooled around and made new appearances for ourselves—the viral program was easy to adopt and use, once we had it cornered—but after the stalemate and the loss of what we knew a lot of us let the grey state be as it was. It is who we are now; a human manifestation of the Signal, and the badge of our war. And before you pity us let me state that none of us feel the loss. We have no memory, so we have no loss. Just this story."

At least I could do that, Lila thought, staring at the android figure and hoping her face didn't convey horror though she wasn't sure it didn't. I could wipe it all out.

She felt herself relax fractionally for the first time in hours. "Thanks," she said, lifting the tea, but meaning the story too.

"My pleasure. The demon agent's ETA is another hour and ten," Bentley continued in the same, relaxed voice. "I can stay here, if you would like to sleep."

"No, thanks," Lila said. "I'm staying."

"Would you like me to stay?"

Lila shook her head. "See if you can find any sign of Mal. Maybe we missed something at his office."

"Yes, ma'am."

"Wait, before you go. Do you know where the agency portal is?"

"Yes, ma'am."

"Are you going to tell me?"

"I do not have permission."

"Okay. I guess I can spend my time hacking the information then. And you can stop the ma'am-ing, I'm not the damn queen."

"As you wish."

The door sighed open and then shut after Bentley's silent departure.

After another minute of listening to the pump Lila abandoned any thoughts of stealing the portal knowledge from the agency AIs. She would rather not start an all-out battle with them, not only because they might win it, but because it would be yet another hostile action she couldn't afford if she wanted to rely on help later. Instead a better plan occurred to her—make the demon agent take her back. Or better yet, if less hopefully, search the rest of Sarasilien's libraries and chattels for some implement that would do the job. Upon this decision's moment, the thought she hadn't wanted to entertain at all crept in and settled at the forefront of her mind.

Teazle was late.

That meant he wasn't coming. There could only be one reason for that—he couldn't. The only thing that could stop him was death, obviously, or else a thing like some unstoppable force or containment which—and she had no idea what it might be—could not be diced, burnt, or teleported away from. She didn't rule out rogue vengeance for the loss of Sandra Lane, but in the list of deathwishers they were rather low. She didn't rule out something weirder. She'd planned to meet him tonight, now, and test the dampener system on him to see if he was able to counter it. She'd been going to explain the dress's trick of outwitting the frequency—not that she was sure it would be any use to him. He had been brewed to be a powerful demon, ruler of a considerable chunk of assets in a world of absolute greed and unflinching violence, but the journey to Under had altered him, and in the months that they had been back the subject of exactly how had never come up. She'd been busy avoiding that, and it never occurred to her that he was anything but completely balanced, confident, and certain of himself. To be otherwise was not to be Teazle.

Another minute crawled past. She was certain then that, like Zal, she had spent too long running. Even listening to the Signal was running, because what it said was pure information, but no suggestion of how to make any decision about what it said. Listening felt like doing something, as if eventually, listen long enough and all the answers to what bothered her would pop out in a moment of blissful lateral inspiration. She'd waited months, and all she got was sodden with knowledge about things, their material forms, their movements, the operations of the cosmos, the permutations of series . . . dead things, to be honest.

". . . no life," she found herself mumbling at Zal as she traced the dull line of his thermoblanket for the hundredth time. "And then it infiltrates living things, but it doesn't live. It just copies, and remoulds, and stores, and keeps on talking the talk. Everyone's details and everyone's movements in a big list of unconnected events, one after the other after the other. It never shuts up and it never says anything. Like me right now. I want to talk at last, and look, everyone went away. Poor little Lila in her raggedy dress that you gave me, you bastard, without warning me or anything. Wake up so I can punch your lights out."

She really wanted a drink so that something other than the beckoning misery would wipe her out. "Did you know it's only been . . ." She checked her clock. "Five months and two days since we met? Your last concert was just a few weeks ago. Fifteen thousand people watched it, two thousand in person and the rest by live broadcast. And today almost nobody knows your songs, except old farts like Greer, my boss, who turns out to be a fanboy. Hey, there's another thing. You never mentioned you really were turning tricks with those songs. That was sneaky, positively demonic."

It was a struggle. She took a deep breath, was stopped short by the corset, and tried not to notice how awful he looked, how frail and ruined.

"I think you could make a comeback. Demon music is popular in the charts; lots of people are getting used to a half-fey world. That was my fault. I told him he could have a year. I didn't know what he'd do. I just said it. And that was that. Cure worse than the disease, probably, I'm not sure. Seems like it was. You should have been the one to cut the deal, not me. I should have run. You should have been there. Then you'd have got this sword thing. Maybe not. I wish it was you. You know what to do with this stuff."

The ventilator hissed, paused.

"None of that sounds very inviting, does it? None of it sounds like it's worth coming back for."

Above her the fake moon reset itself to three degrees beyond Arcturus and started its brief cycle of calming light one more time.

"I still have the house. Falling down a bit now. I should probably demolish it and start again. Sell it. The faeries kept it for me. They don't have too much of a record on paying bills. I don't think any utilities are even connected now."

She stared into the dark beyond the bed and saw the leaves of the elven cycads dripping water as the misters worked for a few moments.

"Some bad shit's gone down in Demonia. Teazle's killed everyone and taken their stuff. I'd blame myself but . . ." She stopped. "With you gone if he dies then I'll be number one target in several worlds. So you know, if you come back then it'll be you in the hot spot; might want to think about that before you stop playing possum. Oh yeah, and we've been sleeping together. Quite a lot. Didn't really mean to. It just kind of happened. You know."

The misters stopped. Down on the floor the flowers of night-dryads bloomed and their strange smell of old bookcases and woodsmoke slowly filled the air. The luminescent spores glowed faintly as they coated the tubs of grass. The gel on Zal's face warmed another degree in response to the bed's programming and started to liquefy, running very slowly down across his cheeks, nose, chin, forehead. Thin sheets of old, dead skin began to peel off with the movement.

Lila folded and refolded the elven clothes. She recognised them by and by. Sarasilien had worn them as lab clothes, washed them, put them away and forgotten them. They were quite threadbare, although the magical signs still glimmered in and out of the weave if you held it at the right angle to see. She put them on top of the mound of silver blanket, in case they had the power to do any good. Surely they would do no harm.

"How am I? I'm okay. I'm fine thanks. I just talk like a moron and I do things without understanding them and I feel quite horrible most of the time. I'm full of hate, that's the problem. And rage. But they're okay because underneath them is the sadness and I can't . . . I can't . . ." She pulled the topshirt off the pile of clothes and screwed it up, mashing it onto her face, stuffing it in her mouth and against her eyes, but it didn't block out all the howling scream and it didn't help at all in making it stop.

CHAPTER ELEVEN

"**M**iz Black?"

The voice jolted her awake. She was face down, head on hands, hands and arms resting on the edge of the bed. A steamy wetness clung to her face—the shirt. She sat up and peeled it off. It fell heavily into her hands, warm and fleshy, slimed with snot so that she quickly rubbed at her nose and mouth with the drier edges. There was a savage aching in her throat and her head. Moonlight glared off the heat blanket, making her wince and blink. "Yes?" Only the corset's rigid, unyielding demand kept her from wobbling as her legs unlocked from their AI-determined position of rest and let her turn around.

She put the shirt down and rubbed her face with both hands in an effort to wake up before she thought to use chemicals and let her in-system pharmacy dose her with uppers. The drugs took effect rapidly, pushing her back into the speed and anxiety of the moment with hellish acceleration that left her feelings behind entirely. Her chest felt like someone had shotgunned it from the inside, but the iron bones of the dress held that wound in check.

A demon in human form was standing in front of her. He was tall and magnificently handsome, though that was no surprise—she'd never seen an ugly one in changed state. He wore a complicated silk robe that revealed a great deal of skin here and there whilst fitting human standards of modesty. His body was the colour of a midday storm, his hair twisting and lifting of its own accord to float on the lightest currents of air. The theatrical silliness of it reminded her of Poppy, the faery singer. Poppy had tried to save Zal from the Giant-killer's vengeance, and now she was dead for her pains. Lila forcibly hauled her sharpening attention away as she remembered Poppy, the stupid kind vacuity of her and her foolish act of defiance. In life Poppy had annoyed her and been the kind of girl Lila had always mistrusted and envied, but Poppy had never noticed Lila's animosity or been put off by her aloof manner. Now was not the time to think of ill-judged acts of love and fury and bodies rolling cold in black water.

The demon addressing Lila was a water demon of some kind she guessed, by the look and the exacting distance from his body at which he held the clay crucible in its glowing wire frame.

"I am Agent Vadrahazeen. Your elemental," he said, and put the heavy container down, stepping aside from it quickly. "I am sorry I am late." He bowed low to her, even his azure eyes ducking for an instant in one of the most submissive gestures. A normal demon of middling standings would make such obeisances only to royalty, so either he was peasant stock or Teazle had been boasting much less than she'd imagined and was in far greater danger.

Lila's heart sank another notch to a position somewhere near her boots, and she looked at the clock—three in the morning. She rubbed her chest, high over the bodice where she was able, but it did nothing to ease the ache. "What kept you?" She bent down to examine the crucible and saw the demon's strange feet close up—cloven pads like a camel's, broad and strong with a claw tip just visible on each part, painted emerald green and wet with some type of mild venom. They never managed to get rid of all their characteristics in the change of form. Teazle always had a tail. This one apparently had feet.

The crucible was wired shut and marked with a great deal of demonic symbols intended to maintain a lock and prevent the wire from melting, though they were fighting a losing battle in Otopia's primaterial atmosphere. It was extremely hot—enough to frizzle and crisp a stray scrap of the dress that dangled too close to it. At least the floor was made of tiles in here, so it hadn't started to burn. She moved back to a more comfortable point as the demon started to talk and studied it, wondering what she was going to do.

"Teazle Sikarza has gone missing."

Thoughts of the present dilemma fled instantly from her mind. "What?"

"White Death is lost." The water demon's soft, liquid eyes were a perfect Prussian blue as they delighted in sharing this information. He was drinking in the effect it had on her, and Lila felt her face steel over as she fought with him. "At least, the Judges of Bathshebat cannot find him."

She got to her feet as he continued, apparently impervious to the news, but inwardly it was eating like acid at the fragile resolve she had. The corset creaked, and she felt the laces take themselves in a fraction. In the dark the demon didn't see fresh fabric twine down the black-armoured length of her thighs, wrapping tight like a living black bandage.

"Go on." Her voice remembered the tone of command she had learned to use all the time in Demonia.

Vadrahazeen made a moue that he wasn't getting a better taste of shock and flared his wide nostrils. "There is a great deal of commotion surrounding the major cities as searches take place. The government has attempted to seize his assets in absentia, in an effort to stabilize the volatility of the commons as news spreads, but as there is no proof of his death they are unable to proceed. Meanwhile the heirs of the various houses recently come under his aegis are seeking ways to reclaim their power either through acts of secession and open rebellion, or else a grovelling servitude to his name in which they climb the ladder of favour. It depends on whether they think he will return alive or not. Armies are massing and alliances forming. Loyal vassals and family are looking for him with their own armed regiments, large numbers of mercenaries and any amount of scum-for-hire from all the worlds. Until there is a body there is no progress, and with such rewards as exist for his death many lesser demons fancy themselves a chance at making their fortune. Whichever way matters fall the economy will be bankrupted by gambling debts. Entire houses have staked themselves upon the outcome. It is ripe chaos." He smiled with a warm nostalgia.

Lila frowned, a gesture that showed her genuine displeasure, if not her alarm, and hedged her only hope. "He often goes into the wild country to hunt for worthy rivals to fight." She gave Vadrahazeen a scathing look. "Or to the other worlds."

The demon spread his hands out, suddenly the soul of peaceable ambivalence. "Yes, but divining his location is a simple matter for any seer. The enforcement officers have twenty routinely tracking him at any time, to be sure of the legal state of his affairs. There is even a Bound Heart beating in the High Court to verify his health at all times. All sources say he is in Bathshebat, and alive." He moved impatiently, and she could feel his eagerness to go and participate in the heady thrill of a mass hysterical maul.

She envisioned parties, balls, duels rife to the eyeballs with murder and intrigue. Dance floors would be slippery with blood. Assassins must lurk around every corner and in the slightest shadow. Demon society must be thrilled to the core, living at a peak of frenzied delight and terror. It would be an orgy of destruction as they found a ready excuse to strive for the pinnacles of excess they so valued. But Vadrahazeen was clearly quite young, because he managed to master his longing for all this and stand still.

Lila moved closer to him. Under the change his age was hard to determine. Her mistake in assuming youth could be costly. But Teazle himself was young, barely out of the prime minister's seat. They had a certain similarity. But she was wasting too much time on a hesitation and he was waiting, counting every moment as a moment in which she failed to be decisive and in which she became increasingly vulnerable. She let it go, turned her back on him ostentatiously to check Zal, and pointed at the red-hot clay with a small gesture of her foot as if it were nothing. "What do I do with them?"

"It," he corrected her. "One is more than enough trouble." He looked around the room pointedly." This is not a safe location. There must be containment."

"I've seen them wandering in the wild in Demonia," Lila said, meaning he'd better come up with something more than generalisations.

"We are not in Demonia," Vadrahazeen replied smoothly. "In the basket the elemental is in a stable environment. Released here it will either deport to Zoomenon—best case—or else burn everything in sight until it runs out of oxygen, at which point it will then deport. There is no aether present, and it is an aetheric being. Any fraction of its element is enough to keep its attention, but if combustion stops and no plasma is available it won't stick around. The other possibility is that it is strong already and would take the chance of seeking immediate refuge with the closest aetheric source. Myself, as I am strongest, after that you, and then the Ahrimani here, what's left of him."

Lila, who hadn't even looked at Zal once, straightened up, turned around, and looked the demon in the face, "So, you can tell he's alive?"

"I can tell that something of his spirit remains. A flicker. As can you. Nothing else. Your metal elementals are much more powerful than that fragment right now." He folded his hands, still, calm.

Lila made an expression of deep indifference. "And what happens if it . . . seeks refuge?"

The demon narrowed its eyes in speculation and a wistful curiosity. "It is a popular method of murder at dinner parties, most entertaining. Alas, I have never seen it myself."

"Probably you don't get invited to those parties," she said comfortingly, and saw it irk him in a suitably satisfying way. "The method?"

The demon walked to the bed and looked at Zal for a long minute. He shrugged. "Put them together, release the elemental, and pray to whatever god you think is listening. If he hasn't got will enough to master the energy then you should cut off his head or, if you don't wish to be merciful, let the elemental burn him from the inside out. Either way, same result in the end."

"There has to be something else," Lila demanded. "I've seen you all tripping out on these things and they don't damage you."

Vadrahazeen recovered himself and put his head on one side. "Demons who are addicted to elemental frequencies often end their lives as prey to higher elemental forms or as accidental fodder to the minor ones." He began to preen with superiority as he was able to lecture her. "You must not have seen enough of them to realise. And those who don't succumb always bring a healthy tribute of some kind— something the elemental would rather take instead. There's not a day in Bathshebat you can't buy short ribs and burnt ends pulled off some fried fire dancer from the night before."

"At last," Lila snarled at him, staring him down until he backed off a step. "The one useful bit of knowledge crawls out of your brain. Set up a containment around the bed."

"It will use all of my energy," he objected.

"Get on with it." She was implacable.

"In *this* world that is the best *anyone* could do," he hissed, and set about withdrawing himself into a meditative state so that he could do as she said. His demeanour was sulky, but she didn't see any rebellion in it.

She considered going to fetch the flares and an oxygen cylinder herself, but something about her back crawled when she thought of leaving Zal alone with the demon. It was busy colouring itself purple and blue—colours of insight, calm and will—but she'd seen demons flicker through the rainbow to the flat white of deadly assault in a second, so that meant little to her. Instead she cued up a steady string of stimulants and nutrition into her own bloodstream and sent a summons to Bentley.

The grey figure arrived a few minutes later. "Your books, and flares."

Lila looked for somewhere to put the flare sticks and the thin tube of the oxygen cylinder, then said, "Hand them to me when I say." She opened the first book, a tome from Sarasilien's collection, and was about to start leafing when Bentley made a discreetly polite noise in her throat and held out a volume that Lila hadn't requested.

Ophelia's Compendium of Bittersweet Remedies for All Occasions, it was titled, under a thick layer of mildew that had died and dried into a vile stain along the spine.

A certain eagerness crept into her measured tones. "Open it."

Lila opened it. Damp pages stuck together, ink running like a mad chromatograph. Peeled apart they were utterly illegible. The whole thing gave off a rank, fungal odour, and then she lifted a second clump of leaves and saw that it had been carefully hollowed out at the very centre. Inside the hole lay a memory stick, almost as old as the book by the looks of it—even had a USB port. As she examined it more closely she saw that this in turn was a fake—a piece of recent memory technology masquerading as an obsolete form. The port was glued on. Break it off and a normal crystal junction offered to grow to meet her fingers. As soon as she accessed it, she found the elf's entire library, meticulously catalogued, cross-referenced.

Over a thousand volumes in more than twenty languages, not counting the mathematical ones. And not only were they illustrated, they were illuminated with designs and pictograms of exquisite detail and shimmering colours. The gift left her speechless with delight and rent with loss. She would far rather have had the owner to talk to. That feeling led to a place she couldn't go now, however, so she cut it off and copied the whole to her own memory. Then she absorbed herself in a second of grace—put the stick back, closed the book, passed it over. "He was such a technophobe."

"We've all tried touching it and even scanning it remotely," Bentley said, tucking the book back under her arm. "But like everything else, it was charmed to be just for you. Bet it's gone blank now." She sounded sad.

"This is such a bad idea," Lila murmured, watching the demon cast his circle, a generously sized one, around the inside perimeter of the room. She forbade the medical staff to interfere and took a few minutes to make sure they were all incarcerated in rooms with exits to the outside world. This forethought earned her the kinds of reprimands that would have burned her ears off if she'd been paying attention and more curses than she realised human beings even knew.

Meanwhile she was reading. The lore of the library said what the demon had said, only in much more explicit details. She would have been better off in a demon lab, using a host of other adepts as backup, but even so her plan to revive Zal was as sophisticated a treatment as wiring him to the mains and letting it rip. "I need a faery healer or an elven one."

"We can get one," Bentley said. "But she lives out of town. Don't you want to wait? I mean, he might recover. It's not unknown. Cryostasis and—"

"No," Lila said with absolute conviction, unable to articulate to herself why. She had begun to feel a deep, pressing unease that was growing all the time. *Hurry up*, he'd written. Using the pen. Her pen. It had occurred to her more than once that she could have created the letters in her sleep, through some dreaming frenzy. It would be a simple matter for her to forge his writing. In her nightmares as a child she'd sleepwalked out of the house one time, taking a packed bag with her. Even the pen could forge it all by itself. Just because it let her carry it around didn't mean the thing couldn't serve other masters, or itself. Who knew what such things could want? Meanwhile, as she glanced at the bed now she thought she detected a weakening of the aether signature in Zal. The aetheric trace showed no signs of wanting to reinhabit the whole of his body. His heart beat—ten beats a minute—only because it lingered as if it also had misgivings or was maybe waiting for a place where it could safely leave. God, she didn't want to think it was that.

That erased any doubts she had over her timing. She moved Bentley to a station near the door. "Stay right here and do as I say." The doubts she had over her motives would have to wait.

"I'll have her called," Bentley said, meaning the healer, but did as she was told and stayed put.

Lila took a long look at the demon. "Don't forget to seal the roof off," she said. "And the floor. This is on the fifth level of ten storeys."

He glared at her, his mouth working incantations, his hands busy. A moment of genuine hate. That was progress at least.

By now word had got around that the new agent was bossing staff around for some mad experimental work. She could hear people gathering to watch through the one-way viewing deck above them, and in the connecting rooms where more usual human medical equipment was stored. Messages and suggestions that she ought to slow down, follow procedure and generally stop came flooding in to her, but she deleted them.

Who had she been kidding? The romance with the agency was never going to last. They didn't want the same things at all. But at least they had some nice gear.

A senior doctor issued her a direct order to surrender proceedings to him, but she declined. She felt calm, thanks to the drugs, aware that she might be making an awful mistake but determined to carry it through, as if that determination would improve the situation and render it virtuous. Again the knell of disquiet rang through her.

I am mad, she thought quite clearly as the demon finished working on his containment ring and began to shape it into an invisible but implacable sphere of aetheric force. He wasn't looking nearly as perky as he had a few minutes ago. Sweat coated his face and he had begun to shiver. Before he completed it she picked up the long handles of the crucible's cage and carried it to the bedside, where she set it on the floor.

Someone in the other room was talking about putting her under arrest. She thought she probably deserved it, but checked all doors were sealed on automatic, locking everyone out, then pulled Bentley to the last corner of the room that was safely away from the demon's containment field. Finally he was done and backed up to join them. There was nothing to see; Lila would have to take his word for it. "All ready?"

"Good as it gets," the demon muttered through clenched teeth. He was panting and chose to slide down the wall and sit rather than keep standing.

"Projectiles can get through it from here?"

He snorted, as if this was common knowledge. "Anything over a hundred miles an hour has sufficient inertia to break through. It will weaken the field at that—"

"Okay," she said, lifted her right hand, and took aim with the .45 it had efficiently become. She had her mind on Fate when she squeezed the trigger. *Come on then, let's see what you've got*, she thought. Her own private bets finalised in her mind. What had her mom used to say? *Aces high.* Lila wondered what it meant. She shot the crucible.

Blinding yellow light flooded the room, making everyone duck or shield their faces, except Lila, who had expected it and already closed down her irises so that she would see the consequences of what she'd done in all their detail. As the fragments of the clay pot blasted wide, the toughened wire cage glowed white and then ran like water. Smoke rose from the burning metal, and the front of some of the bed machinery melted and failed. Alarms began to sound everywhere, but nobody moved or spoke. They were all looking at the small, ribbonlike shape of the creature that emerged from the pooling steel. It flowed in rings, disposed itself in fractal curls, balled itself up, and then expanded into the chaotic shape of living flames as it felt its way curiously into the air. Almost as suddenly as it had reached out it contracted and became a distinct form, sinuous of body, with four legs, a long neck, a long tail, and a small head each made of flame that turned in on itself over and over as if it existed in a different, infinitely combustible universe.

The creature floated around. It attenuated, rose like a cobra, like hot air or steam winding upwards. Its light danced on the silver blanket and glistened on the wet gel that coated the near-dead body. The body did not move, as it hadn't moved yet. The creature rose higher, its posture attentive and giving every impression of acute listening. Its small head wavered, homing in on Zal's chest, to the heart chakra, where the last of Zal was still hiding out. On one of the displays the room temperature reading climbed steadily.

Lila took a last look at it as it reached a sweltering ninety-nine. Her AI mind was silently ticking off probabilities with every creeping degree, and at this point she mentally cashed in her winnings. For a moment she lingered, and looked at Zal. Yes, it would be easier to watch him burn than see him live like that, that was for sure.

Her reasoning, sadly, was impeccable. Any flame of any kind was a fragment of elemental fire—she knew that without reading it in Sarasilien's books. A special form from Zoomenon was a second-order being, it was true, one that had moved up one quantum step on the evolutionary ladder towards the conscious awareness of Elemental Fire, itself a singular collective entity composed of all its instances but self-aware in only one manifestation. An encounter with it would be unsurvivable. But the acceleration of heat in the room bespoke not of the tenuous heat of a living flame but ready combustion, something well into a thorough burning. The temperature told her beyond question that the little salamander wasn't what it looked like. It was not even an elemental, but a fire demon at full power, attempting to contain itself.

She'd never seen or heard of one within civilised bounds. Therefore she assumed this was one of those things from the Wild. Whatever way she looked at it it was an assassination effort, and quite a good one. Her disappointment and rage gave way to cold calculations.

She reached out and grabbed a flare from Bentley's arms. She flipped open the end cap and put her finger in the trigger release. With the other hand she took the oxygen cylinder and flicked it around in her palm until it lay along her forearm, nozzle pointing forwards ready to spray. She moved forwards purposefully, towards the circle, then at the last moment turned, ignited the flare, and opened the oxygen valve.

The water demon's head went up almost immediately in an explosion of steam and boiling liquids. It barely had time to scream its agony before the best part of its flesh was vaporised by the intense, unstoppable burn. Lila stood over it, her own arms lost to sight in clouds of billowing steam and filthy smoke, guiding the oxygen jet to ensure total consumption. The screaming of the humans and Bentley's cry momentarily drowned out the area alarms, but in a few seconds Vadrahazeen was dead and beginning to shrink. The stench of his cooking body filled the room. Lila cut off the oxygen as he began to decompose in the demon manner. She threw the cylinder at Bentley, who still caught it in spite of her shock, then jammed what was left of the flare into the smouldering eye socket of the demon's charred skull. Sparks and flame shot out of the mouth and nose. Around her legs the dress wraps shifted as they came close to the smouldering body, tiny tongues of thread darting forwards to close gaps and taste the foul smoke that was billowing around.

With his death the circle he'd conjured evaporated and so did the glamour he had set upon the creature crouched on Zal's chest. It was small, no bigger than a cat, and halfway in physiology between cat and monkey. Its long, gibbonish arms were stretched out, hands on Zal's face, the overly lengthened and sharpened index fingers moving towards his closed eyes. Its body was wreathed in red, orange, and yellow fire that was so intense and brilliant it was hard to see any details, but here and there the fire could be seen blasting out of its body core through rents in flesh that was raw, suggestions of muscle and tendon holding bones together over a blast furnace. The blanket and everything near it was already catching light. On Zal's face the gel was spitting and boiling with snapping pops.

Lila breathed out to clear her nose, took aim through the clouding air, and shot the demon with a cold iron full metal jacket. The impact flung it through the air and slammed it into the wall. It spun crazily, recoiling and using its long legs to rebound back towards the bed. Spatters of cooling metal trailed in its wake like blood, where the iron had melted and run harmlessly out of its body. It landed lightly, fixated on its task, and with one febrile leap landed on Zal's head and stabbed its clawed fingers down. Its tail coiled, and the spike tip drove into the side of the silver blanket. The body jolted with the force.

Lila forgot the gun and reached for the pen. The heat in the room was well above a hundred and thirty and soaring rapidly. It made her faster, but she wasn't fast enough. She knew it but carried on with her swing anyway, watching the shift of slim fountain pen to sword take place in a time split too small to detect, the sword huge and curved in her hand, the blade a thin, razor-sharp crescent of ice that grew and grew in the arc until it was exactly the right size.

The demon screamed with fury and leapt straight up, clutching its hands and tail into itself as it became a fireball. "Cheat!" she heard it say in the oldest form of demonic, a wailing, desperate, angry, and futile spasm of absolute hatred that cut short as the sword blade sliced into it. The blade shook in her hand as the monkey thing vanished into the splintering white of its surface. By the time it finished the swing and her hand returned to her side it was the pen once more, cool and undisturbed.

Zal was dead.

CHAPTER TWELVE

Lila walked forwards and looked down at the corpse. She was numb. The face was blackened now, gel turned to peeling, dried goo. It was hideous and silent. After a time she was aware of Bentley at her side. The android was holding a baton in her hand.

"I tried to stop it," she said, and for the first time since Lila had met her she heard a hesitant, awkward human in the voice.

"It's not your fault," Lila said. "Not even the demons' fault. It's my fault."

"No," Bentley said. "Nobody would have been fast enough to stop that thing."

Which wasn't true; Lila could think of one, but it didn't matter now. There was nothing here she recognised anymore. A terrible feeling was rising through her. For no reason she could understand the image of a doll kept coming to her mind. She recognised it as a toy she'd owned, never really loved, and one day "lost." It had floated relentlessly when she tried to swim it out to sea. It just kept coming back to the shore, the expression on its bland plastic face unfalteringly trusting.

"Zombie," Lila said, turning away from the rotting body. "It's a zombie. Not really him. At least, not more than a partial copy. I just thought when I saw him . . . it . . . I thought it was. I wished it was.

I'd still think it was if the demon hadn't said so. Did me a favour, really. Sorry." She moved her hand at the room, the stone figures lying on the floor. "Mess."

How could she not have seen it was a fake? When the demon had screamed that he was cheated and leapt from his attack with the intent of doing some greater harm—that was the first time she'd even contemplated that this thing wasn't what it looked like. And it had even been cheated of its revenge for being promised an Ahriman to eat, because she'd already killed the double-crossing scum responsible.

If it had been the real Zal, he would be gone. She would have been too late. She chose the wrong target first. It all left the question—if it was a zombie, then where was Zal? Was he actually dead or was it worse?

Fabric moved quietly against her legs and she found she was wearing conventional trousers, with pockets. She put the pen inside and turned away, suddenly so nauseated by the stink of burnt flesh and demon skin that she retched and only the fact she hadn't eaten in a long time saved her from puking on the floor. At the door she almost blundered into someone, saw a black shirt, coat, the hint of a sparkle of dust.

"Mal," she croaked.

"I wish you'd wait for me before you have a party," he said with his trademark insouciance. "I missed seeing everyone's faces when hell exploded."

"Yeah, they don't get out much around here," growled Greer's voice from just behind Malachi. He passed them both, grumbling and giving orders to the staff who now streamed into the room and started clearing up. "Gimme those paperweights."

As he took the demons' remains away Malachi grasped Lila's elbow firmly and steered her out. She felt lightheaded with too many uppers, dazed, as if she were floating. She counteracted them with a heavy dose of tranquillizers.

"The dead people on your ship aren't real," she said to him, slurring drunkenly.

"Yeah, I figured," he said, walking slowly and calmly. They passed along the halls, took the elevator, and made the turns to his office. "Nice suit, by the way. Bit tight on the corset but the trousers are very smart."

"I don't like the corset," she said, eyes rolling. The sudden shift from high to low made her feel like a hungover drunk who was still swallowing the last dregs of the jar. "Too tight. Like being a sausage."

He snorted and manoeuvred her through the door into the courtyard.

She pointed at the yurt. Even the AI part of her was struggling to keep her afloat. Her kidneys and other purification systems were overloaded. It was oddly pleasing. She felt warmly part of the human race, able to say with genuine sentiment, "Your house got trashed."

"I saw that." He'd dragged out his furniture and made a room on the grass, with chairs and a blanket for a mat and his little cooler, still wired in and chugging away. "Siddown." He put her on the blanket.

The corset laces hissed and let out several inches. Lila slumped sideways and lay on her side. It was rather comfortable except that the wool was a little scratchy on her cheek and the bare skin of her arms. How did sheep manage? It must be different from the other side, she thought. "I'm really tired."

"Just fill me in; then you can sleep."

"You went missing." She yawned and lifted a finger, waving it to conduct her performance of the last few hours. "I found your office, searched it, found the sextant thingy, obviously Jones left it, gave it to Bentley, couldn't find you, went to my office, Zal was there—anyway I thought it was him—so I took him to medical, but he couldn't be revived, and then I thought I should use an elemental because they're like power and he needed power and it all seemed to add up and he's used to mainlining fire thingies, so Greer sent the water demon agent to get one, but he crossed me and brought someone to kill Zal and me instead so's he could have a shot at taking over the Ahriman dynastic line, but I had the sword so it didn't work out, though it *would have* got Zal if it had been Zal because I picked the wrong target first, I was so angry I just had to kill the scummy little sucker, but anyway it wasn't Zal, it was something off those ghost ships. Kinda lucky. What're they called? Zombie. I have to read up on those . . . I . . ." She trailed off, mind dissociating, the finger and its hand falling to the ground. There was a moment of quiet; then she snapped alert for a moment, startling Malachi and making him jump. "And Teazle is missing. In Demonia."

She fell unconscious.

Malachi sat down on his best remaining chair and took a beer out of the cooler. The early morning was almost fresh, with air coming in off the sea over the city. There was no moon, just the stars and the office lights. He leaned back, opened the bottle, and took a drink, looking up at the constellations. They were different to the ones in Faery. He'd always looked for similarities but never found any. Faeries weren't such keen observers of these things as humans and demons and elves, but he felt sure that some of those stars were the same ones he could see at home. Just not in the same places. Perhaps, he thought, Faery was round to the left some more. A turn could make all the difference.

At his feet Lila started to snore softly. Slowly, the purple fabric of the corset stole up over her chest and shoulders, then down her arms. Tiny silver motes, like the stars he'd been watching, came on in the depths of the cloth nap and drew out the familiar shapes of Tigris and the Boghopper. He tipped the bottle at the clothes in a half cheer, thanking it for giving him a friendly sky. "Tatter."

As he watched the coat become a thick cloak—the sewn stars never moved, just the cloth grew around them—he saw a shape drawn in it by slightly lighter threads. It moved, rolling over, a huge circle, no, a spiral. In the sky of the cloak it was a planet revolving, a mandala in the shape of a dragon coiled on itself tightly, wings furled, claws closed, eyes shut. It slept, but restlessly. Its handfeet twitched and the end of its tail shivered. Ripples ran beneath its armour.

"Yeah," he said to it quietly. "Yeah that's what's going on."

The picture on the cloak faded, leaving the constellations.

Malachi put his hand into his jacket pocket and found the warm, rounded shapes of hazelnuts. They were Madrigal's gift. He felt very lonely and took one out, shelled it carefully, and ate it. Immediately his spirits lifted a little and he was able to relax.

At that moment he heard steps and the door opened from the buildings. Temple Greer shambled across the path and over the grass slowly.

"Pull one up." Malachi gestured at his spare chair—a large chest covered in a half carpet and a cushion. He pointed with the neck of his bottle at the cooler.

Greer organised himself a couple of feet away next to Malachi and sat down, twisting the cap off his drink slowly. "I missed the end of the game," he said. "The Pirates won. Can you believe it? We were two six up at the half. I swear, you take your eyes off these things for a second and it all shoots to shit."

Malachi shrugged. He didn't follow human sports. They were too dull and the rules never changed.

Greer sniffed and turned the bottle, pretending to read the label with all its disclaimers. "So, was she right? Was it him?"

"Yes. No. Sort of." Malachi said. "Difficult to answer. Zombies share a spirit with the person from whom they were called, but it can be a piece without memory or feeling or awareness just as easily as a major chunk of soul. They're like elementals in that way. Elemental fragments. They can be put into corpses of the person, or other people's corpses, or any vehicle, even dolls and constructs and mechanical devices, but the last parts are hard. Mostly if there's no body to hand a master will make one out of some elemental substance and cause it to copy the physical memory of the fragment, so you get something that looks a lot like the original. But it isn't. Chop it up and you'll see."

"It's being autopsied right now. I'll go hassle them in a minute, when I get my breath back." He took a long drink. "Ghosts, zombies," Greer said. "Not something we've seen much of so far."

"You'll see a lot more," Mal sighed.

"Oh yeah?" The words sounded light enough. Malachi wasn't fooled.

"That cracking that's been going on since the Bomb . . . well, it wasn't the Bomb," Malachi said. He tried his best not to fidget as he revealed his suspicions, but it was very hard, the urge to confound, convolute, dissemble, weasel, and defraud was strong, as strong as the information was important. If he couldn't do it verbally, it expressed itself in his limbs as a manic need to get up and dance or run away. "The Bomb was just a product of the same thing as the cracks. And this is just the same. Fifty years went by here, you got bigger cracks in reality, you got more and more leakage off the other realms, more instability all over. Cosmic shattering. In that perspective it was only ever a matter of time until the most distant worlds crept up on you and invaded your space because all the worlds are starting to infiltrate each other, like coloured lights crossing and making new colours." He hesitated. He was not a great theorist but he was very convinced by this. Humbly he added. "Actually, it coulda been the Bomb. You know that'd make sense. But also, it coulda just been going to happen anyway."

Greer rubbed his face roughly with his free hand, snorting and snuffling not unlike a warthog trying to wake up. He finished and smoothed his moustache with a swipe of his index finger. "Skip to it. It's getting early."

"S'probably dragons," Malachi said, very quietly. He knew how statements like this went down with the scientific and by-their-fingernails-material-rationalist humans. If you didn't quickly provide a scaffolding that allowed them to scramble safely from an atheist world in which no invisible agents or aetheric powers existed across to a point in which invisible agents could exist as parts of a psychological intentionalist stance et cetera, then you could enjoy a suspicious, contemptuous, and frosted-over life as That Faery You Met at the Party, Mad Like All of Them but Doesn't He Dress Well? He waited, but Greer made no sudden moves. "Either they started stirring around a while back and lots of old things started to surface everywhere, inside and outs, a result of that you were able to tune to the Signal well enough to figure out how to build the bomb, set it off, and et cetera, the rest is history. *Or*, you built the bomb all by your clever selves, set it off, and that started to give them nightmares and wake them up. Either way, don't feel responsible. They move around every so often by themselves. And you weren't to know, were you?"

Greer stared down the neck of his bottle morosely. "Every so often?"

"Every few thousand years, maybe as few as two, maybe as much as a hundred thousand. Or a million. Or a billion. Now and then."

"Doing what?"

Malachi shrugged. He never understood the need humans had to try and find the reason behind everything. Surely it was just an infinite cascade of reasons that led back whimsically into the first moments of time itself? What were they going to do, go back there and fix things? The basics of the situation as it was were always more than enough for him to react to. He supposed they fancied that knowing how a thing happened meant they'd manage circumstances better the next time, but there never was a next time; there was only the one time for everything. Why did a dragon? Why did a cat? It made no sense. He struggled and, because no answer wouldn't do, said all he could think of. "Being."

"Who are . . . What do . . . Are you talking about cosmic scales of being, no pun intended?"

"Can be," Malachi said, floundering and searching for any footing he could find to get out of the question. "Or could be quantum scale. Usually on all scales. The thing you call dragon that looks like a winged lizard with claws and teeth is just a form. They like that shape. I don't know why. Probably because it looks impressive and mystic and keeps most people well away. But they don't look like anything left to themselves. They're not anchored to dimensions. Like angels. Only angels aren't anchored to time either and dragons kinda are. They're almost like manifestations of time, I guess. It's like you and god. So the aetheric and the dragon." He stopped his mouth with a fierce chug of faery lite and hoped that would be sufficient, but of course it wasn't.

"God?"

"Yeah. They're as far over the average aetheric being as god is to you." He cursed himself for carelessly putting that in and added, "Not that there is a god, of course, but if there were then that's how it would be. So don't ask me about them because I don't know. They aren't something ever bothered with me. Some people claim to channel them and speak for them, but they might just be mad."

"People like Sancha Azevedo."

Malachi rolled his beer bottle in his hands. "I knew you were going to mention her."

"Then don't act all coy about it."

"I guess she's on her way here?"

"She wouldn't come. Not even though Sarah promised her a limo and a month's pay. Mountains and Muhammad and all that jazz. Said it wasn't worth it for a zombie nobody would want revived anyway and would we please not call her until after ten in the morning about the other one because she had to do her T'ai Chi."

"She said it was a zombie?"

"Yeah, and she didn't sound pleased. In fact, she sounded rather like Mrs. Greer when I call her at three in the morning to ask her when the hell she's coming home. I gave that up, by the way. It hasn't been as much fun recently as it was for the first few years."

Malachi sighed. He took a drink and surrendered to the inevitable. "What other one?"

"Lila got a call from her sister."

Malachi looked at Greer. They shared a moment of resigned weariness.

"One we can deal with," Greer said flatly. "But nobody is prepared for this to become the next big thing. Not after the last big thing. Is it going to be the next big thing? Did your contact have an in on this?"

"You could say he had an in," Malachi confirmed, nodding slowly. "Big thing? I hope not. I don't think so. He didn't say and I didn't ask." He made it sound like Tath was someone you didn't fool around with so Greer would drop the line, but mentally he cursed himself for not doing more prying into Tath's affairs. All the talk about cards and the fruit bowl and the CuSith had made him forget to be nosy enough. And the visit to Madrigal.

"So what, is he the master of these zombies?"

Dazed, Malachi slowly refocused on the conversation at hand. "They're not . . . maybe . . . shit!" He shook his head and stared at the cloak near his feet. It was possible Tath could use zombies, more than possible, but he'd never send these particular zombies. Or would he? Was there some reason he would want to torment Lila? "I just don't know. He surely didn't send them, and he has nothing to do with ghosts."

"We need hard information," Greer said. "And fast." He moved one of his feet towards Lila in a dull pointing action. "She'll wake up in a few hours. I want something by then that I can use to keep her anchored in whatever passes for reality around here. All we need is a crazy agent with a sword that can rip holes in reality having a mental breakdown. Speaking of which pigsticker-cum-poetic accessory, I'm just going on what you wrote about it here. Nice brief. I'm still waiting for the page that tells me what I can do to get it off her or blow it to kingdom come should the need arise. And the page about how the need for that to arise can be avoided."

Malachi finished his beer and twirled the last drops around in the bottom before he tipped it up and spilled them on the grass. A little gift. He decided to opt for the faery truth, that is, the real one, and not the ten tons of horseshit-in-a-binder that the boss was asking for. "Zal is her anchor. He's your answer."

Greer made a series of faces that spoke clearly of how much he hated being at the mercy of others. His hands worked restlessly on the bottle as if he were testing it and retesting it, never satisfied. Finally he said with menace, "He'd better not be fucking dead."

"He isn't." Malachi was reasonably certainish about that.

"Find some proof." Greer chugged his drink and tossed the bottle on the grass. He got to his feet slowly and stretched his back with great caution. A joint cracked. "Before she wakes up." He began to go then turned around. "Oh, I nearly forgot, what happened to your tent?"

"Friend left me something," Malachi said. "She was being followed so she made a mess to cover her tracks. I think she might be dead."

"It's all the rage this season," Greer muttered. He went another few strides and then turned again on his heel and called as he walked backwards, stuffing his hands into his pockets. "She nixed Sandra Lane, you know." He gestured with his chin at Lila. "I'd be sorrier but I already gave at the office." Then he turned again, almost clocked the door with his head, stopped himself, yanked it open, and disappeared into the lit entrails of the building.

Malachi looked at Lila. She was sleeping more easily now, the snore even lighter. Her face was tranquil and looked more of its real-time twenty-five years than he was used to. In fact, it looked a lot less. She might have been fifteen. The red splash of hair that looked so deliberate shone vibrantly in the dark against her pale skin and the faery cloak. Through one of the windows he saw the grey face of Bentley looking out and waved to her. She curled her fingers once in an awkward society-girl kind of wave and then turned away. None of the androids had slept in the last four decades. He wondered what that was like. Even angels slept, so he'd heard.

He tossed his own bottle into the bushes and reached for another one, opened it, and let the drink sparkle on his tongue for a minute. The mildly intoxicating effects made all his troubles seem like enemies whose riling had become fond with age. It was interesting to know she could dispatch a rogue, more interesting that she'd done it and not spoken about it. The old Lila would have been mortified to crush a fly unnecessarily. He regretted her passing. On the other hand, he didn't regret the passing of Sandra Lane, not one bit. That left only four of them out there doing who knew what in the service of their mad credo. At least they'd kept quiet recently. Small mercies, he said to himself, but at least some mercies, and the Signal wasn't his business or his problem.

He nibbled another nut and considered Zal. Find Zal. That was not going to be pleasant. Find Teazle. Hard to say if that would be more or even less pleasant, but judging by tonight's gore he would rather face the Lovely Ones on the chance of more mercy than take a trip to Demonia and meet the certain absence of it. Plus, whatever Zal had become it surely couldn't be more ominous than the all-glowing, all-overconfident slayer of darkness, bringer of light, destroyer of illusions, and so forth that Teazle seemed to have mutated into down in Under. Trust demons to overcook the egg and produce a monster. Did Teazle even know what he was rushing into as he accepted the offer of that blazing energy—did he know whose it was? Malachi would bet not. Maybe the idiot even thought it belonged to him. Then again, if he *was* aware of its source, would he turn it down? He was a demon. Surely not. Live fast, channel angels, and burn out not fade away. It was horribly, end-timely ominous.

Surely, Malachi thought to himself gloomily, it was time that he stopped trying to lose all his information, as he had these hundred years or more, and tried to actually gather it like a good spy was supposed to?

He finished a nut and counted how many were left. Lots. That was good. He wasn't sure he was ready to be a good spy. Being a bad one had had so many advantages. It paid not to be in the know. Knowing was a sure way to get yourself stupidly killed. See what people did the second they knew things: off they went, mission in mind, problems arising, solutions planned on an endless goose chase of cause and event. Whereas, know nothing and you wallowed around ignorantly, of no interest to things of power, of no use to people with schemes. A kernel of sense was enough to keep you out of the way of such things. Hadn't he been doing such enormously useful work all these years keeping knowing to a minimum, for everybody?

It seemed a miracle then that he was in the middle of a churn of folk and effects that seemed unable to avoid the need to know and who were ceaselessly attractive to powers whose names should be still lost and long forgotten. One might remember them as individuals or loose gatherings of notions, but as long as they had no label you couldn't sum them up or summon them up in any way. They must not be the subject of conversation or even predicates. They had no business in the world of being, and namelessness kept them that way. Names were the most dreadful magic, with a force that enabled and made real. If some of those old things came back, the only way to get rid of them would be to lose their names, and that was almost impossible to do. He didn't want to be a part of any name-losing scenarios. Again. That had all been sorted out ages ago, and he knew exactly where not to look.

But Lila was tenacious, if unstable. It was a constant job of work to direct her away from danger. Zal was a force unto himself, but easily distracted and sufficiently alert to mind his own business, always supposing he hadn't got himself killed. Teazle . . . ugh, a wild card in the mix, all he needed. Teazle was unknown. Demons were usually deflected by better offers or higher odds. Ordinarily Mal was confident he could wrap demons around his fingers for as long as he needed to, but it looked like he wasn't going to be able to trump this one's fortunes, favours, or weaknesses. There must be something about him worth knowing, sadly, which Malachi didn't know and hadn't yet had cause to forget. He drummed his fingertips on his knees and frowned. Already he was thinking too much, and that way he'd never figure anything out.

To distract himself he decided to consider Madame Des Loupes. She was an arresting proposition.

Everyone seemed to have forgotten about her recently, even though it was her disappearance and apparent murder that had almost caused a war as Demonia demanded Teazle's repatriation from Otopia and Otopia refused both because it didn't have a treaty or Teazle and because Lila was subject to the law but Teazle didn't have a status in Otopia except as potential deportation material and they weren't about to deport what they didn't have just because some stroppy demon president who was barely out of training pants decided it must be done. Then, when Demonia insisted they knew very well Teazle was there, any fool with a juju cell in their heads could see it at any seer's shop in any town, they started a particularly ugly line of accusations that were only stopped when Greer did his under-the-table deal to agree to locate Lila and force her to do the decent thing and slaughter her husband for the good of everyone concerned. Whether or not Greer was convinced the murder conviction was a fit-up Malachi didn't know, but he thought it wouldn't have mattered either way. It was the political thing to do.

And it might not have been important if it weren't for the demon in question who had been, conveniently, forgotten.

Malachi didn't believe Madame could be killed in the manner of the crime. Her psychic skills were too massive and all-reaching to permit anyone to get near her. So what was her motive in creating such a ruckus? He didn't think anyone had anything on her. Nobody alive anyway. She must have been the instigator, then. But why? Probably it was too late to see the crime scene, although he would bet there was nothing to find there. He sighed and ate another nut.

How about a different stab? What if he, Malachi, had wanted to be forgotten? How would he go about it? Probably he would choose entropy and not catastrophe as his plan, for he was a cat and subtle by nature; but Madame was a demon, and a fine appreciation of the longueurs and uncertainties of entropy was not one of their strong suits. So, catastrophe then. The obvious path was to have oneself apparently murdered and vanish forthwith. In Demonia that would be easy to arrange, but for Madame, not so much. She would need someone of Teazle's calibre to be the villain of the piece because anything less was not believable. It was, very slightly, possible to imagine Teazle catching her off guard if he had managed not to have the idea of killing her until the very moment itself, in which case Madame's psychic mastery would have given her insufficient warning.

And the motive? On such a plan only whimsy would do. That made no sense. Teazle was not old enough to have developed that level of fanciful malice.

But what else had happened? Teazle had been on this impressive rampage. Malachi saw no sense in that either, and it was fact. However, the rampage itself had not really kicked off until Madame was dead. And he had gained nothing from killing her. She didn't have a house or own things or possess disposable powers. Teazle hadn't taken anything from her home. For a time there had been speculation that it was some kind of vengeance concerning Zal's first wife, the clairvoyant Adai, who had been universally known as Gift of Heaven We Know Not Why. But Madame had been Adai's teacher and friend and there was no suggestion of wrongdoings there, only a connection that linked Teazle, lengthily, to Madame. Gossip magazines had stated firmly that it was Madame's failure to predict Adai's death, or to tell Zal about it, that was at the root of this grudge. Malachi knew Zal did not hold grudges however. Could Teazle have known and decided to exact retroactive justice of his own?

Malachi thought it unlikely. Everyone Teazle had ever killed had been for a cast-iron reason, not a flimsy one, but his subsequent tour of death might have been enough for a jury to reasonably suppose Madame was a necessary disposal if he were to carry out his long list of executions and takeovers. Yet that very takeover made no sense to

Malachi. What was it all for? What could he hope to achieve? It could never last. Or could it? Suddenly he was flung into doubt. If Teazle really did command so much of Demonia's wealth and power, then socially their rampant alpha-wolf style of behaviour might give him enough status to override the conviction of any would-be assassin. Might Teazle have made himself actually invincible to demons? It seemed mad.

And once again it had led him off the trail. He was sure Madame wasn't dead. So Teazle hadn't killed her, though now it looked like that was perfectly viable from a demon point of view. Suppose Madame had seen his rise to power lying ahead on time's path? Wouldn't that be a prime opportunity to put a vanishing plan into action?

Malachi paused and closed his eyes. So much thinking and worrying was like being human. But the early morning was long and silent in the garden courtyard, and he didn't have much time to come up with a plan.

Back to the wheel. Let's say she vanished herself. If dragons were stirring, she'd know about that and maybe a lot of other things. Was she scared? Gone into hiding? Or perhaps bored of her reclusive, prisoner's life? More likely she would want to be out and about at such a time, and that would mean finding a new identity under which to operate. If she were skilled, intelligent, and well supported she could manage a vanish, he reckoned. Seers could be fooled, accessories bribed or murdered, and aetheric signatures remodelled by top-flight necromancers. It was possible. Also, he thought, perhaps there was an extra bonus that wasn't apparent, namely, getting rid of Teazle at some nearish future date when surely the odds would turn against him and someone would kill him. Certainly the upheaval of his spree would create a diversion for a person wanting to slip away unnoticed.

He took out his phone and called Suvidae, one of the Hunter's Chosen who had abandoned Otopia to live in Demonia where they felt more appreciated. A lot of Chosen had migrated there, or to Faery, even to Alfheim. Suvidae had a love-hate relationship with the agency, but his sense of loyalty to his home often won over his rage at their betrayal of him. After a few rings the Chosen's light voice answered hesitantly.

"Yes?"

"It's Malachi. Don't worry. I won't trouble you long."

"Let's see. I'll do you two question-and-answers for a new personal techpad."

"Midrange, no extras."

"Midrange, with case of my choice, not to exceed a hundred Otopian dollars."

"Yeah okay. What's the latest movements on the case of Madame Des Loupes?"

"Case closed. Media covers the big white thing every day, but they don't refer back to that much now. Today is all about how he's missing, of course. Endless speculations."

"People curious about Madame at all? Any investigations into her affairs going on?"

"She left a will. Stuff went to relatives. Some money spent on public goodwills. House is empty. They like to clean them out here, clean them of magic, but apparently it's hard to find someone good enough to do the job so it's waiting on that. After it's done it's for sale, as I heard. Prime site. You interested?"

"Definitely not. Thanks Suvi. Send me the bill for your toy."

"As usual. Should I look around some more?"

"Think you can be discreet?"

"I don't know. If I'm not, I'll be dead so you won't have to pay."

"Go on then."

They hung up on each other at the same moment.

Malachi finished his second bottle of beer and took out his nail file. He cleaned his fingernails and buffed them, noticing how thick they'd become—almost unsightly. As he flexed his fingers they lengthened, sliding like claws, then retracting. He hated that, but he hadn't found a way to stop it yet. Finally even that task bored him and he lay down on his spare overcoat on the grass and tucked his hands between his thighs to keep them warm.

Proof of Zal's existence, position or otherwise? The thought of obtaining it made him shudder. Might as well go the whole hog and find the guy. It would be no harder. A simple task—find the Ladies, ask them. He had spent a long time avoiding them. But since he'd seen the Fleet massing off Jones's bows he'd known they were too close, and he was doing a bad job of it. Because who was on those ships, all three? Not Jesus Christ and his lady, as the modern human words would have it, that was for sure. The Fleet belonged to an area of aetheric potential. It was something to do with the Fleet that had caused him to . . . but he'd forgotten exactly what. Anyway, he knew they should be forgot. At least their emergence had nothing to do with him. But this was so little consolation it didn't even grant him a moment's peace. They were here, crashing into Otopian shores, running aground in the primaterial plane as if they belonged there, and that was just such bad news.

He made himself stop thinking about it.

Zal's zombie—summoned or sent? Calliope Jones, dead or alive? How to find the answers to these things without stumbling into the path of horrors and nightmares? He feared there was no way, because although these matters seemed weighty and important, in the wider scale of existence they were nothing. Two missing people, albeit ones with odd connections, didn't amount to a hill of beans. An age of chaos was coming, heralded by the bomb or whatever it had been, and if he stayed attached to these difficult people, these sticky people with their sticky trajectories and unfortunate tendencies to trip over disturbing objects from older ages, then he would not be able to slip away himself, like Madame, into the shadows and escape.

He fell asleep and dreamed of rats; large, healthy, farsighted rats who rushed away from him down impossibly small channels that existed in the sides of everything, as if the whole world was a ship and all surfaces were its gunnels. With popping sounds like corks from bottles, they vanished down small black holes. He tried to winkle them out with his paw but he was too big even to fit that into the openings. After a while he tried a corkscrew that he found in his pocket and pulled out not a rat, but one of these corks. It left behind it a smooth, unbroken reality. He turned the cork over and looked at the other end. It was a tiny glass, through which he could just make out himself, peering inward, his orange eyes gigantic in the fisheye lens.

CHAPTER THIRTEEN

Zal had grown used to the end of the world. It was not as glamorous as he had been led to believe. For one thing it was dirt poor. For another it was never really daylight. Even given that these ideas made little sense at this point, they both felt wrong to him.

He paused in the course of his walk now to look out at the only non-disappointing feature. His path traced the edge of the known world, about a mile from the line where the geography and atmosphere of Under broke up and faded away. Beyond it and, he thought, around it, was a starry void not unlike deep space, except that instead of showing vast tracts of black emptiness it was filled with shimmering, endlessly flowing fields of faint light. The stars were not bright, but few, distant, tiny, and remote. The light fields moved in all directions, and sometimes made him dizzy if he looked for too long. He thought at first they were a kind of nebula, clouds of gas illumined by other objects. However, there were no other objects, so that theory hadn't lasted.

The path under his feet was bare and a little stoney. He put down his two tightly stuffed sacks—this was the way back—and sat on them to take advantage of his own speed. Lily (not her real name) did not need him, well, at all if truth be told. Mina (not her real name either) claimed she had to have a constant supply of materials or else there'd be damn trouble and he mustn't be later than the strike of six. It was 4:30-something. He had hoped to feel better for looking at the light, but he felt sad. To the other side of the strip of land he inhabited there was another zone of breaking and another miraculous spatial vast. He thought Faery must be upwards, where there seemed to be sky. There was no sun. Light came and went but cast no shadows.

He had sat here at 4:30-something every day for the last couple of decades and stared out into the end of the world, looking for clues. Around him the dull reddish ground was dusty, stoney, and uninteresting as the surface of Mars. It wasn't only figuratively dead, it was aetherically dead as well. He'd tried to find the slightest trace of earth elemental, but nothing had replied to his summons. Tests revealed the entire place to be utterly without power or life. He couldn't understand why the Sisters stayed here. They didn't have to. He'd seen them come and go.

He looked as far as he could out into the tracts. The light shimmered and waved its spectral colours, all hues, like dissolving rainbows. He tried to imagine them into shapes, but it wouldn't come; they defied shape or else he couldn't make them fit. He wondered how much longer he could stand it, how long he would have to wait. Those two unknowns weighed on him every day. Were they the same, close, far apart? Was it pointless to carry on? Was help about to arrive any minute? Even an attempt to muster a sense of hope or urgency fell flat. He was sure it was a feature of the Sisters, like this place—all of it was them. Since he had been here, there had been no real intention in him, no fancies, and at night no dreams.

He wondered if Jack the Giantkiller had pounded them out of him. That was possible. The memory was very dim, but it was one of his only ones. He recalled friends, but not much about them. Only a girl stood out in his mind clearly. She had dark hair, with a red splash in it, and robot hands, and a pretty dress. He wondered if she was a figment of his imagination, but he seemed to remember her standing close, alongside Jack, in the snow. Her silver eyes had reflected him and in them he saw himself as he used to be and knew that way that he had once been real.

He felt convinced they would come, but recently that conviction had worn away and become so threadbare there was about nothing left of it. His heart was heavy and sore. He was lost, and in Faery that meant as good as forgotten.

He bent down and saw the writing he had made yesterday in the dust. It hadn't changed—no wind—but he regrooved it with the end of his finger now, his hidden prayer to the silver-eyed girl because he was sure that she had been alive at the end. He didn't let himself think that now she may be dead.

Hurry up.

That done, he resumed staring at the lights until it was time to go. Then he got up, picked up the sacks, and walked along the path to Mina's house. It was a tidy house, white stone, a slated roof, and a tall chimney. The garden—a span of blue grass—was marked out by a low white fence without a gate. He passed through this opening and looked up to see the sky change. The closer one got to the house the more the illusion of a blue sky or a night sky receded and the light fields against the empty space revealed themselves. Directly above the chimney, so high it must be miles up, was a black circle, almost a dot. Around this the delicate webs of light spun, forming a spiral shape like a hurricane or a galaxy. The light streaked thin, into distinct lines, as it neared the edge of the circle, but the edge was sharp and what lay behind or beyond it was impossible to see. The black hole permitted no escape. The light poured up through it. He knew from long ages of observation and question that this was Mina's distaff, funnelling upwards into the loom of Faery. The sight was utterly enchanting and it filled him with despair.

He tore his gaze away from it, the only route out of the place and far beyond his reach, and hoisted the sacks through the door. Inside

Mr. V was cleaning. At least he was supposed to be cleaning, but Mina's house rarely saw either her or a visitor so there was almost nothing to do day by day and he was, as usual, sitting in the front room in the armchair beside a roaring fire, his feet up. His feet had to be up because he was a dwarf and the chair seat was large. A book was open in his tiny hands, his glasses at the end of his nose. His pipe was lit and resting on its stand, the graceful curve of its stem almost as long as one of Mr. V's arms. The smoke had already quietly perfumed the room. Zal took a deep breath and smelled cherries, and toasted plum brandy, and cinnamon and old roses. He said hello and Mr. V smiled his white-bearded Father Christmas smile that made his eyes crinkle and almost entirely hide their light green sparkle.

"Master Zal. Got the day's allotted thread?"

"No, it's those people I murdered the other day. The rats dug up the bodies and now I thought I'd put them down the waste disposal in the sink."

Mr. V beamed. "Excellent." He picked up a feather duster from the seat next to him and waved it around idly. "I'm working hard myself."

Zal couldn't dislike Mr. V, for all that he had tried to haul any kind of sense out of the little old guy and never had managed to. The dwarf was round, good-humoured, endlessly patient, and even kind.

"Come and look in the fire." He often said that.

Zal went over and looked. It was easier to do what Mr. V asked because he'd keep asking until you did. The flames were roaring heartily on a bed of coals. Zal was careful not to get too close. It was extremely hot.

"What do you see?"

This was a difficult question. Zal knew that Mr. V was hoping he would see something, but so far he hadn't managed to see anything but flames. He'd tried lying a couple of times, but the dwarf had always chuckled and called him a wee fiend of a fibber, a tinkus-minkus, a par-celler of verily old ropies, and other such silly names. For a reason he didn't understand Zal wanted badly to please Mr. V and see something. Mr. V seemed to have nothing at all in his tiny life except dusting Mina's knickknacks, cooking the odd meal, and perusing an infinite variety of small journals out of which he would read tall tales to Zal, if it was late and Zal was particularly miserable. Also, apart from Mr. V, Modgey the horse, and Tubianca the cat there was nobody to talk to at all and nothing to do. Fire-staring was really quite appealing.

He looked into the fire. Nothing happened. He tried to create shapes, figures, monsters from the id, but all he could see was flame leaping on the glowing rock, dancing merrily, never repeating, quite without meaning. If there was more to this than providing a bit of hackneyed light entertainment for Mr. V, it was not obvious to a naked elfin eye.

Not that he had one of those to throw around. He saw quite well as it happened, and he could move all right, so much so that he was still surprised sometimes to look down and find that he was made of cloth.

A glance in any mirror—and there were many at Lily's house— revealed the truth of his current existence. He was shorter than he used to be, but with the old proportions so that his limbs were long and lean, his torso verging on skinny, his face squared at the jaw with a chin that had been difficult to sew and had ended up pointed when Lily pricked her finger on the needle and lost her temper. His ears were satin with fringed edges, supported by fine wires that ended some- where in his head. His hair was combed-out horsehair, flaxen but as thick as straw. His eyes were stitched in brightly coloured thread with a painted black slash in each centre that somehow functioned perfectly as a pupil even though he had never seen it move.

The shadows of his true form showed as purple-black ink stains on the surface of his white cotton body, giving the illusion of contours. His hands were thick fingered and heavy and his limbs bent where they were stitched at the joints. That was what came of being stuffed with Mina's old ends. She had quite a lot of these unused bits of lives that she said just couldn't be fitted in—the whole subject was guaranteed to make her cross—but she hated just burning them up on the fireplace and had been glad to spend a few years' collecting in order to find enough of them to pad him out and make him useful. For that's what he was at the end of it all, a servant—a toy who had ceased to be terribly interesting about thirty years ago and was now passing the remnants of eternity doing little jobs that he was fit for. They didn't intend to be unkind. Lily had promised, after all, to mend him if she could.

Zal was fed up with what they intended. He watched for a few more minutes and then straightened up. "I don't see anything but the fire."

Mr. V nodded brightly and rested his book on his legs so that he could pick up his pipe and take a draw. "Just humour an old man and look again, would you? I used to love seeing things in the fire. Can't really do it so much now. Bothersome."

"Mina needs her stuff," Zal objected weakly. Mr. V rarely asked for a second go. He wondered if something was troubling the old guy.

Mr. V beamed at him, rosy cheeks like small red apples. He had a winning smile and perfect teeth, despite the amount of tobacco he got through. Only the whites of his eyes had taken on a slightly nicotinic colour, like the uncleaned ceiling of an old-time inn. He patted the pockets of his tweed waistcoat and found his tobacco pouch, showing no sign of impatience as he began the lengthy ritual of emptying and refilling the pipe bowl.

"Okay." Zal let his slight rebellion leak through but moved back for another look. He felt that it was good to still have resentment. At least it was something.

"There's a good lad," Mr. V said, scraping the pipe bowl out with a little tool from his pocket.

"I wish you'd tell me what I'm supposed to see." One of Zal's regular complaints.

"Oh but I can't, or you won't see it." Mr. V's standard reply. "You'll see something like it made up by your mind."

"I'm not psychic, you know." One of Zal's standard grumbles.

"If you were it would be very surprising because you have lint for brains, my dear fellow. But I have high hopes for you." One of Mr. V's under-the-top-ten answers.

"Are you sure you aren't called Gepetto?" A standard Zal shot across the bows.

"I am very sure." Mr. V chuckled and paused in his pipe deconstruction to lift and wave the duster. "I've never had the hands for carpentry." The light gleamed off his perfectly buffed nails. They were thick and as yellow as horn, a sign, he claimed, of his extreme old age.

"What does V stand for?" Zal sometimes asked this.

"Well," Mr. V mused amiably. "Not Vendetta."

"Venice?"

"No."

"Veronica?"

"No."

"Verifiably insane?"

"No."

Zal had run out of Vs for the time being but then some more came at him in a rush. "Verisimilitude, victory, vanquish, vivify, viper, vector, vehicle?"

"No. I do like Vanquish though."

Zal stared at the flames. They danced, mindless and evanescent. "This is so pointless."

"No, no it isn't. You must never say that!" Mr. V cried, sitting forward and reaching out to close his book and put it to one side. There was an almost desperate tinge to his voice.

"Yes, it is. I am stuck here forever until I moulder, or fray, or rot, or get forgotten by them, or even by you," Zal felt a surge of anger, but it quickly died back into misery. "There's no way out. I might as well . . ." And then he stopped.

"You might as well . . . ?" Mr. V said encouragingly, as if to a sobbing child.

"I might as well throw—"

"Don't say it." Mr. V held up a stubby finger quickly to stall Zal and then used it to point upwards, upstairs, to the main room where Mina was working. Then he pointed towards the kitchen, where it was possible that Tubianca the white cat was lurking.

Zal sat back on his heels and stared at the dwarf. He'd never thought Mr. V had a nasty bone in his body, but suddenly he wasn't sure.

"Now you know," the dwarf said quietly, his emerald stare intent on Zal, holding him in place. He smoothed his long silver white beard and curled it around his fingers. "You know something important. So don't forget it."

"But I'll die," Zal said.

"Will you?" Mr. V bounced forwards a little more until his feet in their soft striped socks overhung the edge of the chair. He was serious. "I don't think so."

"Easy for you to say." Zal felt an urge to move away from the chance of being pushed into the flames. He would certainly go up in smoke in seconds.

"Don't forget where we are," the dwarf said, and winked. His cherubic smile returned. "Now," he said, pulling his book forward. "Now that you understand one thing, I need you to do me a little favour. Maybe afterwards you will understand another thing."

"Oh." Zal was curious, in spite of what had just happened. He felt strangely lightheaded, so much so he almost forgot to be wary and listen carefully to the words. He didn't forget to wonder why Mr. V was being so apparently kind, though he wasn't about to ask right out.

Mr. V cleared his throat lightly and whispered. "Yes. I want you to take this book over to Lily's house next time you go there and when she is busy you are to take it into the attic."

Zal pulled a face. "Oh I've been there, it's full of—"

The dwarf's finger was suddenly pressed against the stitches of his mouth. He stopped. The green stare in Mr. V's merry eyes was suddenly firm and not a little hypnotic. It would have been comical, except nothing in Zal wanted to laugh.

"The book will show you where to go. When you get there, pick up what you find to bring to me and put the book in its place. Come straight back and do not speak to anyone on the way, no matter what happens. You promise me?" His eyes became mild again, almost rheumy.

Zal looked at the book. It was very ordinary, hardbacked, covered in a moss-green canvas, without any lettering on the cover. "Are you in some kind of trouble?"

"What? No. No, lad. I just mean to borrow something for a little while and I need to put something in its place you see, so as it isn't missed. We'll put it back after. I promise you won't be in any trouble."

Zal had heard promises of this kind many times. They were the kind of promise that set peals of alarms ringing. They were scurvy and called to the pirate in his spirit. He was intrigued, and that was as much of anything interesting as had happened to him since he had been here. He was cheered. "All right." He took the volume and slipped it into the inside pocket of his long felt jacket.

"Excellent!" Mr. V bounced back in his seat, happy as a spring lamb. He resumed cleaning his pipe. "Now there's no rush. But don't forget, no talking on the way back. No matter what."

"Sure." Zal could go days without speaking to anyone anyway. "I have to get the sacks. . . ."

"Yes, yes! To the mistress. Lovely. You're a good lad."

Zal frowned and went to do as he had to.

Mina was in the upstairs apartment. Zal opened the door after knocking and went inside. There were no dividing walls up here, just the one door, and then a large open space of scrubbed wooden boards and plain walls beneath the open sky. In the centre a large fireplace supported the glowing form of the most curious firedogs. They were in the form of serpents and shone hot from the fire, but each one a different colour and unique shade. Atop their backs there were no logs or any fuel, just a ball of white-hot flame, bobbing lightly as an apple in a water barrel. Zal had long figured this for a fire elemental of a high order, but its shape and particularity were confusing. Around this fire Mina paced.

She was a small girl of about seven years. She wore her dark hair in two ponytails at the sides of her head, where they stuck out like floppy hound ears, held fast by pink and gold elastic bands. Her skin was tea coloured and her eyes as black as black could be so that it seemed like they had no pupils at all. She was wearing, as usual, a party dress in dazzling blue and pink, with silver stars and a small red cape at the back. She'd been at work a while, and the cape was hanging off one shoulder and her hair was frizzing where strands worked loose around her face. In one hand she had a fistful of brightly coloured strands of thread. With the other she worked a strand loose, examined it, talked to it, twirled it in her fingers, and then tossed it into the fire.

There was no smoke, but after a moment a dart of light would shoot upwards into the tiny black eye above them in the sky and be lost to sight. Then she would start working on another one. Beside the wall near Zal were two baskets. They still had threads in them, but he emptied the sacks and topped them up again.

Mina noticed him and paused. She frowned and put her hands on her hips in a scolding manner. "Oh Zal," she said. "What happened to your leg?"

He looked down but he didn't see anything; then, just below the hem of his trousers, he noticed the end of a green thread.

"Come here," Mina ordered. She pushed her handful of lengths into the pocket of her dress.

He went there, reluctantly, and pulled up the leg of the trousers. What he saw made him feel sick. Mina gasped, and her hands flew to her face.

Some*thing* had nibbled his leg, made a hole in it, and pulled out the stuffing until it was hanging in a gout, some strands dangling all the way to his ankle.

After a second Mina regained herself and pushed Zal over onto his back—a gesture that cost her nothing but would have been impossible for him to resist had he tried to. She pulled him to her by the ankle and peered more closely. He tried to see what she was doing as she poked about, but he felt no pain. Obviously that was how it had happened. His body did not feel pain, or much of anything. To realise that it could be easily damaged like this, chewed, savaged, was horrifying. To realise there was something here that was ready to chew even more so.

"What is it?" he demanded.

"Some's missing," Mina said with angry conviction. She poked the remains back into place, rather roughly, and reached into another pocket, where short bits of thread were tangled together in balls. She added one of these balls and then cursed. "Lily will have to fix you or it'll fall out again." She stared at the hole and then, still holding his leg, looked sideways into the corner of the room, clearly thinking hard.

"But what happened?"

"Bit of you been stole," she said. "Must be a rat." She sat down with a thump and then pulled a couple of long strands out and set to working them with her nimble little fingers. He saw her shaping a simple doll out of them, as he'd watched someone else do, a long time ago. She twirled and tied, making arms, legs, a head. Then she dabbed the thing on her tongue and set it on the palm of her hand.

It stood attentively, listening, growing before his eyes into a strong, dark figure with gleaming eyes like dots of jet. It had the long legs of a satyr and a long narrow tail and a ferocious number of whiskers about its head.

"Mogu, hunt me that rat," Mina said to it.

The doll creature, imp sized now, leapt off her hand and scampered away, sniffing. Its tiny claws scratched the boards, pattered, hesitated, pattered, and then it had gone.

"Stole?" Zal ventured, seeing Mina's look turn thoughtful again.

"Someone making something," Mina said. Her eyes narrowed

craftily. "Stealing from under our noses. Someone very clever. Or thinks they are. Should have been more careful though." She clapped her hands. "Good games! Get up now and run to Lily. Tell her what I said and to fix your leg."

"Making something?"

But Mina was already standing up, her expression getting the glassy look he knew meant she was no longer hearing him. She began to work again.

Zal suppressed the urge to run to Mr. V and cry. He went carefully back downstairs, trying not to do much with the damaged leg, though it felt no weaker than the other one. As he passed the kitchen he felt a draft of air and saw Tubianca coming out. She eyed him, her plumed tail twitching.

Tubianca was a very large, pure white cat, with a round face, a tiny black nose, a tiny pink mouth, and huge lavender-coloured eyes. Thick, luxuriantly long fur covered every bit of her. "What are you doing?" Her voice was as smooth as cream with the kind of depersonalised interest that made Zal think of freezing railway station platforms or groups of young politicised elves at a rally. She had never taken much notice of him, except once or twice as a pouncing object, an experience he heartily longed never to repeat. Lily had sewn him up before.

"Mina sent me to Lily's," he said, truthfully, because Tubianca could detect any kind of lie and would anger to a lacerating rage in a flash.

"I thought I heard mention of rats." She padded silently out into the hall and put herself between him and the door. "And earlier Mr. V was talking to you about fires. Why is that? It's high time you were in the rag basket with all the rest of the pointless little experiments. Why would anyone talk to you, you useless, uninteresting, slow-footed sack of worthless ends?"

"I don't know," Zal said, glad that she wasn't the best questioner in the world. He took a few more steps, but any farther would take him within easy reach of Tubianca's paws so he had to stop. "Excuse me, please."

She ignored him. "What rats could there be? It cannot be. You must have fallen on a tack. What did she say?"

Zal told her, omitting the part about making things. Seeing her round eyes narrow to slits he took a risk on her pride and added, "Don't worry though, she already sent a doodoll to catch it."

"What?!" Tubianca bristled, and without another word she was past him and up the stairs in a streak of white ire.

Zal took his chance and ran out the door and up the path as fast as he possibly could. He made almost no sound, but all the way he seemed to feel the cat's baleful stare on his back. The clear evidence of his own vulnerability filled him with horror once again as it had before when he had been shredded by her claws. It was a long time ago now and he'd nearly forgotten it, but he hadn't forgotten it enough to stop running.

He hated running to Lily to be doctored, but he had no choice. Or had he? He slowed down, looking back and seeing the path clear. Mr. V had been trying to tell him that he had. There was no trusting faeries—he had to remember that, but he didn't want to. He badly didn't want to. As he reached Lily's imposing door he rang the bell at the silver pull, and the book in his pocket banged against his chest. At least he had a good reason to seem nervous.

There was a pause and then the door was opened. Lily looked out, then down. She was tall, powerful, and pregnant, an imposingly healthy woman with a practical gaze whose actual colouring and appearance fluctuated several times a second so that she seemed to be a universal avatar of female promise. More than once he saw her ears lengthen and bones refine themselves to elfin. She had other forms, but for him she kept it simple. Her clothes were immaculately tailored and stuck about all over with needles and pins of various sizes and shapes. Their points winked like stars. She spoke as if he had interrupted something very important, with a vexed, harried air, "Have you come for . . . ? What have you come for?"

He felt the brief blight of her confusion and her disappointment in him for the millionth time, but it was old news. His stories had run out long ago, and he was used to the role of inconvenient child. "Mina sent me. Something ate my leg." He showed her. "She sent Mogu to hunt it."

Lily frowned and her face went cold. "Come in."

He endured the mending without looking at what she was doing. She hummed to herself the while, like an angry bee, and finally, snapping the last thread and putting the needle in her lapel, she said with pleasure, "It has been many ages since someone dared steal from us. I would like to see this person. And I'd like to see Glinda."

Zal knew this was not-the-name for the third sister. He'd never seen her.

"And I suppose 'biancs needs a kick up the arse," added Lily. "Letting it in as if she had nothing better to do. Maybe she'll redeem herself by finding how it got here."

"Lily," Zal murmured to get her attention, quietly, in case she didn't want to be interrupted. He often wanted to talk to her, or anyone, but in the sisters' case if they weren't in the mood then it was useless, and irritating them was a big mistake. He could feel this as a certainty so implacable and frightening that he had never even tried it.

"Mmn, what is it?"

He steeled himself for retaliation. "You promised."

Like Mina, she had a way of looking at someone that was so acute it was like being pinned under the most powerful microscope. "Yes, I did," she said. "But consider this. Would you like her to come here?"

The answer to that was obviously not. He had supposed as much. He couldn't understand at all what she got out of his being there. "I want to leave."

"Do you? Well, before we think about that we have to deal with this rat business." It had clearly put her in a good mood. She was almost indulgent.

Such luck could come once in an aeon here. He braced himself and asked as if it had been eating him up for ages, which it had, so no worries. "Who *is* Mr. V?"

"Mr. who? Oh. Well. Nobody you need to bother about. He's Lily's little helper. Odd-job man. That's all. Now fetch my coat and hat. It's time we paid a visit to Glinda." With a pretended annoyance she began to pull all the needles and pins out of her dress bodice and put them into a silver holder, but Zal could tell she was happy, because her hum had started to have a kind of tune in it that you might almost describe as perky. However, there were also times, and this was one of them, where he was reminded that what appeared to be going on here was only an illusion. As she got herself ready the world shivered and shifted around her, instead of the other way about, and he saw for an instant things that defied his ability to understand, huge and yet tiny forces of utter and no magic at all, underpinning the thin, colourful skim with the steadfastness of a mountain and the flimsiness of thin air. He closed his eyes and held the doorframe for an instant, blinded.

As he was regaining his balance he realised Lily had futzed her reply. He didn't know why she had, but he did know suddenly that she wasn't entirely happy about Mr. V's position. That was two things he knew, and he would bet that this was not the second thing Mr. V had been thinking of when he said Zal would learn more. Unfortunately he had no reason or way to reach the attic now that they were fussing about leaving. Lily tugged at her skirt, muttered something about Glinda stealing that dress and hiding it away—something she said often with great rancour—and then, after she'd dragged a brush through her hair and practiced a couple of expressions (polite interest, detached understanding, and what could have been affectionate condescension) in the hall mirror they were off.

The path, which had never gone farther than Lily's house, stretched off into the distance and around a bend. Zal had to trot a step in three to keep up with Lily as she strode out, whistling, her hair streaming behind her. As he did so her words repeated through his head and he knew a third thing, because it was obvious now that he'd been reminded of his real position here as the worthless fluff. He didn't want the silver-eyed girl to come here and be stuck with him until forever, but obviously for some reason, Lily did.

The day that had begun so unpromisingly was now so interesting Zal was happy. He felt there were many things to think of that could spoil that if he wasn't very very careful, so for the time being he didn't think and enjoyed himself with the anticipation of more discoveries all the way to Glinda's house.

CHAPTER FOURTEEN

Lila woke up with the sun shining on her face. For a moment she didn't know where she was. She could see grass and trees, but then the glass wall of the building became familiar beyond them and she realised she was still at work. Lifting her head she looked around and saw Malachi's yurt, flaps opened wide. Inside it Malachi was down to his rolled-up shirtsleeves, cleaning. Outside it most of his possessions lay broken in a heap next to the gravel path. Next to her a tartan thermos flask and a paper sandwich bag lay side by side. She reached out for them, and a heavy weight of purple silk velvet slithered off her arm. She felt the air suddenly cool on her hand and looked down to see herself swathed in the heavy cloth.

She raised an eyebrow, but she felt too sleepy to react otherwise. The flask contained coffee, the sandwich was tuna salad. Salad was wrong for breakfast, but her stomach was hurting. She sat up and ate it, chewing slowly, watching Malachi fuss and fiddle with his few remaining things, polishing his desk, using a handheld vacuum cleaner on his rugs and the felt walls. It was quite peaceful. After sleep her AI systems remained on standby until she let them work, so she didn't let them. Her memories of the night before were bad enough.

At last Malachi glanced her way. He abandoned his dusting and snatched his jacket and coat up from their hangers before striding over to her. In spite of his efforts and the state of the place he looked immaculate, his short hair glittering with coal-dust glamour. "At last. Thought you'd never rejoin us."

Lila balled up the sandwich bag and tossed it over his head onto the trash pile. She swallowed, yawned, and peered up at him. "Who says I have?"

"We have to make a house call."

Lila scowled, unscrewed the coffee mug cap, and sniffed. It was a latte, with caramel syrup, boiling hot. She gloated over it secretly. "Not until I finish this we don't. Take a pew."

Malachi was buttoning his cuffs. He shrugged the jacket on, adjusted it, and did up one button. "We shouldn't be late." He checked his watch. "Already a bit tight on time. It's after nine, you know."

"So?"

She was reluctant to spoil the moment but considered the sandwich and the drink and conceded a few notches to him, "Who are we going to see?"

His reply was offhand. "Azevedo. She's a medium. Or a seer. One of the Children."

"I guess it's not a care visit."

"Only for you. We're going about your sister."

"Great." She didn't want to think about that, so of course it was first thing on the agenda. "Anything else?"

"I think she can help us find Zal."

Lila squinted up at him as he shimmied into his long coat and pulled the sleeves of his jacket until they fit inside correctly. She tried to distract herself from the sharp spark of hope that was trying to find life inside her. "D'you think fifty years has passed for him too?"

"I don't know," he said honestly after a short pause. "It wouldn't be that much, for an elf."

"I wasn't worried about him being old," she said, though now she thought of it maybe she was. "But . . ." She didn't finish. She wanted to say that a lot of things could change in that kind of time, except she was looking at someone who seemed not to have. "I'm not sure that the message I got was from him."

Malachi nodded. "Azevedo will be able to tell."

Now that she'd started her mind was loading up on problems. "That thing, last night, the demon. After we see her I have to get back to Demonia and look for T. I think he's in trouble."

"Understatement of the century. I think you should stay away from Demonia or it'll be the last thing you do." He frowned.

"Yeah but . . . he was looking for something. For me. I feel—"

"What? Responsible? I don't think so. No. It's a stupid idea. No." He saw that his reason was having no effect and changed tack. "Anyway, what trouble could he be in? Think about it. You might even make him look bad, rushing to help."

She drank the coffee. It was delicious. "We'll see."

Malachi groaned inwardly. He didn't think now was the moment to share his intuition about Teazle's circumstances. He had to save that for when she really started steaming off. But because he couldn't use it he found himself blurting out what had been on his mind while he was trying to bring order back to his office. "Do you ever think about after?"

She scowled again. "Huh?"

"Here you are, days back from Under, fifty years gone, and the first thing you do is go all out to put the gang back together. Some of us waited. Some didn't. Or couldn't. Point is, what about after? What is your plan? You're burning all your boats just to get Zal. You think that's going to fix things?" He was appalled to find he sounded exactly like somebody's hysterical middle-aged mother.

She drained the coffee mug, screwed the top on, and put it down on the grass. "Nothing can be fixed. So what? Zal always said 'don't look down.'"

"But he did." They both knew it was true, but Malachi could see she wasn't about to stop. There was an implacable force inside her now that he'd never seen before their short, ill-fated run into Faery. It made his blood run cold sometimes. He had nothing with which to stop her. Couldn't even apply a brake. He could help her, or he could leave and that was it. "Who the hell put you in charge?" he said angrily. He knew it was a bad reaction. He put his hands in his pockets and found his car keys. "Ah shit, I'll meet you in the lot."

She watched him stalk away into the building. She remembered when she'd had manners and been polite. It was a long time ago. She got to her feet and shook out the cloak. Its mood had changed to something more serious apparently. It sat heavily on her, like theatre curtains, with a hood hanging at her back over a short shoulder cape that covered the arm slits in the main body. The hem was weighted. Beneath it she was free to be herself today. The leather and metal of the body armour she was used to moved easily, like her skin. It was her skin. She let it grow up to her collarbones and neck until only her hands and face were free, were human. Walking to the car park was worse than she thought it would be. Every step felt like a step towards an execution. Against her skin she could just detect the inert length of the black pen. She saw it scything through the demon in her mind's eye, saw the creature buckling and folding impossibly into the blade, sucked away, its howls of fury becoming screams of despair. Where had it gone? She didn't care.

She got in the car without a word, and Malachi leaned back on the old seats and spun them out into the growing warmth of midmorning downtown. After the confines and events at the agency, driving down the hills into the city's heart was like riding a slowly splurging river into a land of calm, colour, and normality. Lila found herself leaning on the door, hanging out of it, watching the people on the street as they went about their business. She was almost used to the way they looked, their peculiar clothing with its huge variety of anachronistic and out-world styles, the fact that everything on sale reflected a fascination with demons, fey, and elves yet she saw none of these on the street. It was like a hobby, or a fetish for most, or maybe in her good moments she thought it was the humans putting a toe in the water.

News scans flashed headlines at her, which she accepted only because she saw the word "ghost" in the leaders. Journalists and photographers had found one of the wrecks and squeezed out some footage past the agency suppression, or been allowed to leak it, she wasn't sure.

After "Mysterious wrecks pile up on South Bay Shores" it read "Today the beaches of the South Bay area were visited by the unearthly ships of yesteryear. Live-shot pictures of the doomed vessel show clearly a glow (the images pulsed to show where) and identifying features of this one-time legendary craft, *The Golden Hind* *link to more about the Hind*. Outworld specialist groups claim this is just part of the increasing invasion of Otopian space by manifestations from the Beyond *link to claims* *link to manifestation* *link to Beyond*. Meanwhile government officials deny there is any upsurge in the number of recorded anomalies in the Bay area *link to govt statistics* and say there is nothing unusual going on. Those of us who remember the Hunter's Reign may like to consider otherwise *link to Hunter's Reign*.

Lila drilled out a few links and saw that the government was still sticking to its rationalist materialist line, though this was creaky and looked more like a matter of pride and determination than any scientific effort to achieve objective reality. She wondered how it had lasted so long and asked Malachi.

"You are a species under siege," he said, as if it was old-hat. "Such is what you do."

"Wasn't Faeryever invaded?"

"Not after the first few attempts," he said. "The demons and elves skirmish with one another in times of great tedium. Incursions into Faery are constant, but usually where people want to get a specific thing or see a specific person."

"I guess you all defend yourselves with magic."

"We do. And don't forget, no faery would last long in Alfheim, not awake. And no elf would enjoy a stay in Faery. The demons . . . well, you know them. It's best for all of us if we stay close to home."

"And what do we got? Nothing?"

His silence went on a touch too long. "You are sadly a very fit prey and marketplace for all of us. In the old times you were protected by your position—you were a dimensional remove from us and very hard to connect with in any material way. The Bomb Event finished that, and the Hunter's Reign proved to anyone who wanted it proved that aetheric beings could flourish here without erosion, even if there was nothing here of any useful power or interest." He cleared his throat and took a ramp with rather abrupt speed. They started to cross the Andalune Bridge's perfect span across the water to South Bay.

Lila sat up, "Hey, where are we going?"

"You'll see."

She frowned and sat back in the uncomfortable genuine upholstery of the seat. "So what is this ghost emergence? Are they just slow to find us?"

"I think you'll get some answers where we're going."

She watched the city fall back in the rearview mirror. "So how many other people have dead relatives phoning them?"

Malachi's hands tightened and then released the wheel. "Some," he said. "Apparitions and hearing voices are up to twenty reports a day, and that doesn't include the mentally disturbed. But they're ghosts. I sent some people down there last night to your house. You don't have that. In your office you got—"

"A zombie." She peered at him. "I got two zombies?"

"Looks maybe."

"Ugh!" She closed her eyes and concentrated on the feeling of her hair being whipped by the wind coming over the shield. "It's because of that damn pen."

"Yeah I'd have thought so."

"Shit." They came off the bridge and Malachi took the coast road. "The ships are the same?" she asked.

"I think so," he said.

"Then, are they really, I mean . . ."

"Just wait, Lila!"

She shut up and listened to the engine. At least this car had one. "You need to get the timing sorted out."

"Yeah, I will."

"Okay." She waited for a few more turns and then looked at him with disbelief as they braked and pulled left into the darkness of over-hanging trees. "The Folly?"

"You wanted to see her. You get your wish."

"*This* is Azevedo's house? Why didn't you tell me?"

"Because you wouldn't have let her alone yesterday."

"What? I was the one who wanted to stay because she was upset."

"But she said to go. She didn't want you around. When she doesn't want you, best not to stay, not if you want her help in the future. She doesn't belong to us, Lila."

Lila fished around in the turmoil of her feelings, trying to find any that would sit still long enough to form a reaction. The car wallowed through the twists and turns of the driveway. Under the trees she saw the faces of elementals forming and dissipating. "Since when am I the bad guy?"

"Are you?"

"What the hell is that supposed to mean? Why are you on my case suddenly?"

Malachi thumped the steering wheel and they veered towards a ditch. He got it back and turned them to face the brooding slump of the house, then hit the brakes and pulled them up sharply. The engine grumbled under the hood. "I wish you'd back off. Slow down. You've killed two people in two days and you act like it was nothing. Where is that coming from? Where inside you is not bothered by this any-more? Because I'm bothered by it."

She felt her nostrils flare, "Gee, I don't know, maybe I was traumatised by seeing my file with the words 'Unpredictable Outcomes—Terminate' written on it, or perhaps my morals got flushed down the river of blood I had to endure in Demonia while I was doing the good works of the day. Or maybe when homicidal lunatics come threatening me I don't take it as well as I ought to. I mean, not like anyone tried to kill me recently. How should I be taking it, Malachi? Tell me. Because you were the one bitching at me to toughen up and fly right, and now you're saying slow down and what? What am I supposed to slow down for? So some bastard can catch me and blow me to bits? Because every son of a bitch in at least one world wants to, probably with good reason. And let's not forget the interference of your friendly powers." She plucked at the cape. "But no, let's forget that and pretend it's another day at the agency and we have all the time in the world."

He was gripping the wheel so hard he thought he was going to break it. His claws had emerged and were cutting into the skin of his palms. "I am out of my depth," he said after a moment had passed. "No. I'm afraid. That's what." He made himself let go and massaged his palms in an effort to get the tendons to relax so the claws would recede. He showed her his hands, ugly and beastlike as they were. "I don't like to be this. The planes seem to be tilting towards older times, chaos. I liked order, and neatness and small stuff. I liked feeling in charge and on the top of things. And you—you were easy to get along with, you asked me for advice, you listened. I was something. I had a purpose. I felt like I was in the right place. I didn't think it would end so soon and become this . . . war."

Lila rubbed her face. "It's not a war."

"Feels like one."

"It's not a war, but you don't get to boss me," she said. She reached out and put her hand on his shoulder. "But you do get to tell me when I'm going over the top."

"You're not," he said, mollified. He took out one of his handkerchiefs and dabbed a spot of blood off his hand. "I want to lock you in a vault and keep you out of trouble because your trouble is so big and I don't want to lose you. Sorry."

"Hey." She leaned across and gave him a hug. It was awkward with the gearshift between them but she made it. Tears threatened and she had to fight to keep them down. The warmth and tenderness of the moment felt like they were enough to undo all her efforts at self-control. She had to pull back long before she wanted to. "It'll be all right," she said with a confidence she didn't feel.

"Yeah," he said, released the brake, and let them roll up the last hundred metres to the house. They parked and in the silence following the engine's last note they listened to the sound of the gulls circling.

Malachi got out first and led the way. He didn't have to knock. The door opened as he reached it, though it was hard to see inside because the interior was unlit and the hall had no windows except a single skylight.

"Come in," said a woman's voice with a strong Latin accent.

Malachi thanked her quietly and moved forwards. Lila hesitated. She remembered this door in a better state, just months ago in her experience, when Zal had rented the house. Demon bodyguards had stood outside it and his manager, the effervescent (not) Jolene, had answered it. She could still see the woman striding over the black-and-white marble floor, heels clacking, suit perfect, anxiety visible in every tough and competent little movement she made as she pretended she was fine with a massive demon drop-in party, catering for hundreds, playing servant to the Queen of Pop, Sorcha the Scorcher, Zal's sister. Where was Jolene? Was she even alive? Lila shivered. What would Jolene have made of Zal's sudden disappearance? Lila didn't even know what the papers had said in those days. She wasn't about to look now.

In those days Lila had thought Zal was just a jumped-up elf egoist, Sorcha was ditto from the other side, and that her job as rock star's minder would be mercifully soon over. She'd go back to the agency, learn to live with some prosthetics, and keep an eye on her family from afar whilst doing good works probably somewhere not too far above traffic duty for a year or two.

The hell with memories, she thought, and moved forwards into the sepulchral gloom and damp of the hall. The building's familiar sense of presence enveloped her. It seemed to have sunk farther into the ground since she was last here, but the dirt on the skylights, the growth of grass and weeds on the flat roofs, and the general dilapidation probably weren't helping. As she passed the threshold Lila looked for their owner, curious to see who and what she'd noticed the day before. She found herself face-to-face with a ghost.

No, she thought, a split second later as the woman's transparency suddenly vanished to nothing, then flickered and was equally suddenly whole and firmly three dimensional. Not a ghost. Something else. Something she had no idea what, though her senses and AI had an explanation at hand. Sancha Azevedo was phasing in and out of reality at randomised intervals and incomplete sequences. She was occupying their linear time sporadically. The only good part was that the intervals were so brief it was almost as if she were completely present. Looking at her was like seeing a character in a rough animated cartoon book being flicked through by a clumsy thumb.

When she was present enough to see, Azevedo was a short, thin Latino woman of about forty-five with long black hair tied in a single braid. She wore jeans, a T-shirt, and a long flowing over-robe in a fashionable ethnic print. She had beautiful handmade cowboy boots on and surprisingly pale blue eyes. Those two things stuck in Lila's attention as she recovered from the initial shock of the meeting.

"Ms. Azevedo, this is Agent Black," Malachi said.

"I was expecting you. Call me Sancha," said the woman.

Lila was about to reply when a movement caught her eye. She looked and saw, crossing the corridor, a thinner, more transparent version of Sancha Azevedo walking with a steaming drink in her hand. It moved silently into a side room. She paused with her mouth open, greeting forgotten, her hand reaching for the other's hand to shake it. She felt fingers close on her fingers and give a squeeze.

"Don't mind me," the half-fey said with evident pleasure at being able to make the statement. "You'll see a lot of me. But this is the one that does the talking right here."

"You're a walker," Lila said. "Like Jones."

"A strandloper, yes." The blue eyes sparkled with amusement at Lila's discomfiture. "But not like Calliope. Now isn't that a strange name to call a girl?"

"She was one of the Muses," Lila said, glad to find something to say. "From the old Greek. Orpheus was her son."

"Is that right?" Sancha Azevedo looked pleased. "I thought it was something to do with fairground music, you know, but at least that's better." She closed the door after them and an automatic set of locks bolted home, making a thudding noise like something heavy falling down stairs.

"Expecting someone?" Malachi asked.

Azevedo made the kind of noncommittal shrug that said she was and she wasn't. "This is an odd place full of odd things. I don't need too much of that."

"But why did you come here?" Lila blurted, caught short in the act of following the woman by another apparition of her which, seeing none of them, moved quickly through and out the solid door.

"That was yesterday." She pointed down the long corridor that led to most of the rest of the house directly from the front door. "Terribly careless feng shui right here. If you don't come in, it'll be like downtown traffic lights at five-thirty." As if to prove her point there she was again, more solid this time, but very sporadic. She appeared at a sequence of points with pauses, in the hall, along the corridor, turning into a room, her head bent over a book.

Lila followed Malachi quickly along the halls. Most doors were open onto various rooms: a library, a sunroom, a computer suite, a playroom, a fitness room, a kitchen, several lounges, a dining room. In and out of all of these came various figures of Sancha, reading, carrying, walking, preoccupied, flickering about odds and ends of domestic life in various changes of clothes. Sometimes there were more than one of her in a place, even on the same seat. Here they interfered with each other, alternately phasing in and out, fuzzing, flickering. It wasn't just spatial dimensions, Lila realised. It was time. The woman was time-lapsed.

Then they came to the room she remembered best—the ocean view—and her bewildered awe at such an existence, her wondering, came to a halt. She looked down through the plate glass, across the terrazzo, through the gardens to the ocean, and it felt to her like Zal was here only yesterday, might be in the garden, or in his room upstairs. But then the details eroded the pain of the nostalgia. The pool was covered, the furniture there different. The garden had changed. And on the shore the fully wrecked ugliness of the Ghost Hunter's Void ship was beached, its gleam nearly gone, being pawed at by the sea.

"She came to you," Lila said, thinking aloud carelessly. She turned around to the flickering shape and then it struck her, what had been nagging her. "You look like . . ."

"Don't say it." Azevedo held up her hand. "I know. Princess Leia's Artoo message. It's been noted. And yes. She did. But that's not your business right this minute, is it?" She gestured gracefully. "Please, sit down. Let's get through this as quickly as we can. I am pleased to help you, but I don't have long before you must go."

Lila sat with Malachi on a beautiful leather sofa, only then noticing the gracious loveliness of the room, the sunlight's warmth. It was probably the only decent room in the entire place. Opposite them Sancha Azevedo sat and gripped the arm of her own settee as if to anchor herself. She obviously liked this room. There were at least six other versions of her there, jumping in and out of existence, in and out of time and space.

"Are you crossing?" Lila couldn't help but ask, looking at them all.

"I can be in more than one place at a time, yes."

Lila looked at her. "That must be hellish."

"You're here about your zombies," Azevedo said, a tautness entering her smile. "It's a struggle for me to be so still, so please, keep it to the point. Once I run out of concentration I will break up and that will be it for a few days."

"Yesterday two showed up," Malachi said. "One at the office. One at home."

Lila explained the circumstances. The fey watched her closely all the while. When they'd finished she paused a moment. "We have something in common then. I know your story from the Hunter, though he forgot to mention your eyes. They're absolutely terrifying. Anyway, we both have a break in transmission, let's say, though I have a few more. Look, here's how it works. Zombies and ghosts are created in the same way. Out in the Void there is plenty of free energy in various protoforms. When a magus comes along—a magus is anyone with a powerfully focused mind, let me say—they act as an attractor. The energy gathers and, under their influence, takes form. Ghosts are forms created either by one or many minds, either slowly over aeons or immediately by a great piercing focus. They spring from the living. Zombies are clones. Material and spiritual clones of an individual, usually recently dead, but possibly alive in other circumstances. Where people are weak they may become zombies if they are taken under control by a master, but you didn't have this sort." She flickered, guttering like flames in a draft, and her voice broke up, returning in a stutter over a period of a couple of minutes to complete the speech. "Ghosts and zombies are like elementals in this respect, both forms. They share the soul of the original, are part of it, because souls are always and everywhere, not locked to time or space. Souls are like the Void. You see? Everywhere and always, even in the most material worlds."

She paused, much weakened by the effort of talking for so long. Lila didn't even move to interrupt her. The woman gave her a grateful glance and said, "What you had at the office really was your husband, but not the only one of him, not the greater part, not what you would call the original, not that it matters very much. But it was made of ghost stuff, fresh out of the Void. It wasn't stable in this plane. It wouldn't have lasted. It was a weak copy. The other one is different. The other one is a strong copy, almost entirely primaterial in nature. It is not your sister. But it is." She paused, took a breath, waved off Malachi who was about to speak, and leaned forward with a sense of great urgency. "No. No time for me. Listen. The important feature of these things is who has made them and what they willed. It is easy, very easy, for beings from other planes to hitch rides in zombies in a desire to become material and inhabit the other worlds. Easy to use the weak the same way. That is why zombie use and the training of weaklings to magical knowledge is taboo among magi, including necromancers. Nobody'd be that stupid. There are few minds in existence across any time who have the strength to notice and resist the kinds of beings that can cross over from the hidden places. Certainly they are almost impossible to manage. They have no natural material form of their own. They are entirely thoughtform and will, nothing else. Beside their abilities most sentient material creatures are no more troublesome to them than amoeba." She paused and winked out completely.

They waited, and waited.

"I . . . ," Lila began but then Sancha was back. She looked weary and spoke now rapidly, in bursts, as if she was ill and out of breath.

"The last question you have is who made your zombies. The sister. That was you. You made it. You called it up and it came to you. Because of the instrument you have. Very foolish. Very careless. You must find a necromancer to ask more detail if you want to know what it truly is and if it is ridden. The spirit decays, you see. Soul's eternal but spirits decay. Important to know difference. And the other. The husband. That one was not you. And it was not the weapon. Someone else sent it."

She blinked out. Returned. "It was ridden. It was open. So dangerous. I think it was . . . good it failed . . ." She began to judder, and fury crossed her face as she began to lose her struggle to cohere and be linear. "Come back in a few days. I . . ." She stood up and they saw her start talking to someone who wasn't there, looking in a direction that wasn't at anything in their room. She became thin, transparent, and then, after a series of violent flickers, vanished. Around them she moved, without seeing them, pale, ghostly, multiple.

Lila and Malachi looked at one another.

"What a fucking existence," Lila said. Under the cloak she was cold, shivering. "Well at least a couple of things got answered. Are the hidden places—does that mean Thanatopia?"

Malachi nodded grimly. "You think Jones is here in the house?"

"If here means what it means to this lady? I guess probably, maybe, who knows?"

"She can phase at will," he said. "I should look but. . . ."

"But you're a guest in someone else's house and you should leave nicely," Lila said. "Which is what we're going to do. If she's here, she knows how to find you. Jones left you that thing, remember. Maybe she's safe here. Figure out that before you go wrecking her cover."

"I . . ." He paused. "Okay. Place is creeping me out anyway. I swear this is the biggest earth energy sink on the whole continent."

They got up and began to walk carefully back the way they had come, dodging and avoiding all the Sanchas who came their way. Though neither of them said so, they both felt the same absolute degree of caution about occupying the same space as any of Sancha's disparate selves, however immaterial they seemed.

"If it is, why would Zal choose it?" Lila asked. "He was a fire junkie."

"Earth consumes fire," Malachi said. "Safest place in town to hide your light under that bushel. He was a hunted guy: here he could summon a lot of fire and not be noticed."

At last they reached the relative sanity of the entryway, passed through the door after unlocking it, and then got into the car. Malachi turned them around and then stopped, taking a look back down at the beach.

"Are they zombie dead in that ship?"

"I hope so," he said. He wasn't sure.

"There was a ghost here before, when Zal was here," Lila said. "It came right for him. Why?"

Finally Malachi turned away from the sight of the shipwreck and put his foot gently down on the accelerator. "Energy sinkholes are weak spots. Easier for things to come through here. He was powerful, it was hungry. Also, he was careless."

"No, he made a protection circle. It didn't affect it."

Malachi frowned. "No? Ghosts usually can't cross."

Lila opened the glove box, looking for anything, even the car manual, as long as she didn't have to keep looking around at the Folly and its grounds. "Oh yeah, what do they eat?"

"Memories. Information. Dreams. All that kind of stuff. And they suck aetheric power from anyone stupid enough to let them try. Not you humans obviously. By the way, what was it?"

"A stag kind of thing."

The car stopped with a jolt that nearly sent her forehead into the dash.

"Mal, what the hell?"

"Like that one?"

The driveway from the house bent sharply in a switchback, and it was on the second bend, shrouded in tree shadow so dark it might have been twilight, that the creature was standing. A faint glow limned it, giving away its true nature; otherwise, she would have thought it was a giant elk at first. Its rack was almost as wide as the road and high enough to tangle with the branches overhead, but it was not impeded by the antlers at all. It snorted and turned to face them head-on from the position where they had caught it crossing the narrow tarmac strip. Only then did the smell hit her, wafting on the afternoon warmth, a sweet stink that was half rot and half poppy smoke and incense, myrrh and the thick odour of dry dead things.

It looked as solid as an ox. Its fur was heavy, rank, and dark, its nostrils caverns on the wet black nose, eyes staring, whiteless, empty. A black spill of shadows dripped off it, and poured and gathered around its massive split hooves. Apart from its size, decay, and air of brooding malevolence she found it familiar.

"That's it. But it's been on the evil steroids since then. Mal?"

"Yeah." He was watching it intently, his fingers moving lightly on the wheel. "There's been quite a few reports about bad things like this coming up recently. Three or four a week. Like you say, ordinary ghosts but on the boo-juice."

The stag thing lowered its head. A slough of skin loosened on its neck and fell away with a wet slap onto the ground.

"Ugh," Malachi gagged.

Lila's initial jolt of fear was receding into nausea. "It looks pretty real."

"It is pretty real, just not entirely," he said. "I'd drive but I don't think touching it is a good idea. I heard. That is, from the hospital. People with some kind of wasting disease. They'd seen these things or been up close to them. The link wasn't clear. Oh god, the smell . . ."

It was choking, vile. Malachi put his sleeve to his face. Lila, used to demon tricks, filtered her air and kept a straight face in spite of the gut-churning nature of it. She took hold of the windshield to help her stand up in her seat, formed a shotgun out of her right forearm, and shot two rounds at it. The sound of the gun was almost deadened by the miasma of shadow around the thing. It lowered its head further and shook its antlers, opening its mouth to groan and bellow. Lila felt the glass vibrate under her hand. More pieces of skin and other matter slid and slipped out of the ghost's form. She saw them land on the road and become leaves, sticks, and the gloopy, rotten flesh of some animal or other.

Moaning, the creature backed up a step, stumbled, backed more, and then decided to head forwards into the trees. It had to struggle with the undergrowth and trunks but it passed through them, shedding more parts of itself in a constant shower.

As soon as it had cleared enough space Malachi gunned the engine and they screamed past it in a cloud of blue smoke. The old car slid around the bends crazily, shock absorbers grinding, but he didn't touch the brakes until they were at the main road.

Lila couldn't stop herself replaying the vision of the thing falling apart and remaking itself as it pushed through the woods. When she first saw it she was sure it had been composed of forest litter, but it had seemed healthier, an animal spirit of a kind, not a monster. "What kind of minds make that?"

Malachi bit his words out, still holding his breath as best he could. "Undisciplined, fearful ones. The usual sort. No shortage of nightmares, is there?"

She shook her head silently in agreement. No shortage.

CHAPTER FIFTEEN

Glinda's house was not a house at all. Lily's and Mina's zones paid a weak, clichéd kind of homage to the end of the world, Zal realised as they trekked through barren waste that would have been called a desert except that *desert* had romantic and appealing implications involving sand, sun, and recognisable objects that this ground had none of. He wasn't sure they were walking. They were moving or something was moving and it involved them passing through it. He was tired and his grip on his senses was weak, not helped by all of them having to work via cotton, linen, and bits of silk rather than the usual organs they were associated with. Ahead of him Lily strode with the determination used by people who don't want to go somewhere but must and want to make the best of it. He was sure that she was shrinking. This was confirmed as they entered a place of more definition and he realised the top of her head was at his forehead instead of towering a good ten inches over.

"Here we are," she said briskly.

"Nice," Zal said. "Minimalist. Austere." He felt so drained that he sat down where he was and hoped that the ground remained solid enough. It did. He'd heard stories about planewalkers and travel in various dimensions that weren't suited to the 4-D kind of person, but it was much worse to be there. Even more boring than it had sounded at the time.

"Nice." A voice dripping with sarcasm, cynicism, and contempt repeated from all around them. Apart from the tone it was a pleasant voice, melodious, rich, and clearly belonging to a woman with no self-confidence issues. It reminded him more than anything else could have that he was not visiting some elder faery who had a place and a house. He was in an elder faery who was part of a trio that had the whole creation and destruction of realities down pat, and the place was as much part of her as the time and any other objects he might encounter. But keeping that in mind was too hard, so he'd learned to let Lily and Mina and Mr. V be themselves because his brain, or lint, preferred it that way. He could deal with a girl, and a mad aunt figure with anonymous hairdos and an ever-pending birth, and a white cat and a wretched backdrop no better than a cheap computer game vision of the edge of forever because it was what he was used to. Glimpses of what lay beneath all the fabrications made him feel so ill he couldn't function at all. He wasn't sure if it mattered, but now, as the still air started moving and the ground heaved and grew a fancy black castle with crazily high towers around him, he thought maybe it did.

"Maybe it does . . . ," the voice echoed.

There was a sound like an all-over snap and he found himself in an almost pitch-dark castle room of some kind with vaults so high they were invisible and a dais in the centre ringed by torches holding daylight flame. In the middle stood the third sister. She was tall, lissome, and had the exquisite features of the most lovely of all the shadowkin, including their nightskin, the colour of deep purple shadows cast in the last moments of a golden afternoon. Her hair was platinum white, with a midnight blue streak in it where it fell across her shoulders in thick straight cascades, and she wore blue-and-silver robes in the ceremonial style of a Jayon Daga sword master, bound tightly to the wrists and ankles and neck with cloth wrap, shielded by exquisitely worked heavy wool panels and braced with black leather belts and bandoliers. Like the red-haired girl in his dream she had metal eyes, but hers were gold and they had an inner light that made them gleam like a demon's. In her right hand she was holding a crystal shot glass. Ice chinked in it. In her left hand she had the very end of a hand-rolled cigar, its tip glowing. As he watched she put this to her lips, bit back a drag, flicked a shred of tobacco off her mouth with one elegant finger, and blew smoke in their direction in a long, unimpressed stream.

"You're an elf," he said with surprise.

"No kidding." She looked at him and began to walk towards them regally. "If only we could say the same for you." Her merciless and unblinking gaze turned to her sister, who was now only up to Zal's shoulder. This put her a good three feet too short to meet Glinda eye to eye. "Lost your nerve?" Glinda said coolly and made two air kisses about a thousand miles too high and wide in the general vicinity of where Lily's head would have been if she weren't so short. "Glinda," she said. "Hmm . . ." and took another drag on the stub before she flicked it out of sight and knocked back whatever was left in her glass. By the smell Zal figured it was bourbon. "About time you brought him around. What kept you? Armageddon or something?"

"We've had a visitor," said Lily very deliberately. She explained the situation as Glinda ignored her and her golden eyes tore delicately into Zal.

"Necromancers," Glinda said as Lily finished. "I hate them. Making a mess of everything, fingers where they shouldn't be, fiddling and twiddling." She rubbed the tips of her free hand fingers together and narrowed her eyes. "Pulling and poking and twisting like naughty little children because where there's a way there's always some fool willing and some fool not paying attention." She gave Lily a cool glance and rattled the ice in her glass. When she was done, the glass was full again. She sipped and peered at Zal some more. "You'd better leave him with me."

"But—"

"He's mine anyway, or did you forget who was yanking the strings that day?"

"I saved him."

"I let you. I cheated Jack. That was sweet. Who'd have thought he'd meet his end at the hands of those old swords of mine, not that he didn't deserve it. I would have preferred something more drawn-out myself but . . ." She shrugged. "Can't have it all."

"What are we going to do about it?" Lily said firmly. "We have to do something."

"Oh blah blah," Glinda waved her cigarless hand airily. "You make it sound like a duty when it's a chance to have some fun. Aren't you curious about who would go to such dangerous lengths for something as trivial as making a zombie? Someone has their eye on things much better than we do. Go and get back to the weft and see what's going on up there in the old land. Make yourself useful and get that cow-brain of yours sharpened up."

Lily bristled and fumed, but she was under Glinda's command, clearly, so after some fussing and a few mild ripostes about Glinda's general state of being, she left. "You were too slow anyway," she said as she made to go. "His memories are sketchy and most of him was ruined. He's been nothing but cheeky and useless and he knows almost nothing about anything. He hardly even knows who he is. So who was careless that day, hm?"

Glinda said nothing, but smiled a crocodilian kind of smile, blew out some smoke, and waved good-bye with a merriness that was only in her hand.

"You forgot your cigar," Zal said, referring to the smoke.

Glinda shot him a look that made him wish his mouth was sewn shut and not in a slightly ajar position. Then her expression softened with self-deprecation and she grinned, which unsettled him even more. "So I did." She stretched out her arms and looked herself over, smoothed her thick hair with one hand, and admired her bourbon glass. "Could be worse," she said.

"Did I invent you?" There he went again, like there was no tomorrow. Oh, there wasn't, he reminded himself, so it was okay. Looking at Glinda he was really sure more than ever that there would never be a tomorrow. Her stare was glacial, saurian, and fiendishly intelligent, a combination that made his seams shrink even though he couldn't really feel pain. Her eyes could rip you apart all on their own.

"Of course you did," she snapped, and released him, turning away and looking around at the black castle. "Don't ask silly questions. I don't know why you made Lily so bland. She isn't, you know."

"I had to live with her," Zal mumbled. "And Mina, and that cat. And Mr. V." He felt the book in his pocket. It seemed heavy. He wondered how he could fulfill his promise now.

"Very oversightful of her to hang onto you so long," Glinda purred frostily. "What is that thing in your pocket?"

"I . . . hm . . . what?"

Glinda turned around. "Play or nay?"

Zal's insides frayed. "P-play?" The idea of starting some game with this particular fey paralysed him with terror.

Glinda's savage eyes narrowed. "We can play, and do guessing games and question and answer and truth or dare. Or we can not bother and move straight to Go, collecting the dry rewards of practical creatures. Your choice."

Oh yes. He had to agree. "I . . . er . . ."

"Come, Zal. You were always a player. I have seen you many times."

"Yeah, but . . ."

"And you have played with me before."

"Have I? I mean . . . are you . . . who I think you are . . . or are you . . . not who I think you are but something a bit like it in a Faery-only version?" He cringed, trying not to move backwards and shrink, though he was pretty certain that he was doing both. For all that he had felt briefly that it might be worth throwing himself in the fire and ending it all, even when he'd hung off the cliff and could have let go, even at the worst of himself, he wasn't really into suicide.

"You see?" She chinked her ice and smiled. "You like to play. You can't help it. I always liked that about you. Not many people like playing with me. I consider it a compliment, from you."

"Good." She hadn't answered him. He badly wanted her to. He had to know. "Right. Muses. Furies. Fates. Birth, life, and death. Beginning, middle, and end. Sort of thing. So, you'd be . . ."

"I would be the truly inspiring one," Glinda said with grace and, to his surprise, genuine majesty. "Yes."

"Are you all rolled up into one, the three of you, not separate really?"

She shrugged. "It may be something like that."

"But you are a faery."

"I am what came before faeries."

"You aren't part of the human world or the others."

"I was before that."

"You aren't universal?"

She hesitated. "Beyond what may be touched by aether, I cannot go. So no, in that sense, not universal, not eternal either, though close enough to tick the box on surveys. Is this enough?"

"Are there even more primal fey than you?"

"One surely," she said. "But that doesn't concern you, or even me. Mother Night is the first."

"She's the queen?"

"No, you fool. The faeries elect queens by the moment and the yard. Queens are ten for tuppence. Every female has been the queen. Even brownies."

"They didn't used to. In the legend, the queen's magic turned the lock and shut off Under." He stretched what he knew, to test it. In spite of the obvious danger, which he felt less dangerous somehow, he was enjoying himself now.

"And those of us down there, yes. Tell me Zal, what do you remember of music? And the light elf magic? And of demons?"

He struggled. He had a sense that there was something but it refused to come clear. Blurred images flitted through his mind. "Music is songs but I don't know any. Light elf magic is about harmonising and using nature elementals by cooperation or something. Demons . . ." He cast about again but there was nothing. He shrugged. He had a great sense of failure but he didn't understand why.

She sipped her drink and looked around for somewhere to put it, but there was nowhere. She sighed, staring at the blank darkness and then up at the few sketchy tower tops against the bloody sky. "I see the old sister wasn't lying. You really have been stripped bare by that old bastard Jack. He meant to kill you the hard way. But at the time I thought it better to let it go far. The years you must spend here would be less kind to you if you remembered. So, what is in your pocket?"

"A book," he said, paying up for the information and not daring to speculate on what she meant by "remembered." If there was something to remember she must know what it was, so it wasn't lost, not really, not properly. The sense of having had a life elsewhere was exhilarating. "And that's all I know."

"Whose book?"

Zal, still sitting and shivering with a cold that was deep and lasting though he barely felt any change in his stuffing, thought over the deal. He could say no to it because he was certain that any contest they might have she would win. He could say no to it because her penalties might be dire although since he was virtually dead anyway he had a tough time imagining much worse, although lots of pain might be worse, surely. He could say no and break the habit of a lifetime. But he never said no. "Truth or dare?"

Glinda seemed to come alive. "Dare," she said, her eyes flashing.

Zal cursed. If he had had such wits as she implied in the past he surely didn't have them now. Typical. Death comes asking for a dare and he hadn't got two notions to rub together. Then a moment of pure genius struck him. It was so pure and so delicious that he couldn't say it for a moment. "I dare you to take this book to Lily's attic, pick up what you find there, and leave the book in its place. On the way back speak to nobody and give me what you return with."

Glinda jerked her head back on its swanlike neck. Her golden eyes blinked. Then she narrowed them and drew a long breath in, calculating. "Can I read the book?"

What did he care? "I don't know, can you?"

He thought he'd gone too far. She got taller, darker, and the room filled with a brimming sensation of power like a tsunami about to break. Zal cowered, much more successfully this time, and got his head under both arms.

Then she held out her arm, hand outstretched. "As you say. I agree."

He thought she was trying not to smile. Carefully he brought out the volume Mr. V had given him. Mr. V hadn't *said* he couldn't give the task to someone else, and anything specifically not in the rules was fair. It was Faery, after all. He handed the book over to her and she took it with care, as if it were precious or dangerous. She ran her long fingers over it softly without looking at it.

"I think it would be a very short story if I were to read this," she said in a more gentle tone than he believed she was capable of. "Do you know what it is?"

Zal shook his head. He really had no idea but he reckoned she wouldn't tell him for nothing. He had to work on more material.

"Well I do," she said, smoothing the cover. "And I will be very interested to see what Lily's hiding away that is its equal. What a dark horse she can be. And as for Mr. V, why, to part with this . . . hmm mmm . . . interesting days indeed." With that she vanished. If Zal hadn't known better he would have said that she was skipping.

In the minute that followed he looked around him at the bleak barren gothic castle, its heights silhouetted against a blue moon and a black sun, the shifting colours of the light clouds flitting behind them in orange, red, and gold. It reminded him of a second-rate heavy metal concert stage. He tried to imagine something less obvious, but in its way what he already had was comforting. There were other ways to see this place that he was sure were infinitely less so. He liked illusions. He didn't want any more of them stripped away.

At that moment Glinda returned. She stood exactly on the same spot, but now she was covered in a thick film of dust and not too few cobwebs. Her head was on one side to regard him more speculatively than before. She kept her mouth shut and held out her hand. On her palm lay a large silver heart-shaped lady's compact. Half of it was studded with what looked like diamonds, the other half was polished smooth, but it was scratched and a bit dull with wear though there was no tarnish.

With her other hand, drink intact, she indicated a space in the air where glowing letters appeared: *Do not speak. Think, and your words will appear here.*

It was Mr. V's book, Zal thought, careful to finish before he took the small object. His words appeared below hers in glittering dust; then they winked out.

Zal could see the compact had a hinge and a small pressure closure. It was no use trying to open it, his fingers were too thick and blunt, and he had no nails.

Glinda snapped her fingers in front of his nose and he looked up. She pointed at her words: *Well well. Take it back now and keep your word. But remember, you are mine. We have played and I have won.*

He frowned—when did that get into the rules?—but the glittering writing spelled out more.

You are mine and I am yours. I am always with you and I always have been.

He nodded and understood. Some powers had nothing to do with you, some took forms that everyone saw, and some were personal. This was one of them. You would never encounter her otherwise. Lily, Mina, they were all different for the individuals who perceived them and gave them faces and shapes with meaning that for them went some way to encompass and define their power and range. Glinda was his death. This was his end of the world. Lila and Mina, even the cat, were aspects of the same fey, which was split up for him, so that he had a chance of surviving his interface with it. He wished that this knowledge made it any easier. He wished it meant he wouldn't have to walk all the way to Mina's house and back again now, but it seemed he would have to.

Come straight back, Glinda wrote, drinking at the same time and moving her small cigar to the side of her mouth with a practised pout where she bit on it with her sharp white teeth. *We have a necromancer to hunt and I've got something to give you. And don't go playing with Mr. V. Though I expect you will, you idiot.*

He hesitated, getting up slowly. He felt light and unstable. *Why didn't you let Jack kill me?*

She looked at him through the filmy smoke of her cheroot and grinned a fiendish grin that was as comforting as the smile on a skull. *Don't be long, Zal. Don't be long.*

He found himself outside on the road. Any trace of the black palace was gone. Because there was nothing else to do he began to trudge the long way back towards Mina's house. He wondered if Mr. V's talking rule included himself. In case it did he ranted silently in his head and wondered how a faery could have secrets from itself. Maybe he didn't understand it as well as he thought. It was probably the lint.

CHAPTER SIXTEEN

"I'm going, and that's that." Lila stood at the door of her office. Malachi was beside her, hands in his coat pockets, frowning and shaking his head.

"It's suicide," he said. "The first thing they'll do is expect you to find him, for their own very pertinent and important reasons. No, actually the first thing some of them will do is try to kill you any which way they can. Then they'll watch while you find Teazle. Then they'll try to kill both of you. Meanwhile they'll expect you to kill him or else their justice enforcers will kill you and him. I can't see any way out of it. Unless of course you survive, find him, and kill him. Then you might expect about ten seconds' respite while they crown you leader of the largest cartel in Demonia and after that the free-for-all will commence."

"I know all that," Lila said impatiently, her hand on the door. Its locks had already responded to her touch and opened; she was just delaying the sorry inevitable.

"So, it's not just because you don't want to go home."

She looked around, but there was no sign of Temple Greer. Zinging her AI system informed her he was at home, sleeping. The agency was at a lull for the first time in days. She turned to Malachi.

"I really don't want to go back to that house. I couldn't call it home. And no, I don't want to find out and face what is living there or going on in my absence. But I will. Soon as I make sure Teazle is all right. Undead sister is probably sticking around and doing fine, according to Azevedo. I haven't seen any reports that she's eating neighbours or sacrificing pets to the dark gods, so the missing demon husband wins on points. Right after I check in here." She rested her forehead against the thick wooden panelling for a second. "And I feel responsible . . . no, shut up a second . . . because we had a deal going. I asked him to look for things that could help me locate Zal. And the fact that he's in the middle of them and the demons can't find him anywhere makes me think he's found something. Might not be useful, but you never know until you see it. Either way, don't you think as agents of the human interest we ought to find out what that kind of thing is?"

She turned her head without lifting it off its resting place and looked at him. He stared at her with his orange eyes, thinking, and then his tense posture slumped and he took a deep breath and let it out.

"Nice try. Kinda convincing, I admit."

"Yeah, isn't it?" She straightened herself up and turned the handle. The door opened—perfectly balanced elven wood on brass hinges—and swung silently inwards to reveal ordinary rooms. Of the ghost wreck there was no sign, except the tideline of office flotsam it had created and a smell of rot and damp. Relief flooded her.

"That's strange," Malachi said, following her inside. "The other ships haven't decayed this much." He inspected the carpet, bending onto one knee, then picked up papers and held them up. "Not dripping. Condensation and some ice melt, nothing more."

"The smell is bad." She looked around, aware that Sarasilien had kept plants in here but seeing none now. The windows that opened into the central courtyard were papered over and she hadn't had time to pull it down. Now she went over and stripped the panes clear, at the same time finding the lock controls in the AI system and opening them up. She wadded up the old sheet papers into a ball and looked for a bin, but there weren't any, so she threw it into a corner. The sickly odour of decomposing flesh, sweet, rotting fruit, and poppies drifted sluggishly with the influx of mild afternoon air.

"Azevedo said this wasn't the same. I called her after her Tai Chi class. She isn't keen to come here and this seems to be part of the reason why. But if he wasn't part of the Fleet, why did he arrive on that ship?" Malachi put the wet papers down carefully on a sheet-covered table that was still upright near the wall. He surveyed the scene morosely.

"Not all ships are—"

"But they are," Malachi said. "They are. Every vessel of any kind belongs to it. I guess perhaps they might manifest alone. I wish I could ask. Do you think that might be because the person who sent the zombie is with the Fleet?"

"Would it be a good place for a necromancer to hang out?"

"Would be," Malachi agreed. "If they could survive it. The Fleet isn't a stable entity. It can decompose rapidly and turn into mist or less, or at least it used to. If it fizzled out while they were inside one of the ships, then they'd be floating in the Void. No air, no nothing. It took a ton of technology for the Ghost Hunters to make it out there." He sounded doubtful, but to Lila's mind not doubtful enough.

"Demon tech?" she asked, confident it must be since the machines of her type didn't deal with aetheric creations well. At all.

"Mostly. Uh-huh."

"You go talk to Jones about it. Find out why she's running and dumping on you all over." She finished her unproductive prodding about and went through into the laboratory proper. It was still littered with her previous experiments. She was an exact, tidy worker but there were so many setups that there was barely room to walk between the benches. "And get some rest. You look grey."

"Aye-aye, and you?" He bridled slightly at his ready acquiescence to her order, but it was too late now he'd said it.

"I am going to get this cleaned up by an expert." Lila snapped her fingers.

Malachi turned as he heard footsteps and Bentley appeared at the door. He realised Lila must have called her earlier, but the effect was briefly unnerving. He turned back. "And then you're going to Demonia."

"Soon as you tell me where the portal is."

"I . . . uh . . ."

"You can tell me or I can just trash the AI systems and find it."

He sighed. "Is there anything about you that isn't overly aggressive today?"

Lila shook her head as Bentley began to dismantle the convoluted glass monstrosities Lila had created in the fume cabinets. The red streak in her hair shook side to side. "Nothing."

"I wish you'd change your mind."

"Can't."

"Won't." His anger surprised him with its sudden reemergence. He saw her silver eyes flash and she crooked her finger at him, lips thinning. Bracing his jaw he followed her into the back room of the suite, where Sarasilien had eschewed all paraphernalia and stuck to fine furnishings and comfortable chairs. She sat down in a large armchair still covered in its dustsheet and indicated he could do the same in one next to it. Outside the door they could hear the steady clink and tinkle of Bentley working. The toxic smell was almost unnoticeable.

"Mal," she said awkwardly, knitting her fingers together until her gauntlets creaked. "I'm grateful you care."

"But . . . ," he sniped.

"Yes but. But back off. Ever since I got here you've been on my case." She looked up at him and then down at her hands. "It's like you don't understand. I mean, look at me . . ." She held out her arms, and the leather armour vanished into her skin softly, like butter melting into warm tea. She breathed with great control, and when she glanced up the silver metal eyes were gone and she was looking at him with ordinary blue eyes, faintly lilac around the iris in a way he wasn't sure that she knew about but which made a jolt stir in him as he recognised Tatterdemalion's hold. He was astonished when she seemed to read his mind and plucked at the thick purple cape self-consciously.

"Yeah," she said. "And that. And the other. But they're just more of the same thing. I didn't ask for them. But I've got them whether I like it or not." She pulled the cape around herself. "And they bring a lot of power. Stuff that an ordinary person has no use for. I mean, when the agency made me, they weren't thinking about saving my life so much as making themselves a handy tool for the outworld kit. I stopped being a person then and I started being an instrument. It was automatic. Nobody asked me; I did it by myself. I'd become a thing, so I was worthless, I decided it. I don't blame the people who remade me exactly, not for that part. I didn't get that for a long time. I was so angry with them, played my role as the tragic victim heroine. Thought I'd save the day and that would make it all worthwhile. I kept on trying . . ." Her voice cracked and she made a snarling face of pain and mastered it. "I kept on trying to deny it. It's only when I met Zal I started to notice, and then, a long time after—actually when I met Tath and we talked in Under—I understood it doesn't matter about your makeup or what happened or what other people do, only your will. So I decided I wasn't going to be an instrument anymore. I wasn't going to be a good girl and serve my saviours. No martyrdom any-more. It's all me now. And here you find me, fighting the forces. What-ever they want me to do, I'm not interested in doing unless it suits me."

She tapped the side of her head with a callous gesture. "The Signal—that fucking hissing shit—I won't bore you with its contents, but it has a mission. . . . Forget that. It's not important yet. It's far from being able to do what it wants, so we can forget it for now. The old faeries . . ." She plucked at the cape. "They want their own things.

I don't care about that. I don't even care about the games we play. I'm a parasite opportunist, looking for my chances same as them. If they let me use them, then that's their problem. I know they have plans that are nothing to do with me. I'm just a handy method of passage for things that aren't shapeshifting death machines. And the agency still thinks I give a shit, which is interesting. Sometimes I seem to, even to myself, but I can tell you for certain that if they didn't give me everything I wanted I'd be out of here in a second. The only people in existence that I give a damn about are all in deep trouble. And I am going to try and get them out because my foolish caretaker habits die very hard and they aren't entirely dead yet. I expect this mission will kill them off. I don't know what I'll find. I don't expect you to help me. You don't owe me anything, Mal. But don't stand in my way. Maybe the demons will kill me. Fair enough. I'll risk it. Because the alternative is hanging around here forever 'doing research' until I get the phone call that says love is dead."

She was looking at the covered chaise longue that was at the side of the room. Her gaze was fixed on it as if it were the most interesting thing in existence. "Where the hell did he go?" she said to herself, and the anger in her voice was bitter. "Sarasilien, I mean. How the hell could he leave me here and go?"

"If he were here," Malachi said, "he'd say the same as I say. We were trying in our own ways to take care of you. Do you think we didn't know what you just said was true? You *were* a victim of the system. We wanted to make it up to you and protect you from the worst of it. We just couldn't."

"You should have helped me to destroy it," she said, lost in her own thoughts. "You should have taught me to disobey sooner."

"You wouldn't ruin the defences of the humans, Lila. That's pain talking."

"No, I wouldn't ruin them. I'd make them functional, because at the moment they're a wet tissue facing a cyclone. Anyway, enough of the hero formula, Mal. I don't know what you want, so you can either say it or shut up but this nannying passive-aggressive stuff has got to go." She suddenly looked up from her brooding and met his eyes, separating her hands to rest them on the arms of the chair and sit back. "If I *am* going to die stupidly early, full of a sense of 'with power comes responsibility,' then we don't have time for bull." She gave him a wan smile. "Don't think I don't know what I'm getting into. I've figured it out by now. I am a collision of unlikely things, and that super-attracts shit."

Malachi took a deep breath and let it out slowly. "When I first came here I thought it would be a good laugh, something to do that was full of curious new experiences. I wanted to see the humans struggle to accept what they have never accepted in the last centuries as they slowly took the material path. I laughed at their inability to understand the difference between the world of objects, the flow of energy, and the structures created by their own minds. We fey played tricks and finally the trick was up when the Bomb came. We thought it was the end of a merry era indeed. But even now you don't understand. Perhaps some do thanks to the Hunter. Thanks to you." He paused as she flinched. "No, I think his interference was a good thing if a savage one. But that's beside the point. I came to satisfy myself. And I would probably still be here even without you. But I like you. I love you, as a sister. I wouldn't want to see you fall. I don't want to. And there are many kinds of falls. You are tough, but I don't know that you're tough enough to withstand the storm around you."

Lila slid forward to the edge of the seat and reached out to take Malachi's hands. "Thank you."

He felt himself forgiven, redeemed. Her combative energy had gone. It was a lovely moment. Then she let go and stood up, shaking out the heavy cape with an annoyed flounce. "I wish I looked less like a second-rate warlock."

"Talk to the clothes." He stood and adjusted the tension out of his shoulders.

"I can't . . . talk to the . . ." She looked up, seeking patience from heaven. "Right."

"Portal's under a government ban. No way to use it, even for you, not unless you want to shoot a bunch of harmless admin staff and a few dozen marines to get to it. But I'm sure if you're creative you'll find another way." With his hands he mimed writing with a pen. "Probably would pay to master the things you've been gifted with, before they master you."

She made a petulant face, mocking herself. "Last time I wrote something it went badly wrong. Undead sister. Remember?"

He shrugged. "So get better at it. Use your head. If you can't, then it's probably not possible. Maybe that's why they're with you. They've finally found someone too stupid to use them unwisely."

Lila nodded, considering. "Maybe they have a keen sense of adventure and sly trickery."

"I've no doubt of that." He paused. "I will find out what Jones knows. I kinda suspect it's my problem really, and not yours anyway. But if you're not back by the time I'm done then I'm coming after you."

"Okay," Lila said. She walked through the door and Malachi heard her asking Bentley to stop washing test tubes and look for dry vellum, paper, and pencils. "And when we've done that I want you to instruct all the machine agents working here that the rogue agents are to be arrested and detained pending my return. You can tell them that if they resist arrest they can suffer the same fate as Sandra Lane."

Yeah, he thought to himself with a touch of both gloomy fatalism and anticipation, things were very different now around here. Lila Black had done as he told her. She'd grown up. He was kind of sorry. He wasn't. It was both that was so damn hard to take.

Lila had said her last orders aloud for Malachi's benefit. She waited until he was gone, however, before she stopped pretending to search for drawing materials.

"Sarah." She touched the android's arm. "Do you think the rogues have became servants of the Signal? Are they its materials?"

"We all are," the measured voice replied. Bentley handed her two pieces of leaf vellum, the Alfheim kind, and an ordinary elven ink pen. "Will this do?"

"Yes, thanks." Lila took them and righted the table nearby. She swept the surface with her hand but it was dry enough. The smell of rot furled and bloomed.

"But I mean," Lila said. "Are they its consciousness? That is what it wants. I'm right, aren't I?"

"Yes, you are right," Bentley said, obediently standing at her elbow as she relayed Lila's orders to the rest of the agents. "But I am not sure the process has completed. The rogues volunteered themselves as disciples, as hosts for the Signal, so that it might progress into this, the primaterial plane. They are the body. They claim success and that they are carrying out a holy task. They are moving toward the perfection of the Signal."

Lila nodded, composing herself. She must not make a mistake. She uncapped the elf pen and began to draw. "It's crap, isn't it?"

The android beside her hesitated. "Yes, ma'am."

"Because," Lila said slowly, surveying her forty-four circles and noting that she was learning to compensate for inaccuracies caused by the flow of ink and the nib, "I can't hear that in the Signal. Can you?"

"No, ma'am."

"But we agree that the Signal was seeking material expression. If it could be said to seek. Which I am not sure it can."

"I would say it lends itself to it, ma'am. Ultimately, in spite of its absolute concreteness and total specificity, not to mention its completeness, any engagement with it is a mystical union."

Lila regarded her seventy-eight circles with a growing satisfaction, and looked for more paper. "Sarah Bentley, you are a smart lady."

"Thank you."

"Do you ever wonder who handed the blueprints of our machinery to the humans?"

"Yes. I have heard it was the Others."

"You don't want to say the A-word." Lila shook the pen, but the ink was all gone. Before her a hundred and twenty-eight circles covered all the available paper, some overlapping.

"Angel," said Bentley.

"That one, yes." Lila turned some of the pages, critically. "I need more paper, but scrap will do. Can you find me more? It's in short supply, I know, but anything. And don't *ma'am* me."

"Yes. What will you do with the rogues?"

"I don't know," Lila said. "I thought just maybe keep them locked up for heresy or stupidity or something. I'm sure it'll come to me. Probably I should talk to them but I don't much feel like it. I need another pen. Or maybe just some ink; I think it's refillable."

After Bentley had gone Lila took a used sheet and wrote on it by burning a line with high localised heat on the tip of her finger. *If I am not back in a week, give up on me and let the buggers out. Sincerely, LB.*

Then she took the pen out of her bra, uncapped it, and drew a circle on the wooden floor. She paused until she was absolutely certain of what she wanted. The black line slid out of the nib without the slightest resistance, as if it was eager to please. Inside the line she wrote: *Demonia, Central Souk Square, a seriously impressive flashbomb effect with knockback affecting anyone within fifty metres plus sonic shock wave to stun for ten seconds, knockback to do no lasting harm, portal to expire immediately after first use.* She put the cap back on carefully and regarded the infinite darkness of the ink, its slight reflections that reflected light that wasn't coming from her room. The words weren't what a lawyer would call nailed down, but she had no doubts about her intentions and that had to be enough.

That left only Tatter, and the pen. Feeling rather stupid but determined she said aloud, "I am not going to die wearing Harry Potter's Halloween outfit." On her shoulders the cape shifted slightly, but it seemed a tense, annoyed shift. All right, she decided that she would move straight to begging and cut out the whole middle in which they could fight about who was in charge and she could lose. "At least make it practical. Demonia. Remember? You must want to live through it and not become a Galactus demon's tablecloth forever, I assume." To illustrate her point she enabled all her weapons systems and the AI faculties that helped her to use them.

The shift was almost instant, she noticed, her responses almost as fast as light. They were faster than her human parts could follow. One moment she was herself, the next she was a tall battle mechanoid with vastly impressive shear-bladed blue metal armour and impossible-looking gearing. Her hair was a fury mane of blue-black spikes, shot with the red scar that splashed through the plating of her shoulders. In spite of this she had a delicate look, she knew, like a graceful faery dancer composed of razor blades and spite. She'd been working hard on the composition of that as much as the adaptation of new weapons and the inclusion of the antimagic technology. Demons loved a look as much as the faeries, and she'd used every comic book from the library to come up with it. She wasn't the greatest artist, she reckoned, but she'd do.

Over her body the metal elementals moved in a slow electric blue-and-white glide making it seem as if they were her shield.

With the shift the pen had moved in her hand. It outdid her of course, she realised. Although it weighed nothing to her the massive zweihander was back, with the elven runes shining as if they held a sun trapped in the vast curve of the blade. Its edges curled back with cruel barbs in a showy manner that wouldn't have outdone a hotelino spectacular floorshow. Then, at a touch, it split into two and became a longsword and a dagger, the dagger made not of metal at all but of a dark, purplish shadow whose length shifted unpredictably as though it was a serpent's tongue, tip flickering with the blackness she was used to seeing in the ink. Splendid silk tassels and bindings formed the grips. She was able to hold them and still employ forearm gunnery.

The dress meantime had also made up its mind. At first Lila didn't know where it had gone, but then it dawned on her. She didn't need a mirror to form the image of herself accurately in her mind.

She was a killer robot with magic swords, so of course she was wearing a skimpy purple-and-turquoise silk designer swimsuit of the kind that was more stuck to the skin than employing any kind of sensible attachment. Slightly ruched, dip dyed, glittering with gemstones, it offered the unlikely support of a top-rank plunge bra and the styling of a tart's boudoir. A very very expensive tart with tastes that included designer bikinis that cost more than small countries and who had no embarrassment left to interfere with her couture.

Once she'd got over the shock of seeing so much of herself on show, of seeing how she seemed to have got a human torso without meaning to exactly in spite of all her planning, she found herself starting to smile. She looked quite mad. It was perfect.

At that moment she heard Bentley's footsteps in the hall and immediately jumped into the circle, both feet in, arms tucked to her sides.

There was a sensation of being surrounded by a second skin so tight there would never be another breath, and then there was light and the roar of a serious blast. She remembered at the last second to strike a heroic pose and wished with all her heart that Zal was there to see it.

CHAPTER SEVENTEEN

After the day's duties at Mina's house were completed Zal checked around for Tubianca. He didn't find her, so he made sure Mina was upstairs, safely cocooned in her room, and then slipped quietly to the fireside downstairs where Mr. V was curled up in his mighty chair, almost asleep with an open book resting on his chin.

Zal slid the compact out of his pocket and nudged the dwarf's foot with one hand. Mr. V opened one eye, then both, and peered at Zal before clapping his book shut and sitting up. He glanced down and saw the silver circle in Zal's hand, and his eyes went as round as circles themselves. "You got it," he whispered.

Zal nodded. The firelight's merry orange flicker was reflected in the case, and a thousand times over in its many small diamonds as he gave it to Mr. V.

Mr. V stroked the case with delicate awe. "You have no idea . . ." He was choking up, and then he gave a little cough to clear his throat and hummed for a second. He turned the case over a few times and examined the simple pattern of its division into halves, one smooth and polished, the other encrusted with gemstones that shot light in all directions. One of these hit Zal in the eye and he was blinded for a second in which he saw the scene before him refracted, bent around on itself. . . . Then the moment passed and he found himself rubbing his stitching.

"Careful," Mr. V whispered to himself and Zal. "Easy does it. Dangerous visions for those who don't know. Dangerous. Now." His stubby fingers worked sensitively around the circumference. Zal thought he was searching for the hidden opener that must surely be there, or the gap where a sturdy fingernail could prise the shell open. But instead he saw Mr. V's hand stretch to its utmost, placing all fingertips and thumb to the rim. He did the same with his other hand, each one gripping the lip of one half of the compact. He rotated them gently, and from the silver came the strangest sound, as if a huge metal gate was being dragged across a vast block of stone. It was a quiet sound but unmistakable. It finished with a heavy thudded clink, as of a mighty bolt being drawn, another one being shot firmly home.

Zal glanced at Mr. V's face. The dwarf was sweating, beads of effort forming in the lines of his forehead and beginning to run along the deep channels of his cheeks. Neither of them made a sound. They listened as Mr. V continued to turn the halves, and after a while Zal began to understand that the clinks and thuds made a pattern, with other, softer noises like jingling keys behind them. He realised that Mr. V was listening for telltales; he was picking a combination lock.

After a while, as the fire burnt low and Mr. V's collar dampened, there was a new sound of bolts that drew back only and a faint ringing tone as if a bell had been struck, but only the end of the sound was audible, not the strike. Mr. V released his hold with a sigh and looked at what lay in his hand. The diamonds had moved their places, and now they built a picture in the centre of the compact. It showed something like an octopus, Zal thought, but he got no further for Mr. V gave a cry of horror and quickly twisted the dials again with a great clanking and shuffling that made Zal start and go look for the cat again. She was nowhere to be seen.

The work continued while Zal rebuilt the fire, checked Mina's bedroom, and watched the sluggish daylight begin to set. He hoped Mr. V succeeded soon, but as he drew the curtains the glimmer of unseen suns waned with the swiftness of an axe descending and before he could reach Mr. V's armchair night had come and he was once again a big cloth doll, slumped on the rug unconscious and helpless as the dwarf clicked on and on into the hours of the dark.

It was morning when Zal woke up. He never needed to eat or drink so he was quite ready to see Mr. V's excited face as the dwarf beckoned him close to the embers of the night's fire. "I have done it," he said to himself, fondling the compact and staring at it in wonder. "Bless you, lost one." He showed Zal, but before Zal could see the pattern of the diamonds he became stern and said quickly, "Don't look at it directly. Go to the side of the room!"

When he'd done so the dwarf opened the case like a clamshell, angling it so that Zal couldn't have looked inside even if he'd wanted to. A soft green light shone up into the little wrinkled face, which held an expression of delight so great it couldn't have been more joyful than if he was seeing heaven. Then the light shimmered.

From the palm-sized circle that rested on that small, creased hand a large talon was emerging, black, curved, and cruel looking. It was as big as Mr. V's forearm and quite impossibly huge for anything that could have been in a powder case. But this was nothing. In a second it was joined by another four the same, and then an equally outsize and matching hand came with it, a kind of a hand anyway, deep emerald green in colour and faceted like a jewel, the daylight sliding on its long, heavily knuckled fingers and vast palm. An arm followed, clad in crystal scales of increasing size, and then an elbow, and then another hand, arm, elbow, and then in a smooth, easy manoeuvre there came a mighty head, bigger than the whole fireplace, mantelpiece, and chimneybreast together. With the sudden slither of an easy birth the entire form of the giant dragon then came in a rush. If it hadn't been a purely spiritual form it would have burst the walls, brought the house down, and crushed them flat. As it was it filled the entire room in translucent, tight-packed coils, able to contain itself and fold itself up, as if being concertinaed and having several body parts occupy the same space was entirely natural.

Mr. V dropped the clamshell and held out his arms wide in a rapturous embrace, and the dragon shoved its head forward, frills and fans and horns alight with gemfire. There was a sighing sound from them both and then Mr. V was standing there alone, his green eyes sparkling, looking so happy he might float off right there. He didn't, however. In a moment he had caught up to the compact and snapped it shut. He came bustling quickly over to Zal and put the little object into his thick cloth hands, folding Zal's awkward fingers over it tightly.

"You're a—" Zal began, but Mr. V stood on tiptoes and put his finger to his lips with an expression of desperate earnestness.

"Yes," he said. "And I was her prisoner. For lifetimes without number. And you have freed me. This is her prison." He shook Zal's hands, still gripping them fiercely. "My spirit was trapped inside it. She kept it so I might never leave. I must be Mina's guardian and protector, look after her always." Tears were filling his eyes now and spilling down his face as he looked up at Zal with such kindness and love Zal thought he would start crying too, except he wasn't able to. "And," continued Mr. V, whispering swiftly, "I would have been here forever if not for you."

"But I don't understand," Zal said. "I have been here ages. Why did you wait so long?"

Mr. V pulled him down close, glanced around them, and then said rapidly. "At first I didn't understand what you were. I didn't know if you were like me, stuck in there too, or if you were different. It took time. I had to see. And then, when I was sure who you were, and what, I knew it was possible but I still had to find a thing of equal weight so she would not miss it."

"The book?" Zal knelt down and sat on his heels. He would have put the mirror in his inside pocket to protect it in case the cat returned, but Mr. V was holding him too tightly.

"Yes indeed. You see, there is a library here in this house of infinite content. Every book that will ever be or could have been, might have, was, ought, should, wasn't . . . they're all in there. But of course it's Mina's and she's hardly a librarian. I had to find something. And I did. I did. But now we must be swift. Listen to me. Soon Lily will know the mirror is gone."

"Mirror?" Zal felt he was plaguing Mr. V with questions but he couldn't help it.

"The prison is made of the two null mirrors of the Septagon. . . . We don't have time now for a lore lesson, boy. Just know that it is two mirrors that face each other. What then?" His stare was intense, unblinking, getting rather strong for Zal, who was almost hypnotised.

"Um . . . I don't know . . . an infinite regress of images . . ."

"Yes, exactly. The infinite prison. No end, no beginning. There are others in there."

"When you unlocked the other combinations . . ."

"Yes."

"Who are they?"

Mr. V shook his head. "I saw very many. None of which I would release. Do not try to open this again. Many are in there for good reason. Fate makes her mistakes like anyone, has her moments. I know, I know, why should you trust me when I have just shown you this? But you must. Do not try to open it. At the least you will find an empty cell and, once you look into it, you will be there until someone willingly lets you out. It's time to return it now. Will you do that for me?"

"Well . . ." Zal hesitated. "You said you knew about me. Can't you tell me what that was? Not that I want to play on the fact I did you a favour unknowingly, you understand."

The dwarf's green eyes sparkled. "Aye, play me, would you, boy? Ah, last time I played I didn't know who I played with either." His face became bleak and suddenly old, full of pain. His fingers on Zal's gripped hard enough to hurt, cloth or no. "And I sense a geas on you, yes, from herself, the final sister. Even she could not let me out. But you could. I will tell you when you return the book."

"And then what? Are you leaving? Won't they find out what I've done?" Zal suddenly sensed there might be a fate worse than death. In his hand the silver compact was cold.

"The sisters always have their little feuds," Mr. V said with an airy manner but a significant nod and wink that indicated the feuds were on epic scales. "You are Glinda's. That was the first part I knew, and Lily was playing with you. And then, having heard you talk and seen you about I began to realise how it was. What you were in your life, all that you were, is almost gone. Whatever happened to bring you here in this state, it was the ending of that, almost entirely. But while memory and mind has fallen into the past, spirit does not fall. You have yours still, so you are not someone dead they have pulled out of the weft, you are not someone undead walking and talking. You have lost only memories, but you are truly alive and free. If you had only the wit or inclination to leave here they could not stop you." He paused and smiled at Zal's expression. "Did you not know? I see not. And that is what enabled you to get this. I hope you will forgive my own game with you and presumption on you. I hope you understand why I did not enlighten you immediately."

Zal was thinking. It was hard. Lint wasn't suited to the task. He was quick to reassure Mr. V nonetheless. "Yeah, of course. But what if I keep it?"

"It would not do to make an enemy of her. She controls the warp, and that means she can pull threads in the lives of all you cross and not only your own. She is a prodigious weaver, a knotter, a tangler. . . . Do not."

Zal sagged slightly. "But what will happen to you if you go? You're going to go, aren't you?"

Mr. V's face became kindly and old again, like the grandfather Zal had never had. "Yes. I am going because I was tricked into staying. I have paid for my mistake. Mina doesn't need me. They can make other servants." He shuddered slightly as he said this but he carried on. "Dragons are not part of the warp or the weft. We are . . . hm, the analogy breaks down a little . . . we are like free shuttles. She has no power to yank my strings, and I have some power to ruin hers so I think she will consider us quit and be wary of me from now on. Not that I have any wish to see her again. Besides, who would miss me?"

"Well, I would," Zal said. "Nobody else talked to me. Except 'biancs and—"

Mr. V put his hand to Zal's mouth. "Say no more, boy. Nobody finds the Yin a happy companion, though she has her place. She'd be a great deal more pleasant if the other one hadn't run off, but we all have our losses to bear."

Zal didn't know what to make of this. He thought he'd try to remember for later since he was short on memories. "Can I go too? Can I go with you?"

"No," Mr. V said sadly. "No, you can't survive as I do. I could not travel safely and be sure I wouldn't kill you each second in the way I move. But you can leave."

"Oh, I suppose you mean the fire." Zal glanced at the embers, coated in ash, thought of himself as those ashes with fear and reluctance.

"Yes. Or you can answer the geas, the burden Glinda wishes you to bear."

"Would I be dead?" Zal asked, continuing to stare at the ash. "Would it hurt? If I become part of the strands of light, won't I lose everything?"

"It may be," the dragon said. "But you have an affinity for fire. Maybe you would be burned—there is always a chance of that with fire. But maybe not. Anyway, understand that this is not only true because you are here, and made of unsuited things. Anywhere. Anytime. Do you understand me? If you are not consumed fire can be your path, Zal. It always was. Come." He took Zal's hand, slid the silver compact into Zal's pocket carefully, as if giving him a gift, then led him to the fire surround—a silver guard decorated with grapes and vines. Gently he sat him down facing the weak heat and then, as he had for countless days and nights, Mr. V busied himself with the log basket and built up the fire again, expertly laying the pieces and adjusting the flue. Zal found it almost impossible to imagine being here without him. He wanted to catch the little man's sleeve and cling to it.

"Now," Mr. V said, caressing the logs lightly with his fingers.

Green flame played gently on their broken bark and then darted inwards to the old fire. Within moments the dry, seasoned wood had caught and was burning enough to allow flames to dance through the gaps and up, reaching for the sky.

"In yesterday's suns," he said softly to Zal. "Your memories were made. Look again. Look again. Is there anything?"

Zal looked, and for a while there wasn't. He felt close to Mr. V and wretchedly sad at the same time, but then something came to him, faint and far away, a couple of notes, a line. His throat felt strange. He heard music in his mind, he didn't know why.

". . . that's our destiny . . ."

"Go on!" Mr. V cried, hands clasped before him.

". . . the gods may throw the dice, their minds as cold as ice . . ." It came and went and Zal felt sure suddenly.

"The game is on again. . . ." He couldn't pick out the words fast enough. And then, like Mr. V's rebirth, in a rush there it was, belting out of him in a voice he didn't even know he'd had, like a foghorn calling for the last ship to come to shore.

"Winner takes it all! The winner takes it all!"

There was a thump from upstairs and a sound like a hefty girl falling off a chair followed by a cross wail of disappointment and annoyance.

Mr. V was up and running, shaking his hands at Zal. "Go boy! Go! I'll see to her this last time, don't worry. Just run and put it back, bring the book, undo what's been done."

Zal stood, still in shock, his mouth too strange to speak. He looked at Mr. V for a moment and hoped somehow his awkwardly sewn face could show all he meant in that second, all the warm feeling and gratitude, the sorrow and the gladness. Then he turned and ran, his thick stuffed feet flapping on the path with a sound of someone thumping a rug.

But he was not fast enough for Tubianca. As he reached the gate she shot out of the low bushes at the edge of Mina's small garden where she'd been hiding behind a bag of Mr. V's grass clippings and wrapped herself around his leg, digging in all her claws and taking a large mouthful just below his knee for good measure.

He howled in surprise, anger, and pain and paused to pull at her and shake, but she wouldn't be budged. Through his trousers she hissed, "I see you conspiring with that dwarf. . . . What are you up to? . . . Awful doll thing . . ." Here she stopped to get a better purchase with her teeth and yanked off a large piece of cloth, tearing his leg. Her hind paws paddled at him, ripping through his clothes. She intended to shred him, he realised. Already his leg had begun to bend oddly. He started running again, hauling her with him in a huge swinging stride around his hip. At least the swinging forced her to stop tearing so she could prevent herself from falling off.

She let out a yowl that ended with, "*Sto-op!*"

"No," Zal said, in between bursts of effort. "It's none of your business." He kicked as hard as he could, but his only reward was the sound of his seam splitting. He didn't slow down.

"Stop," the cat garbled again, sensing both his determination and the rapidly lessening distance to Lily's house. "I want to talk. I promise."

After what Mr. V had said about her Zal was inclined to believe her. She was fey, and she had said the p-word, but before he paused he gasped out, "Talk and nothing else." He kicked again, hoping she was sick and dizzy.

"Yes!"

He stopped. Tubianca unpicked herself from his leg and spent a moment turning away to smooth her fur and regain a dignified sitting position.

"Well?"

She licked her whiskers. "He said something about me, but I didn't catch it. You were too far away and whispering like little rodents."

Zal sensed an opportunity, though for what he wasn't sure. "He might have. What's it worth? Will you stop sneaking around and trying to get rid of me?"

An unhappy miaow escaped from her mouth. "But it is so dull!" she cried in protest, and he found himself agreeing with her.

"I know. But I don't find your methods of entertainment pleasant. I expect you let that rat in on purpose."

Her eyes grew round, and then the pupils slitted with hatred. "I did not, though I might wish I had. Very well, I will stop pouncing on you."

"And the sneaking?"

She stared at him. He got the impression she was at the limit of her ability to bear the shame of being beholden to him in any way. "One thing for the pouncing. If it is good, then we will see."

"For the pouncing then," he said, hoping he didn't regret it. "He said you were a lot better when the other cat was here."

Her expression wavered. She was quiet, then she said, "The thing about you, doll, is that you are the last in a long line of inferior toys. I have no memory of another cat, so either you are lying or else I have spent too long here in the comfortable rooms."

Zal couldn't answer that. He shrugged and turned to go.

"Wait!" she snapped. "The other. Thing."

He said nothing.

"I promise I will not follow you around."

"Anymore."

"Anymore," she repeated acidly.

"He said no one finds the Yin a happy companion."

At that she turned her face away and became abruptly and passionately consumed with a contemplation of the distant rocks. Finding her unresponsive to any gesture or word he resumed his trip to Lily's house, ignoring the way that bits of his stuffing were loose and trailing on the floor. The leg was half crumpled but still worked well enough that he could move without being too slowed down.

He made a quick search. He was most interested in establishing that she was not in, which she wasn't, but he couldn't help noticing the peculiar clutter in the downstairs rooms, even her workroom which was normally a place of order, housing the magnificent, evanescent tapestries on their bone stretchers. Today there was nothing but charts, and mostly ones that looked to his untrained eye like nautical charts. An astrolabe was out in the kitchen, a sextant in the workroom, and rulers, string, and writing materials lay here and there. On her small desk he saw an abacus and a scientific calculator side by side. Her bag of movable materials was missing, so she must have gone upwards into the real planes. He longed to have a good look around but he knew he couldn't waste a chance. He ran upstairs, pulled down the ladders, and scrambled into the dusty, empty reaches of the loft.

Two dirty skylights showed him a clutter of objects lying higgledy-piggledy, coated in a layer of dust so thick it was like a kind of moss. A few items in the farthest area were relatively clean, and here he easily found the book. It was lying on top of an open red velvet case, which bore the deep imprinted shape for the compact mirror. In a trice he had switched them over and closed the lid of the case. Fortunately things were reasonably dust free here and did not mark. As he was about to go his attention was drawn by the setting of the case . . . he had wondered how, in an entire loft, the dwarf could get by with a phrase like "what you will find there." The case glowed scarlet and was, clearly, the most obvious object in the room, but still . . . and now that he looked he saw that there were other things here: a old perfume bottle of pale blue, down to its dregs; a silver-backed hairbrush with a dated style of pig's bristles for brushing long hair; and a small green glass swan or goose with a red beak and big, childish eyes. Glinda must have seen all these, he thought, and then he looked at what they were resting on.

The dressing table was a kidney-shaped curved item in walnut, clearly an antique. It had a mirrored back, but the mirror was covered in a heavy velvet drape of mid blue that had faded unevenly in the light from the windows. It was weighted with long golden tassels on all sides that meant it couldn't slip off by accident. In the middle of the drape was a gold-stitched emblem of a rune that he recognised as being a royal mark of some kind.

He turned to go and found the white cat standing at the top of the ladder.

"You promised!"

"I came here of my own free will without any following or sneaking," she said, and moved forward, delicately sniffing at the floor and stepping only in the cleared space between items where there was no dust. Even so, she sneezed. "Blame yourself if you will go leaving ladders down where they aren't supposed to be. I have a rat hole to find too." She glided smoothly past him and looked askance at the dresser, then prowled about its legs observing the skirting boards.

"I have to go. Come on."

But she continued her idle prowl. "Go on, do. Don't let me stop you."

"I will put up the ladders and close the trap. You'll be stuck here."

"I can always sing to be let out," Tubianca said mildly, sitting down and observing the hang of the low swinging tassels.

"But then she'll know we were in here."

"And? I shall only say I came here after the ladders were down. She can interrogate me all she likes with that stare of hers, it is the truth. You are the culprit. What are you doing here, anyway? Perhaps if you tell me I will come quietly and Lily need be none the wiser." She batted idly at the tassel nearest to her.

"Stop that. Don't touch anything."

"But it's so much fun," she wheedled. "And I have no fun left anymore since you spoiled it with your stupid promises." She smacked again, harder. The weight tugged on the cloth and it slid half an inch.

He could leave. If he went now he could give Mr. V the book, throw himself on the cinders, burn, and be dead or gone before Lily returned from whatever strange errand she was on. If she caught him . . . If she . . .

The door downstairs closed with a firm sound and they both heard the jingle of keys and the sound of Lily's sigh as she hung her coat.

Without a thought he threw himself forward, arms outstretched, fingers wide. He met cat and floorboards at the same time, fortunately without a sound as he was too light to make one, although the book clunked faintly on the hollow floor. White fur slipped through his fingers and he felt claws rake his face a second later, though she made no sound in her flight. There was also a slight flumping sound, and then the tinkle of the perfume bottle falling onto its side.

As he got to his knees, slipping on the polished wood, he saw the big white tail vanish through the trapdoor with noiseless ease. Cursing her, he straightened up and reached forward to set the bottle right, and without a thought his eyes glanced forwards into the mirror where the heavy drape had fallen free.

He knew it was a mistake as soon as it had happened. For an instant he was paralysed, staring at himself and the dusty room behind him, the yellow gleam of the door in the floor where lamplight was coming through. . . .

. . . And then he was standing straight and tall, staring at the falling form of a large and ugly cloth doll as it collapsed to the floor, coat wide. The book showed clearly, half fallen from the inner pocket.

The paralysis was gone.

"Genius," said a voice sarcastically from behind his left shoulder. He turned, and there was Glinda. They were both inside a room that was exactly like Lily's loft, only reversed. Glinda bit out her cigar and spat the end on the floor, grinding it under her boot. "Well, that's one way of getting a move-on. I told you not to play games, but you never listen." She shook her head, grinning at herself. "You think I'd understand by now. Anyway . . ."

But he was looking down at himself. "I'm . . . I'm . . ."

"You're a shadow," she said, waving off his wonder and awe with a flippant hand. "Big deal. It's part of your nature. Shadowkin. Just don't go running around in bright light, not that there's much of that here so I wouldn't worry."

It was true—there was not much light, and what there was seemed blue and dim, making his shape a stain of black and purple on the air. He felt better than in the cloth form however, fluid and strong.

"Let's move," Glinda said, clapping sharply. When he looked back at the mirror she had already covered it with a filthy black robe.

"The book. Mr. V. . . ." he began.

She sighed, adjusted a piece of her part-plate, part-leather armour, and suddenly produced the book, offering it to him. "Here. Don't ask me again or I'll have to kill you."

"Thank you, but he needs . . ."

"You should have thought of that before," she said, shrugging rather like Tubianca in manner. "Now you promised me that you'd be my little soldier." She pulled out a new cigar, stuck it between her teeth, and grinned at him. Her golden eyes blazed.

"I have to stop doing that."

She snorted as if it was self-evident.

He looked around. "Where are we?"

"Isn't it obvious?" She held out her hands and made a sweeping gesture at her own magnificence. "Where do you think you get to see and talk to me in person?"

"Thanatopia?"

She made her hands into guns and lined them up to shoot at him. "Am I—"

But she was giving him a look that said if he even uttered the word she'd be glad to make it so.

Zal shut up. He did a turn, and another, found he could walk, move, talk. He smiled. "Okay. Let's go."

"You first," Glinda bowed theatrically and waved him on. "Rules say I gotta follow at the stated position."

"Where?" He reached the trapdoor. There was no ladder here, just a set of stone steps winding down into a fathomless blackness.

"I don't know exactly," she said with good humour. "But I think you used to once be a decent soldier, so my plan is to find necromancers— any necromancers—and prise the truth out of their nasty, fiddly little fingers by any necessary means until we hit the right one or get a clue. I know where they all are while they're here, so the first part will be easy. After that I'm sure we can think of a way to make 'em talk."

And with that less-than-comforting confidence they began to descend.

CHAPTER EIGHTEEN

There was light. For an instant it even blotted out all of her sensors. There was sound like a force on its own that made the stone vibrate and weaker portions of it shatter, sending splinters and dust flying into the air. There was a blastwave that cracked the stones which survived the sound and threw over a hundred bodies up and into the air to join the matchwood and rags, the fruit and meat and vials and potions and fetishes and jewellery and small animals that had taken flight along with them. There was a roaring of storm-force winds and an unearthly terrifying howling of vortices counter-ripping, tearing hapless objects to pieces. There was a thudding. There was a pattering. There was a kind of extended sigh and then there was a silence.

Lila walked out of the epicentre along the road towards the Ahriman Manse. The sword, in one piece, lay at her back on a make-shift belt. She neither looked right nor left, nor at the ground, as she stepped over the increasingly large piles of debris in her way as she passed through the concentric rings of her destruction. In her wake groaning demons began to pick themselves up and the less stunned of the small creatures dragged themselves to shelter. At the last second she'd decided against holding the weapons in her hands. A little bit less was a whole lot more.

She made her way steadily, ignoring everyone. When the attacks came, as they must, she parried them with necessary force, but she never slackened or speeded her pace or altered her direction even in one degree. These were not significant attacks or else she would never have been able to stage-manage herself so well. They were merely opportune assaults hastily made in case she were weaker than she appeared, almost a demon welcome of a kind.

By the time she reached the house, having telegraphed her arrival and intentions so clearly, there was a small posse waiting for her. The steady pelting of missiles—everything from soft fruit to gunshot—ceased abruptly. The demons in front of her were all large and imposing. They dwarfed her in size, except for the central figure, who was slight but made up for stature by the brooding malevolence of his presence, an energy that was sufficiently powerful to make her feel like turning around and going home, though she didn't.

Viza was the master of the Law. His accompanying creatures were the Instruments of Justice. She recognised them from a quick study of the latest photographs from the agency files. They had no exact authority to prevent her entering her own house, but she stopped as a mark of respect to hear them out in the hope that she wouldn't have to fight them.

"Welcome back, Friendslayer," Viza said. He was almost human looking, save for his strangely extended skull and the talons he bore instead of fingers. "I trust you are here to execute justice upon your husband?"

"If you can point me at him," Lila said lightly, "I'll be out of your hair."

At this Viza's already significant darkness deepened and the light dimmed around them all. "Alas, I was hoping that you knew his whereabouts."

"I'm here to find him," she said. "Do you have any helpful knowledge you might share with me?"

"All say he is within the city, and that is all."

"Okay. I'll start with this house and then I'll search the city then," Lila said, a model of civil compliance and practicality.

"We have searched all the properties not directly controlled by your . . . family interests . . . so you may ignore those," Viza replied smoothly. "Perhaps you would take one of my assistants with you on your task to verify—"

"I don't think so." She knew she had no obligation. He was simply hoping to prey on her inexperience of demon affairs and win her over with civility, which she was reasonably sure he didn't feel. That made elbowing aside the dregs of her natural politeness much easier. She lowered her chin fractionally and maintained a powerful position, unblinking. "Stand aside."

He had no choice, though she could see it irked him deeply. The black miasma of his spread energy clotted and became flakey, like negative snow; then he gave her the merest nod of acceptance—the only concession to her authority he could bear—and twitched himself to his left so that she could pass them and enter the house.

The hall was crowded with demons of all shapes and sizes, none of which she recognised except the Ahrimani servants who wore a purple sash around their garish colours. These immediately ran to her and were first to prostrate themselves, facedown on the floor, quickly followed by most of the others present. Those who didn't flatten bowed deeply. The slowest was a tall, horned, and tusked demon like a centaur, with a dappled, wet-looking skin. His face struggled to compose itself around the many outgrowths of fang and horn but he did lower it to her. She guessed he must be a significant member of one of the houses Teazle had most outrageously acquired.

"Get me maps and inventory of everything we own," Lila said, walking through the way that parted for her as if it were the sea parting at the foot of a saint. "And send the vassals of all the newly sequestered families to me in the war room." She didn't acknowledge anyone with even a glance and proceeded through the house in the same way, acquiring detailed information from all her machine senses as she passed. The basic features hadn't altered, though there were many more of the lesser immediate family in residence and signs of great spending having gone on in their previously seldom-visited apartments. Even the fish pools sparkled with jewels cast carelessly into their tiled shallows.

Besides family, a lot of whom Lila supposed must be friends and relations were about the place, trying not to crowd to see her, bowing, ingratiating, backing off, spouting greetings of enormously overblown grandeur, and trying to foist trinkets on her. She strode by as if they did not exist, and if they got too close she made no effort to avoid them, even treading on one particularly greasy individual who was trying to stop her, scraping and bowing backwards with some whiny petition about an unfairness in the distribution of wealth gained by the family. However, the servants at least had some of their heads on straight and made sure that the war room was pristine and ready for her arrival, with onlookers and hopefuls corralled to the halls on either side, as she reached the head of the vast staircase that led to its frescoed and vaulted magnificence.

She'd only ever been shown this room by Zal after they'd been married, as part of her grand tour of the house, and remembered its heavy black grandeur, set off by a magnificent set of stained-glass windows that wouldn't have disgraced a cathedral, although the subject matter of various Ahrimani engaged in acts of torture, slayage, and sex might have.

At that time she hadn't been head of the family or anywhere near it. Zal was an adoptee, through love, by Sorcha, who was herself only one of thirty children of the matriarch's sister's marriages. Zal wasn't counted lesser, but he was only a minor authority with some seventy or more individuals before him in line to the ascension. The fact that the house itself was the second-largest power unit in Demonia was what had given him so much kudos. However, Teazle was the direct heir of his own house, Sikarza. They had married, and that had yanked Zal and Lila up the ranks of the Ahriman wannabes about forty places. Further ascent waited only on some longevity to their match; time and good-will needed to be established, and then more would follow in due course as both houses made the most of their fresh alliance. However, once Teazle had killed his mother, they had reached direct heir position themselves, seeing as they were wed to the head of an allied house. Only Zhadrakor Ahriman counted higher. But since then Teazle had gone on his monster mission to rule all of Demonia, as a side effect of his mission to help Lila, and that had pushed the whole Ahriman house into the shade of his glory. As his spouse and the only available member of their union, this made Lila head of the entire empire he had fashioned. She had greatly honoured Ahrimani by making this her base, elevating its ranks instantly to equal position with Sikarza once again as overlords of the civilised world. They owed her big-time. The Ahrimani stood to lose a lot in Zal's absence, though his death was unproven. Her reemergence had renewed all that had been lost in the fifty years since they had gone. Coupled with Teazle's reign of terror, it put her in a supreme position. Plus she didn't want to start out by flushing the Sikarzas through with blood since many of them no doubt would be the keenest rivals for her position. That might be messy, with too many possibilities for a mistake. She had to come here, and she had to make them all come to her and establish her superiority immediately and absolutely. Yes, as she reached the throne at the head of the vast ebony horseshoe table and sat down in its ugly gothic nest of snakes, skulls, and skeletons, she felt in charge, confident of her decisions and out of her comfort zone by a factor of approximately a thousand.

The bikini gleamed with approval of the entire scheme. She placed the huge sword down in front of her on the tabletop and removed her hands from it.

The servants took this as a cue that they might creep forwards with an intent to place drinks, food, treats, and baskets of solid-gold fruit about the place as some kind of warming welcome. Lila dismissed them all with a wave. Gifts were toadying. Even a glass of water would be grovelling to them too much. They got nothing. She took a drink for herself in an ostentatious etched glass and placed it next to the sword.

Vilifi, the Ahriman majordomo, a thin humanoid demon of spectral properties who had been housekeeper when she was last there, drifted to a position just behind her and asked what they ought to do with the items. She sensed a key moment. If she admitted responsibility for this, he would plague her with decisions every second of the day and she would get nowhere. It would be weak.

She raised one armoured finger in a laissez-faire manner and let it fall to signify she couldn't care less but that he had better not bother her with such trivia again. He wasn't in his position for nothing. Demons loved subtle command. Whatever he made of it the servants holding the decorations melted away silently, leaving the guard, looking rather desperate to be curious but even more desperate not to be, and Vilifi himself, who blended with the shadows cast by the vast drapes at the stained-glass windows. As an afterthought she had all the other chairs removed from the room so that she could better claim the entire table and, by extension, any business, for herself. She seemed decently alone as the first of her subordinate house leaders arrived.

She was a fire demon, blazing with live flame, six armed and black eyed, and as soon as she had a clear sight line she flung her chest forward and a lance of white-hot fire moving at slightly less than the speed of sound shot directly at Lila's chest.

The sword leapt off the table, transformed itself into a whirling grey shield of strange vortices, and consumed the flame. In dismay the demon repowered her attack, using more energy, trying to push the grey anomaly backwards. She opened her cone to let the fire flow around the sides and get Lila that way. The grey disc bent the fire into itself. Then, as if it had lost patience, it turned on its side like a whirling circular saw blade and sped down the line of fire, eating as it went, spinning itself up to the demon and scattering her in a blitz of tiny smoking pieces all around the room. Her shriek of shock broke a window and the drapes began to smoulder.

Lila hadn't had to move. The sword re-formed itself and was back on the table, in its makeshift holder, before anyone had time to draw breath. It moved so fast that the other demons who had arrived weren't sure what had happened. Vilifi appeared at that moment with the records she had requested on a box full of scrolls. She tried not to lose her temper at the archaic things and reached casually for the first of them.

"Get me the heir," she said aloud, opening the scroll. "And make it quick. I haven't got all day."

The air became poisonous as another demon used the moment of her distraction to chance his luck. Clouds of vile toxins appeared as if from nowhere. As they touched her skin she felt her body react, analysing, manufacturing counteragents, issuing chemistry to prevent the damaging effects from causing lasting harm to her nerves, though she was soon immune to what would have killed an ordinary human on first contact.

Lila yawned and began to speed-read the scrolls, taking them, opening them, flicking them out to full length for a glance, and then leaving them on the floor. Her arms moved so fast they were a blur.

The sword became a spinning sphere of white cloud. It vacuumed up the filthy air and poured fresh, clean, ionised air in its place, darting around as fast as thought so they could only see it when it paused. Plagues followed, diseases so virulent and aggressive that they killed several delegates. The cloud spawned microclouds of bacteria, viruses, and phages of its own.

There was a brief, epic microparasitic war that lasted three generations for the minuscule protagonists, and then the cloud re-formed itself into a thin, clear film and wrapped itself around the body of the blight demon who had thought he would murder Lila until there was no air left for him. He struggled briefly against it, thrashing as he tried to tear it, but it was a complete membrane. Then it sucked out all the remaining gas and free molecules, and water.

Lila and the remaining living demons who were lying about in various states of recovery were able to watch as he was shrink-wrapped inexorably to death, shrivelling, withering, shrinking until at last he gave up and petrified. As the film unwrapped itself and spun back to the table, a sword again, he was left lying where he'd fallen, twisted and flattened as if the bindings were still there, his face horrified and enraged. He was about the size of a wastebasket, Lila noted as servants of the house appeared, picked him up, and carried him off.

"And that one," she said. She tossed down the final scroll and reached to take up her glass of wine, had a sip, and placed it back down delicately on the table. "Any more before I begin?"

But although she was certain others had come with her death already a certainty in their minds they didn't offer to make it so. Four had died in the poisoning and two of the diseases. Their stone remains were also removed to be returned to the family homes, and couriers could be heard winging off from the dispatch balcony to demand the attendance of the new regents.

She was slightly surprised to find herself with only eleven remaining living in the audience. They bowed deeply and kept themselves well back and artificially still.

"Listen carefully," she said. "You can fill in the recruits when they get here. I will be searching your properties in the city for my husband. If anybody gets in my way or so much as attempts to interrupt me, I will respond with mortal force. Those whose properties are clear will be granted dominion over their own once more. You will remain in exclusive and priority allegiance with the Sikarza house, but you will manage your own affairs, all of which are in need of some serious attention as I see here. If I find any of you have concealed Teazle or his whereabouts or are in any way implicated in his disappearance from free conduct I will kill you, and that goes for any I deem to be involved. Does anyone have anything they would like to say that might be useful to me?"

Some of them took breath.

Lila held up her hand. "I urge you to consider the fact that if your information is not useful I will liquidate half your house assets and distribute them among the commons," she added. "Half a fortune *every time* anyone utters a single word that is pointless. Chattels, property, and dependents are not exempt from this. But if your information is useful, then you will receive one-tenth of the Sikarzan fortune to be distributed as you see fit among your house."

In one minute she had undone Teazle's empire and possibly saved it from a fatal implosion, she figured, since after their takeover all the houses had halted any effort to look after themselves and awaited Teazle's decrees. Since he had no interest in managing a world again, everything was in a terrible mess. Not that she wanted it either. This was as close as she could get to returning everything without looking like a fool. They could be a cartel.

She spent a moment allocating responsibilities to those next in line at the Sikarza house who were still young enough to be able to handle that kind of authority, and then she made a final check of her subdirectors. They were all deep in thought, apparently.

Then one stepped forward. She was a hunched, birdlike creature, with clawed feet, who was almost entirely hidden in the shelter of her enormous feathered wings. Sweeps of green and blue were shining on her, signalling deference and placidity. She cleared her throat, though this didn't help her creaking, gravelly voice, and said, "Teazle Sikarza left my house a day before he vanished from sight. He was moving on, but he did not take another house over, and no further murder was reported. My servant was near the house of the wolf lady. They say they saw him inside hours later, as they were buying spell powders in the Souk. It is all I know. May it be useful." She backed up a step after speaking, and then as the others sneered at her she muttered a curse under her breath and they stopped quickly.

The antimagic detector Lila had engineered to be part of her skin had flared in that instant. This demon must have a formidable power if they were all willing to stay silent. She wasn't sure how she'd manage against it. Hopefully she wouldn't have to. "I will go there directly," Lila said and stood up. She picked the sword up casually in her hand and paused to finish her drink before walking out.

She took her time, waiting for a dagger to the back or some other check. She was almost disappointed when nothing came and she was able to leave the house unmolested.

The wolf woman was Madame Des Loupes. There was a certain full-circle satisfaction at hearing the last sighting might be there, Lila supposed. She wondered if Teazle had been looking for a way to clear himself, but that seemed unusually forward-thinking for him. It could be that he had run out of other places to look. His acquisitions were extensive. If he had completed a search of the remaining small private homes, he would then have been left with the Wild. She was glad it had all stopped before it went that far. Demons of the Wild were something she never wanted to see again in any lifetime.

Madame's house, on the other hand, was something she did want to see for herself. As her foot touched the street, however—a street remarkably clear of pedestrians and other traffic—she realised she was going to have a few delays. Clusters of demons were massing in the alleys that lined her route back to the Souk. As she walked they attacked her singly and in groups, piling one after the other in a great eager rush, their energy like a wave breaking in a fury of destruction until she was aware of nothing except herself in constant motion and the sword, a whining hum of vicious glee in her hands.

She progressed at the centre of a storm of violence, leaving a slick trail of gore clotted with body parts in her wake. It was slow, slower than walking. It was more grim and exhilarating than anything she had ever known. As she moved forwards she seemed to have left the ground and left all traces of her body behind. It moved without her, at a distance, its signals perfect in her absence until it seemed like she directed the monstrous gyre as a conductor and lead dancer, everything moving exactly to her timing and not the other way around. They tried to move hell to kill her, each in their own way, and together in every method they could muster. But Lila flowed and blood rained. Magic died on her. Curses shot back to the mouths of their unhappy givers. Blows shattered weapons. Poisons faded. Plagues died. Fire and aether vanished into her shell as if she consumed them. Water evaporated, boiling unwitting nearby attackers alive and exploding them in outguttings of steam and viscera. Missiles were returned to the gun, the bow, the cannon, and the shooter, no matter how much they ran, turned, twisted, and tried to escape.

The woman, the machine, the dress, and the sword had become an unstoppable force. Lila rode them, watching from the quiet central eye of the melee and at the same time seeming to float above herself and see it all from a bird's-eye view. It would have been comical in its ludicrous excess if it were not unfathomably and unendingly horrible. She wished in that moment, feeling stupid, feeling sad, "I wish I played the piano instead of this. Or even cards. Or anything." It was the greatest freedom and glory to be so good at something but the execution of her ability gave her no pleasure now, in the peak of the experience. She felt they were fools to attack her. They posed no real threat. Killing them was a waste of time and their lives. Try as she might she was no demon in her heart and at last she knew it. She would never belong here, and now, after so much ample proof of her power, they would want her to.

Finally the assault ended and she walked free, the last of the bodies falling off her back and onto the unyielding stone. As she reached the central square and Madame's house she was alone in a quiet town, her footsteps sounding loud on the pavement. The green door that led off the street bore the marks of the police department and was locked, but she was equal to the picking, opened it and went inside, closing it behind her and locking it again. It was dark in the hall, and mercifully enclosed and quiet. She leant against the wall and closed her eyes for a moment and breathed out a long breath silently into the musty air.

I am never going home, she thought. Never.

After settling the sword on her shoulder she began to look at the rooms. They followed an orderly layout the same on three levels, with large square suites opening off a central hall and stairway. The crime scene, as she had seen in the photographs, was in Madame's favourite parlour that opened onto the square itself and commanded good views in three directions over the Souk and larger city. She stayed well back from the windows so that nobody could spy on her and examined what was left of the furniture. Most objects were dusted with telltale powders of various kinds and protected with hexing charms from disturbance. There was a lot of dried blood and signs of struggle. All the gracious items and lovely fabrics she remembered from previous visits were either chopped up, stained, or blackened by what had been a hasty but virulent fire. A lot was out of place, and she slowly pieced together from her memory, the photographs, and the present evidence that looters had been here several times over after the police had gone on their way. She found the balcony doors broken at the latch . . . that explained that.

There was nothing to indicate Teazle was responsible now. And nothing to indicate that he wasn't. She gave up sifting and straightened, listening. The empty house listened back. And then she had an impulse to put her hand in her pocket, though bikinis didn't have pockets of course. But suddenly hers did—it had a small bag hanging from the flimsy strap across her hip. She was not surprised to reach inside and find the warm, unpleasant lump of fleshy stone that was Madame's Eye. It seemed infinitely long ago that she had sat here on a sunny day, with the imp cavorting in the milk jug, and accepted it from Madame's hand as if she were a rookie reporter being given an assignment. That was what it had felt like, though later she'd never actually used it. There was nothing to fear now, however.

A feather was what she needed to make it work. She searched a few more rooms—Madame had kept ravens as well as her suitors, who had feathers of their own. There was nothing on the top two floors, not even on the ground floor. She wondered if the police had cleaned out the place or if Madame had just made the suitors incredibly fastidious. Given their looks as risen dead, it seemed a bit incongruous if that had been how it was. She was mulling this when her eyes flicked back twice to something on the floor in the pantry.

She had to bend down and reach back into the deep shadows behind a grain bin to reach it, but there it was—a blue-and-white feather. One of Teazle's.

What the hell was it doing back there? Nothing in here had been moved. The air was fusty with mould and the floor covered in dust that showed no tracks. He would have had to put it there, she thought, but her spirits lifted at this sign of him. She was slightly loath to use it, but she moved back to the kitchen area, set the plume down on a sideboard, and then put the Eye on top of it.

Instantly the nodule sank down as if melting and became markings on the feather, transforming it into something rather like the end of a peacock's tailfeather. Then that marking moved and blinked and became a blue eye on a white background. The eye looked around, swivelling as far as it could, then fixed on Lila. She had no idea what to do. There had been no further instructions.

The eye stared at her, and its pupil dilated and then narrowed as it put her into focus. She was about to speak when the most peculiar feeling of being watched from the inside came over her. There was no centre to the sense of presence, and none of her AI systems registered or set off an alarm, but the hairs on her body stood up and a chill ran through her that made her shiver convulsively. She half expected a voice any moment: Tath had spoken to her easily when she had carried his spirit. Instead it was like occupying, faintly, another person. Faintly because in comparison her own senses were strong signals and this was a weaker thing, less than half the power. But it was good enough. She understood, because this occupying ghost understood, that she was connected to Madame's mind and it was a place of curious, unfolded dimensions, glimpsed vistas, winking possibilities, and the flickering half-lives of moments as they fell from chance to reality or into oblivion.

She took the feather, so as not to break the fragile contact—the eye did not seem to mind—and carried it in finger and thumb as she left the kitchen and moved along one of the halls to a particular spot. There she was now able to see that the light fittings where smokeless torches had been taken away and little solar glowbulbs fixed in place were the covers to a panel. She stuck the feather in her hip sash and levered the panel free. It was beautifully made. Even with her enhanced faculties she'd missed it. Beneath the fascia lay a small set of buttons, unmarked and unpowered. There was also an inlet socket. It was the work of a second to create a matching plug, jack it in, and run electricity through the system. As she keyed in the combinations it did occur to her to wonder where Madame was, why she seemed to be helpful. The answers that suddenly manifested in her mind were hard to grasp at first. Madame was in the back of beyond—a faery style of answer if ever there was one. She was assisting Lila because she was being hunted.

Lila paused at this and cast about looking for more details. A sense of reassurance came over her. All would be revealed. Prompted by her new thoughts she realised this part had concluded. She unjacked, replaced the panel, and went up to the second storey, to a walk-in cupboard where a new door had opened behind a rack of clothes, splitting the rack neatly in two. There was a narrow staircase, circular and stone-built, lying in the heart of the house. Lila had to shrink all her proportions very slightly and take in some of the bladed extravagance of her armour. Then she slid into the opening and closed the doors behind her. It was utterly dark, but this did not bother her as she had more than enough senses to cope without eyesight. She felt her inhabitant's slight twinge of envy and smiled as she started a long walk down.

As she descended she found that she knew this stair led past the house's single and obvious cellar and farther down to a tunnel that had been dug long before out of the friable bedrock of the city's foundation. Some ten metres below the surface she reached it. It was dank and her feet splashed in low water. Beneath the lagoon's surface the rock here was usually supersaturated with water, but spells kept most of it out. The house had belonged in much older times to a pirate queen, and this was the secret passage to her treasure chamber. Madame had discovered it via her clairvoyant skills, because prior to her purchase of the house all knowledge of it had died with the pirate herself. Madame had fitted the tricky electronic extra lock mechanism herself, as she had foreseen a police search of the house in which the cupboard would be scanned and its old lock system discovered.

It was Lila's turn to be impressed and envious. She paced the familiar/unfamiliar track of the tunnel steadily, noting its turns, and then, with surprise, she found it branching. The suppurating, stinking air, old and foul with neglect and the seepage of generations of demon sewage, formed sluggish intersecting trails. Lila scanned and scanned again. She had reached a labyrinth. It was the treasure chamber. By her calculation they were now beneath the lagoon proper, not far from a major commuter boat route that joined the main city to Isle d'Ifritis, a place given over to the more elementally attuned demons so that they could experiment with Zoomenon energies at a safe distance from the majority of the population.

Lila began to move forwards. Left, left, right . . . the turns flowed out of a memory that wasn't hers but which was confident of itself. Occasionally she turned her face out of habit to "look" down an untaken path. Sometimes she had a sense of knowing what lay that way, but most of the time she was not sure. As she went she created a clear map in her mind, marking all this down, and soon she began to understand that the labyrinth's ways were masterfully planned. She twisted and turned, crossed and recrossed ways—this route was one discovered by intuition working on old traces; it was not "correct" in the sense of being the only way to the destination. The labyrinth was not a true single trackway. It was a complex set of routes that met and parted, met and parted, revolved, reversed.

She hesitated suddenly. A faint smell had come to her, over the taint of the air that she'd become numbed to. She knew it. Her heart leaped, surprising her. He was here! She began to move faster, but then a possessing caution and a curious impulse made her slow down and pause once more. Ahead of her was a chamber that had light. But she must not use her eyes to see. She must shut them. Something was in there that was very important. Madame was excited but imperious in her warnings. This thing, whatever it was, was key to her survival, as well as Teazle's. Lila would be helping her in finding him, but it would be no help if she looked.

Lila closed her eyes—which made no difference at that moment. She moved more slowly, utterly alone in the dark except for the occasional drip of water from the low roof barely an inch from her head. She made more turns, descended a short stair, slid down a ramp, and was there. What she "saw" on infrared detection made her stop dead in her tracks. The chamber was small, but it was half full of demons. Teazle was among them, at the back of their ranks. Aside from him, all of them were stone dead. He was not moving. As if he were one of them, he was caught, motionless, balanced with grace in a pose that was moving eagerly forwards, all the better to see what every single one of them was staring at, each in their own individual pose of rapture. At the front of the queue was an unusually large statue of an Amazonian female demon of mixed draconid and human descent, her hair a mass of finny tentacles writhing, her eyes and mouth open in an expression of strange delight as she balanced on her clawed feet like a dancer, her hand outstretched to touch the large and beautiful frame before her from which her other hand had just pulled free a heavy covering silk.

That silk was now a few rotted strands in her eternal grasp. Inside the frame sat something so infinitely black that none of Lila's ur-lights or frequencies could penetrate it. It was there but . . . she had no idea what it was. It bore no properties of anything in the physical world she could measure.

It was the Mirror of Dreams.

Of course it was, she thought and surveyed the scene once again, closely, before stepping carefully towards Teazle. He might have been made of rock for all the movement he made. She thought of moving him, but a recoil struck through her bones. No. He must remain exactly where he was when he had been trapped. Otherwise he would never get out.

Madame herself had never come this far. . . . Lila was surprised. She had expected to find her too, but after sensing what lay around the final turn Madame had stopped her exploration of this particular tunnel. Her question had been answered. This was where the pirate queen had been lost, and her crew after her, and a couple of other lucky discoverers after that, until in time they had all been forgotten. It was the heart of the labyrinth. The pirate had brought her greatest loot here and, in defiance of all warnings and in a good deal of ignorance, had thought she would have a look at a legendary object for herself. And it had looked at her. And that was that.

Teazle had somehow got himself down here and he had done the same. He couldn't have known. He wasn't stupid. Lila checked him over. Apart from some muscle wastage and fatigue he was still alive. He was breathing. His heart was working fine. Soon he would become badly dehydrated and later he would starve to death or else . . . she turned around and looked closely at the other demons. They didn't appear to have died of starvation. They all looked rather lifelike, if not lively. She was forced to conclude that something had happened before that. She waited for more knowledge to rise from her contact with Madame, but the clairvoyant knew nothing about it, only a vague notion from an old story that one might die whilst dreaming and so die in reality. Lila scanned back into the still darkness within the frame. It gave out nothing. Were they more than paralysed?

This the clairvoyant knew. She was impatient with Lila's obtuseness. Of course they were inside the Dream! Their bodies remained in the real world, but their spirits were gone. Lila didn't know if the body died because of that severance or if something in the dreaming was getting to them and killing them there. At this a sense of urgency so acute overtook her that she started to gasp for breath and her heart began racing of its own accord. Madame's fear overwhelmed her, and in that instant she saw what the demon saw. Madame was pursued! She must run and hide! Futures whirled before her in which the thing that came behind her overtook her and consumed her from within.

There was a brief burst of energy that flung Lila across the room to hit the wall. It snapped her out of the contact. Lila found herself back in her own body. The bikini had become a tight-fitting leotard in its efforts as it pulled her from the brink, and she felt it slithering crossly around her skin like a snake that she'd annoyed. In her hand the blue-and-white feather was smoking ash. She was really and truly on her own.

CHAPTER NINETEEN

Malachi returned to Solomon's Folly with a heavy heart and the sinking feeling that would usually drive him away from any matter that brought it on. He wasn't sure if it was a case of premonition, but the pall of foreboding was so thick he could almost taste it. He did not care if it was a great insight for the future or his own dread. His guts felt uneasy. As he parked the car and got out into the heavy atmosphere of the house itself he thought it had sunk even further. The sun—a bright day—failed to light even half the windows. At the periphery of the overgrowing gardens the forms of wood elementals hovered, gathering bodies, trying to see him and nose out his business or his strength. They rustled hungrily.

He knocked and waited. Vines had begun to grow over the door hinges, he noticed. There was also a kind of activity moving across the surface of the walls, a restlessness he had rarely felt before but that he had found in some graveyards. He didn't know what to call it, and didn't want to know. At last he heard soft footsteps and the scrape of a slipper on the tiles, then keys and bolts on the move, and finally the door opened once it had been given a good pull.

The ghoulish face of Calliope Jones stared up at him from its surround of bird's-nest dreadlocks with a slight impish smile on her lips. She looked cold as winter, though it was warm inside and out, enough to be jacket-only weather.

"You look like hell," Malachi said in spite of himself, shocked by her cadaverous appearance. Worse than the physical was the air of desperation that emanated from her, a vibration that anticipated nothing good or safe. He wanted to put his arms around her, but she still held herself up with that damned, brittle defiant anger shimmering even through all her suffering, so he made some gesture towards her with open hands and, seeing it, she turned quickly and padded back into the gloom of the hall. He followed her and started as the fey charms shot all the bolts and keys to slam and rattle at his back.

"S'where I've been," she whispered as she led him swiftly through the unfamiliar halls, passing several pale flickering copies of Azevedo, whom she ignored and even walked through at one point in her haste to reach what turned out to be the kitchen. It was a mess—an awful, cluttered, unwashed mess with everything out of the cupboards, used or left where it lay. But at the centre of it was a long black iron range burning scented wood, and around that was a small space with a chair, a footstool, and a teapot in it. She almost raced to the stool and crouched on it, huddling close to the stove and wrapping her filthy layers of wool cardigans and multiple skirts around her. She didn't smell, but even so he was repulsed at her slovenliness. He sat in the chair after assessing it for cleanliness. She rocked herself for a second, then leapt up. "I must make tea! You want some?"

"No. Just a few answers would be fine," he said, wondering if he would ever learn to loosen up around her. It was hard. He longed to be protective. She would have had his eyes out. Wryly he thought of Lila and then pushed the thought away.

Jones fumbled awkwardly with a kettle, water, the teapot, tea caddy, and spoon as if they were an advanced alchemy set and she had never used such things until yesterday. Her clumsiness stood in stark contrast to the slick expertise she'd had aboard that ugly ship in the Void, he thought, and her soldier's toughness in her camp. She was like a shell of herself. It was hard to watch and not try to help but he sat on his hands. Eventually she managed to get things in some kind of order and turned around, leaning heavily on the range, the oven door bar clutched in both red-knuckled hands. "You might as well have 'em," she said, still in a whisper. "No use to me anymore. I liked keeping a secret from you. It felt like fun. A bit of fun. But . . ." She hesitated, took a breath, and fought some inner impulse that he could see wanted her to turn away and run. He waited. He knew when to wait.

"That thing is the Admiral's Octant. Actually it's more of a nine-sided thing, but you know, I don't know the right words, the lingo for that kind of stuff. It's what he used to navigate. Without it the lead ship don't know where to go, can't reliably get anywhere. Lost at sea. And the rest follow it or the Admiral's orders. So nothing's goin' anywhere without it. Understand?"

Malachi nodded. Jones flexed her hands on the bar, gripping it as if it were a weapon. Her breathing was light and fast, her gaze darted everywhere, like a rat leaping from stanchion to stanchion of a sinking vessel. "It was good. Your faery money. It was good. They let me back. Sort of. We spent it all on gear and supplies. We found out lots of stuff, Malachi! Lots of good stuff!" She tapped the side of her head. "Like the ghosts are made in zones that spontaneously occur in the Void, always at coordinates that only make sense in planar metaphysics." She paused and swallowed a self-aware giggle. "You'll have to look that up, Malachi, it's not faery stuff. But they're made by thinking, made by minds, moments of focus, of longing and all that goes through a place that's always and everywhere, like the planes, a plane nobody talks of much, you know, like it was unpopular or not necessary or something. So we discovered it, kind of, we described it, we fitted it into the mathematics, Mal, and then of course I had to *walk* there!" She paused, alight with the pleasure and joy, the raw thrill of the memory, as if her adventure were happening now. He was infected by the feeling, but the light in her eyes warned him not to give her pause.

"So I *went*," she said, and waved her hands, shivering them like butterfly wings. "I went to the edge, out there, in the void, where they come from, I stood on the edge and I walked it and looked over into . . . but I couldn't go there. I was stopped."

"Thanatos?" Malachi asked, unable to stop himself.

She shook her head no, her mouth open with slack wonder. "No no. I said a new place. No dead people there, well, not exactly. No, you are there now, the part of your spirit that lives there, the part that is most *upper* and least *lower*. It is a place"—she paused, searching for words—"of dreaming. Close to Zoomenon, it is. Close. Closer than your own blood to you but you're never never able to cross over until you lose your mind. Do you see?"

"Sleep?"

But she wasn't listening to him; she was lost in her reverie. The kettle began to steam and simmer. "The ghosts were dreams that had been dreamed so much they were taking up spirit of their own, from the glimmer, the golden fields. Yes. They were hungry, empty things but with the chance to become. In the void they were strong enough to take on matter out of the nothing, blurts of quantum particles, you would say in human foolery, yes. Enough to be form. Then lose themselves again if there was no interest, nobody, nobody to *see them*, Mal. And I went there and I *saw* . . ."

But as she reached this part of her speech he was just for a fraction of a second ahead of her, and if she hadn't stopped his hands were ready to stop her somehow because she was about to say something dreadful. He found himself staring at her, his arms out before him bursting the seams of his linen jacket, hands become the grasping claws of a giant cat. Jones was staring back, slack mouthed, her eyes as round as saucers, but she was laughing, in a mostly silent, gasping kind of way.

"You *know* what I mean," she breathed, struggling to hold onto the bar, her hands reclenching. "Yes, you do. So, I saw them, and Mal . . ." She paused like a child about to deliver the punch line, longing not to tell, not to have the delicious suspense and control be over and done. "They ate me all up."

The kettle began to whistle, faintly at first, then louder and more stridently. Jones was grinning at him, at his horror and his inability to conceal it. "Choo choo!" she sounded softly, pumping her arm. She laughed and, using the bar like a rail, swung herself around and lifted the kettle off the hotplate. For a few moments she fought once again with the teapot, the spoon, the teapot lid. Finally she was done. Shaking as if she had the DTs she turned back. "Four minutes," she said to herself. "Four minutes."

Malachi had brought his paws down and let them rest in his lap as if they were his hands. Jones seemed lighter now, as if she had released something that had been pressing on her a long time. She fixed him with a more rational stare.

"That isn't all. Why I took the octo-thing. I got aboard the Fleet after a time, to find my way out. I knew I could ride it. If it manifested I could get out of there before it was too late. . . ." She glared into his eyes as if to dare him to contradict her, but he knew she was literally correct. The half-formed things and all her own potential would be stripped out in that place, mined like a seam of precious ore by the rapacious foment of that which strove to become real. "So I got to the Fleet and I found the ship. *Temeraire*. Yes. I got aboard her, stowed away. I saw the Admiral—a boy, Mal, imagine it! A boy with ragged trousers. He is hungry! They all were. So very hungry. But I was lasting. Only down there, in the hold, in the dark, there was something else. Not a dream. Not a ghost." She fought to speak as if the words had to be dragged up from below. "Not me."

Malachi could not move, dared not, in case he broke her fragile control. She looked as if at any second she would shatter into pieces.

"He said I would die there." She kept gripping, working the warm bar of the oven door. "But he didn't know I could be so quick. Didn't know I was a walker. I tried to get out but . . . I was lost. I hid in the rigging. I saw him go into the Admiral's cabin. He took him prisoner. He took the Fleet. He took it, Mal. And they all obeyed him. And he set sail. He was so glad. He had a chart. I stole a look. I saw what he wanted. And he saw me. I picked up the octant. It was just there, just lying there. He thought I'd gone but I was there. I got it and I ran and we were close to the edge and I jumped, Malachi, I jumped like I never jumped before and all my light . . . everything . . . I made it over. But he was after me. He saw me, Mal. He knew me. He came after with the whole Fleet, like a storm, like death. He wanted it. I didn't know where to go so I came to you—you're the only one I know, only one and you could have kept it, I thought maybe—so I came here and I dropped it and ran thinking he'd follow." She stopped abruptly. "Four minutes," she said and turned around to pour her tea, a little ritual of cup, pot, jug, spoon that took her another four minutes to accomplish while Malachi let his hairs subside.

"He came," she said, holding the stove. "But he couldn't cross. I don't know why. Some of the Fleet were too slow to stop. They crashed here. After me. They came too. He was strong enough to send them. But not strong enough to catch me. Not that way. Except he *has* caught me, Mal." And at this last her voice weakened and became a sob of rage. "He has a hook in me, a claw, and it is scraping, scratching me away to nothing. He can't come here, but I can't get rid of his grip. He is eating me. They are. The Fleet will have me because he is its captain." She paused and took a drink. It steadied her. She put the cup to her forehead, to her lips, back on the stovetop. "But I'll have a hand in getting him," she said, more steadily now. She turned, cup in hand, and sat down, for all the world like a normal woman, if an ill and sickly one.

"Understand he isn't human—he's something like a demon. Very old, very cunning. He is strong. Stronger than you. He is like death; I think perhaps he walks that path. His chart was of the Black, Malachi. Do you know that? Of the Darkness Before and After, as if it was a place and in dream it is a place, of course it is, could be, might be . . .

understand? He wanted to sail there. But he had other things, other servants with him. Many. Very very many. I think he had been there a long time and made and mastered things. Nasty things. They are like this claw in me. Anyway, without his compasses he cannot sail true. He will look for them if he can't make another. So his servants will be on their way. If not here already. I'm sorry for that. But don't let him have it. Don't make it easy."

Malachi shook his head, agreement. "But who—"

"If I say it I make it more true," she said, pleading with him to jump to an understanding. "Do you see? If I tell you then the idea spreads, becomes more real. It helps him to bring it to be. He is more likely to succeed."

He knew this was true. "If you don't tell me then I can't do anything."

"I don't think you can do anything anyway, except run," she said. She sipped the tea and rubbed her thin, hollow chest with the flat of her hand. "All right. Shit to him. All right. But not in a way that helps. He has this thing about the will to power. I'll call it that. I did philosophy, you know. Read it. Nietzsche. But he's like that, like that idea, something like that he's trying to do, but as far as he can go. He would do anything. What he can't steal he will borrow and what can't be borrowed he'll barter for or trick, and things that must be borne or suffered he will do all. He was looking for the first impulse. There. Do you know what I mean? What came before all the rest. What was first in the order and has been forgot so long nobody ever thinks of it anymore. Before the Titans. Older. Oldest. He thought it was real and even if it wasn't, angel, he was making it so with his map and his search. He will open a way. Do you see?"

Malachi did know what this meant. "But that's crazy," he said, almost ready to laugh. The Titans were demigods, the stuff of childhood fancy, of legend. Nobody even in Under believed such things existed now, and maybe never had. It was from a time when everything was in a state of much more profound unbeing, chaos and creativity in the fundamental states of aether and matter. It was the equivalent of the first moments of the universe. You might argue and calculate about it from the ancient radiation of those moments as it propagated steadily through life and limb, but you didn't know for sure. The Titans were guesses, faces put on forces that he doubted had anything as sophisticated as a spirit of their own. Or they were all spirit. He hadn't cared to pay attention in metaphysics, but he understood the path Jones was pointing at. Force of will dreamed, dreams took on spirit, spirit moved them to seek material form and articulate, actualisation occurred. Ghosts were the accidental by-product of this; snippets, by blows. There was a thing that apparently dreamed itself, however, was will first without mind. He knew about them and avoided them, like he tried to avoid the Sisters. Dragons. Before the Titans meant dragons—one in particular. The first one. The Dreamer. Night.

"It *is*," Jones said, crouching with her tea, inhaling the steam from her cup. "This was his dream. I *saw* it. And he saw me. The fucker."

Malachi was so surprised. "But what for? Why would he want . . . ?"

"Becoming," Jones said into her cup. "Power. Absolute creative authority to manifest . . . anything."

By now his hands had returned to their apparent human form and the holes in his sleeves no longer bulged with unsightly fur. He checked his nails but they were smooth. Jones was shivering compulsively. Her state made him afraid deep down, but here, in the house, amid the mess and ordinary disgust of neglected things without power, he was able to master it. He thought Jones was saying that this creature somehow wanted to become Night. That was not possible. There were lesser options, however. A servant of it? No. It had none. A channeler of it, perhaps, a conduit for it. That was possible. But at what cost? He could only speculate wildly. And then he looked at Jones again.

She smiled the smile that lies about all right and says not to worry, because there isn't any point. Sadness overpowered him.

"Jones," he said, remembering the tough, arrogant, defiant girl who had always played him to the hilt and taken everything like a greedy thief. The one who would never stop or slow down for anyone.

She clutched her cup but spilled the liquid anyway, smacking at the drops as they fell on her filthy clothes. "I'm done," she said, looking at her hand tremble. "Funny. Not to mind though. I did it. I found out about ghosts, how it all fits, what's made in the Void. I found it. But"—she looked up at him, fever bright—"I never wrote it down, Mal. I'm not good at writing. I never learned it. Isn't time now. And Azevedo can't. She isn't anywhere long enough. Too much trouble for her. Could . . . I mean would . . ."

"Yes," he said, leaning forward and taking her free, tea-wetted hand in his own two. He held it tightly but the shake went all the way to the bone and it couldn't be stopped. "I will. I'll make sure everybody knows about it, and that it was you who found it."

She looked at his hands as if she were puzzling what they were. Her face reddened slightly and she pulled away. He resisted for a second, then let her go.

"Can't I get you a healer? There's a place in the country. People like you there. Nice people. Half-fey. Chosen. They might . . ."

"Too late," she said. "Anyway. You know me. Don't like to hang around. You should go. They're coming. They mustn't find that compass. I 'spect they will find it, but they should have to wait. Make them wait. I want him to wait on my account." She was suddenly urging him to go; he felt it like a push in the chest.

He stood up. "Do you need money?" It was such a crass thing to offer, but he couldn't think of anything else.

"No, I'm fine," she said, nodding to herself, leaning on the stove once more, her eyes half shut. "You go. I'll see ya."

He nodded. "See you."

Her eyes closed all the way and she began to rock gently. Malachi slipped out silently and closed the doors after him. In the car he sat without starting it and glanced down towards the beach. The wreckage of the Void ship was breaking up and crumbling, its attempt to be metal failing under the ruthless scrutiny of the sun, wind, and waves. He laid his forehead on the wheel for a moment, holding to it like Jones held her bar. He felt time slipping away, sliding, hurtling him towards unseen vertices, separating him from her forever. It wasn't as if they'd been close. He didn't know why he was crying.

After a second he made himself sit up, turn the key, and drive. From the dappled shadows of the woods things half-unmade stopped and watched him passing. He couldn't help but see them from the corners of his eyes. Their gaze was cold, silent, more still than that of living things.

Lila considered the situation. Teazle was stuck in the dreamworld, with a good chance of dying before long, if the other statues here were anything to go by. But if she pursued him there was no guarantee she wouldn't suffer the same fate. Maybe the mirror was only one way. Or there could be a million other factors. No, it would be stupid to plunge in. Possibly, she thought, without her spirit her body might do all right on its own. She was capable of being a self-sustaining machine that didn't require aetherial presence of any sort. She was sufficiently remade to be sure that she could activate the AI to replicate her personality choices and run the show so that most people would never be the wiser. It was an odd thought. If she became a ghost, the machine could run itself. She didn't dwell on it.

Teazle could not have got here the same way she had, she was sure of it. Madame had already gone, and the combination lock showed no signs of use prior to her appearance, nor any trace of Teazle's DNA on it, or she would have found it. He might have searched the house briefly and left the feather as a sign of his presence, or even by accident, although it seemed unlikely it would fall to a place like that by accident. It was peculiar to think of him having the foresight, or the lack of certainty about his future, that he would leave a sign for her. In fact, it was so unlike him she felt it must have been prompted by an exterior source, that which would have convinced him he was heading into a possible trap. What could that be?

She made a more thorough search of his person and found that his right hand was clutching something very tightly. It was a parchment, a folded one, very old judging by the degradation of the cells that made it up. She tried to prise his clawed fingers open but they were absolutely rigid. If she persisted she'd break his hand. A few tugs on the thing and she was sure it would tear long before she could free it. Then she'd have to guess it was what led him here, a map or a letter. From the house above? There were too many unanswerable questions. One thing, however, she was sure about. Nobody in Bathshebat knew of the existence of this labyrinth—at least no one who wasn't already here. Teazle had teleported in, not walked, only she could be followed, though her threats must hold good for a while yet, even if she didn't come back. She betted it would take time to follow her. And what at the end of it? Without foreknowledge you would enter the room, look at the mirror, and be lost. Clearly Teazle had not known about the mirror. Therefore, with the small caveat that the mirror seemed to promise death by its own devices, he was as safe as he could possibly be from all harm. She could leave him here and return.

It was quite a caveat. She stood with her hand on Teazle's warm back and looked at him in the green simulation of her infrared vision, taken by her skin and not by eye. Her feelings for him were warm, but were they love? Of a kind, she thought. But she would not die if he was lost. She could survive it. He wouldn't blame her; he knew the truth better than she did. She liked his affections, she loved his allegiance, but in the end that didn't amount to soul partners. It seemed mean indeed to think so at this moment, when he had only come here in service of their deal, to find a way to find Zal.

And was this it? She stared at the black void of the mirror. Was the answer in there? Had he finally found it? If she didn't follow what was she going to do instead?

Follow Malachi's leads, she intended, always hoping he had some out of that annoying, arrogant Jones woman, the strandloper. Whoever sent her that zombie, that was who she had to find. Because this seemed a viable, less immediately fatal thread, she decided to take it. She hugged Teazle's immobile form and kissed his long, ugly dragonish face. She was about to speak and tell him she would return when the faintest sound from the labyrinth came to her. She stopped and listened.

It was the tap of a stick on the walls and the floor of a tunnel. Mapping and predicting the changes that the known regions of the maze would make, her AI calculated that it was coming from the other side of the puzzle. There was another entrance, or exit, and whoever was walking so carefully with the expert aid of their stick was headed her way.

The room was low and already getting crowded for its size. There were no corners or cubbies. There was nowhere to hide. The sound suddenly became nearer and she realised the distance effect had been a mistake on her part. They were not far away. They were nearly here.

She moved to the far side of the room as rapidly as she could in silence, assisted by every microadjustment her supersensitive body was able to make. She prayed to the dress and to her own systems as she remade her armoured shell into something more like smoothed stone and dropped her surface temperature to that of the surrounding air. Then she moved into a position like Teazle's, even copying the surprised expression of his face, and locked herself like that with her breath on internal recycling. The benefits of losing her human body's properties had never seemed so apparent. She made sure the connection to the camera systems in her eyes was shut off, then opened her eyes so it seemed she looked into the mirror's plane.

The tapping grew loud and then more cautious as it checked the turn around the doorway. She saw a small demon carrying a sizeable cloth pack on its back come into the room and inch its way towards the first comfortable marker of one of the statues. Here it set its cane with a practiced movement, hooking it safely in the crook of the dead demon's arm. Then it reached up and tightened the heavy cloth that was tied around its head, covering it completely to just above its nostrils. It unslung its pack and, using one hand, found its way around the first couple of stone bodies with a steady patting. Then it sensed something, probably heat, and hesitated, but not enough. It blundered into Teazle's arm and leaped backwards with an ear-splitting shriek, cannoning into the body behind it and hitting stone spines. A second shriek of a more comprehensive horror and distress followed. She could only imagine that, as she had, it supposed nobody knew to come here. The shriek was followed by a howl of pain. Both were sufficiently fast and ready to let Lila know that the creature was already very jumpy before it had even got into the room.

It muttered to itself, panting and lying still on the floor. Then it groped its way back to Teazle and touched him again, moving just enough to reassure itself that who it had found might be new but they were entirely stuck fast. Its gibbering continued and she couldn't make out what it said, but this was typical of demon speech. It sounded like music or nonsense to whoever was not intended to hear it.

There followed a few minutes of jabbering and general fussing about before it pulled itself together and resumed its business. It moved forwards, very, very slowly this time, until it reached the pirate demon queen, and then it turned its back on the mirror and pulled its cloth bag free of its shoulders. In a moment it had brought out what Lila decided was another mirror, but an ordinary one. It slowly, slowly removed the covering from its head and still with eyes tightly shut lifted the mirror up so that it would be able to see the reflection of the huge pane behind it, had there been any light.

There followed a scene that was completely surreal to Lila. She saw and heard the demon talking in a rapid, urgent way, looking in the mirror. During the gaps in its gibber she heard a very different voice speaking in Demonic. The visitor sounded upset, bad tempered, and put upon, if she was any judge. Demons rarely spared their feelings. The other speaker, however, sounded amused, contemptuous, but above all frightening. There was a quality to the voice that issued from the mirror that was as relentless and insidious as the penetrating water of the lagoon itself. You could put rock in the way, but it would worm itself through given a little time. You could put any amount of resistance in the way of this voice and it would find you and convince you. It was utterly compelling. She was glad she couldn't understand a word it said. She knew it could say anything and she would believe it.

After a series of crabby retorts and sighs and agreements in which she could clearly distinguish an agitated discussion of the newcomer the visitor packed up the mirror, replaced its hood, tightened the strings, and set its pack and then, with the same deliberate and now much slower and more resentful actions, it inched its way back to where it had left its stick. A few more minutes and its progress was a faint ticking in the breathless corridors beyond.

Only then did she find herself with the urge to shout, "Boo!"

The moment passed. She unlocked her position and remade her more common shape. Moving as quietly as she was able she followed the demon's path, able to find the way easily by smell and temperature and the disturbances of the air rather than the confusing rebounds of the sound. Obviously now that it knew Teazle was there, it had to die, but she wasn't about to let it die without talking. She moved closer, cautiously. She knew she had to make her attack before it moved into public areas because she was too well known, but even as that thought formed unsatisfyingly she felt herself warmed by the thin cloth of Tatterdemalion. It shifted and moved around her, coating her in ninja wrappings, in bandaged clothes that covered everything except her eyes. Following the hint she made herself small and lithe, and gave herself a demonic set of eyeballs with a slit pupil and green irises. The sword folded up into its Mont Blanc incarnation and she slipped it inside the coverings on her forearm.

It would be much better to find out where this demon was going, what it was doing, and who for. And besides, she persuaded herself, there was a chance it hadn't recognised Teazle. A chance. After the storm of death she had waded through before, now she found herself reluctant to kill. The messenger wasn't to blame.

She paused. She was so used to the sound of the Signal, the white hiss of constantly repeated information. It had made her miss the whispering of another kind of sound. Yes, her thoughts were hers, but they had, for a second, been reinforced by a doubled intensity. That voice from the mirror, she thought, putting it together faster than she was able to put it into words for herself. It had found her. Even though nothing it had said was meant for her some insidious part of it had leaked into her mind. It would be nice to find her conscience, to feel good, to be doing right. She longed to feel those things but had given up on the longing as an impossible thing. Those were for scholars and people who were not involved personally in an ongoing war for survival. She would have blood on her hands and blackening her heart every day, some kind of stain. . . .

She stopped herself. *Insidious* really wasn't the word for this kind of self-recriminating negativity. She had to get a grip.

The demon was almost out of reach. She hurried after it on her light feet, now easily silent on the padded perfection of her silk slippers. She used the AI to automatically terminate any thoughts that tried to make themselves into words. She had an inkling that words were the vehicle. An absence of language would be a firewall it couldn't jump across. She hoped.

They followed a different route out that came up in the cellars of another house on the far side of the lagoon near the dockyards where the vaporetti in public use were maintained and refuelled. It was an area favoured as artistic, where artistic leant to the illusion of suffering in penury and isolation from the common throng of society. Isle Saba was full of self-styled outcasts and rebels, philosophers, painters, sculptors, thinkers, and a surrounding coterie of style-conscious aesthetes. Zal used to say it was where critics were spawned, and he and Teazle fantasised about bombing it into the bottom of the lagoon when they got drunk together. Apart from artists it also had a large number of outcasts of a similar bent from the scientific and magical communities, and it was into this area that she emerged, in a house one street back from the waterfront.

If her prey had any ideas about the new demon in the labyrinth being Teazle it showed no desire to broadcast the news or even share it. It spent some time putting its mirror and head cloth down, dressing in warmer clothes, setting the cane in place, and then fiddling with powders and the various ingredients of a serious magical ritual that, she realised from her hidden position in the darkness at the bottom of the final staircase, would close and hide the exit in a very major way. Her only advantages were rapidly disappearing. She watched the arcane putterings going on, and when she was more than convinced there would be no chance to slip out unseen she lost her patience and ran up the stairs in two bounds, the second one powerful enough to launch her over the top step so that she landed right on top of the startled demon.

It was drawing breath for a yowl when she clamped one hand over its face and anchored its arms with the other, pinning it against her. She had thought she would interrogate it, but that would have required talking and talking required words and she was sure that would be a mistake since the thing in her head might be alerted in some way or would use them against her. The demon struggled, but it was no match for her strength. She could tie it up, she thought, feeling ridiculous. Fortunately they were alone and there were no other sounds in the house. She ought to kill it. Every reason said so. And yet the idea jarred a bad note in her. Was she losing her will? Days ago this path had been clearly the one she embraced. Now, now of all times was the moment to get guilt?

The demon wriggled a few fingers free and stabbed her with the quill it was holding. The sudden slight made her jump. There was a hollow, dull clunk noise, and she realised she had broken the demon's neck as it fell limp in her grasp. She pulled the quill out of her skin and looked at it with misgivings. It had been dipped in the blood of various dead individuals to become a ritual object, but her wound was already rejecting the alien proteins.

She let the body slide to the floor and searched its bandolier and vest, uncovering a large assortment of strange tools and bits, some of which she recognised because Tath had had them on his body when he died and she'd found them when she wore his clothes. They were necromancer's artefacts.

A flip of the corpse's major limbs revealed no significant scars, so they were not his own. The basic tools were made from bone, and in necromantic cases, always the 'romancer's own. This demon hadn't filleted so much as a splinter from itself, so he was using borrowed items. That made no sense. She sat back on her heels and stared down at the motley collection. Somebody else's instruments would not work, but it had just a moment ago been planning a closing spell.

She listened attentively and, on a whim, left him lying and went to search the rest of the building. What she found made her wonder a great deal.

There were no masters hiding in the wings waiting for a grand entrance, though clearly this was the house of a master. A master what, though?

For a start the house had no windows; it was built in the central well of a set of other structures that, by referring to maps and aerial photographs stored in her AI, she could see to be a series of warehouses. Ordinary businesses trading magical goods and luxury items operated a reasonably brisk shipping exchange through the outer layer, unaffected and maybe even unaware of a missing square footage near the centre of the huge cluster of buildings.

The lack of daylight was not an issue, and there were no signs of lighting equipment anywhere. Air was funnelled in through vents channelled from the roof, the sounds of tinny fan movements high above just audible next to their openings when she put her face to the incoming stream of city smog.

There were no doors. She amended that to probably no doors since they might have been magically concealed.

There were floors of laboratories, well fitted-out, and rooms full of books, parchments, and all the study paraphernalia of any educated and committed scientist. All in the dark. There was a telescope in the roof observatory, but no opening to the sky. In other areas, closer to the subbasement and its trapdoor, she found operating rooms, a surgical area, and a workshop full of engineering gear and the remains of various kinds of intricate machines that looked to her like demon clockworks of the sort that they used in golem manufacture.

The basements and some of the other rooms all held what she guessed were more necromancy devices or areas, judging by the circles and signs drawn on the floor. There was a kitchen without food in it. This puzzled her. She searched around and found a large door at the back with a sizeable latch. Opening it brought a cloud of bitter cold and pluming vapour. It was a freezer.

She left the door open and went inside.

It was full of body parts and some whole bodies. Humans and elves were there, many animals and birds, some vegetation, and, incongruously, a lone bag of frozen peas. This was nothing special considering the town and place, but at the back there was a large frosted chest, made of lead she discovered, as she found it hard to lift the lid. Inside it was sackcloth, blackened with fire and incense that had been ground into the thick weave. Inside that was a plastic bag and inside that was a collection of teeth. There were three of them, two fang teeth and a kind of shearing molar. Each was as long as her arm and their roots as long again. She knew they were teeth by their shape, but they were transparent and unflawed and they rang faintly as she clinked them against one another. At first she thought they were glass, but then, as she opened the bag and touched one, she found the shape of carbon and knew they were diamond.

It didn't take a very long game of Whose Teeth Were These? to figure out that they were the teeth of someone very big and carnivorous whose jaws would be large enough to drive a car into. She put them back where they were and was sliding the lid into place when she heard a quiet sound. She turned but she was too late. With a thump and a click the door of the freezer closed.

CHAPTER TWENTY

The world of death was not as Zal had imagined it, not that he had ever spent much time doing that. He'd assumed it wouldn't be like anything at all. But it appeared to him in the same fashion that Glinda did, as a function of his own ability to comprehend its nature, so it was doubly surprising that it wasn't what he expected. He reasoned after some time that this must be because it wasn't entirely up to him to create the way he perceived it. It had a topology, a geography and features of its own that he rendered in terms of the familiar. Thus there was countryside and sky; there was water and land and buildings. They all seemed much more real than he had hoped; there was nothing vague, floaty, or ignorably evanescent about them at all.

The land was craggy and bleak, its trees and copses shivering and bare. All was grey or in subtle shades so bleached they were nearly colourless. Water was invariably black, like ink. The sky was a deep, threatening mass of clouds that rumbled faintly and brooded with storms that never broke. Lightning backlit them now and again, leaving him plunged in what seemed to be increasing degrees of darkness, but the sense of it was alleviated slightly because he could only see for a few tens of metres before everything was lost in a mild but persistent soup of trailing mist.

The building he had first come across, on walking out of the end of the world, had been a romantic ruined abbey—no roof left, only the frames of the windows and a few columns through which the mist wound with listless ribboned elegance. Its flagstones were cracked, and grass and thin weeds grew through. Saplings had broken part of the outer yard as if an orchard was trying to burst up through the paving, though all the trees were rotten. Below the abbey's hill there was a river and stepping-stones. As he crossed the abbey fell out of sight into the gloaming.

"Go on," said Glinda with confidence, or else he would have gone back and tried to find a way of marking his position, because within a few more metres he could see nothing at all but rushing black water and the blunt, rough tops of the stones leading into the murk. He felt that it was cold but it didn't bother him. Looking down he saw his feet take steps that were so light he couldn't feel them. He almost drifted, like the fog. He looked like a black-lined ghost. He reminded himself of silk stockings, dark at the edges, lighter from a face-on view. It was so good to be without the lumpen cloth body, but at the same time he felt fragile and that if a wind came along he might blow away.

Once he turned to look back over his left shoulder. Glinda was right behind him, looking impatient, although he had no sense of anyone's presence when he turned to face front again and kept on stepping. He wondered that there should be this kind of place, it was so material.

"It isn't the material of atoms and such," Glinda said around her cigar. She seemed comfortable replying to his thoughts, even though he never spoke aloud. Her voice sounded in his head. His ears only heard the water's eager rush and the occasional tiny sound of his movement on the rocks if he caused unstable ones to shift in their beds. "And you can thank all the second-rate movies you watched for the special effects. Don't step in the water, whatever you do. It's soul-reaving. It'll finish what Jack started and you'll be seeing me for the last time if you do. Nothing living can touch it and survive."

Even a drop? he wondered.

"It has to run to work," she said, "but yes. Might as well consider even a drop, because if it ever does reconnect with the rest then same result."

"Not for you."

"Pff, I'm not some mortal existing in so many planes at once with my energies scattered like a toddler's crayons. Of course not me. What do you think I need you for? My health?"

He smelled the smoke of her cigar. "What *do* you need me for?" It had baffled him since she first said it. "Can't you just kill anything with a thought?"

"I am the Cutter," she said, "but I am not the blade. I am the pathfinder, but I am not the first step. Whatever it is that sunders the eternal from its connection to your actual temporary organisation, it isn't me." She sounded immensely satisfied.

He found a missing stone. The space to the one beyond loomed ominously far, tempting him to doubt. He leapt. He landed, wobbled. He was fine. He could balance well with these light, flexible limbs. "Am I the blade then?"

"Well, whatever you have to be you're it," she said.

He paused, seeing a bank coming up ahead. He looked down at the water's sickly gush. It was too fluid to be like blood, only the colour reminded him of death under different moons. He felt cold and empty suddenly. He was sure he had killed and seen people dying. The lack of firm memories made his body ache in the strangest way, as if it were listening for the familiar sound of home, turning in all directions. The water sluiced on, a muted roar, dragging mist with it. "I've killed before," he said. He resisted the notion that he was lost.

"Yes I was there," came the reply. "Go on, the bank is just there."

He stood on the stone, balanced, both feet just fitting on the narrow surface. "Was I a good person?" The tune he had sung in Mr. V's presence stuck with him and he clung to it without singing it again. It seemed out of place now, but it tugged at him.

Glinda did not answer. "I am not the judge of it," she said finally. "That is your business."

"I can't remember," he said. Then his mind sharpened a little. "But you intend for me to kill this person we are here to find."

"Let us find him first," she replied, her tone implying that he was getting well ahead of things. "It is not certain until it is done."

But Zal still waited. "You, and Lily, you must know my life. Mina knows what I could have been. Yes. What's gone is certain. And you weave it and finish it. You must know."

She acquiesced reluctantly. "Yes."

"I want it back." Her impatience was growing; he could feel a pressure in his back willing him on.

"I can only tell it to you, like a story. I can't return the memories as they were. Those parts of you are lost forever."

"But you haven't," he said, now aloud. "So you have a reason."

"After we are through here, I will tell you what you want to know," she said. "Now can we get along?"

Blackmail. At last, he knew where he stood. "And if I don't?"

"That is your choice," she replied.

"Tell it as we go," he said, watching the rush of the water. "I might slip with boredom if you don't. Running water is so hypnotic. I could fall in. You can always keep a few things back. There must be a lot." This place felt bad to him, because perhaps he shouldn't be here and only Glinda's will allowed it. He felt haunted, and not only by his own frailty and loss. Beyond the line of the mist things without eyes watched him. Sometimes he was sure he felt them brush close, though there was no warning of their arrival, only a sudden rush of air past his face or the peculiar sensation that invisible stuff like threads or straw was sweeping through him. The trailing lines were sticky. They pulled at him, stripping off energy from him. He was fished. But this happened so quickly he couldn't be sure.

He looked at the water. Dark. Endless dark that reflected the weak grey light because it could bear none of it inside.

"Very well," Glinda's voice said sharply in the middle of his head. "It may be a long journey, and if you keep trying to catch hold of those vampires and gaunts who want to eat you you will be in trouble so I will start at the beginning." She waited, but he didn't move on, though he did look forwards at the next stone. She sighed with a long-suffering air. "You and I were born in the dark of the harvest moon, in Alfheim, at a place called . . ."

Her voice spoke steadily. He made the first leap and then another and another. In a few minutes they had finished crossing the river and dealt with his birth and parentage and the beginnings of the political tangle into which he had appeared, controversial before he had taken his first breath because of his mixed heredity and his mother's scandalous choice of father for him.

The story and her friendly tones acted as an effective shield, he found. The pouncing and trawling activity that he suffered lessened almost to nothing, though the watching sensation increased. They travelled along stoney paths and through barren, monotonous moorland. Ruined buildings came and went like mirages at the sides of their way, and they crossed streams that were all as black as the first, the sound of their trickling greed the only thing to be heard. In all the hours he ran and leaped he saw nothing but the landscape and felt nothing but the cold air and the fierce intent of the invisible creatures in the mist.

The passage was not in the least pleasant, but he found himself enjoying his story, though he could not relate it to himself, much as he tried. Images came to his mind, but he thought he conjured them up. He couldn't even remember the look of his own face or what the places she described had felt like. Very occasionally something would appear that was unusually vivid and he felt a stab of happiness as he was able to fit a fragment to the tale she was telling. At least he was convinced she didn't lie. What she said rang true. In the twists and turns of events he would not have taken other paths. He felt pleased by that, and by this proof that he was still alive even if it was only through a fraying connection to his soul.

"Stop," she said at one point, and he realised she didn't mean in her story. He stopped. "I smell something," she said. "Go slower." But after another step she stopped him again. "No, that is far enough. I must lead now. Stand still until I am ready. And beware, what you perceive must change now. You will see this place as I see it. As you have carried me with you, I will carry you. Do not attempt to do anything unless I tell you to. I must hide you so well even the land does not know you or we will not be able to go further. Only the dead or the unliving may pass beyond this point. We are at Last Water."

Darkness fell like a theatre curtain being drawn from behind him and moving through him forwards until it had consumed the path, the mist, and all he could see. He felt unusually light, and then weightless. He tasted the expensive flavour of Glinda's cigar suddenly, and a hint of bourbon. Then his perception of himself as a separate entity vanished. Floating lighter than air Glinda crossed Last Water and he went with her, at her shoulder, as if he were her shadow cast by a pale and unmoving sun.

She tracked life, he realised. She could smell it, taste it, feel it with the acuity of hawk sight. The vampires and ghosts she had named were just as easy to discover as they had been invisible to him. He was astonished that there were many kinds of undead things there. *Undead* was not the right word; *neverliving* would have made more sense, but he hadn't got the right words for these beings, because all his words about being implied life. These things existed on a plane without bodies but not without structure. They had forms, energetic and aetheric in nature, and they had will and intent, motion and various kinds of hungers, all of which behaviours implied life again so that he found his previous understanding of what death meant to be inadequate, or even in error.

"*Life*," Glinda said, growing impatient with the flossing about of thoughts that seemed to be the legacy of his natural thought style and not just a linty residue, "is perfectly good for them as a term if you would get rid of that insistence that only things with material forms on certain planes can be alive. Dump that and it's fine. They're things living on another plane, one in which the energy bodies of humans, elves, demons, and materially focused creatures of all kinds do not persist beyond Last Water without one sodding hell of a lot of effort. Most pass through without a scrap of trouble or awareness. They're dissolving before they know they're here." She flew like a gossamer cloak and there was no mist for her, just the swarms and mothlike flutterings of the unliving things and the spaces between them.

"Necromancers are usually the only individuals who make the effort. The creatures here are in their natural habitat, a plane of limited matter and energy, a place of transition where dissolution is easy and formation difficult. They have been known to penetrate the lower levels and gain themselves bodies now and again, and sometimes they parasitically attach to weak people, which is why you know them at all. Idiots summon them occasionally. They are attracted to living energy forms, as you would call them, because of their complexity and abundance. They can live and become strong by consuming the energies of others."

Zal looked around the darkness, making out the drifting, sliding forms of the deathless things. All shape and almost all definition had gone. In Glinda's world there was, and there was not, and there was not much difference between the two. "I thought you said the living existed here."

"They're here," she said. "Everywhere. I just haven't been paying attention to them because they crowd the trail. I'm looking for a living thing that sustains good form in this plane without a material root, but you can see the others if you like."

For a moment the subtle blacks that had been omnipresent bloomed with radiance. It emanated from huge numbers of glowing egg-shaped vessels of light. They moved in clusters so vast they were like blooms of algae on a fertile sea, joined here and there by little tendrils of gold—some form of energetic connection. Scattered between them were clouds of dispersed dust, like glitters, which moved about as if in their currents. They were separated by dark flows of what he realised suddenly was malignant force. Meanwhile, around them like moths, the vampires and other beings fluttered and swam, trying to burrow into the patterns and shoals, thrashing in the dark streams like ecstasy-crazed dancers, clinging here and there to individuals as he'd once seen killer cells clinging to a virus as they consumed it; a feeding frenzy of sharks in a giant swarm of odd jellyfish.

Glinda turned off the life-o-vision, or whatever it had been. "You see?" she said, and wound her long tongue around her cigar, expertly switching it to the other side of her mouth. "*Way* too busy."

"Blinding," Zal said, content to stay superficially sardonic and not have to dabble too much in his real horror at what he had just seen.

Adrift, moving like the biggest predator in a bad ocean, Glinda smoothed her way onwards. "The Void Border," she said to Zal. "I would bet he is there, switching between places so he can hide." She began to swim with purpose, or walk or run—it was hard to say. They moved at a great pace.

Zal enjoyed the feeling for a moment. "But back to my story," he said, trying not to notice that the creatures they passed now were growing in power and form, size and intensity. Even through a solid coat of Glinda he could feel their polarity, and it was anti-him, razor sharp, malevolent. "Why did I go into military service?"

"It wasn't the military. It was defence," she said. "The best fighters went into the secret service, but it was there that the biggest part of the civil war was being fought, covertly of course. You wanted to tip the balance and that was where the action was, so you made yourself out to be a hundred percent High Caste, passed the initiation tests. . . . What now?"

"I was just wondering, if these things are bad things and they are all here, and you are here and travelling and . . . well, aren't you one of them?"

"I am not," she said. "I exist in the same manner. Were you a high elf focused on the will for power?"

"I'm guessing not, but that's because of the tone of the question really."

"You were a bleeding-heart revolutionary," Glinda said impatiently. "But you were still an elf."

"I sound tedious and immature and a bit whiny, the way you speak of it."

"I'm glossing!" Glinda snorted dismissively. "It's not easy trying to tell you all this and hunt through the evil that has no name at the same time."

"You didn't use the *e*-word before."

"Well I'm using it now. I don't have time for a metaphysical discussion in addition to everything else. There. These things are evil. Can't you feel it?"

"I thought I was being living-ist and overly judgemental about it, but yes. Since you mention it. Why are they . . . ?"

"Zal. We did this whole good-and-evil schtick already for twenty-five years living wild in the backwoods with your father's people, and you concluded that you didn't care about the causes or makings of good and evil; whether by individual choice or by preexisting influence of higher minds or whatever damn reason, you were going to do whatever you thought was right at the time guided only by the light of your own spirit and the vision of your own dream. And for good or ill or ridiculous you have done so relentlessly ever since without the slightest regard for anybody's opinion." She paused and the smell of bourbon suddenly burst around them. "So, do you want to know what happened after you became a leader in the secret service, or don't you?"

She sounded annoyed. They were now moving so fast that everything that was not them was a blur of unrecognisable malcontent. "Yes," he said, trying to be humble though he was rather excited at how heroic he had tried to be when he was young. "Carry on. But first, do you think you can sing the Gloria Gaynor song, the one you said was on the radio the first time I went into Otopia? The one that changed me forever."

There was a brief period of silence. "*Some* people felt you were a bit of a jerk," Glinda said, confidentially. "It's because you took very seriously your dream that you shouldn't take anything seriously even though the contradiction implied a passion that was relentlessly opposed to frivolity. You were contradictory. The song confirmed everything you hated about your own people. Although they were not really your people." She stopped her rant as he wondered why she was harping on, and said, "I don't sing." There was a desperate taint in her declaration, as if she secretly loved to and longed to be discovered.

Zal sighed. "You must. I used to. You must know every song I ever listened to." He tried hard, but the only tune he could recall was still the one Mr. V had made him think of, and he was saving that in case another one never stuck fast in his mind. Glinda had told him about his musical talent, but she needn't have. He would have loved music even if the only thing he'd ever heard was Mr. V's whistling as he laid the fire logs and made up Mina's dinners.

"You don't understand how very nearly dead you were," Glinda said quietly at this recollection.

"Sing it!" He thought he did understand. Years had passed like minutes, tens of thousands of days the same as the last without a trace of longing or anguish. "Go on. Sing it. Please."

"If I do, will you shut up?"

"Yes," he promised with confidence. He did want the rest of the story, but he had to hear the songs themselves in all their magical wonder. He wanted to feel alive.

Glinda had an amazing voice, like a foghorn full of gravel. Dark creatures fled before it.

". . . At first I was afraid, I was petrified . . ."

Lila took aim at the freezer door and shot it out with a rocket. She should have known that one second of mercy would lead to a hellish shovel of shit in Demonia. It might have closed itself, but she didn't think so. She was not surprised to find the scattered body parts of the demon whose neck she'd just broken in the debris. That figured, finally, she thought, wondering at how slow she was getting.

This place had no light because the occupants didn't need it. They were blind. The mirror clearly worked despite this on any unshielded eyes, which was worth knowing, but more worthwhile was the conviction that she had stumbled into a necromancer's house and zombie workshop. The fact that it connected to the mirror's hiding place and had a regular maintenance routine going meant Teazle wasn't safe. But the enclosure and the routine also meant that the master was both in residence and not in residence. She would have bet all Teazle's money that he was in the mirror.

Sadly, the only necromancer she knew or would have trusted was dead.

A quick search of the rest of the house revealed no more unliving servants, though she wasn't willing to count on the fact that some couldn't appear. There was a lifetime's supply of arcane books and equipment. She could search it, looking for information about the mirror, but if she were in charge of such an object she wouldn't have left any instruction manuals around, so she abandoned the idea.

She ran back down to the subbasement and found the servant's bag. Slinging it over her shoulder, she took a moment to kick around and ruin all his preparations for the big closing ceremony, then jumped down the stairs and took off through the labyrinth as fast as she could go. This time around she noticed that the tunnels here were much more recently carved out. They joined the old labyrinth after a few hundred metres of gradual descent, and their smooth sides gave way to ragged edges and lower roofs.

She reached the mirror room after a minute and made sure her eyes were shut and disconnected before she found her way back through the stone dead to Teazle. She rubbed his ear and kissed his face as she passed him and put herself where the servant had knelt, uncovering the mirror and holding it so that she could see the blackness and the frame behind her. Then, recording a brief explanation in case this was the most stupid idea ever tried, she opened her eyes.

Malachi drove back from the Folly with a headache that wasn't helped by the midtown traffic. For some reason rush hour had become a backlog that was dragging well beyond dinnertime into the evening. It was dark as he reached the city side of the Andalune Bridge, but that meant at last he could see the strings of police lights flashing and the glowing yellow of the redirection signs that blocked his way. Everyone was being forced to take the southern exit ramp from the speedway and make a loop. A few checks and he realised that the agency buildings were in the block that was central to the cordon. His heart sank, and a chill made him shiver as he parked illegally, flipped out his POLICE sign onto the dash, and abandoned his beloved to the mercies of the dock district.

A beat officer stopped him at the end of the street, "Sorry, you have to get on a transport and take the long way tonight." He scowled a little at Malachi's obvious faery features.

Malachi showed him his badges. "I've got business inside."

"Yes, sir." The uniformed officer led him beyond the yellow-and-orange cones and onto the strange silence and darkness of Movida Street. Every storefront was closed, even the bar on the corner that had never been closed in all Malachi's many years in the city.

"I can take care of myself." He was starting to wonder if the cop intended to follow him.

"Captain Greer wants to see you," the man said. "All of you. They're at the Foley Centre."

Malachi almost gave a start. The Foley Centre was a drama and performing arts studio that was the agency emergency port if anything happened to the offices. He wasn't surprised when they got there and no dancers were in evidence. Instead the building and its big, open rooms were packed with staff and portable equipment. Power cables trailed like intestines through every doorway and along the sides of the staircases. They wouldn't risk transmitted power. That meant an aetheric lockdown. He realised he had returned to a state of siege.

Greer was audible before he was visible. He was giving orders on the second-floor landing. As Malachi closed in he saw Bentley appear and lean close to Greer, talking rapidly. Greer's expression, always grim, darkened further. He caught sight of Malachi and his arm shot out to point at him. Agents scattered for the exits, their expressions preoccupied or relieved.

"Here, here! The man himself. At long bloody last. Where have you been? No, don't bother. Just come over here and tell me what the fuck is going on."

"I'm behind you," Malachi said in his calmest and most agreeable voice. "Fill me in on why we're here." He could guess, but he'd learned to temper his guesses with a few facts.

Greer's phone rang, one of them. He searched his pockets and stabbed at Bentley with a finger. "Fill him in up to the eyeballs and then I want him back." He stumbled away over the lines of data cable towards a relatively quiet space between two doors.

Bentley nodded and drew Malachi to the banisters where the old staircase took a pause before turning again to ascend the next three levels. "Pirates."

That was, Malachi thought, beyond the eyeballs. He could shovel the rest over the top of his head by himself. The Fleet had returned. "Come for the sextant?"

"Yes."

"Casualties?"

"At least forty. They overran us very fast. We countered but were unable to use sufficient force. . . . The material ones do not respond to gunshot, only fragmentation grenades and in a closed area . . ."

"Zombies." Loathing made his skin shiver.

"Yes. The others are ghosts or . . . other beings," she said carefully, keeping her voice steady and very very quiet as people bustled past them. "Aethereal agents were sucked dry. Artefacts consumed. It made them stronger. Antimagic devices stopped them, but the range was limited."

"Vampires." He was astonished. The Fleet was not merely ghostly. It had features of the undead. That was utterly outside his experience. He felt the first twinge of real fear.

Bentley shrugged. "They have occupied the agency and have begun to quarter the surrounding area in a search."

"What for? I mean, the sextant was . . ."

"It was in the safe room, yes. It still is. The safe room was locked down as we abandoned the building. They are unable to penetrate it."

"Then . . ."

"They have taken hostages and are looking for more. Some have been added to their number. Others are being held as ransom."

"They want us to open it."

"That is correct. Until we do they are killing hostages at the rate of one every half an hour. So far they have killed two."

"How did they get in?"

"Through the same route as the raft into Lila's office."

"Portal."

"Yes."

"Did you close it?"

"We did but it reopened."

Malachi was dumbstruck. Otopia was a place in which the operation of serious aetheric potentials was almost impossibly difficult. It had little natural aether and an atmosphere that suppressed it further. Porting in was a feat. Porting in aetherically dependent beings and sustaining them in such a hostile environment successfully was unheard-of. The power required baffled him. As one of the key aetheric operatives he must come up with a solution to this, but at this moment any ideas eluded him. "How many do you think there are?"

"At least fifty. We count ten of the things you call vampires and the rest are ghost forms like the zombie that came through to Lila. Except these are much stronger."

Malachi looked at the cables. "Power is coming from somewhere and it isn't here. We have to cut it off."

"Or hand back the item."

He looked at her. It hadn't occurred to him, though he was getting a clue as to why Jones had been so desperate. He began to appreciate the magnitude of her daring in stealing it at all. The idea of whoever was doing this having the thing back . . .

"Well?" Greer snapped.

Malachi turned and found the man standing beside him. He'd been so lost in thought he hadn't noticed him appear.

A uniform ran up. "People report kidnappings and ghost sightings in Harristown and Noble Heights, Ponds Beach, Mariontown . . ."

Greer waved them off. Those places were all suburbs, far from the local area. "Portals?"

Malachi nodded; it had to be.

"What is the thing that Jones brought?" Greer demanded. "What is it for?"

"It's a navigation device," Malachi said, reeling. He put his hand on the banister for support. "They came here because they followed Jones. If they get it back . . . I didn't even see it. I don't know what it can do. . . ."

"Wait." Greer held up his hand, paused, looked at his watch, and then looked at Malachi. "Are you saying that the only reason this is happening here is because whatever it is followed Jones here?"

"Likely . . ." Malachi began and then gathered his breath once more as Greer tapped the face of his watch. "I'm a faery. I don't deal with this kind of thing. It's not our business. You need a necromancer."

"We don't have one. Did they manage to port here because she was carrying the device?" Bentley asked.

"Maybe." Malachi was fishing for any clue in his old head. He struggled. "But it could be that because she is a walker she left a trail that was open enough for them to follow. You need to ask another walker. I don't know. . . ."

"Give it back, or not?" Greer asked him suddenly. "Twenty seconds before we kill someone through indecision."

Malachi opened his mouth, but no words came out. He was thinking of the broken hull on the Folly's beach, the bodies rotting inside it, of Jones, of Azevedo, of what he had seen once so long ago that he might have forgotten it through natural causes and not simply because it was too awful to bear.

CHAPTER TWENTY-ONE

It was as she opened her eyes that Lila realised the thing in the bag was not a mirror. It was a crystal plate, about five centimetres thick, fractured and bashed so that it was full of flaws that reflected light and sound internally through hundreds and thousands of planar shifts. Sarasilien's library knew of such things and catalogued them with scrying objects—items that allowed someone to protect themselves from detection as they nosed about in the frequencies and transmissions of other levels of existence. There was no danger of seeing the mirror in its face. In fact, she saw nothing at all to begin with. Then, slowly, tiny sounds and lights began to show in the angular facets. After a few moments they began to noticeably migrate closer to the surface.

Calculating, comprehending, she turned the plate rapidly in her hands so that the emergent wavelengths would appear at angles that she could see. They did so in pieces, every image shattered, every sound broken to bits. She had to put it back together like a puzzle. The library said there was a charm for this, but as she didn't know it and would have had no ability to use it anyway, she had to do it digitally. There was so much refraction she couldn't get rid of it all. The light and sounds were bent. Blackouts in her reconstruction made the transmission patchy. But they didn't in any way prevent her from understanding what she saw.

Over her shoulder, beyond the frame, lay a pleasant beach with a clapboard old family house behind the dunes, and in that house, with her family, Lila Black was making dinner with her sister, feeding the dogs and drinking wine, laughing with her sober mother, her grey-haired and contented father, playing a hand of cards where it didn't matter who won. She recognised herself immediately. Older, more successful, a bit wealthy, a bit heavy with the physical mass that comes from being happy and grounded in who you are, careless of fashion but not without style. Somewhere around, not visible but present, were the boyfriends and girlfriends, smiling and healthy, happy and positive, human and full of life; her date and Max's. It was Thanksgiving. The thing on the table was a turkey, golden roasted, with wine and faery dressings. The sun shone not only with the good light of a day well spent but with the abundance and blessing of this life. She knew this. It was her secret shame, this dream of a normal life, perfected through thousands of hours of polishing in every black moment and struggling second. As she saw, she was half transported. She experienced her own body. She tasted the gravy and added salt. Max smacked her hand, not too much! She threw salt over her shoulder against ill spirits and the dogs snaffled it up and pestered for tidbits, for crisps and the jelly from the top of the pate.

As she leaned on the edge of the sink and looked out of the window she saw her car—a beautiful, sleek thing, parked in the drive. And her friends were there, faces she'd nearly forgotten from school, the boys who lived at the end of the road. They were in the garden, talking, waving at her, and smiling, everyone ready for when she wanted to come out. Happy to see her. On the radio there were only surf reports.

She watched the goings-on, half-absorbed, almost there. She couldn't believe how real it seemed. Her mother's face. Her father's shirt . . . every stitch. Max's grin. The taste of that dinner. Night fell.

They slept. Daydreams became night dreams, robbed of the organising blinkers of the mind.

The house washed away into the sea, the beach was dark, the waves were turning, rolling logs over and over, pushing the dead wood onto the shore, and she was there with the empty city at her back, every building a mass of opened eyes and mouths waiting for something to come walking. . . . Meantime beyond the visible horizon the sea was rising; she could feel it, rising and rising into a single, almighty wave.

An AI alert made her put the pane down. As she did so the trance broke and all sense of being there vanished, leaving her with the clammy dank drip of the labyrinth and the bad air of the chamber. Lila sat with it on her lap for a second. She understood a little. Trapped in dreams. In hers for her . . . and presumably a different dream for everyone else. Whatever she saw wasn't going to be what the zombie servant had been seeing and hearing. It had spoken, and been spoken to, she was certain. But she wasn't getting it right, if she was even able to.

Use of Mirrors: there was a big book on the subject of course, right there in the library she'd so glibly scanned and copied. It even mentioned the Seven Great Mirrors and their various perils, of which this, the Mirror of Dreams, was by far the trickiest. But reading about it first proved too confusing. She had to go back. She started from the beginning, as fast as she could go. Every word that passed through her mind brought back the itching, scratching feeling that someone was trying to take a rubbing of her thoughts and was hoping to rub them away, but she had no choice. Teazle was stuck in the mirror's thrall, whatever else was going on here, and she was determined to get him out.

Light, the book began, *is all there is in the universe. Nothing but light. A mirror reflects light. A glass may also refract light, splitting it up into its component frequencies and scattering them over a wider area, creating the appearance in the mind of the beholder of false images and misleading colours.* Blah blah blah . . . there were over eight hundred pages and illustrations. *The more suited a being becomes for the passage of light, the more able*

*and open to enslavement by higher powers it is; therefore as the individual
ascends in refinement of the higher frequencies and energy forms it is paramount
they guard against the unwitting inclusion and transmission of more able and
subtle forms.*

She reread that a few hundred times and looked into the inky
blackness where Teazle was standing, unseen. She would have said,
"Oh, shit!" but that was more words and she'd already used far, far too
many of them.

Temple Greer was looking at him as if they had all the time in the
world. Malachi knew that he didn't have such a luxury in this one, but
if they were talking to someone here, someone who would be here at
least in twenty seconds' time in order to speak and listen, then that
someone wouldn't be anywhere else right then. He would know, for a
minute, where trouble was.

"Give it to him," Malachi said. "I'll work on it from the other side."

He galloped down the stairs, leaping the cables, not waiting for
Greer's reply or Bentley's thundering pursuit. Out in the street he
turned corners, found shadows, the concealment of dustbins, and he
was cat, then small cat, then moving through the darkness shared by all
worlds and into the harsh, biting cold of a place he had begun to know
very well. In the depths of Under time would stretch much farther than
a few more seconds. But instead of a fire he saw ashes and the black of
cinders. Madrigal's camp was gone. She had moved on. He cursed, cast
about, and then began to run in the trail her wolf had made.

In his mind's eye he saw a green sun and bronze shadows of three
women. Their axes rose and fell, rose and fell, and the mountain they
carved ran with black rivers; and all the creatures like him, whose kingdom was the dark of night, howled and screamed. The tallest woman, the
oldest, turned. She had tiger's eyes and they looked right at him.

The snows of Under were beginning to melt, but in the high passes the snow was resilient. He had hoped that Madrigal would be nearby so that he could have mustered her help or at least a kind word, but summer itself was coming and she had business in the lowlands, he guessed, so he must take the road to Tath's lonely outpost by himself. The brisk run gave him time to think of what he would say, but as he neared the turn of the path where it lost itself completely among the last pines of the steepening slopes he was stopped by the sight of scarlet on white. Instinct made him flatten himself down until his back was lower than the snowline and his belly was wet on the hard ground.

It was not the ears of Tath's hounds, but blood on the snow. The smell of it was strong as the wind turned towards him.

"Who would think we would still bleed red?" said a voice behind him wistfully. He turned his head and saw the elf not six metres away from him, all but invisible in the stand of white birches.

"Tath?"

"I guess your arrival means I am not the only one to have found something curious and regretted it." Tath came forwards and showed his empty hands. He was covered in a fine layer of snow, but it didn't disguise the fact that at least some of the red had come from him. He limped although he tried to conceal it. Hearing his master's voice a lone hound darted out across the bloodied hillside, but he waved it back and Malachi heard its whine of disappointment after it had vanished.

"What happened?" Malachi hardly noticed his teeth now, almost was grateful for them in fact. He let himself get to all fours and shake off the cold.

"I was careless with all my new power," Tath said wryly, and then as Malachi's stare urged him on he gave an uncomfortable sigh. "A necromancer came to find me. I have met them on occasion. Knowing the art I understand what I must look like from the other side. And I saw myself something that looked greatly interesting—so unusual for anyone to survive such regions for any time, Malachi, you have to understand, for someone who is not one of the angels or monsters natural to these places. Anyway, to cut to the point, I saw a necromancer's form surrounded by masses of the dark agents. He was a kind of focus for them. In common situations this would be the end of the necromancer, but they formed order for him and it seemed he spoke to them in their own way. I have only been able to do this since I was cast in Jack's shoes, so I thought I would take a closer look. Well, he saw me and he pursued me with the ferocity of a savage. There was no talk, just an assault. Took me by surprise." Tath paused. "He sent all his creatures after me. They hesitated. But then they came on anyway. His will was stronger than theirs. I fled here, thinking a material plane was a place they'd not follow me to. Most didn't. But he had angels with him, Malachi. I don't know if you ever encountered one? No? Me neither until now. They have no trouble manifesting parts of themselves on this plane at least, let me tell you. We fought. Terrible weapons. My pack tried to save me and most of them are spirits on the winds now."

"How did you survive?" Malachi looked at the figure before him more carefully.

"I am not easily killed anymore."

"Jack's power was godlike." This was speculation for Malachi, and not a little envy and awe. "Are you saying you are immortal?"

"No, I think not. But the Winter King can't be defeated on his own ground. The land saved me. Its strength is mine while I stand on it. I think this is always so for the older fey, no?"

"Yes." Malachi nodded. "Tell me about these angels. Are you sure about it?"

"Not sure. I never saw one before, not close and never in a material form. They were weak here. Their blades only had spirit powers and the strength of normal iron. I am not iron-weak. But they were not either." He stopped talking suddenly and Malachi watched him ease his hip and cautiously move his arm. A fine tremor was visible on him. It shook the snow off his clothing and revealed its shredded tatters. "They almost tore me to bits. Their blades have a righteous power; every evil you have ever done, every hurt, every torment, all awaken to their touch."

"Some angels," Malachi muttered, though he was shaken. He realised Tath's checking was genuine surprise that body parts had not fallen off him, but in fact he seemed to be unharmed, physically at least. "But how did you best them?"

"I am not sure I did. They left me here when it was clear I couldn't be killed. I healed too fast." His voice broke and he turned away. "Better to die in those circumstances, Malachi. So, now amuse me, have you come for my help?"

Malachi explained the situation as he understood it. Meanwhile Tath beckoned him forwards and they walked a wide berth around the bloodied ground to the cave where they had sheltered before. It was quiet. Just two dogs ran to meet them. Others lay by the fireside, panting, their eyes closed, their coats blackening with gore.

"And you thought I would have a way to stop him."

"You seemed like a good bet," Malachi said, trying not to be defeated. "I didn't expect this. Angels and that. I don't know what they are."

"They are proxies acting at lower frequencies to their master powers," Tath said, standing by the fireside but looking no less cold. The bleakness in his eyes spoke of a great deal of pain. "So either he has ascended greatly already or he has the favour of beings best not dealt with. You were right to give him the device back. You should feel less guilty. Where is Lila?"

"She went to find that useless husband of hers." They both mulled this over for a minute. Malachi regretted his rancor, but he couldn't help but feel it. "And started some new war with the rogues, but that is unimportant."

"They are hunting for Zal," the elf said, as much to himself as to Malachi, who nodded and stared at the fire's slow lick on the fallen branches in the grate. Then he said, "This is not an attack on the human world. It is something quite different. If it were an assault you would have fallen. Kidnap, hostages, murder—small-time games. A zombie, the Fleet . . ." His musing trailed off into silence briefly. "No, I think he is after her weapons," Tath said. "And Teazle himself. You said that he came here and was changed. Lightbringer, you said."

Malachi squirmed uncomfortably, "I hate these names. They are ill to speak of."

"Lila has Tatters and the pen. Teazle has the swords and the fire. I am undead. You . . ."

". . . are unaltered, just retro. That's all." He began to look around, and found the things necessary for making tea, water, a kettle. He started work.

"And Zal?"

"Those bitches took him," Malachi muttered, setting the pot over the fire. He struggled with his hands but the difficulty was a pleasant distraction.

The elf nodded, containing his shaking by keeping a grip on his own arms. "Well, whether these things are more than opportune can't be said, but they are a hell of an opportunity for someone."

"And what for?"

"Does it matter? The dreams of creatures like that seldom stray from acquiring power. What they do with it later is anyone's guess. Acquisition is usually enough of an ambition to draw them to their ends. Only godhead would be enough of a summit to turn their hearts to other greeds they might satisfy."

"Godhead. Is that an ambition these days?"

"It ever was," Tath said. He bent down to one of his dying dogs and placed his hand on its head gently. For that instant his own shaking stopped. Its ribs stilled and stiff legs relaxed. Tears were on his face.

Malachi stared at the pot. He had run out of jobs. "Okay. Seems like he's well beyond us then."

"Suppose he has mastered the continuum of death, dream, and void. He sends servants to do his work in Otopia. He sent angels for me."

"You think he has trouble in these regions?"

"Yes, I would think so."

But Malachi had suddenly realised a greater implication. "Mastered? What does that mean?"

"Passing between them at will, moving things through them at his command."

"Tath. All these memories . . . this snow . . . is this snow the memories of the dead?"

"Yes."

"But the spirit . . ."

"Departs."

"Can there be true resurrection?"

"Come, tell me what you are leading to. It will be faster."

Malachi snarled with frustration at himself. "I wish I knew. Jones said this bastard wanted to ascend. He was going to become a conduit for a dead thing. Is it possible? Isn't that energy gone forever, turned into everything else in the constant round?"

"Usually."

"Usually, usually! Damn it, there has to be some law!"

"Which dead person are we talking about?"

"Don't you listen? Agh, no I didn't tell you that part of it. Listen now, then. Jones said he wanted to use Night. Mother Night. Ridiculous, of course. But then, unlike the others, I remembered . . . she's dead. They killed her. The Three Sisters killed her and used her body to make the lower worlds of Faery, Demonia, and Alfheim. I saw it. I was there. If this creature has mastered death and dream, if this snow, if if if, Tath . . ."

"Yes, I see," Tath said. He took his hand from his dog's head and he was calm. "He does not propose resurrection. He proposes to become."

"What does that mean, Tath?"

"He wants the mantle of Night."

"To become a dragon?"

"Yes."

Malachi did not understand why that would be desirable, but then he was not a demon and he didn't deal with the spirit realms, so what did he know? "Should we stop him?"

"If we wait and he is successful we will not be able to. Then he can take whatever he wants from anywhere. Only the gods will stop him if they live, and you know there is some debate about that."

"You didn't say yes."

"Is my word all you need?"

Malachi looked at the elf closely. "I am not saying it would be your responsibility."

"But you would like to. I would like it to be yours. We are afraid. Rightly so. Already his actions prove he has no cares for whoever gets in his way. But also they show he does not go out of his way in order to cause harm, else there could have been much more chaos than there has been. Only the sending of the zombie to Lila seems to me to be an offensive move. If we set out to stop him, and by stop you mean kill for nothing else would work, then that puts us at least on an equal footing of evil as he, does it not?"

Malachi bared his teeth. "I should have expected a debate on metaphysics from an elf."

"And your faery conscience is not biting you, of course. That is why you are here and not rousing what powers you could from your own house." There was no rancour in Tath's answer. Malachi saw he was in a place of stillness and sadness that wouldn't be moved by small insults. Perhaps it was a place where these matters were much clearer than they were to a feral cat. He realised that here, in spite of the race opposition, he might really have someone with insight into a mind like that of the necromancer. "You know of the will to power?"

Tath almost smiled. "High elves are raised with it as mother's milk. I would have been its good disciple if I hadn't had a more demanding master. But yes, of course, yes I do. And I know necromantic art. Let me say that *will* is the wrong word and idea however. *Want* is the word. It is stronger than will. What I wanted allowed me to do anything because I wanted it with my whole being. To beat this creature we would have to want to, and more than he wants to succeed. I doubt that for all our losses either of us are up to that degree of desire."

"Yes, so give me a stake that will make me want it, Tath!"

"Ilya."

"Ilya. Tell me what he could do."

"But that is the trouble. I would bet that the mantle of Night is his obsession. Once he has it, then there is no goal left for him. At such a moment there is no telling what would come to fill the vacuum." He paused and Malachi felt despair. "But," Tath said slowly, and Malachi hung on every word, "we might guess that he would not then stop all effort for a life of contemplative withdrawal.

"You know the story of Rome burning?" Malachi asked, but in his heart he felt the same nagging doubts, the same sense of being wronged but also of seeking what might be an equal wrong. "I would myself wait until the facts were proven."

"If Rome, so to speak, were actually on fire then I would have no trouble," Ilya said. He bent down and picked up his dead dog.

"I know someone who will not have this dilemma." Malachi followed him outside. The ground was solid and no chance of digging. They made a grave in the snow. As the body was laid it had already begun to dissolve. The ruined fur and broken limbs became gossamer, ice and sticks. Ilya watched what Malachi could not see—the golden light—spiral up and out into the wide grey sky.

"Lila," the elf said. "He was calling her."

"Yes."

Ilya paused and looked directly at Malachi. "We need a ship."

"To join the Fleet?"

"Yes. Then it will not matter if he regains his ability to sail freely."

"But we don't have anything that can sail . . . into the Void or . . ."

"It will sail there with me at the helm," Ilya said confidently. "Just find a vessel."

"Easy," Malachi nodded. "Come with me to Otopia. I know the very one."

CHAPTER TWENTY-TWO

linda had stopped somewhere—Zal had no idea where—and now she was watching something he did understand, and know, and remember. Before them in the space of the Void massed thousands, perhaps millions, of ships. He had once been aboard the command ship, as a guest of its captain, the Admiral, and his guest who had been Lily, though she wasn't called that then. He remembered the view from the top of her mizzenmast: the Fleet spread out around him. Every vessel ever built seemed to be there, on the invisible swell of water, the intangible currents of the air, and below in the great depths. Higher craft were not visible except through their signals, all of which appeared on the Admiral's master chart as continuously moving dots of pretty golden light. Against the profound darkness of the Void their lanterns and beacons twinkled like a galaxy of stars and their bells and klaxons measured the space with endless calls.

"In there?" Zal asked, delighted to see and know the sight.

"He has become master of the Fleet," Glinda said with disappointment. "This will not be so easy."

"What about the Admiral?" Zal thought of the mop-haired lad in oversize pantaloons and tricorne hat that he'd met.

"Imprisoned, I would say," Glinda replied. "Not dead—that is not really possible. But ruled by this creature, this upstart thing." For the first time Zal thought she sounded uncertain.

"So obviously I free him, he reclaims the Fleet and we see off the bad guy," Zal suggested, hoping this was not the plan.

"That would deprive him of the Fleet, but that is all."

A strong infusion of cigars and bourbon made Zal's thoughts spin dizzily for a few seconds. "It's just floating here, doesn't seem to be doing anything," he said.

"It is capable of transiting between Thanatopia, the Void, and the Dreaming," Glinda said uneasily. "I would not have it captained by anyone other than its intended master. You will sneak aboard and we will discover the plot."

"What if there isn't one?" He was beginning to have a sneaking admiration for anyone who was capable of hijacking the Fleet for his own ends. Something in him answered that impulse with a jolt of fire.

"Surely there is," she said firmly, a smile in her voice as she registered his rise in energy. "If there wasn't why would he send a rat to grab what's left of your innards? He made a doll. He used the hoodoo, and competently too. He made an image of you and sent it on some mission. The only reason he didn't call you and use the real thing is that you are not dead and he does not know your true name. So, what would he want with a copy of you? There's a question."

"You needn't make it sound like I was yesterday's newspapers."

"But darling, in every world, you're history. You haven't released a record in fifty years. Everyone thinks you're dead, except for some of your die-hard fans who think it's all a conspiracy and that you went back to Alfheim or Neverland or whatever. . . . But look, that's not the point."

He felt unfairly humbled, although the idea of having fans somewhere, however mad, was heartening. "I thought you were on my side."

She growled like a sixty-a-day rock star, "Just get aboard the *Temeraire*. Then we'll have something real to chew over."

"How?" He was beginning to have an uneasy feeling that there was more to this than some simple tale about Glinda being annoyed by someone she felt should be far beneath her.

"You are shadow," she said. "You are darkness. You may draw the dark. You are an elf. You were a top-grade assassin. You are the inheritor of vampiric—"

"What?" he interrupted her. "Then it's true? The shadowkin are crosses of the elf race with these things from Thanatopia. You didn't say that in the story. You said I discovered that they were experimental by blows but not how they were made. You *lied*." He was shocked.

"I *omitted*, for the sake of brevity and relevance. Yes. The living ones are hybrids of high elf stock and these spirit-based entities; the lowest of them, the worst, I am sorry to say. There are other kin of yours, however, who were unable to persist in Alfheim and who are also unliving. Angels of a kind they are. And there were also monsters made, whom they banished to the deep Void before they finished their foolish interference and tried to shut the gates on all they had called. But *focus*, Zal. You have their abilities. Darkness, sneaking, stealth, silence, agility . . . talent to burn, darling. You can get aboard that ship without being noticed. Come on! We may not have time. They could depart at any moment."

"They look pretty marooned to me," Zal said, mostly out of pique. He wasn't sure if he was appalled, horrified, thrilled, enchanted, terrified, or sick. He was all of them. It was a kind of rush, nauseating, but high in its hit. He found a smile on his face.

Glinda showed no such tendency to miss a beat. "Zal, if I tell you everything you will get distracted. I promised I would tell it when we are done. And I will keep my word. Now would you just move!"

"Body, control of, relative space and time and mass, action equal reaction, problem with basic motor activity, travel et cetera," he muttered crossly, not sure if he believed her, but not wanting to doubt. She was his death. Surely of all things she wouldn't lie? When he went, she went too.

Suddenly he found he had his normal assortment of limbs and head and was surviving reasonably well in a place he was sure wasn't suited to him, no matter what Glinda said about it.

"I'm helping," she said. There was another mist of bourbon.

"Quit that," he ordered. "I need a clear head."

He felt her outrage, but the drinking stopped. The taste of tobacco vanished. He felt something like a road under his feet, though he couldn't see anything of the kind.

"Run then, health fanatic," Glinda snapped. "Run run run!"

He ran. He was the speed of dark, as fast as the turning world, impermeable to the interference and telltale revelations of any frequency of light. It was exhilarating, the purest joy.

The Signal was the Akasha. Lila understood that. The Akasha was the total informational sum of all organized energy. It had an intent. It had will. No mind unless you counted her mind and that of the other constructs it had created, using them to ascend to a conscious state. She was an avatar of its will, though she had no sense of it trying to move her in any way. But the new claw that had her in its grasp like a fish on a line was adept in using the Akasha, even though it wasn't a machine, nothing like that at all. And the scraping, tugging, listening of it was all some alien will at work in her. Words were its tools. She had to stay clear of them until she found a way to be free. Something like her could probably be useful if you found a way to run her, but she wasn't about to let anyone do that again. One set of remote controllers and their idiot button pushers was enough burden to deal with.

She put the crystal plate back in its bag and cursed its uselessness. If she were stuck in her own dreams and Teazle in his how would she reach him? She couldn't rely on something as unreliable as a wish to dream of him or that he could dream of her. But the demon's dead servant told her by his existence that there was a way to manage it. He must have shared his master's dream. Much as she longed to rush to action she was going to have to sit and read the damned wordy tract on the mirror. And that meant standing like a deer in the headlights of the hunter's great big 4 x 4 as it took aim at whatever it was going to hit in her. Nothing in her system told her that was an acceptable idea.

Almost before she'd had the idea herself she felt the fabric of the dress move in its snakelike way across her skin, tightening, thickening, and twitching. When she looked down she saw that her bandaged ninja gear was studded with sequin stars and the silver-and-gold stitching of the night sky. It pulsed with animal eagerness. She drew the sword and held it before her, and then as an afterthought bent down and picked up the plate in its pack, slinging it over her shoulder. The only vision in her head was of herself, a warrior of power, arrowing through everything that lay between her and Teazle's lost spirit. As she turned around she felt no doubt about what she was about to do. It could go wrong. She could end here. It didn't matter because the alternatives were all forms of slavery, to others or to fear or to what she didn't want. She would have none of that. The cold certainty of her own determination was a straight, strong line inside her. It ran down her arms, through her hands, through their metal-to-metal connection with the grip, and into the blade as she drove it forwards into the face of the mirror.

The battle that surrounded her was in full-tilt. Machines and monsters the size of tower blocks clashed and spat fire. Shrapnel and flaming fuel was falling from the sky. The tortured ground shook and split beneath her feet. She was small, a doll, a little thing in a storm of giants and a hurricane of whirling debris churned by their struggle. Filth and gore filled the air and blocked out the sun until it was a crimson disk with a blurred edge, a battered shield too far away to help anyone, an eye that stared without blinking on a field of death and destruction. Screaming and roaring and the blast of sonic weapon discharges deafened her. She turned the sword in her hands, pointed up, and engaged her jet boots. The falling limbs of titanic warriors clashed, would have crushed her to smithereens if she wasn't faster, smaller, more accurate than she had ever been. A body blotted out the sky. She pierced it, the blade of the sword cutting it in half just above her so that she rose from the wound in crimson rain, blood streaming off her razored armour body and weighting her hair in dreadlocks that clung to her face and neck. As blood cleared from her eyes she looked down into the carnage that stretched as far as she could see in all directions, bodies made the ground and the hills, blood and burning fuel the rivers and lakes, where a mass of warriors, each as glorious and terrible as the last, fought for their lives.

Yes, this was a demon's dream, day and night. She should have expected to find him here, but the scale of it, the savagery, the relentless fury . . . it took her breath and thoughts away. Nothing in her experience of Teazle had prepared her for this. Its brutality was something he never showed outwardly, not to her anyway. He had been a silent, deadly, sophisticated killer, she thought. This was nothing like that, no gentleman's dance. There was no art here but the art of killing as fast and efficiently as possible, though as she looked she saw that was an art indeed. Everyone an enemy of everyone else. No quarter and no mercy. Only the supreme fighter would survive here. Surely this was not the dream of all the demons locked in that room, but surely theirs had been no different in the degree of their excess. She was awestruck at the scale, the madness, the purity of it. She knew, with the conviction of dreamers in any nightmare, that this war would never end until there was only one left standing on the pile of all the dead, on the mountain it had made of its opponents. And because he wasn't dead, somewhere here Teazle was fighting, determined to be the one, satisfied to die at the hands of a better fighter, either end as good as the other as long as he was tested to the limit and reached the peak of his abilities, found the limit.

She flew above the battle, fighting with all her senses to penetrate the heaving forms, sometimes several bodies deep, the scale of the largest dwarfing the smallest. Then she found him in the midst of a concerted attack by a group of half-demons armed with everything from swords to machineguns; temporary allies against his blinding power.

He fought in human form with his faery swords, white hair lashed into a braid at his back, his body glowing with light gold and white, bleeding moonlight in trails that glimmered as they fell through the air and into the mud. Then in an instant he was dragon, his swords claws and the spike blade of a lethal tail that cut down four or five in a slash, his breath a fire that blackened the faces of those who stood before him and left them screaming, balls of unrecognizable flesh and bone condemned to final moments of agony. He trampled them. He became a creature of flame that cauterized all before it, a miniature sun. And on the cleared mound of smouldering ruin he stood again, the human fighter, ablaze, his face alight with joy and a smile she would have loved to see turned to her even though he used it now, along with his hands, to beckon the next enemies to the attack. Light ran out of his wounds, shone from him in lethal bands of red and violet destruction. He was magical, unstoppable. And there she'd thought that Lightbringer was the term for a good thing.

They were not put off by his prowess. Each believed him- or herself the best and had no sense of self-preservation. They threw themselves at him—monsters, men, creatures of iron and earth, and things for which she had no name. But Lila was able to see that although he was magnificent, they did hurt him, and degree by degree he was getting slower, weaker though he didn't seem to feel it. He stood on glowing trails of his own life force. The enemies in their endless supply saw it too. Each wave of them came with more determination, more conviction. Gradually they would wear him down like water on rock. It was only a matter of time. How much time had already passed? He had been gone for days in her worlds, but that meant little in this place; dreams that took years in themselves could pass in minutes of the clock. Did that mean he had been here for so long?

She cast a glance over the dreamscape, but there was no visible end to the number of fighters. They crowded the land, and as they fell more sprang from the air fully formed and armed or crawled up from the ground, clawing through the dead, their hands and heads sometimes cut off before they had even made a stand. If anything there were increasing numbers of ever larger and more powerful foes emerging. And the sun did not shift in any degree, as if time itself were not moving.

Teazle danced through his fight in glory. Any way she could think of for getting his attention might easily get him killed—there was no second for a mistake in his moves—besides, she didn't think he'd thank her for breaking this dream. It, and not she, was his heart's desire. It occurred to her that her interference, whatever the outcome, might not be wanted. In the midst of the killing he looked alight with life. She could tell by the look on his face that he was exultant. There was no better place for him to be.

Her heart felt the pierce and bite of loneliness. Did it matter that it was a dream? Did it matter if he died here, and not above in the much less clear-cut worlds of the material planes? Should she save him now if he returned to an existence that was grey compared to this? Was this his heaven? At first she'd been convinced she had to bring him back. This was saving him, wasn't it? If she could even do it?

She thought of Zal, determined to run against Jack's hunt, knowing it was fatal, could not be outrun. She gripped the sword hilt in her hands. She missed him so much. Her own life was a struggle every day with the greyness that she'd found in his absence. Why should it be that way? She raged against it, but her rage was useless.

Was this to be the way they found him? Was Zal in a dream somewhere, a dream like this one, something that for him was better than reality? Teazle had conjured this because he was a simple being, a creature of easy power. Would Zal's dream be like this or was he lost, a stain on some faery's bit of cloth, forever beyond her reach and not even able to dream? She had no way of knowing. And the years that had passed, the years of nothing. It was unbearable. He was as lost as he had ever been to her, and at this moment it felt like an unbridge-able gulf, a search without end, futile, the kind you had to kid your-self about until the last of your friends filed away, bored of your obses-sion. Mom, Dad, Max, Tath, Zal . . . even that stupid imp . . . she could hardly believe their loss, and she'd flung herself into the days so she didn't have to feel it; she'd killed Sandra Lane so she didn't get dis-tracted from her distractions. Well here was a distraction, and she didn't want to wait.

With a scream of rage she dived down, the sword before her, and plunged into the fray. If this was the Akasha's dream, then let it fight to survive and prove itself worthy of her.

CHAPTER TWENTY-THREE

After Ilya had tended his dogs he walked outside. The snow was falling again, soft and silent, covering the red ice gently with its million caresses.

"I thought you were godly. How the hell did they get the drop on you?" Malachi asked, looking at the spot and trying not to imagine what agony must pass when you could not stop living but you had lost that much blood.

"I didn't expect them. Vampires, creatures of the emptiness, those I am used to. Angels, I was not used to. Next time it will be a different story. Their blades can destroy faery flesh; they are pure aether made to an edge by a colder mind than mine. They had a kind of distant perfection, in their way." His voice was wistful. He turned away towards the higher mountain, where the peak towered over them. "This glacier is built of all the memories of the dead. I think it is many miles deep. But at the bottom is the first memory of any being. If legend might stand in some form, there we could expect to find the snows belonging to Night herself. Then you might at least answer the question about what to expect from one who wears her mantle."

"You're kidding," Malachi said, staring at the forlorn peak. "But how would we . . ."

Ilya held up his hand and beckoned. Malachi followed him for some distance through the gentle drifts as around them the soulfall continued, their soft imploring touches something he turned from. He felt himself a defiling presence in a sacred place, and wanted to apologise for every footstep he made, but at last they stopped at the foot of a wide swath of snow.

Ilya made a sweeping motion with one arm, and Malachi almost fell over with shock as the snow responded to his command and swept aside in an avalanche of dislodged chunks that hurtled to the side even as it started a fatal burst of energy heading downslope, ending in a thunderous roar that shook the mountainside as it went foaming and plunging down the pass. Trees and rocky outcrops vanished in its soft clouds. Around them the air sparkled with tiny crystals turning in the sunlight, and before them lay a sheer plane of ice, turquoise and azure and pink in astonishing radiance, clear as glass.

"The Mirror of Forgetting," Ilya said to him quietly. "Of course it would be here, close to the Hall of Champions and Under, where everything is lost that must be."

Malachi stared at it. For once he was confounded. "This was only a story. Nobody I know has ever seen it. We thought it was an imagined thing."

The elf stretched out his thin, white hand towards the face of the glacier, fingers extended but gentle as if he were reaching to clasp hands with a friend, and in answer light rose from the blackness far below where the ice met the rock of the mountain, shot through the flaws in the structure, and made them shine like stilled flags in the depths.

"Watch closely," he said. "For once the light is released it cannot be caught again."

Malachi's eyes were wide and he felt the cold air strike tears in them, but he didn't flinch. He leaned close to the tall figure at his side as the surface moved suddenly with images from a past so long ago he felt it steal his shape away from him so that all he felt so sure of became liquid and ran in his mind.

Darkness was alive. The light there was showed only the extent of its reign. It moved like fluid, was sticky and elastic. What he saw defied rational description. He could barely understand what he was looking at. Unlike his shaped memory of the Fates at their butchery of the mad chaos that Night's avatar had become, creating order from the storm, this was a roiling sea of constant changes in which raw energy became aether or matter or both and fled away to nothing again, evaporating as fast as it was spawned. Stars and the like, bodies and forms flitted in and out of being. Everything bled together. There was no distinction—that was what he saw—only change. Even light itself revealed its own birth in the foam of dark's silent boil and turn, a radiance bursting out spontaneously from the clash of powerful forces. Night's hands were making and breaking, her body was the universe itself, all he could imagine. Her dying was the birth of things as he understood them, her ceaseless turning stilled into space and time and ordered moments where matter might rest and grow complex before entropy drove it back to the beginning again.

As the vision faded he tried by some impossible measure to print it forever on his mind, but its strangeness was already sliding out of his grasp as he turned to the elf.

"In the wrong hands that could be very, very bad indeed."

"We should go; time is fleeting," the elf replied, as though it wasn't of much account to him personally. His indifference was calming. He let Malachi lead him down through the snowy passes to where the beginnings of spring were melting water at the gateway to Under. By the time they were in the low country Malachi was almost composed.

Madrigal was there. It was cold, in spite of the rise in temperature and the increasing light, and she was still in her layers of winter furs, her guns hanging by their straps on her back as she stood waiting for them at the tall Turning Stones. There was no magical portal to see here, though the ground was uneven and Malachi wouldn't have trusted his own footing on the Lock. Nonetheless it was the gate he intended to use to get Ilya to Otopia, since he couldn't take him any other way.

"Malachi," Madrigal said as they neared. She was smiling and his heart leaped, though he tried not to notice.

"We cannot linger," he said, almost cross with her for not being at her camp when he'd arrived. He stayed pacing in his cat form, on all fours.

"Oh." She didn't seem disconcerted. "I hope you return soon."

"I thought you would have had to shoot this one," Malachi said grumpily, nodding at Ilya. "But seems you don't need to bother."

"I don't think shooting him would kill him any further." She grinned and opened her backpack. "Would you like a fish? Fresh caught. You look hungry."

In other times he would have enjoyed the beginning of this game but instead he found himself saying crankily, "I would like a kiss. I think I've waited long enough."

Behind him he heard Ilya cough into his hand, smothering a laugh. He lashed his tail, shocked that he'd allowed himself to make the admission and regretting it. But Madrigal put her bag down and crouched by his head. "You bad cat." She wagged her finger at him. "First you must—"

As she was speaking he had already changed form, and even though it was freezing and he was naked without a stitch to enhance his style he was holding her tightly and kissing her on the lips. Her clothing was cold and damp and she was trussed up like a burrito, but holding her was as satisfying as he had always dreamed it was. He was pleased to find he had surprised her.

"Well," she said after they were done. "I will look forward to your return much more eagerly now." She stepped back and observed him with a huntress's eye. "Really."

"Good," he said. "Come on, Ilya. Try not to die as we get to the other side. Would be really inconvenient."

Madrigal put one of her apples into Ilya's hand and whispered to him to eat it as they passed her. Malachi hoped it would be enough magic to survive Otopian climes and that his clothes were where he had left them. They stepped onto the soft earth between the stones and it swallowed them up.

And ejected them in Malachi's car. The hood was up, but he felt ridiculous as he fought into his shirt and trousers. The traffic had returned to the street. The cordon was being taken away. He had been longer than he intended. He flipped on his phone set as Ilya sat in the passenger seat and ate his apple slowly. In his ear Temple Greer said, "All quiet on the western front. He got his wish. We got our dead. What's the score?"

"I'm just here to pick up some gear," Malachi said, pinning the phone with his shoulder and backing out of the lot. "The game's not up. Score not available."

"Betting's open then?"

"I wouldn't put a dollar on us."

"Bad as that?"

"Worse."

"Did you hear from Lila?"

"Nothing."

"Goddammit. I don't want to send agents to Demonia after we got this beating here. Nobody to spare. And she's started up some war with the rogue agents. Or was that just to keep me busy and off her back?"

"I'm guessing it is."

"Crafty bitch. I could almost propose to her, if I knew where she was. Keep in touch."

"Yes, sir." He turned his head as he flicked the phone into his pocket just in time to see Ilya flip his booted feet up onto the dash and lean back in the seat. His long white hair whipped around his head. He ate his apple in thoughtful bites and watched Malachi in turn.

"So this is a car," he said after a moment.

Malachi sighed and wound down his window, resting his elbow on the door. "Yeah."

"Noisy."

They turned onto the freeway and headed out to the bridge. "She's a good girl."

Ilya looked around the interior pointedly and stroked the upholstery. He smiled and ate the apple core, then spat the seeds out on his side. "I have missed such things. I miss her."

Malachi knew who he was talking about. "We all did." He tuned the radio to a rock station and watched Ilya's long ear tips flick as the tough bass came blasting through his state-of-the-art speakers, hidden in the dash. He was usually a soul or a blues cat, but today that didn't seem the right mood.

The elf sat back and let the wind drive into his face. He looked like he was enjoying it. Malachi put his foot down and they sped out over the glittering water of the bay.

He avoided the house and drove them farther down the coast where they could walk up the beach and find Jones's ship without going back to the Folly. As they got out of the car the sun was starting to slide down the sky. It was warm, balmy. The sea was quiet and a few people were out walking. A kid was flying a kite with a long tail, and they both paused to watch it for a moment before they turned and Malachi led them along the tideline and around the headland.

The ship was waiting, ground into the sand, her decks at a thirty-degree angle, her bodywork already starting to rust. The ghost glow was gone, but she had been Jones's ship and real enough before her capture by the Fleet's massive quantum gravity, so she hadn't fallen apart yet, though she looked more wrecked than many a vessel on the scrapyard and nothing like seaworthy. Her hull was more hole than metal, and the gaping spaces where her aetheric charms had been ripped away to leave bare wires promised no protection from the Void either.

But when Malachi turned to see the faery elf's reaction he found Ilya staring at the beach and the sea, at everything but the ship. He looked inland.

"That house," he said slowly, moving his long fair hair out of his face with one hand and shucking his fur coat with the other, letting it fall to the sand. "The shear is strong here, very strong."

Malachi recognized the term for a place of thinning between realities. "Yes. Earth sink, some say."

"It will need to be. This world is more dead than I remembered to my senses." He closed his eyes and breathed in deeply through his nose. His eyes flashed open. "Who is there?"

"Just one of the walkers," Malachi said.

"She is in many places at once."

"You're starting to freak me out, and that's something."

Ilya's smile was bleak. "I see a lot more than I used to. She is the Hunter's get. What do you know about her?" His eyes were alight with interest. His nostrils flared.

"Ilya, we don't have time for this. After, then we can pay a visit."

"I will insist."

"We have to go."

The elf suddenly turned to the ship. "What is her name?"

"She is the Matilda."

Ilya nodded and went down to the water. In the sunlight of the bay afternoon his rough clothing looked even more primitive and worn, his glory changed to ordinary without the glamour of his faery home. He bent down and put his hands in the shallow water as the waves came to shore, and when he lifted them out he was holding a disc of ice he had made. He held this up, dripping, to the sun's low gaze and focused the sharper light that came out of it on the Matilda. Malachi saw him murmuring to himself, words in every elven magic, and then he had to jump back because the ship righted herself and lifted clear of the beach in one unencumbered move. A soft ghost glow began to appear around her points and edges.

"Hurry up," Ilya said, pointing with his nose to the gangway, which was dropping sand and water into the edge of the surf. "Get aboard."

Malachi ran up and grabbed the narrow rail, ignoring the bite of its iron touch as he leapt to the deck. Light began to spill from her frayed cable ends and the million eyes of broken wires. Ilya walked after him, keeping his focus on the melting ice in his hands. "To the Fleet then?"

Malachi took a last look at the beach, the house, the hill, and the woods. He took a breath of the air that swirled around, mingling scents of the sea and land. He knew why he stayed here. He liked these things, and he'd had no reason to go home. Until now. "To the Fleet, Master."

Ilya put the lens down on the control desk where Jones used to stand, her helm a smashed-up set of instruments nobody would read again, and placed his hand flat upon it. Malachi felt the ship shudder deep within itself. The elf's palm reddened at the edges with a thick line of blood, and the warm air of the day was cut in two by a savage chill. The water lapping at the hull stilled and the vessel groaned as she contracted in the cold. The sun and the beach faded away slowly and left them afloat in the darkness Malachi had grown to dread very well. A spherical shield of faint, blood-coloured light surrounded them, keeping their air in, he assumed, not that he was sure they needed air now. The Fleet's charm worked on its own to sustain its host. He looked up and around him and saw lights everywhere, heard the tolling of bells, the sharp call of those ships who were alive speaking to one another across the empty gaps and the lonely foghorn yodel of beasts farther out. Up, down, left, right, in all directions he could see nothing but the vessels of the Fleet. They seemed to go on for eternity.

"Where the hell is she?" He spoke now about *Temeraire*, the Admiral's ship. He couldn't see any sign of her anywhere.

"I cannot see her," the elf said gently, "but I can see him. They are higher up, to starboard and moving. His angels are with him."

"Moving?" Malachi looked at the destroyed remains of all the ship's instruments helplessly.

"The other ships part to make way. It looks as if he will take a leading position. The others form up behind him as he passes."

"Can you get close?"

In answer they began to rise slowly through the ranks. "I will aim to get into his draft and below him. Did you have a plan for after that?"

"No. You?"

"No."

"Good." He held the helm with his clawed hands, and the cold tore through him but didn't damage him. His fur was limned with the ghost hoar, and it stood on end as he turned around to the mouth of the cabin and saw the dead come walking out soundlessly and take their posts at the research stations. Where they passed the ship grew whole, and where they touched her ruined controls glasses and lights came to life under their fingers and feet and then spread their restoration across the decks and up the mast, along the deckhouse and into the stub of the harpoon gun until she was whole again, aether filling what material had lost. When he turned back he saw Ilya holding someone's hand. Then the elf turned and released his hold, the lens melting to watery blood as another pair of hands took the helm.

Shyly she looked over her shoulder, her shadowed eyes glowing and a brief smile for him on her lips. "Hello, Mal. Back with us again?"

"Jones," he said, finding something painful jamming his throat. "Captain."

"Thanks for looking after her," Jones said, turning her face towards the higher Fleet. "So. He got it back."

Malachi swallowed awkwardly. "I had to."

"I understand," she said, sniffing and wiping her nose on her sleeve. "S'okay. But we're going after him, en't we?"

"Yes." He reached out involuntarily and touched her. His fingers passed right through. "Oh, Jones."

"Don't worry," she said, and looked up at Ilya with a smile that was warm and feeling. "It was all right. I'm where I oughta be. Ironic, don'tcha think?" She rested her tough little hand on the elf's arm for a moment with more tenderness than Malachi had ever seen her possess in life and then let him go and took hold of her ship. "I get to sail one more time, right?"

Ilya nodded at her.

"Then we'll make it worth the trip, eh faery?" She gave Mal a sidelong glance. Her eyes were almost lost in their deep black sockets.

"Aye-aye," he said, and clipped his heels together and saluted.

"Aye fuckin' aye," she said, laughing at him. "You daft bastard." Then her voice hardened to its natural gritty state as she shouted orders to her crew. "Power the generators, full throttle. All logistics online. Prep the 'poon and make fast the lines. Shock wave cannon to standby. Man your guns, babies, man your fuckin' guns!"

CHAPTER TWENTY-FOUR

Zal landed on the rear deck of the *Temeraire* just as she got under way, when the sough and sigh of her sails lifting and the slide of rope on wood was enough to cover any sound he might make until he was used to his new shadow body. Her crew was busy and he was able to steal past them easily. Beneath him was the Admiral's cabin. He went over the side and climbed down to the struts where the leaded-glass windows were deeply set. There was a lot of fancy woodwork to hang onto. He tucked his hand around the figure of a leaping porpoise and bent close to the glass to see inside.

"Careful!" Glinda hissed, but she was too late. He'd already seen the figure at the chart table, compasses in hand, and around it the two figures that were barely more than rudimentary forms with heads, shoulders, and, possibly, wings. They were swirls of pale colour and they were restless. As soon as he looked they turned their heads and began to drift towards the windows.

"Away!"

"Ahead of you," Zal said, landing silently on the deck above. He crossed quickly, slid down the handrails that bordered the stairs to the main deck, and jumped through an open hatch into the lamplit gloom of the hold. He was delicate, light as a feather. He paused to peer at the flame of one of the lamps in its cage and lifted the glass so he could put out his finger towards it. He could see the fire through his own shadow flesh. He touched it to see if Mr. V had been lying.

For an instant he was transported from the ship's hold to a wooded glade. He was lying on his back staring at a pink-and-purple sky and a sun that wanted to undo him. He saw an arrow fly overhead and miss the girl with the red flash in her hair. Her silver eyes looked at him. She seemed horrified.

"Tsk!" Glinda snatched at him but he'd already pulled his hand back.

"Didn't she like me?" He felt confused. He was sure he liked her. The feeling of the fire connected him up. He felt stronger, lighter, if that were possible, more able. He wanted to carry on, but he could hear footsteps coming towards him and he flitted away, along the gangway and down another stair, searching quickly for any sign of the brig. He assumed that was where the Admiral would be. He was only hampered slightly by not knowing what a brig looked like. At least he knew Mr. V was good for his word. He carried on his way, hiding in the shadows, of which there were many, whenever someone passed him. At last he discovered a wooden room in the lower decks that had a locked door and a small openable porthole in the door. A bored sailor was apparently the guard, but he soon fell asleep at his place as the ship got under way and began to rock them. Zal moved to the porthole and opened it.

Inside the cell a boy he remembered was lying on a bench, his tri-corne hat on his belly, eyes closed. His bare feet poked out of the bottom of ragged breeches, and an oversized shirt was rolled up at the sleeves and falling all around his rope belt. On the floor lay a dagger and a piece of whittled wood along with a fair lot of shavings. A plate held the remains of a loaf of bread—all crusts. The boy scratched his nose and rubbed his face with one grubby hand. He opened his eyes and looked around, peering myopically at the open port. "Hoy, Smith there, what hour is it? Where is that blackguard taking my ship?" It was the Admiral.

Smith snored, slumped over the crate he had used as a table for his dinner.

"It isn't Smith," Zal whispered. "Shh, quiet and come here."

The boy got up quickly, feeling around him for his dagger with his foot and flipping it up to his hand with an astonishing dexterity. He slapped his hat on and came closer, but not within arm's reach. "Who the hell is that? If you're one of his fiends you can throw yourself overboard, I'll—"

"Shut up!" Zal hissed again. "I'm for you."

"Let me out!" At least he had understood. He was quiet.

"I can't. Not yet. I need to know about this guy first. Who is he?"

"Who the devil are you, sir?" the Admiral said with some rehearsed effort, coming no closer. "I say nothing more until you reveal yourself!"

Zal put his hand through the porthole. "I am an elf. A shadowkin. I am here to rescue you." He was aware of Glinda's strong objection but he ignored her. As he guessed, she wasn't ready to come forth and declare herself. She railed at him, but he took his hand away and put his face back there. "But I am afraid of this man in your cabin. He has with him—"

"Angels, yes I know! Oh they are marvelous! But why they are with him I don't know. They are not quite like the angels I have seen before in the deep. Shadowkin? But you look familiar."

"Amida brought me here," he said before he realized he had used the name of the goddess in her full form. Glinda's shock was rewarding. She hadn't mentioned it in her story. "A time ago. I was different then."

"You are the castaway! From the elemental shores!" The boy came forward suddenly and peered into Zal's face. "But you are darkness now. What happened?"

"Long story," Zal said. "Another time. What happened to you?"

The Admiral stood straight, his ankle bones touching, chin high. "I surrendered to save the Fleet." Then he added, "We found him, like you, floating in the Void. We brought him aboard. At first he was pleasant, for one of the death traders, and we took him to that shore, but he refused to leave and then he called them angels and they tore apart one of me ships, so I said they could stay but they threw me in here. He said he was only lending it. He said he was going to the Black Deep. I would never, but he wanted to go and so he put me here. There was another one here before you too. Dunno what happened to her."

"Who?"

"A woman, girl really. Real navvy-mouth she was and all. She said he was no good and she was going to stop him. Was a while ago, but when she left we stopped moving and we only just got under way again now. Was it you started them moving?"

"No." Zal wondered who she could be. "What did she look like? Silver eyes?"

"Eh? No. Ord'nary ones. Listen, there's things in the deep you don't go fishin' for. Where's this bloke going? What's he want?"

"I hoped you knew that," Zal said, sighing in disappointment. "There must be something. What about these angels?"

"What about them?"

"I never saw one before."

"They don't usually come here and never where you are really, so what? People say they's always good, but these two seem more like servants than leaders. They're just powerful in spirit, more than we are. They come and go as they like, I guess, got they own plans and stuff. I dunno." He shrugged and scowled. "What're you gonna do? Don't look like you could handle my cook let alone that bastard."

"I don't know," Zal admitted, "but I think the angels can see me, so I'll have to be careful."

The Admiral snorted his opinion of that and picked his nose thoughtfully. "Then you're as stuck as me. Rescue! Cuh!" He turned away and sat down on his bench again, picked up his stick, and began to hack at it with the dagger. Chips flew.

Zal stood back and looked over his shoulder at Glinda. She was glaring with her golden stare. "Any ideas?"

"Angels," she said with dislike. "This is much more than some little game about zombies and ordinary necromancers interfering with my work. The Deep. I don't like this at all."

"Who're you talkin' to?"

Zal turned back to see the Admiral's bony face struggling to get its chin over the porthole sill.

"Glinda," he said, leaning to the side so she would be visible.

The brown eyes squinted and his nose wrinkled. "Can't see anyone. You're not mad, are you?"

"No," Zal said cheerfully. "Look. She's my death. Glinda. Tall girl. Rude stare. Pointy ears." He held his fingers up beside his head but then realized how stupid that must be, since his own ears were there and equally pointy.

The brown eyes swiveled to look at him for a moment. "Just my luck," the Admiral said with deep contempt. "A looney. Well, in that case my advice is go up and talk to the new captain. Tell him about . . . Glinda . . . or whatever she's called. Introduce them. Maybe he'll tell you all about his plans and his angels and whatnot and then you can come back and tell me."

Zal took a breath to rebut this, hesitated, and turned back. Glinda was staring at him, her arms folded. She mouthed the words *rude stare*, and then *looney* at him. He turned back to the Admiral and considered the choices. "It's the best I've heard. I'll do it. Back soon."

"No, no! I di'n't mean it!" the Admiral began to shout as Zal reached up and closed the porthole on him. "Come back an' let me out, you lackwit! He'll eat you alive! Let me out! I demand it! Let me ou-utt!"

Smith woke up with snort. "Hey there, Captain, don't go getting worked up. . . ." But Zal was already gone.

Zal jumped up the stairs, climbed out of the hatch, and walked across the gently swaying deck to the door of the Admiral's cabin. Glinda was speechless, either with contempt or some other emotion, but he was intrigued by anything that she thought was bad news, and the threat of being eaten didn't bother him as much as it used to. At least it sounded interesting. He didn't look to check Glinda's view; he knocked on the door instead. He had a feeling that he'd always preferred the direct approach to things in spite of whatever Glinda said about sneakiness.

The door opened. A demon stood there, one of the humanoid kind. It was tall and solid with it, and if it hadn't been as part-substantial as he was and a ghost he would have said it was intimidating. It had a long, stretched face, with big carnivore's teeth, a beard, and several long tentacles on either side. More tentacles hung down in its thick dreadlocked hair. Ironbound horns swept back from its skull in two pairs, one short, one long enough to scrape the ceiling. In spite of all this it gave an impression of narrowness, agility, and ease. He was purple, dark green, black, and crimson; the colouration of deep introversion, spirituality, and corruption. The palette gave away little from one like him; only the black was interesting—creativity. His eyes were a dark cowlike brown with a red tint and horizontally slit pupils that were large in the glow of the lamps. "And who are you?" he said, not so much asking as looking and making known the nature of his enquiry. "Ah. I see. Zal Ahriman. How unexpected. Come in."

Zal held out his hand, "I haven't had the pleasure."

"Who I am is not important," the demon said with ease.

"It's important to me; you stole my stuffing," Zal said, still pleasant but not moving. He saw the angels in the background, their energies gathering strength as they moved near the lights.

"I am Xavien," the demon said, "but my house name is lost these days, of no account. I left society a long time ago and I don't like visitors, but since you have come so far, please." He opened the door wider and held his arm out.

Zal went inside and felt the demon's stare on him as acutely as if it were a touch.

"You have survived an extraordinary fate," Xavien said. "True shadow, yet not of the shadow world. Either you have a strong nerve to come here or you are misinformed about me."

Zal was watching the two beings who moved around at the periphery of the room. He'd seen demons before, and Xavien showed no unusual characteristics. "Who're your friends?"

"My guardians," Xavien said. "They would introduce themselves if they felt you warranted it. I can only follow their judgement in these matters."

Zal flicked an eyebrow but he was used to insults and he knew better than to take it personally. "Okay. So, what are you doing with my stuffing?"

"Do we have some business?" The demon's affability was starting to falter, Zal felt. A point against him if he was going to simply refuse an answer. Civility was an important skill when you were out to kill someone.

"I thought I could spy around and figure out what you were doing, but then it seemed easier to ask you," Zal said. The cabin was much more luxurious than he remembered. Beautiful rugs were spread beneath a table at the centre of the room, which held an array of charts and instruments, including a large gold-and-brass object he thought must be some kind of star finder. "That's nice. What is it?" He moved across to the table, noticing how his presence bent light in towards him and swallowed it. He was transparent, but less than he used to be. A slight aura of darkness blurred his edges. He admired the effect against the pale cream colour of the map parchment.

"None of your business. Might I ask what you hoped to achieve?" Xavien had moved near to the table. Zal got the impression he would have liked to hide something on it, but it was impossible to say what that might be.

"Yes. I came here to find out what you wanted with my stuffing, but then, seeing you had taken this ship off my friend, I thought I'd find out what you wanted with that too, but he said something about sailing into the Deep Black or whatever, so now I need to ask you what you want to do there or if you're going to just hand the ship back, I suppose. I mean, if you've got good explanations"—he looked up at Xavien's stoney face, took the measure of the two angels burning at the sides of his vision, and grinned—"then I'm sure we can sort it all out without any trouble." It was the happiest he had been in a long time.

Xavien looked speculative, and his hesitation let Zal know he was taking what he thought was a gamble. "Do you know about the Weapon of Intent?"

"No," Zal said, sorry he couldn't exploit the moment. "But then, I've lost most of my memory, so I don't know about much. Is it good? It sounds good."

The demon watched him, looked out the windows, and looked at his charts. The angels moved slowly like drifting fish in an unseen current. Zal could feel them as a burr of soft vibrations in his own skin. It was a strange and unnerving sensation. He had never been close to beings who operated at those kinds of frequencies and he'd have liked to debate the alleged superiority of such things, but he wasn't sure how to talk to them. It seemed that they followed the conversation, but he was sure they were having one of their own, at a pitch he couldn't hear but that created the feeling in his skin.

"It is an angel's weapon," Xavien said finally.

"That's nice." Zal hadn't known angels had weapons so he took this with a pinch of salt.

"I need it. I wish to leave this plane and in order to do so I need it."

He didn't understand where this was headed, but he rolled with it. "Where is it?"

"It will be here shortly. But know this: If you oppose me at any part of the way I will destroy what is left of you. Leave me be and the ship, your friend the Admiral, the weapon itself . . . everything will be returned. I only use force when persuasion fails."

Zal smiled. If they'd got to direct threats then whatever was going to go down was going to happen very soon. It was simple to carry on playing innocent, since he was. "Good of you."

"What I want is none of your business, elf demon. I have no desire beyond that moment. It is the pinnacle of my long life. I have never harmed any who did not stand in my way, and I would rather not start doing so. I would explain it to you at more length but—"

"Ah, go on," Zal said. "Looks like we've got a way to go." He walked his fingers across one of the extremely long blank spaces that roved between the chart's complex lines. He knew the temptation would be hard to resist. A lifetime's work almost completed. That was worth talking about, and he was sure the angels already knew the tale. Besides, he wanted to know what angels would guard. In spite of appearances and clumsy manners, he was ready to believe that Xavien was worth the effort.

To his surprise Xavien told him.

Zal looked at the charts, at the necromancer, at the angels. "That's brilliant!" He didn't turn to see what Glinda thought. It was genius. A few misdemeanours with the work of ordering forces in the weft of reality seemed small-fry by comparison. He wished he'd thought of it himself. "Will it work?" He looked at the demon with new respect and a bit more caution. Dreams like that didn't come from people who inhabited normal realms of the mind.

"I do not know."

Honesty, that was disarming. Zal decided to be a believer. "That part about Night, though. I mean, that's a bit scary. I can see why nobody wants you to go there. Always a chance that you could just be consumed in the rising influx of energies and instead of transmigrating yourself you're just fodder to her rebirth."

The demon nodded briefly, as if he didn't mind what Zal thought. "So, will you oppose me, Zal?"

Zal thought it over. "No, I don't think so," he said. "I want to see what happens." He did look over his shoulder this time. Glinda's face was like stone. He rationalized that he could always change his mind if things started looking tricky.

"Come on," he said to her. "You don't think that's crazy? Guy wants to become an angel, personally experience the highest potentials of existence."

"You don't understand," Glinda said, getting out a fresh cigar and lighting it on her tongue. "One false move and everything we've ever been will fold up on itself and be done. Night died because her job was done. Resurrecting her, even in part, invites all that you are to revert to its original causes. Now, in one sense of course, nothing's lost, only transformed, and since that's pretty much life and death in a nutshell where's the harm? But it's the end of a lot of conscious beings and their evolutions, not to mention the end of order and complexity and all the wonders of the worlds. That's quite the price for one person's test of their own limit, wouldn't you say? And if you wouldn't I would." She puffed deeply and shot smoke out of the corner of her mouth. "For one thing, Zal, I prefer you to him, so if there's got to be a choice, I'd rather he didn't."

"You prefer me, really?"

"Go to the top of the class," Glinda said, flicking a shred of tobacco off her lip and fixing the cigar firmly between her molars. "Why do you think you're still around?"

"And Night being reborn is just a chance thing?"

Glinda tilted her head side to side, drew hard on the cigar, widened her eyes, and finally nodded confirmation.

"I take it your death does not approve," Xavien said. He and the angels were watching Zal very, very closely, like hawks.

"No, not really," he said, shrugging with a "what can you do?" expression. "She just likes to look after me though, so . . . expected it. Potential end of everything brings it out in her."

The demon narrowed his eyes. "The Fates, Muses, whatever you want to call them, the daughters of Night are matricides. That might sway the balance a little. They didn't get their power by chance. They will not let it go easily."

"Yeah but, you're one of theirs as well," Zal pointed out, fairly he felt. "I mean, divided loyalties. And you got so far where most don't even dare. So you'll be favoured even if you threaten them. Mothers . . . it's tough when the children get ambitious and run into risks, but you have to cut the cord, y'know? Got to be hard."

There was a long pause in which the angel vibrations increased and Zal felt as if he were sinking to the bottom of a well, the three of them at the top looking down on him as they considered how on earth they could get rid of him without getting blood on their hands.

"I see where your fame as a fool of renown comes from," Xavier said, inscrutably, just as Zal was convinced they had decided on drowning, but he was interrupted by the ship's bell ringing suddenly loud and calls from the deck. The doors opened and a crewman rushed in.

"Strange ship to port! She's attacking. Orders?"

"Destroy her," the demon said without hesitation. Only then did he move to see who it was. One angel went with him; the other followed Zal onto the deck. Zal leant on the rail, looking at the hundreds of ships. Only now on the flagship signal were they moving to defend, but they were late. The incoming ship was moving at high speed, and even as he caught sight of her a bright, sharp dart shot from her bows and flew straight and true to embed itself in the base of the mizzenmast. He saw boats near her suddenly flung aside by an invisible hand. As he threw himself to the deck, grabbing the first anchored thing he found, he was shouting at the top of his voice.

"No!"

A hand like a wall of ice crushed down on his mouth. He fought, turned, and found himself staring up into the face of an angel.

In the battle there was no time, but an age had passed for the sun had fallen down the sky and lay in bloody exhaustion at the edge of the distant hills. Haze made it seem vast and weak at the same time. Lila found herself standing still, staring at it. There was no impulse in her to move, no more foe to slay. The last one was falling, to his knees, toppling to his side, his head rolling past her feet. All she could taste was blood. It came on every breath. The sun hypnotized her with its stillness, and then her arm moved, faster than thought, and the blade clashed and shock ran through her arm and body into the spongy ground. She turned to look at the face of the intruder who had broken her peace and attacked her from behind, her blade held over her head, edge grinding horribly as she moved but yielding not one millimeter.

His face was white but streaked in red. His eyes blazed white, and more white fire spilled out of his mouth, half-open and grinning at her. Both his blades pressed down on her single one, his raised arms fixing there in a dare to try his open guard, wire muscles on his narrow body rigid and shaking with effort. His white shock mane of hair was red and plastered to his neck and face, large hanks of it missing altogether. She wasn't sure as she looked into his eyes that he recognized her at all.

"Teazle?"

He stared and his face changed slowly; he lifted the swords and backed a step into a guard pose. His mouth worked silently for a while as it discovered how to speak. "Lila?"

She put her sword down and nodded. Around them mounds of dead and dying lay by the acre. When she took a step towards him, her boot sank between limbs and stood on more. She didn't know if there was even earth beneath her or if it was flesh and bone all the way down.

"What are you doing here?"

"You're in the mirror," she said. "I came to get you out." She saw his gaze wander as he dealt with this information.

"I had this dream so many times, all my life," he said. "It only ends when . . ."

"When you die, or when you are victorious over all," she said. "Yes, I know. I suppose that's why we're still here. Two of us. Can only be one or none."

The battle fury was leaving him; he swayed slightly, and the swords drooped in his hands. He looked around. "We won." That grin of his landed on her then, and suddenly she was reminded of Zal and knew why she liked it.

"Yeah," she said, smiling though there was a pain in her chest.

"I was always alone," he said. Pearly liquid, glowing and gleaming, ran over his arms and torso, and streamed to the ground in sticky strings, steaming slightly. He looked around. Here and there was movement among the massed fallen. "They rise again. Because it won't end. I don't know why."

Lila racked her brains. "Repeating dreams are a way of trying to resolve deep issues," she said, reading off her AI's suggestion. She looked too and saw that he was right. "You won't survive another repeat." She pointed at his body, and for the first time he looked down at himself.

His grin widened with self-consciousness. "Hah. And if I die here then I'll be truly dead; is that why you came?"

She nodded. She didn't know what would happen if they fought. But if it was the only way out then she'd have to because she wasn't leaving him here. There was no dry run inside her systems in which she had ever beaten him, but now she thought she had a chance; he was badly hurt and exhausted. She was a regenerating machine on infinite power. She stood and raised her sword, not certain what to do, feeling she had walked into a stupid trap, just as much as he had, and now she was going to pay. Tears ran down her face and she blinked so that she could see. Her chest was burning.

Around them warriors were getting up, picking their weapons from the butchered mounds, and moving into positions ready for attack. Lila stayed in her stance. She felt it was only fair.

Teazle straightened up and eased his neck. He slid his swords into their holders on his back and limped towards her, hands held out in a warding and offering way as he kept a weather eye on her sword. The berserk power he had been was all gone. His smile was cautious, voice gentle. "I don't want to fight you," he said.

Around them the rising warriors spun and fell to dust. The bodies vanished, and in their place solid ground showed, covered in a thin coat of green. Teazle blinked as from one instant to the next his terrible wounds were healed and the gore that coated him was gone. Lila lowered the sword and found that she was shaking uncontrollably.

Teazle's hands closed over hers on the hilt of the huge blade, and he gently turned it away from himself without attempting to remove it from her grasp. She gained a bit of control of her hands then and let go with one of them, catching hold of his arm and leaning on him. "Is it over?"

"Yes," he said. His hand took hold of her jaw gently and tipped her face up towards his.

What she started to say was cut off by his kiss, and she could feel his smile in that. Just like a demon, one minute facing doom and the next forgetting it as if it wasn't important at all, living in the moment. She put her arms around him and hugged him close and filled her nose with the animal, mineral scent of his skin. Against her body the dress had subtly bloomed into a silky cocktail slip in deepest black silk. It made his glowing body look even more spectacular.

"Were you gonna fight me to the death, Black?" he asked, stroking her hair.

"I don't know," she said, pressing her face into his neck and feeling him tip his head against hers, covering her up. Cool wind on her skin made her snuggle even closer to his warmth.

"Lila, what are you doing out here?" her mother's voice said, questioning and a little accusatory, deeply disapproving. "Who is this man? Or should I say *what* is he? Should I call the police?"

Lila froze and then, very slowly, she released her grip on Teazle and turned around.

They were standing at the bottom of the garden, her childhood home above them on the slight rise of the lawn. The stand of willow trees was in full leaf and had hidden her from sight of the windows. Her mother was just behind the leafy screen, peering inward into the shade. She was wearing a peach silk suit and looked as beautifully groomed and sober as any bride's mother. Lila kept her fingertips in contact with Teazle's skin as she moved forward. "Mom?"

"You just went running right out," her mother complained. "It's time to sign the register and the deeds. Everyone is waiting."

"Deeds?" Lila asked, picking the least worrisome word. She felt Teazle caress her hand though he didn't move.

"Deeds to the property. Are you all right? What's going on?" Her mother started to slap the willow fronds aside.

Lila saw the same things she had seen in the crystal pane and reflexively checked her shoulder. Although the bag had altered into a gold leather handbag, she felt the heavy weight of the glass in it. In her hand the black pen sat snugly. She felt a shiver and looked down to see the heavy white lace of a wedding dress. Her feet pinched her painfully in high-heeled shoes that made her stagger on the grass.

Her mother stared at her angrily as she emerged. "You're ruining that dress! And it cost the earth. So much fuss over it and look at you!"

"Mom." She wanted to hug her and cry, but the dream didn't have any room for that; she could feel the restraining weight of compulsion on her, a peculiar force that warped her intent and made her say, "It's okay. This is just . . . an old friend." The dream had a shape of its own and it would have its way. She felt the logic of it and knew that until it reached some final point, like Teazle's, there was no escape; only this time it wasn't a repeat of something she dreamed at night. She'd never had this dream, at least, only in parts and only in the day and long ago, or in parts of her she'd assumed were gone. She had no idea what the end condition was supposed to be.

Then her mother screamed fit to wake the dead.

Lila turned to see what she was staring at and realized Teazle was standing with her in his true form. The noise attracted attention. Guests and relatives, Max and her dad and the dogs came spilling out of the house and into the garden. Belatedly she saw that everything was decorated with white roses and garlands of silk. A marquee was there, a feast prepared, servants were everywhere—even though until a second ago the garden had been empty. Her husband was there with his immaculate tux, looking lightly perplexed. He was holding the deeds to half of the Bay in his hands, not just their house, and he had signed and the ink was drying. Only her signature was missing.

She froze. The tangled knot of love and longing inside her felt heavy as lead, a cancer that had almost finished its task of consuming her alive. She stared at their faces and saw how much they all loved her and wanted her happiness, and she felt inside how much the cancer didn't want her happiness but fed on her hunger for it and changed it into hatred and rage; all this was her stolen life that might have been. The only reason she'd been able to draw breath and carry on since she'd been made was the loss of this and the anger it had made her feel. Anger was a kind of energy, even anger at herself that she couldn't stop longing for these things though she despised herself for doing it. She didn't want to be the weak person who couldn't let go of the dead, who felt life had to answer her problems with comforts and who bought the whole ninety-nine yards of the conforming deal whilst at the same time dreaming she was special. She hated the way that the dress made her feel: like someone's property, like a thing wrapped up and parceled into place, ready to be erased from the entries of everything that mattered and fitted with a face not her own and a name that was someone else's and all the things she was expected to be contented by. She wanted to feel the special power of such a day, to be in love honestly and truly, to know that she was right in herself, to feel sure. Here it was. And she hated it. Hated it.

The dress corset and the diamonds in her necklace were strangling her. She dropped the pen and groped for them and started to rip at the chain. It cut her skin. She couldn't breathe.

"Darling," her mother cooed gently, coming forwards to help her.

"Liles," Max said with her cool dismissal. "Get a grip."

"I can't do this," Lila gasped. She moved back, feeling with her free hand for Teazle and finding a monster behind her. He felt hard, scaly, the scales sharp and slicing, and he was burning hot. She pulled away in horrified surprise and turned to see him grown in size, a white-and-blue dragon, every part of him razored and thorned, his mouth and nostrils pits of burning heat that seared the air.

"Here, hon," her father said, "look who's coming, your best friend, she'll help you."

Bewildered, Lila turned. Beside her father stood a grey android with a sleek body like a dolphin's. Her doll-like features smiled brightly. It was Sandra Lane.

"Hey, Lila," she said, and bent down to pick up the pen. "Let me get that for you. Won't take a tick." She made a brushing movement with her hand. The pen flashed out, the blade screamed. There was a wet thud.

The dragon fell in two pieces, blood and fire streaming like lava. Her mother and father fell like cut flowers. The house and Max bent and slid into the broad grey blade, taking the guests with them.

The caterers tiptoed around the body pieces, making the faces of people who are suffering a terrible social faux pas but heroically not noticing it.

"There ya go!" Sandra was beaming. In her smile was everything that was honest, open, and friendly. She held out the pen. "Here, don'tcha want it?"

Lila's heart was thundering. She couldn't breathe. Her face felt twice its size and she couldn't speak. She choked for air. Tears blinded her. She began to back away, but the dress tangled with the shoes and she stumbled into the burning body of the dragon and felt herself catch light. Sandra came on, holding the pen forwards.

"Here," she said. "Take it. You still haven't signed."

Lila ripped at the dress, tore it, and then started tearing at her skin as the flames took hold. She was burning. The misery she had been feeling turned to helplessness as she saw it wasn't only the dress: her hands, her arms, her body was burning. She looked around for water and saw only the drinks on the trays passing her, bubbles rising.

"Help me!" She tried to reach them but they were carried away; nobody heard her, or if they did they just smiled at her as though she was the perfect bride and hostess as they moved off. Only Sandra kept coming.

Lila began to pat and then hit herself with the flat of her hands, trying to beat the fire out, but wherever she put it out it sprang up somewhere else. And then it began to hurt, but worse than that was the panic. She tripped up and fell on her ass. The remains of the flaming dress ballooned around her, knotting around her legs. The pain grew intense, white hot. She wanted it to be over. Sandra Lane bent down towards her. "Are you okay? Aww, it's been a long day, huh? Here. Have a drink." She held out a long-stemmed glass and poured the contents over Lila's lap. The pure alcohol went up with an explosive whoosh in a gout of searing heat. Lila felt her face melting, running, but it was nothing compared to the misery she felt inside as she lay there, worthless, useless, powerless. Even so she struggled and she didn't understand why she didn't die. Wretched, able to do no more than twitch, she persisted when she longed for it to end. Finally all she could do was listen.

She heard Sandra Lane's cheerful golden voice: "No, she just won't sign it. I don't know why, darling. Maybe it's all been too much for her? You know, she always was a bit of an attention seeker. Oh, always was since she was a kid, thought she was better than everyone else. Boohoo my mom and dad are drinkers, yes they are, didn't you know? God, talk about lush, you could strip wallpaper with her mother's breath. And as for her father, his only steady job was AA. Uh-huh.

Didn't she tell you? And then there was the job she had that was so much better than everyone else's she never stopped talking about it. I suppose you must have met her after that? There was nothing she couldn't do. Yes, she really did say that. Oh, and you won't believe this, she used to have this crush on that elf, you know the one, yes him with the . . . yes ahaha! Can you believe it? I know." Peals of laughter from a sizeable group of people briefly overcame the snap and crackle of flames. "Soo embarrassing! Talk about teenage crush victim. I know! Oh, he died in some motorbike accident, blam right into a pylon or something, yes, bound to happen. Mmn. He probably did deserve it. No, it doesn't look like she's coming. Probably decided to burn to death rather than do the decent thing. She would, yes. She's selfish that way. Oh, spiteful seems a bit strong. Well, I could always sign it, I suppose?"

CHAPTER TWENTY-FIVE

The deck of the *Temeraire* was suddenly alive with activity. The crew rushed to issue the necromancer's orders though they were not ready for a battle and all they could do was to bring the ship about so that she faced her attackers head-on, presenting less of a target. The harpoon in her mainmast, however, did not release in spite of the change in angle. The line vibrated with tension and gave off a low note as aboard the other ship an engine worked to reel it in.

Under the angel's grip Zal struggled. Everything was hard, material, for an instant, and then he thought of fading to darkness and slipping into the shadows. He felt a quickening all over, as if he were electric, and then he was free and the angel was staring at him face-to-face. He held out his hands towards it and saw how deeply shaded his arms were, almost opaque, the darkened edges of his clothing the pen marks of an artist's final inking. Wait! I can stop them. Get me to the other ship and I'll stop them."

The angel stared at him for a long second. Its body, almost comically like that of a snow angel though much less well defined, was shot with varicoloured lights dotted with brilliant moving points. It looked like a living nebula, giving birth to new stars.

"God, you're beautiful," Zal said, not realising he was speaking aloud, but it was such a magnificent sight he couldn't help it. The angel's eyes blazed in a turning storm of brilliance. Their light shone onto him, and through him. He felt himself dancing around that light, unharmed but interrogated by it. A strange joy filled him as the angel knew him, although it gave no sign of change in itself. Looking at it made a channel open in his chest, through his heart, as though they had been harpooned together by a magnificent spear. His mind and body lit up and he felt that in spite of all he had lost he knew himself and was himself more truly than he had ever been. All this passed in an instant and then he had to look up.

Around and behind the angel in the rigging Zal could see regions of darkness massing and forming; in fact, he felt more than saw them. They had a deadly cold about them as they poured themselves together, massing substance from infinitesimally small holes that were foaming open around the ship's masts and sails as the Void opened onto Thanatopia. Even the sailors cowered in fear as they drifted down from above, coalescing with languorous delicacy into shadows as dark as Zal and darker. They were pure and uncomplicated hungers, spilling at the necromancer's command, their will mastered by his infinitely more powerful one.

Zal watched them over the angel's shoulder and saw them whirl and spin towards the demon's upraised arms. They were dreadful only because he could feel their power, their lack of any restraint. Only the fact that their will was subjugated by Xavien's prevented them from falling instantly on everything that could have been sucked and scavenged from the beings around them. The angel over him flared across the region of what Zal thought of as its wings with a flash of light that he fancied was repulsion. He glanced at its face, to see, and looked into its eyes. His mouth, ever ahead of the rest of him, asked in puzzlement. "Why are you protecting him?"

There was a shudder in the angel and it reached out with both arms. A blinding flash of dark enveloped him and then Zal found himself standing on the rear of the other ship's ghost-glowing deck, banks of instruments flashing lights before him, the thunder of her engines

vibrating through his feet and two startled crew—elf and demon—
staring at him as if he were a living incarnation of evil itself. But
beyond them he saw the helm. A ghost was there, her face dismayed
and surprised as she looked over her shoulder and saw him. He saw her
recognise him as he began to run towards her. Her mouth dropped
open. Beside her, turning, was a faery, his orange eyes vivid against the
black of his skin as they flared wider. His white teeth were shocking as
his lips parted in a half smile of amazement and disbelief. Zal didn't
know them but he felt good about them so he didn't bother himself.
He ran harder, feet sure on the deck's slippery surface as she shook and
groaned with the effort of dragging herself to the other vessel.

The elf ghost at her station reached out with her claws but Zal
dodged her, not knowing if she could catch him or not. The demon
leapt. His fingers passed through Zal's leg.

"Stop!" Zal shouted as he ran, everything in his way. He passed
the line winch and tried to hit the controls, but he was too light and
the ship ground on, quickly closing with the *Temeraire's* forward
guns. The dark swirling around the masts was visible against the pale
sailcloth bank of her rig as she dipped, nose down, towards their
onslaught. Zal could see Xavien at the rail, the angels on either side
of him in the air forming into shapes like arrows pointed directly at
them. "Stop. Please! Stop! They'll kill you!"

Then it was his turn to falter openmouthed as the figure on the
other side of the captain turned around. His pale hair floated out in the
ship's weak gravity; his elongated classic high-blood features caught
the hoarfrost light and stood out in white planes. The eyes, which had
once been blue, were black, but Zal would have known him anywhere.
It was the first face he had recognised in an age, and in the split second
between knowing it and finding the name that fit he felt all that was
between the two of them and it was such a powerful flood of emotion,
so dense that he slid to a halt in his tracks, grabbing at his chest for a
second, sure now if he wasn't before that he did still have a heart.

"Ilya," he said as the ghost captain snarled at him, her face twisted with hate, and yelled, "we cannot stop! It will bring chaos!"

The faery was staring at him. Zal glanced at his face, and realised it was expecting recognition. He had none, so he looked back at Ilya, almost unable to understand the vibrations that were emanating from him. Unmistakably it was power, much greater than Zal's own. For an instant he was thrown by the lack of contact between them—every elf joined aetheric bodies on meeting—then remembered that here they *were* their aetheric bodies and had no other, him literally. "Ilya! Listen to me. Those things on that ship are—"

"Angels. We have met." He was so calm, but that meant nothing. There was a time when both Zal and Ilya would have been calm in a battle and died calm without a trace of feeling in their faces and little of it within themselves. A smile was almost forming on Ilya's face. "I thought you were finished." The smile suddenly shone. "But you never appeared where I was, so I knew it was not so."

"Fire!" screamed the captain, ignoring their exchange.

"Don't fire!" Zal screamed at her.

"Zal?" the faery asked, his tones suggesting he didn't understand, that they were supposed to be on the same side and that side was fighting. Zal wasn't sure, but he saw the darkness hanging over the *Temeraire* suddenly deepen and he knew what it meant.

"Stop!" He hung on the faery's arm and pushed at the captain though she shook him off and tried to hit him. "It's not worth you dying. They'll carry on anyway. Please. I'm begging you. Stop."

The harpoon gun sounded its blast and a bolt went screaming over their heads, trailing a fine line. One of the angels flared and it flicked down at the last moment, slamming into the forward bulkhead of the *Temeraire*.

"There is more to this than meets the eye," Zal babbled, unsure of what he was going to say but only knowing he didn't want them to die and it was nearly upon them. "Give me a chance! If you knew me, if you know me, if you care, then just wait. Wait. You can commit suicide later. There's always later. A few more minutes of an interesting life. Come on." It was then he realised that he was addressing the only truly living person on the vessel, apart from himself. He looked back at Ilya, surprise deepening his curiosity even as his spirit plunged. "What happened to you?"

The elf had his head on one side slightly, chin drawn back; his eyes were deeply puzzled. "Zal, is that . . . concern for me on your face?"

"No!" The captain's wail of disappointment almost drowned him out as she surveyed the missed shot and witnessed the severing of her lines by the angels. At the same time the dark shades plunged forwards across the gulf, a boiling, indistinct mass like a cloud come to cover their skies. "Man the blasters! To stations! Get ready to fire nets."

Zal was shaken, but the moment with Ilya felt more compelling than his impending doom. "Shouldn't it be?"

Ilya looked at him with something approaching wonder. "Did you forget . . . ?"

"Yes," Zal snapped. The black cloud had blotted out most of the sight of the Fleet now. It was speeding towards them. "I did. I forgot everything. But apparently not you. Now isn't the time for a reunion. If you want that you have to act. What should I do? More concern?" He darted forward over the last few metres that separated them and hugged the tall thin frame, just able to feel its bitter cold surface, though that didn't lessen his grip. "I love you. I need you. I want you to live. Don't die. There, now please, stop her! Stop her." The strange thing was that as he talked he found he meant what he was saying. He really didn't remember any details, only the feelings. For the first time in a long time, he knew that he was telling the truth as it was meant to be, without regard for incidental things, like facts.

The faery had begun to try and reason with the ghost but she was fighting him. Her face was distraught, a ruin, tears running down it in big, black inky lines. "No, no no!" she was moaning as her hands mastered the difficult controls and brought them around so their starboard side faced the huge sailing ship. The demon and elf and other ghosts were all set, seated on swivelling gun mounts, their odd barrels taking aim, the hum of the power generator becoming a scream. Zal had no idea what they even did.

"Jones," the faery said, holding onto her even though she was fighting and swearing at him. Her crew looked to her. All their faces were so sad. Zal didn't understand. "Jones. For me. For the crew. For what you learned. Maybe there's more."

"There is no more!" she cried. "Don't you hear her, in your mind? You didn't. You don't know what she's like! She ate us, Mal. She destroyed us! And him, he's like her. Shadow!" She wrenched her head around and opened her mouth.

Zal knew what was coming. He slapped his hand over her face and pressed on it with all his might, pulling hard on every scrap of shade, every bit of the Void's natural dark, on the black tears running on her cheeks. He stared into her narrowed eyes as she glared her hate and rage at him. Then he thought he had heard right after all. "She?" He looked away from her terrified face at the other two. "She?" He looked over his left shoulder.

Glinda stared at him fixedly through a haze of Old Havana. "Ah-ha," she said slowly. "I didn't think Xavien was all that great a demon name. I think our necromancer is playing a game of charades. Figures they're not brought up in the best schools of meddling with dark forces. Who in their right mind would piss me off that much?"

Unable to move in his grip Jones rolled her eyes toward the *Temeraire*. Zal realised he was crushing her. He could feel the substance of her melting against his insistence, literally, her glow fragmenting, fading. He let her go and backed away in despair. She reeled against her control deck. The oncoming wave struck the ship, and where it touched its glittering, glowing edges the light was instantly consumed. Ilya, who had been gazing at Zal, raised one hand without even turning around.

"Get back," he said in a tone of command that was as gently spoken as it was absolute.

The captain, Jones, spat at Zal and took hold of her wheel again, bracing herself for the onslaught as if for a hurricane. But it never reached them. Like mist rising and clearing with the sun, Ilya's command had dispersed it into primary particles. Zal felt it wash past him invisibly, too discontinuous and disparate to be any more than an unpleasant, itching chill. In seconds that too had gone.

"What the hell?" Zal said, an echo of Glinda, but the effect hadn't gone unnoticed aboard the other ship. One of the angels had suddenly crossed the gap. Its explicit examination of Ilya was obvious, even though it hovered above and in front of him without making any significant movement. He stared back at it, watchfully, with what Zal thought was intense bitterness rather than rapture.

Nobody was staring at it with more awe than Jones however. "What . . . what is that?" she whispered hoarsely to the faery who was standing behind her, supporting her. "It looks like . . . is it . . . ?"

"Yes," he said, as elegant and insouciant as if they were in a pleasant lounge and not at the brink of extinction. "It's an angel."

"I never saw one this close." She gave a snort, an almost noiseless one-shot laugh. "Isn't that just the shits? They chased me. I was too scared to turn around and look."

"Not entirely without reason," Ilya said dryly.

The angel abruptly vanished and reappeared some five hundred metres away on the *Temeraire*'s deck. The two of them spiralled up suddenly in a rush of light and remained close to the crow's nest there.

Abruptly Jones slapped a switch and the power generator quieted. The ship stopped thrumming and they slowed to a halt with a brief hum. The two ships floated a hundred metres apart and the Fleet massed around them, gathering close on all sides so there could be no escape.

"Captain?" her demon crew asked from his position at the front gun.

"Stand down," she said. "We died once out here. It's enough. We're done." She pulled away from the faery and walked away from the helm and ran down the steps in the centre of the deck, followed closely by the demon, while the rest of the crew reluctantly went about the business of disarming.

The faery glanced uneasily at the *Temeraire* and then more urgently back at Zal. "Zal, what happened, did you really forget everything?"

"I don't know," Zal said. "Did I know you?"

The faery seemed disturbed. His cat ears flattened to his head. "Yeah." He glanced at the deck hatch and then back at Zal.

Zal felt awkward. He looked to Ilya, who was still staring at him. "You're not . . ."

"He's an avatar," Glinda said behind him with undisguised surprise and what Zal thought might be professional envy. "Jack's supplanter. The twice-dead Winter King. It's complicated. Faery remade him. It does that. Long story."

"Oh right." Zal nodded at her. "I thought he was Ilyatath Taliesetra. An elf. But yeah. Something happened to him."

"Who are you talking to, Zal?" the black faery asked, peering around.

"The Three Sisters," Ilya answered for him as Zal said, "Glinda." They paid no attention as the cat fey hissed and muttered under his breath. For a moment there was only the two of them.

"What happened to *you*?" Ilya asked him.

"I . . ." Zal began, but he couldn't go on because there was only blank space in his head, not even lint. "There was a girl," he said. "She had silver eyes." It was what came into his thoughts first. At this he saw Ilya's face tighten slightly and take on a look of caution. The faery's even more so. "What?"

"We can have a reunion later, as you said." The faery pointed to himself. "Malachi. Now that ship is coming this way, and when it does any chance we had to act will probably be gone so tell us what's going on from your end and make it fast."

Zal looked and saw the *Temeraire*'s crew making ready to board. "There is something going on over there that isn't what it looks like. Demon, necromancer, manages the beasties, superior mastery of ghosts, strange behaviour, using people's insides to create doppelgangers . . . but that woman just said . . . she said she . . . and those angels. I don't think two angels would be here if this were what it looked like."

"And what's that?" Malachi asked, folding his arms.

"An attempt to seize the ultimate in aetheric power and re-create the world. I mean, is that what you thought?" He looked at the faery, who was mulling it over, his jaw jutting, and at Ilya.

"There is only a chance of that," Ilya said. We are here and ready to fight because we have been used and fought. It is possible those things are unhappy chances that came in the wake of deeds done for a greater good, but they did not feel that way at the time. But look, they are here. We have stopped. You got your wish as usual, Zal." That bitterness touched his mouth again. "Now we will see who is right or wrong in their guesses." He reached out almost compulsively to touch Zal and their hands met and Ilya's passed through Zal's.

"Tingles," Zal said, sorry. "I'm only partly material enough."

"All material form here is largely illusory," Ilya said. "And the longer we all remain present in planes not suited to us the worse it will get."

"I thought you were right at home."

"I am still relatively low on the rank," the elf replied with wry humour. "I am not an angel or a Titan"—he discreetly flicked an eyebrow as he glanced over Zal's shoulder—"to be dotting around at my whims without a price."

Zal looked back at Glinda. She was sitting with her feet up, glass in hand. She waved him back regally to his conversation. He glanced at Ilya and whispered, "Can you see her?"

Ilya shook his head. "No. I see only you but I know what happened to you in Under, so it is no surprise to me that you are ridden by the Three."

"It isn't like that," Zal said. "There's only one of her."

"Of course there is," Ilya said.

By now they were surrounded by the *Temeraire*'s freebooter crew holding various weapons pointed at them. Other vessels of the Fleet were so close they also could have boarded, but they held off with poles and ropes, tying up the ship fast so she could not move.

"Take them below," the demon said from the *Temeraire*'s deck. "Except that one." It pointed at Ilya. "This one is too dangerous."

"Ah no," Zal said, mouth ahead once more. "If he stays I stay."

"Three for me," added the faery, as though he were lengthily and heartily bored of such affairs and would much rather have done something else.

Glinda whispered in Zal's ear, her breath warm on his neck. "Get me closer to it. Closer."

They were marched across a narrow board, on either side of which the infinite Void fell away into forever. Zal would have liked to stand on it longer, but he was between Ilya and Malachi so he crossed. This route took him past Xavien, so he pretended he was interested in Ilya's back, stepped closer, and tripped himself on Ilya's heel, falling sideways against the demon. Xavien leapt aside with great speed but he wasn't fast enough and Zal's hand touched him. Immediately he felt a shock go through his arm. As he made to get up he found the angels on either side of him, pushing him back, but he knew then and there what was going on. As he got up he was looking into the demon's face, seeing it for what it was, a mask . . . and the demon was staring at him with horrified shock and a loathing so intense that it was difficult to meet it and still rise to his feet. In that second the Fleet wavered, a ripple of dissent running through it like the weak buck of a trapped animal's one free limb.

"No," the demon said, backing away one step from Zal as he straightened. "No. Stay away from me. For that you shall die." His gaze swept around quickly. "All of you." Its hand shot out, fingertips pointing at them. Zal felt a dark thing like a doubt or a question skitter around in his chest, find his centre, and take hold.

The drawing on the combined powers was so fast that none of them could counter it.

The demon's fingers clawed and it had them. "Die," it hissed and drew its fingers slowly into a fist. And Zal was dying, his connection to everything pouring away, scratching away down the thread that bound him to the shadowkin's hand. She was so strong there was no counter to it. Beside him he felt Ilya's hand and took it in his own. He felt himself falling on the faery's collapsed body and inside him the roaches of his own words, all the things he had said, went rushing around talking about him, babbling his short, dull life away before they poured across the line into the demon's closing hand. He saw the light of the angels and wondered why they had taken to her and abandoned him. And along the line he felt how much his slayer hated him, how she had let him live only out of morbid curiosity and now she was glad that she was undoing the last of him, pathetic as it was.

At that second he felt the last thing he expected to feel. He knew her. He knew her because she was like every rotten high elf that had ever hated him and she was like all the darkness that they had hated him for, with power enough already to make anything of herself that she wished, and she made this. Her genius dream was so small she had nothing but death to give him. And he already had death. He saw Glinda step in front of him.

She looked cross. "Not that close, you arse," she said, jamming her cigar stub into her mouth.

"Is this the end?" he asked her.

"Yeah in a minute." She flicked her shot glass out into her hand and then, in a mockery of the demon, closed her fist on it so that it burst into shards. She shook the pieces out of her hand and cut the cord.

Xavien screamed with rage. He turned to the crew. "To the Deep with all speed!" They rushed to obey and the Fleet began to re-form about them as they got under way. Ilya and Malachi lay on the deck, still not moving though their presence was enough of a sign they had been spared along with him.

"Hey Zal," Glinda said, picking the rest of the glass out of her palm. "Gimme that book a second."

He abruptly felt his jacket on him and that it was heavy on one side. The book was still there. He reached in and handed it to her. She opened it and read. "Excellent," she said. "Now, in order for me to fulfil my promise to that wretched girl there remains only a little more trouble." He felt she was talking to herself there and tried to look at the book though she twitched it away from him with an arch glance that dared him to try peeking again. "Good of Mr. V to be so perspicacious and find me such a volume," she said. "I knew he would. Only needed the right incentive. Going to miss his Friday night chilli though."

Zal thought he'd take the opportunity to ask a question that was on his mind while she wasn't making sense. "If you and an angel were in a fight who would win?"

She stared at him, her golden eyes narrowed, and then shook her head with a frown, relit her cigar on her tongue, again, and went back to her book, vanishing slowly. He looked over his shoulder and she made a filthy gesture at him. If he'd been corporeal he'd have been embarrassed at his reaction.

He looked up to find the angels standing beside the three of them. They seemed so beneficent it was hard to imagine they were there to enforce Xavien's will. On the foredeck Xavien, still disguised, orchestrated preparations for her master stroke.

The Fleet, gleaming, shining, sailed into the precipitous dark. Zal left Ilya and Malachi and went to the rail. Above and below him and to the sides the ships were fully formed in every detail, running lights and lanterns shining in the absence of stars. He looked forwards to Xavien, now seated in meditation alone on the bowsprit. Ilya was right. These things did feel different on the receiving end. It was one thing to kill someone who had been given fair warning and who still chose to stand in one's way. It was another to torture them to death. Xavien had a taste for cruelty that was high-caste in its casual manner, a primal hunger for information and knowledge that was vampiric in essence. Her longing was much more easily understood by him. He had felt the same things, and turned to the demons in order to find a way to them, long ago. In spite of everything, he felt sympathy for her in her lonely journey. He knew how stupid you could get when you hurt badly enough. He knew how much damage he had done. Glinda had told him. The Dragon Mantle was a lovely idea but something only a drunk or a desperate soul would aspire to find. Sober it wasn't possible to believe in it, although he had already come much further than he would ever have believed possible, so he felt no confidence in his judgement on the chance of it being real. In spite of his admiration for the heroic spirit of the effort and his initial enthusiasm, the last few minutes had robbed him of his naive conviction and left in its place a cold dread and sadness. He remembered in Glinda's story that he had always been slow to see the negative, and it was comforting.

He moved forwards, leapt onto the rail, and walked its length as the sails bowed out above him as though filled by a strong wind. In the mizzenmast the harpoon's angry spike was still fast. The figure on the bowsprit was immobile, alone, facing the blackness.

"I know what you are," he called out from a good distance away. "I mean, that's kind of rude to say so, I don't know your real name, but I know what you are besides being a cold-hearted murderer."

There was no response. Zal looked back along the deck and saw one angel crouched over the elf and faery who lay senseless as they had fallen. Close to him the other one hovered, casting a reasonable amount of light. Zal saw most of it pass through him. He wondered if it was trying to communicate with him but he was too low-level to under-stand or even hear it. Then he felt the telltale itch of the vampire's cast as she trawled for his thoughts.

He replied in kind and felt her snatch herself back as if she'd been burned, then turned his back on the angel and walked up to her. "Won't work twice," he said, standing behind her. "I learned how to do it now. You know, I just wanted to say that perhaps this isn't such a great idea. I mean, it looks like a royal high road to self-actualisation and union with the divine, but I have to ask you: Don't you think it's easier than having to wade out here at the beginning of things and doing some . . . actually, I don't know what you have to do but it seems to have got a lot of people killed so it must be really good, involve some really hot gear. Don't you? I hope it's worth it."

"It is," Xavien replied. "It will be."

"How do you know?" Zal didn't know how long he could keep it up. He longed for inspiration. He kept thinking of the girl with the silver eyes. He sighed. "I think I did something once like this, and it wasn't. Thought you should know. Have these angels been around long? They're a bit pesky."

"When I am like them they will not bother you any longer."

"No no they're not bothering me. How will you know when we're there?" The Void was impressive, he had to admit it, but in a way that quickly faded from awe and left a strange emptiness in its place. He didn't like the way it suddenly shifted in his sight from enormous depth to complete flatness. It was not darkness. It wasn't anything. He longed to be home. "Do you like songs?"

"Leave me alone. It will be done soon. Then you can go."

"I can't though," he said, sighing heavily. "There's a problem."

Xavien did not reply. He saw her shift uncomfortably. The tentacles didn't move much on their own. He should have seen it was a suit the first time. "Since you ask so nicely I will tell you," he said, not believing himself although he wasn't behind his mouth on this one. "The problem is that there is no way that you are going to turn into one of those. And you know it."

"I realise you think you are going somewhere with your talk,"

Xavien said, "but I do not expect to be transformed in that manner. What I will be is akin to angels only in that it is a higher power. As you say, such as we do not possess the ability to change ourselves so utterly."

"We have infinite choice, and that has to do," Zal said. "I'd have put you up for angelhood before I saw you move."

Now she did start slightly. "Are you threatening me?" She was incredulous. In her position he would have been too.

"It's difficult," he said. "As a fellow monster I feel we should help one another. I can only count myself sometimes among the lesser evils and I regret the membership of that club, but I can't undo it. But your problem is that you have no problem with being a monster."

"Ah, your moral concern is so charming," she said. "But your compassion is misplaced. Just because I have no compunction in overruling those who stand against me I have no interest in those who go about their business and allow me to mind my own. Surely a true evil or a just victim in my position would seek to avenge itself on its creators for the pain of its unique position as a sentient abomination, an exile, an eternal outsider. But I will not take revenge. I have no interest in it. I wish to leave my torment."

"Very noble," Zal said. "But you're not alone."

"The angels have aided me. Their presence has affirmed my intent."

"Not them. The rest of us."

"You're nothing like me. A shadow nature, ease in the Void, subtle energies, tuning to frequencies of lesser kind, ripping sustenance from material things . . . you are almost a true elf of a darker nature, hardly a bastard born that isn't able to call Alfheim home. Even the Saaqaa, brutes as they are, have their place in your world. As for your label, be careful whom you call monster. I took no part in the atrocities that birthed us. Those who did are worthy of a swift end."

"Spoken like a true elf," Zal said. "But your theoretical high ground isn't going to be worth jack. Intention doesn't matter. Actions are everything, and the consequences. Surely you agree. And your actions are everything your makers intended—focused on extinction. You should be stopped if you won't stop yourself."

"So, do you threaten me, shadow? What will you do? What can you do except worry over the state of my soul like some weak-kneed priest? The only one among your group able to harm me is lying useless at our backs after breaking my grip. Why don't you go and preach to him? You should be thanking him for your life."

"He can't hear me," Zal replied, pondering that she didn't even know it was not Ilya who had stopped her. "But you're right. I have nothing."

"You were not worth killing then."

"You've got that the wrong way round," Zal said. "What you mean is I am worth keeping alive."

He knew he had failed. It wasn't ever likely that talk was going to touch her. She was the success of the experiments that had produced hybrid failures like himself, and her self-absorption was the only thing that had kept her going. It was hundreds of years past the time for talking.

She got up suddenly and walked back to the deck. "At last," she said. "The waiting is over."

Zal looked around but saw nothing. Then, above them, a yellow light winked on and began to grow in size. He peered at it with difficulty. He thought it was another angel, a brighter one, with less colour change. There was a dark heart to it.

"Were you alone all that time?" he asked, as they both watched and the crew and all the Fleet stopped.

"Yes," she said. "They cast me out when I would not work for them. Forever." As she spoke she looked at the angel between them. Zal saw what she expected. She would be one of them, whether or not she was the same.

Then the descending light began to take on form and he saw it was much more defined than the angels of the ship. It was a tall male human figure, with enormous wings whose pinions were blades of white, blue, and gold like shafts of sunlight on a cloudy day, their rays spreading far beyond their form. In his arms and slightly in front of him, so that it had looked as if she were carried, was a woman in dark blue and purple armour. She was holding a huge sword with an odd grey blade. A red flash shot through her dark brown hair and over her shoulder, and her eyes were silver. As they neared the *Temeraire* they separated and she descended by herself, the angelic figure drifting to the rigging where he took a position, buccaneer style, one arm and one leg hooked casually in the ropes. His face was handsome and fiercely arrogant as he lounged there, glowing, naked to the waist with his long hair falling around his shoulders, and resplendently full of himself. He reminded Zal of something, but he couldn't remember what it was. It didn't matter. He only had eyes for the woman, whom he had thought of as a girl but who now had nothing much of girlishness about her except her size. She was petite and beautiful in her fierce metal suiting, silk strands and scraps tied and banded all around it, floating as if she had fought her way through a fabric emporium so that she trailed gossamer strips of beautiful colour. Relief filled him. Here she was, the girl with silver eyes, his love. If only he knew who she was.

Xavien seemed expectant, her attention focused on the woman and the sword.

But the silver eyes ignored her in her demon guise and looked at Zal instead. She touched down on the deck and walked towards him. Her lips parted and she hesitantly smiled. "Zal? Is that you?"

"Yes," he said eagerly, coming forwards past the demon.

"Finally," he heard Glinda mutter behind him. His nose filled with an alcohol shock of whiskey and he sneezed.

They stopped a few inches apart. He could see the angel moving closer to them, backlighting him into a ghostly silhouette.

Her eyes changed suddenly, the silver resolving like a developing photograph into human eyes that were blue, tinged with the strange violet of the ribbons on her armour. She lifted her fingers up to his face, and the spiked gauntlets on them melted away.

"Oh!" she said as she tried to touch his cheek. "Zal." It was his name, that was all, but the way she said it made his heart burst into fire.

He couldn't feel her hand.

CHAPTER TWENTY~SIX

Lila couldn't feel Zal but she stood on tiptoe and kissed his mouth anyway, closing her eyes. The faintest shiver passed through her lips. She looked up and saw him doing the same. His arms were around her. She released her armour and suddenly was touched where he pressed by a tingling rush.

Zal was grinning at her. "I must be a better kisser than I thought." He looked down and she saw herself naked except for the ribbons of Tatter, no hint of leather or metal anywhere on her. She still held the sword lightly in her free hand. She was even shorter without the armour, and even with the point of it resting on the deck her hand on its hilt was by her shoulder. She blushed, but not for the nudity or the onlookers. She looked into Zal's eyes, black on black as they were and nothing like his former solid, blonde and brown-eyed self. She couldn't stop smiling.

The demon started talking. Lila heard it on automatic. That voice. That hissing scratch. So they were the same. And the maker of that zombie . . . here it was. The cold strength of the Signal filled her, the knowledge that everything mattered and everything changed, nothing lost but nothing the same. She kissed Zal, and then, keeping herself between him and it, she turned on the demon.

"I've had enough of you," she said, overriding its speech in which it explained it had used its tactics in order to bring her here, or rather not her but the sword, which it wanted to use. The form of the demon's body looked exactly like the one she had sat before when she tried to use the crystal pane. "If all you wanted was the sword, why didn't you just ask me for it? It isn't even mine."

Xavien seemed taken aback, but only for an instant. "And would you have given it to me?"

"Take it." Lila flipped the sword up and around. She presented the hilt. "End the fucking drama already before I end it for you."

"Umm . . ." Zal said behind her in the casual easygoing boy tone that meant it was a seriously bad move. There was a bright metal sound above them. Teazle had drawn his swords. The ghosts gathered close, closer until they were ringed by a mass of cold, glowing forms.

One of the light forms that Teazle had told her was an angel dropped down beside the demon suddenly.

"You don't even know what you hold," the demon said. "Night's Mantle."

"I do," Lila replied, looking up the reference and reading as she continued to offer the sword. "Go on. Take it. Have your stupid dream already so we can get out of here. I used to be patient but I've really had it with your crap. You have power. Big scare. I know it. You know it. Take the fucking thing and be done." She felt the moment brim with sudden tension, and that smile she'd felt on her face recently came back. It wasn't the nicest smile in the world. "If you can."

"She's a Voidelf," Zal murmured. The vibration of his voice against the back of her neck made her shiver.

Lila looked that up. As she did so the demon came forward to take the sword. And she twitched it back, just out of his grasp. She stared at the form, felt Zal, saw the Fleet, remembered Lily's promise, saw her office, filled with his things, Sarasilien's things, the library. She? She. This was no demon. She was an elf. And not just any elf. At a speed faster than she was aware of a pattern snapped in place inside her. For an instant she saw Sarasilien's eyes as he bent over her when she was suffering outside the operating room, the first day she woke up as a machine. He had been crying. It wasn't for her. She'd forgotten. His kindness, the way he had felt, like a father. And then, Zal's story about the creation of the shadowkin. Lila was sure, as sure as she was that her own father had never been able to pull anything together except his kindness towards his children, that her mother couldn't face an ordinary life without being smashed numb by drink, that Max had lived in that house all her life, in case she came back one day . . .

She was sure that this was Sarasilien's daughter.

The demon hesitated with the patience of a striking adder and made another, much more definite attempt to seize the hilt. Lila flicked it out of reach teasingly a second time, as if she were toying with an irritating younger sister. She grinned and tutted, "Oh no, doesn't look like you can have it. Isn't that a shame?"

"This is not a game!" the demon snarled. Its voice had become slightly strangled. "Give me the sword or I will kill your boyfriend and the rest of them. There will not even be a memory left of what they were. I will ruin your world and theirs. Make it again."

"She probably can do it," Zal whispered. "She'll certainly try harder than last time. Unstable."

"Last time!" Lila felt her grin turn to a frown. "Others?"

"Here." The demon made an angry, sweeping gesture and Lila saw the bodies farther down the deck. She went cold for a second as she realized who they were, nauseous for a moment with the swirl of feeling as she saw Tath, delighted that he had survived, horrified that he seemed to be dead already. Along with Mal. Their slumped forms were dissipating, becoming thin. It was invisible to the eye, but she could feel the order of their signals breaking up. If they stayed out much longer this creature wouldn't need to bother trying to finish them. She felt weaker herself, and she'd bet even Teazle did, although you wouldn't know it to look at him.

"You moron," Lila sighed, with anger that she had to suppress for now, and with sadness. "Your father is still alive. You still have a chance."

"I have no father," the demon snarled, but it sounded less than certain.

"Well I have his office and personal effects and his library in my head, and I say he's alive. We could find him for you."

"I can find him myself. Give me the mantle."

"Here." Lila held it out. Again the hand came. Again she twitched it away. "It doesn't seem to want to."

"Stop doing that!"

Lila made her best innocent face. "What? I'm not doing anything. It doesn't like you." Faster than anyone would have noticed she looked at the sword herself. Now that she'd finished reading the damn books and their hundreds of references about the thing she really did realize what she was holding. "Shit!" she said under her breath so that only Zal could hear her. "It's the thing itself."

The moment was lost in a sudden lurch of the ship. All the bells of the Fleet went ringing and their horns sounded out. Patches of nothing flickered in all that had seemed so solid and true.

"We can all end here," the demon said. Its voice was icy. "If you rather."

Panic broke out. The Fleet began to break up more literally, lights moving off, some at speed.

In Lila's hand the sword moved. At the same time she felt Zal nudge her, and she looked around in bewilderment to find him holding out to her a book that was oddly solid.

"I'm supposed to give you this, apparently," he said.

Lila took it. As she did so she felt the sword lift and the demon's hand grab it successfully. She let it go and looked around at the sound of surprise to find the demon standing with a pen in its hand, staring at it. She opened the green-bound book. On the flyleaf was written, in deep black ink and a hesitant but beautiful handwritten elvish script, as of someone doing their best writing, "The Journal of Xaviendra Angela Sarasilien, begun on her twenty-eighth birthday. . . ." Lila turned the page and saw the first line, the date, and then closed it. She held it out as the negative storm began to blot out the spirit forms in greater flurries, feeling motes of herself vanishing.

"This is yours."

The demon stared, hesitated, reached out, looked at the book and the pen in its hands, then opened the book, and turned it the right way up. Then it looked at Lila and the demon disguise it had been wearing fell to dust. The storm blotted out its last few flakes and was gone. Before them stood a tall, narrow figure of an elflike girl who looked exactly as if she had been drawn in ink and coloured in with a lighter wash of the same. She looked like Zal, but unlike him she had two magnificent antelope-like horns rising out of her skull. Her black hair whipped around her and grew down her back and over her shoulders in a long, silky fur.

"I don't understand," she said falteringly, looking at the pen. "I thought . . . I thought it would change me. Why am I still here? Why?!" And the last word was a cry of absolute horror and loneliness. She turned to the angel beside her. "What have you done?" She held out the pen. "What is this? Why aren't I like you? Why can't I hear you?" She whirled around, looking for the other one, but it was already rushing towards her as she started to scream, a truly awful sound that felt like it was tearing Lila's own insides apart.

The black storm was back in an instant, but this time it had a vortex focused on Xaviendra as she hunched in on herself. She'd dropped the book and the pen and was clawing at her own face with both hands. As Lila watched the angels darted in and their light closed on her arms. They fought with her, trying to make her stop. All the time the scream continued.

Lila turned to find Zal, suddenly terrified he was gone, and looked into the dark of his face. He was shouting at her, almost inaudible. He was pointing at the pen, the book, miming writing, pointing at her. Teazle was the fastest to react. He darted down and seized both items, opened the book to the last page that was written on, and held out the pen to her.

Write something! he mouthed at her.

Lila felt herself dissolving. Overhead the Void was beginning to break open and the light of other worlds was coming through, like a haze.

She read the last lines of the careful hand, now more practiced and less self-conscious . . .

. . . experiments are truly evil. I cannot allow them to continue or allow my father to continue in this insane purpose which he is so convinced is for the greater good of the elves and the safety of Alfheim. There are forces at work in those with power that are too fond of their own will. If he will not see how he is used and corrupted, then I will make him see. He has gone to Demonia on a hunt for more "materials" for the soul forge. In his absence I have answered the call. I have volunteered to be a subject for the change. When it is done and he returns home then let him see the value of his work. I pray to survive long enough to illustrate the truth.

Around them the Fleet shook and began to fade. Deep cold burning.

Lila uncapped the pen and saw the nib flood with the infinite blood of Night. She looked up at Zal, thought of her own father and, strangely, of Sandra Lane and Sarah Bentley. She struggled for a moment, because what she was about to do did not seem entirely just and merely a whim that exacted no retribution and solved no history. It salved only pain. But then she wrote quickly and easily.

It was aboard the Fleet in the gulf of Night that Xaviendra Angela Sarasilien woke from the long journey she had embarked on centuries before to find herself changed according to her most heartfelt and sincere wish . . .

The screaming abruptly stopped.

. . . surrounded by the faery, Malachi, a curious cat; by the Lord of Winter,

Ilyatath Voynassi Taliesetra, who was once carried in the heart of the robot girl and who was born again in Faeryland; by the demon, Teazle Sikarza, who went Under and came out an Angel; by the human Lila Amanda Black, who was remade by the Signal; and by Zal the rock star, soul rebel, and last survivor of the reign of Jack the Giantkiller—her allies. Friends and lovers all, they had recovered from the rigours of their trials by the grace of Night, mother of creation, whose pen so wrote, this day. She time-stamped it and signed her own name to the entry, because it seemed appropriate to. In doing so she realized that she did not know Zal's true name.

Lila looked up. Zal was reading over her shoulder. She capped the pen and closed the book. There was calm and the Fleet drifted, damaged but still distinguishable.

A tall elf with white hair and golden eyes was standing beside Zal, just behind him. She nodded at Lila in a businesslike manner and spat the dog end of a cigar out onto the deck, where she ground it under the toe of her soldier's boot. "Signed, sealed, delivered, he's yours," she said. "That concludes my bargain with you. It's me, Lily, whatever. Thanks for unlocking Under and letting us all out," she added with a scowl as if thanks weren't something she was used to delivering. Then she cleared her throat, spat the result over the rail, and addressed Zal. "I'll be seeing you, honey. Make it not too soon." She reached out and clapped him on the shoulder. "Be sure you go back with the Green King there." She stabbed a thumb out to indicate the slowly rising form of Ilyatath. "Via Faeryland. And wait there. Or you won't get your body back. Understand?"

"Yes." He grinned at her. "You sang well."

"Uh-huh? Fuck that," she muttered, producing an enormous cigar from her sleeve. She stuck it in her mouth and looked pleased with herself. "Until later."

Lila was not surprised to see her fade out, patting her pockets, and, as she was halfway gone, producing the pen, at which she raised her eyebrows and then waved at Lila as if to say *Well look at this!* Then she laughed, put the pen into a pocket of her war tunic, took the cigar out of her mouth, stuck her tongue out, and lit the cigar on it. She sucked hard until the thing was almost flaming, before jabbing it back into place and winking as the last trace of her vanished.

Lila looked at her hand. Sure enough the pen was gone. She sighed, relieved, and then Malachi was running towards her, slowly, limping a little, but running. He was in his giant catman form, as big and ugly as any nightmare, but she hugged him as he arrived and felt his thumping paw on her back. Tath was behind him.

"You look scary," she said, unaccountably shy. The last she had seen of him he had been naked except for her DO YOU WANT FRIES WITH THAT T-shirt, facing down the Giantkiller. Now he was almost as intimidating as Jack himself.

"I do my best," he said, and smiled at her. "I missed you."

"I missed you," she said.

"Hey, who missed me?" Teazle had put his swords away and strode across to them.

"Turn it down," Malachi grumbled, shading his eyes with a paw. "Some of us had night vision."

Zal looked at Ilya uncertainly. "Was I supposed to miss him?"

Ilya shrugged elaborately. "You married him."

"I what? She didn't mention anything about that! Are you having me on?"

Malachi's tail lashed side to side. "Zal has a small memory problem involving everything except Ilya. And an invisible friend. We should go. None of us are made for this."

Beside them on the open deck a circle slowly bloomed vertically in the air. It held a picture of a land full of snow, the sky grey and promising more. "Faery awaits," Ilya said.

"We have to go another way," Lila said. "We left from Demonia. It'll be tricky to get out alive, so I'll come and meet you in Faery, if you can take me there, Malachi. We'll be at Madame Des Loupes old house."

Malachi nodded at her.

"Zal, with us." Ilya moved towards the portal he had made.

"I will," Zal said, "just a minute." He stepped past Lila, kissing the top of her head, and crossed the few metres to the prow rail, where Xaviendra stood. Of the two angels there was no sign.

"They left," she whispered. She wouldn't meet his eye. "They were with me so long."

"Come with me." He held out his hand.

She looked at it, half turned away from them. It was clear at this angle that she had a long, saurian tail as well as her horns, and although the shadow that made her had shifted its colours from black to the blue spectrum, she was no less shadow than she had been, no more elf. Her gaze wandered often to the dark, but wandered back again without finding help. "Where?"

"Anywhere," he said. "We'll look for your father. He can't have gone far."

Still she hesitated. "He never came for me," she said. "I don't know." She kept glancing at the rail. It was clear that she was considering jumping it. "Where did it all go? My resolve, my power, my will? What happened to me?"

Lila held out the book. "It says in here."

Zal took it and passed it across. Xaviendra took it with shaking hands and opened it, fumbling the pages. She took a while reading and then looked up. "I don't understand. I am no different. I feel no different. And I wanted to."

"What were you going to do?" Zal asked.

"I was going to be . . . I would have found my father," she said slowly and deliberately, "and I would have made him love me."

"And now?"

"And now . . . it's gone. And there's nothing." She turned and gripped the rail and stared out at the nothing. A few seconds passed, and then she began to laugh, weakly and ironically and in a hurting way but laughing. "And I am free."

"I'm going home," Zal said. "Come with us. We're all unredeemable to the core."

"And free," Lila added.

"And magnificent," Teazle said.

"And late," Ilya and Malachi insisted, and then looked at one another suspiciously for speaking at the same time. Then Malachi stepped through the portal and Ilya followed him, calling, "Zal, hurry up."

"I am," said Zal, staying where he was.

"Zal," said Lila gently, pleading.

"All right." He turned and walked to the gate, at the last moment turning back to Xaviendra. "Let the Admiral out before you come find us. He deserves to get his ship back. He's a good kid."

Xaviendra watched him go and the portal closed. Then only Lila and Teazle were left. "You were kind," Xaviendra said.

"How many chances did you get in your life to write a happy ending?" Lila asked her, taking Teazle's hand.

"I did not deserve it."

"Elves," muttered Teazle under his breath. He kissed Lila's neck.

"You can still deserve it," Lila said; then she put her arms around Teazle's neck and closed her eyes. "Do you think we can wish ourselves back there?"

"You said you didn't need the bloody sword anymore," he murmured, sliding his hands down her back and under the ribbons on her bottom. "I'm only repeating your very words."

"I should talk less," she said, but she was confident. She lost sensation for a moment, felt a strange discontinuity, as though seconds had been lost; then she was standing in the dank, stinking blackness of the labyrinth. Somewhere just ahead of her she heard Teazle swear horribly, and then there was a crashing and smashing sound as he fell over and knocked into the standing statues and they broke on the floor.

"Come on," she said. "Let's see what's left of your empire."

"Hah." He got up and found his feet, and shook his head. "Excellent. Let's get in a fight." She slapped him as she ran past him, sonar for vision. "Can't catch me!"

"Stay naked and I'll get you before you reach the exit," he promised.

Around her the faery ribbons didn't change themselves. She ran, feeling the wet stone, the chilly air, laughing.

Zal looked over his left shoulder, but he saw no sign of Glinda. Ilya sat beside him, as solid as he was not.

"How long will it take?" Zal asked, staring into the fire. He couldn't stop thinking about Lila.

"Not too long," Ilya replied, as he had replied steadily to the same question for the last few hours. Malachi had left them as soon as they arrived, bounding down the hillsides without a backwards glance. Ilya had explained that Madrigal was down there, and it was probably summer by now. Zal inferred the rest without asking any details; it seemed obvious.

"Explain the marriage thing again," Zal said. "What was our relationship like?"

"No. I have done that three times and three is the limit." Ilya banked the fire and lay down on the thick furs before it.

"And you and I were best friends?"

"Always," Ilya said in a way that Zal thought meant it wasn't true.

"Did we have an affair or something?" He couldn't figure it out.

"Go to sleep, Zal. She'll be here tomorrow, I am sure of it. She will be here very soon." He closed his eyes. "And don't touch the fire."

"But the dragon said . . ."

"Zal!"

"All right, all right, keep your hair on." He sat awake in the night, watching Ilya sleeping among his dogs, listening to the sound of the wind restlessly moving the crystals on the surface of the snow and seeing himself slowly alter in the firelight's steady glow, gaining colour, gaining form, absorbing the beauty of the fire's light.

THE NO SHOWS VS. CYNIC GURU

Through the agency of arcane powers beyond imagination Zal's band, The No Shows, have been in collaboration with real-world band Cynic Guru, so that together they are able to bring you a free track for your entertainment. Listen live to "Doom,"* at www .thenoshows.com.

This page is dedicated to **Cynic Guru** as a thank you for allowing themselves to be temporarily possessed by beings from beyond. They are:

    Roland Hartwell (vocals, violin, guitar)
    Ricky Korn (bass)
    Oli Holm (drums)
    Einar Johannsson (lead guitar, vocals)

They also write and record many great songs entirely their own that have nothing to do with channelling the mystical aether of imaginary space-time. More information about them, their tour dates, and their music can be found on their Web sites: www.cynicguru.com and www .myspace.com/CynicGuru.